MW01625684

PEACE AFTER WAR

· *Volume Two* ·

CLUNY CLASSICS

Visit WWW.CLUNYMEDIA.COM/CLASSICS *for other titles from the Catholic literary tradition, including:*

RICCARDO BACCHELLI
The Mill on the Po

ROBERT HUGH BENSON
Come Rack, Come Rope
Dawn of All
Lord of the World

GEORGES BERNANOS
Joy
Under the Sun of Satan

G. K. CHESTERTON
Wanderings over the World

MYLES CONNOLLY
Dan England and the Noonday Devil
Mr. Blue

ALICE CURTAYNE
House of Cards

GERTRUD VON LE FORT
The Veil of Veronica

MARIELLA GABLE, O.S.B. (EDITOR)
Many-Colored Fleece: Short Stories

JOSÉ MARÍA GIRONELLA
The Cypresses Believe in God
One Million Dead
Peace After War

RUMER GODDEN
A Breath of Air
Five for Sorrow, Ten for Joy
In This House of Brede

CAROLINE GORDON
The Malefactors

CARYLL HOUSELANDER
The Dry Wood

SHEILA KAYE-SMITH
Joanna Godden

ELISABETH LANGGÄSSER
The Quest

BRUCE MARSHALL
Father Malachy's Miracle
A Thread of Scarlet

FRANÇOIS MAURIAC
The Desert of Love
Thérèse: A Portrait in Four Parts
Vipers' Tangle

DOROTHY L. SAYERS
Whose Body?

IGNAZIO SILONE
Fontamara
Bread and Wine
The Seed Beneath the Snow

SIGRID UNDSET
The Burning Bush
The Wild Orchid
The Longest Years

HELEN C. WHITE
A Watch in the Night

Peace After War

· Volume Two ·

José María Gironella

Translated from the Spanish
HA ESTALLADO LA PAZ
by Joan MacLean

CLUNY
Providence, Rhode Island

CLUNY MEDIA EDITION, 2022

This Cluny edition is a republication of
Peace After War (Foreword, Part III, Part IV, and Glossaries),
originally published by Alfred A. Knopf, Inc., in 1969.

With the exception of actual historical personages,
the characters are entirely the product of the author's imagination
and have no relation to any persons in real life.

For more information regarding this title,
please write to info@clunymedia.com, or to
Cluny Media, P.O. Box 1664, Providence, RI 02901

• • • • •

VISIT US ONLINE AT WWW.CLUNYMEDIA.COM

ISBN: 978-1685951467

Cover design by Clarke & Clarke
Cover image: Francisco Gimeno Arasa, *A Village in L'Empordà*,
1918, oil on canvas
Courtesy of Wikimedia Commons

CONTENTS

Peace After War

VOLUME TWO

TO DOCTOR ADOLFO LEY AND HIS WIFE, SOLITA,
WITH MY AFFECTION AND GRATITUDE

In order to come close to freedom and happiness, it is not enough to change systems; the minds and hearts of men, of the governing and the governed, of the powerful and their subjects, of those who command and those who obey, must change, too.

PAPINI

FOREWORD

AFTER *The Cypresses Believe in God* (the period before the Spanish Civil War) and *One Million Dead* (the war period), I now offer the reader *Peace After War* (the postwar period).

This book will not close the ring, however. The entire work I conceived to center around our national drama will not be a trilogy, as I announced earlier. I have taken into account that the historical and political phase that began in 1939 has not ended yet, and that many of its circumstances are still operative. Hence I have decided to devote several volumes to the postwar period. It seemed to me to be not at all valid to bring my historical series to an end with any particular year, say 1945, 1950, 1958... It would not be feasible either to try to fit such a long span of years into a single volume. I chose, therefore, to write the story of the era in sections, as a sort of *Episodios Nacionales*, which might end on the day when the successor to the Chief of State comes forth.

Accordingly, the present volume covers only the immediate postwar years. The next will follow events until the end of World War II, more or less. And the others will follow in succession.

Peace After War takes place almost entirely in Gerona, except for the scenes in which the exiles appear. The characters have returned to their homes, and the Alvear family and their friends, old and new, again play the leading roles in the novel. They live once more in family groups, after the inevitable dispersal into settings in which the manifestations of the conflict that divided Spain into two zones forced me to place them and that made necessary the alternation of scenes in *One Million Dead.*

As usual, I singed my eyelashes in my effort to tell faithfully and impartially all that happened, even though, as in any narrative, there must inevitably be an underlay of personal interpretation. And also as usual, my most firmly held purpose has been to write a work of fiction and not a historian's dissertation. Events, the *Official State Bulletin*, speeches, and the like, provided me with nothing more than background music. To change the figure, I have used them as a platform, or a trampoline, in order to go on with my task of analyzing "the virtues and defects of our race."

Consequently, the rhythm of the work again resembles that of *The Cypresses Believe in God*. I believe that every subject demands its specific formula of expression. Describing battles between tanks is by no means the same as dealing with individual or family conflicts. Peace is not at all the same as war. Nor is talking about Lister or El Campesino the same as speaking of El Niño de Jaén, fascinated with flamenco dancing, or Agustín Lago, Chief Inspector of Elementary Education and a member of Opus Dei.

Ignacio Alvear is still beset by doubt, is still striving after a truth that will satisfy him. What can we do about it? Isn't doubt one of the stigmata of the present period? And am I not a man of my time?

I thank the authors of the books I have consulted. I am grateful to the newspapers that have been incomparable sources of information. My thanks go also to the many people who have said to me: "That same thing happened to me." "I experienced this." My thanks also to the many readers who still follow this difficult pilgrimage of my pen all the way through the fascinating problem of my country.

José María Gironella
Barcelona
April 1966

PART THREE

April 1, 1940, to March 30, 1941

THIRTY-TWO

ON the first of April the parade celebrating the first anniversary of the victory took place. Cannon, a couple of tanks, machine guns, and troops passed along the Rambla, the scene of the solemn Way of the Cross a few days earlier. The usual authorities and the Governor, wearing his Army uniform, reviewed it from the grandstand. The loudspeakers that had transmitted the religious evocations at the Stations of the Cross were now sending forth the usual patriotic songs. The Bishop was not the hero of this occasion, however; the torch had passed to the General.

According to *Amanecer*, the following day, April 2, had been chosen to start work on what was to become famous as the *Valle de los Caídos*, the Valley of the Fallen. "The gigantic monument would perpetuate for centuries the exploits of those who died in the Crusade." The first drill bored a blast hole. The newspaper report datelined Madrid and published by Warning Voice explained that the site where the *Valle de los Caídos* would be constructed had been chosen by the Caudillo himself after many days spent flying over it and touring the passes of the Guadarramas. His final choice was the spot called Cuelgamuros, near the Guatel and Boquerón creeks. The enormous basilica would be petered from the living rock; it would be big enough to contain the bodies of three thousand men. A cross some three hundred and sixty feet high, the largest in Christendom and visible from a great distance, was to be erected above the basilica. The work required would be comparable to building the Escorial, which had taken twenty years; and it would be done in partnership by private enterprise and battalions of "workers."

In connection with the events of those days the newspapers burst anew into praises of the Chief of State. In Gerona, Jaime, the newspaper deliveryman and sometime bookshop proprietor, was not happy. The cause of his discontent was his unswerving partisanship of Catalan independence, which was outraged by one of the encomia to the Caudillo rendered by the monks of Montserrat.

Indeed, the news further revealed that the abbot, Father Antonio María Marcet, had journeyed with some of the monks to Madrid to bestow upon the Caudillo, in the Palacio de Oriente, a very beautiful little chest made in the Red prisons and containing the cedula of the Sisterhood of Our Lady of Light, an honor conferred upon Charles I and Philip II in their time. The cedula was inscribed on paper dating back to the tenth century which had been carefully kept ever since then by the Benedictine monks in the monastery. It symbolized Spain's revival of her glorious past.

"We'll get nowhere this way," Jaime muttered behind his counter in the book kiosk next to the Soler factory as he handed a novel about the Far West to a workingman who had once collected for the Red Relief. This same man wrote verses in Catalan on the nights when he could not sleep.

IMMEDIATELY afterward, as spring reached its lush apotheosis, a series of transcendental events burst over the world, touching the conscience of mankind and keeping the ears of the Gerundians glued to their radio sets.

The first of those events was a cease-fire between Finland and Russia. The preliminary accord was signed in Moscow. Doubtless it happened because the beeswax and wine sent to the Finnish Catholics by Spain had been all used up.

By the terms of the peace treaty, Finland agreed to cede to Russia the Isthmus of Karelia—most of its inhabitants chose to move at once to Helsinki—and a military base on Hängo Head. In Moscow, Cosme Vila's wife, who had never understood why Russia had attacked its peaceful neighboring country, said to her husband, the former Communist leader of Gerona: "I don't see why Russia couldn't conquer Finland. This is a defeat, isn't it?"

The second event, on April 10, was the sudden occupation of Denmark and Norway by the German Army. The operation came as a stunning surprise, which proved the statement that Goebbels had made to the newspapers: "No one knows the Führer's plans in advance." Denmark accepted the situation and surrendered unconditionally. Norway, on the other hand, with the help of an expeditionary French-British corps that landed at Narvik, put up a weak, futile resistance. The royal family moved to Hamar after Oslo was occupied. Hitler claimed in his official speech that he had made his decision in the hope of blocking "the obvious plan of England and France to cut off Germany's supply of raw materials." In Gerona, however, the armchair strategists who sprang up like toadstools claimed that what the Führer was actually attempting was to begin the encirclement of England from the north, for most certainly England had become an obsession to him.

A month later, on May 11, the third event happened. This one was of much greater importance: the lightning-swift occupation of Belgium, The Netherlands, and Luxembourg by Germany. With this move, the war, which Mosén Alberto pronounced "the mortal sin of men," penetrated to the very heart of Europe. The importance of the action was emphasized by the Führer's own words: "The struggle that I have initiated will decide Germany's future for the next thousand years." The entire world was stunned by it, for there had been no provocation. The response of the Allied democracies was very weak in the opinion of the Governor of Gerona as Churchill took Chamberlain's place in the English government as Prime Minister. "What can Churchill do? He's sixty-five years old. He can't be the man he was during the 1914-1918 war." Be that as it may, from the military point of view, England was absolutely unprepared. Churchill himself recognized that in his address to his people. And although Switzerland discreetly ordered a general mobilization, its act was tantamount to rolling stones down the mountains. The United States, on the other hand—which did indeed constitute a mighty force—had declared its neutrality.

The most disparate commentaries were the order of the day. Everyone in Spain recalled the discipline and efficiency of the German forces and the technical staffs—Mateo remembered Major Plabb vividly—which had intervened in the Civil War. In his "Windows on the World," Warning Voice became a sentimental fan of young King Leopold, who took his place at the head of the Belgian troops attempting to resist, and he praised the attitude of Queen Wilhelmina of Holland, who said to her people: "Let everyone do his duty; I will do mine."

But now the question was how to hold back the avalanche. This was what General Sánchez Bravo said. True, the Dutch engineers flooded a part of their land by pressing the famous button readied for that purpose. True, French troops moved exhaustedly toward the north and England sent another expeditionary force to the Continent. But the German air raids were devastating, the motorized troops of the Panzer Divisions, conceived to act independently, not to be attached to the infantry in the traditional manner, advanced everywhere, and Germany introduced another innovation which brought from General Sánchez Bravo an admiring exclamation that almost split even Doña Cecilia's eardrums. Hitler had used paratroopers to seize the airfields at Amsterdam and The Hague by surprise. "Do you know what that means?" the General asked his officers grouped in front of his map of operations. "This was a stroke of genius. Occupying enemy territory behind the lines from the air!"

The ardor in Germany's favor spread throughout the city and became blatantly obvious in the conversation groups. Even under the present circumstances, how could people forget that "the democracies had taken the side of the Reds during the Spanish war?" The Governor, Mateo, Marta, Don Emilio Santos, José Luis Martínez de Soria, and a large portion of the population regarded the Führer as a kind of incarnation of omnipotence on earth, bound to crush all his enemies in no time at all. Dr. Chaos, for his part, seemed happy. His admiration for the German methods of scientific investigation had increased apace. "Now, with the war on," he said, "the German surgeons will perform miracles." Dr. Andújar was more cautious. Aside from the fact that he did not put much stock in the efficacy of the "emergency surgery" that had developed from the war, he himself viewed the Führer more or less as a man possessed, and he told all his eight children to pray ceaselessly that the ambitions of that man, apparently guided by astrology and not by God, might be checked some day. "He might at least respect the civilian population," he said. But the bombs falling from the sky had no brain with which to select, and no heart either. As for Notary Noguer, he kept repeating helplessly: "Poor France, poor France!" His theme song was that the Germans would raze "Paris, the most beautiful city in the world" as though drawing an eraser across a venerable life.

Julio García and his wife, Doña Ampara Campo, had finally moved to London. His two friends, Fanny and Bohlen, were reporting from the Belgian front. If the authorities and the Germanophiles of Gerona had heard the ex-policeman's comments, they would have split their sides laughing. In the first place, Julio García believed in Churchill and his extraordinary personality; he was still a "lion" in spite of his years, Julio said. In the second place, he agreed with Dr. Andújar that the power that ruled the sea would win the war in the long run. In Julio's judgment, the sea was in the control of the Allied fleets. Finally, he agreed with Manolo and Esther that the potential strength of the British Empire and the Commonwealth was incalculable, particularly in conjunction with the Dutch Empire, the third largest in the world, with rich and prosperous colonies in the Pacific, not to mention the Belgian Empire, which held a dominant position in the center of Africa.

JULIO's thesis was lucid; it was the fruit not only of his frequently accurate instinct, but also of his renewed contacts with the Masonic lodges in London. "The English are slow," he said. "If Hitler had on hand a secret landing force with which he could assault the British Isles right now in a surprise attack, he'd win the game. But if, on the contrary, he's counting on demoralizing the English people through air attacks, and if he gives Churchill time enough to get his genius for organization going, he's lost."

Julio García's arguments would not have made a dent on anyone in Gerona, for Hitler's successes, still so frequent and swift, were repetitions of the battle for Poland. On May 29, King Leopold of the Belgians surrendered and became a prisoner of war, in disregard of *Amanecer*'s "Windows on the World." In the opinion of Warning Voice, any attempt to struggle was senseless. A few days later, the German armies crossed the French frontier and General Gamelin's troops were in retreat everywhere. The famous Maginot Line had turned out to be a tactical joke. So many thousands were taken prisoner that the French Chief of Staff told his men in a pathetic address: "All the troops that cannot advance must let themselves be killed." The order was pitifully futile. Both the soldiers and the civilians were fleeing to the sea in the grip of total confusion bred by panic and infiltration between their lines of English-speaking Germans dressed as British officers, who gave orders that sent the convoys astray.

On June 17 another startling event occurred: Mussolini came in on the side of Germany, thus disdaining the supposed pressure for peace applied by Count Ciano, declaring war on England and France. That represented a strong reinforcement for Germany, the forging of the Axis. In vain, Agustín Lago and many others thought that the Duce was guilty of an inelegant act by stabbing France in the back while the war was still not decided. The fact spoke for itself and had its own importance. So much importance that the incredible operation of occupying Paris was moving closer in giant strides. The very name of Paris was so evocative that the eyes of the entire world were centered on it. Could it be possible that the German machine would not be attacked, that it would not break down somewhere before it could overpower the French capital? Paris was not merely an idea, it was a sentiment. Something so specific that any intruder would automatically become a rapist. "Occupying Paris," Notary Noguer exclaimed, "is like occupying the Acropolis or a whole civilization." And if the French defended their city, would it be destroyed, and thus confirm the notary's worst fears?

None of those possibilities happened. The German machine did not get stuck and there was no "need" to destroy anything. On June 15, German troops entered Paris almost without resistance. The German Army paraded triumphantly from the Arc de Triomphe along the avenue Maréchal Foch, and German soldiers stood guard over the Tomb of the Unknown Soldier and Napoleon's tomb in Les Invalides.

Two months, then, had sufficed the Führer to force the great democracies to abandon the struggle on the continent of Europe in a retreat that reached Dantesque proportions at Dunkirk, where by a miracle of collaboration and order, British boats and barges of all descriptions managed to take aboard and remove to safety a total of three hundred thousand English and Allied combatants while columns of smoke rose skyward from the coastal area ammunition dumps, which were being strafed by Stukas.

The French Government moved to Bordeaux after the occupation of Paris. England demanded that France keep on fighting, but by that time the Bordeaux government could do nothing. Consequently, at the instance of Marshal Pétain, an armistice was signed, with the Spanish authorities acting as intermediaries who took the necessary steps. To be sure, General Sánchez Bravo was again almost struck dumb with astonishment when he read the conditions of the armistice. "How can that be?" he said to his aides. "The Führer has left a part of the South of France free, and he hasn't occupied the French possessions in North Africa; he hasn't even demanded the total surrender of the French fleet. What's the reason for such generosity? Upon my word, I don't understand."

At the moment, the objections voiced by the General seemed of no importance whatsoever. The deed was consummated, and from then on, the auguries seemed to have been confirmed. The next objective would be England, where even the cannon from the museums had been hauled out. And Germany no longer had an enemy at her back. Her entire strength would be concentrated on the Atlantic coasts, aimed toward London, toward Oxford. The words of the Governor seemed to have come true: "What can Churchill do against that hell unleashed?" Marta declared: "It's not likely that England will become another Alcázar of Toledo."

The repercussions from that disaster wrought by the German National Socialists and Fascist Italy were endless and varied. Thousands of people from France, Belgium, and other countries had no choice but to seek refuge in Spain—one of the paradoxes of history. They entered through Irún and over the border with Gerona. Consequently, Colonel Triguero suddenly had to increase the personnel in his office in Figueras—Ignacio had escaped by a whisker—and while he awaited orders from the Governor, the Colonel did not know "whether he ought to treat the refugees like gentlemen," or "whether he ought to expose them and put them in jail." The Grand Duke of Luxembourg, several members of the Rothschild family, and the King of Nepal were among the people entering Spain. Those personages intended to move on to Portugal, or indeed to North Africa, and in many cases, the Spanish Government agreed to let them. The internment in concentration camps of other fugitives of lesser rank could be foreseen. Detention camps would be opened in Miranda de Ebro and other places—and that was going to intensify the problem of food beyond all expectations!

Another of the dramatic phases of this complex of events was the problem facing the Spanish exiles living in France. They were in a state of utter confusion, afraid that the Germans would either shoot them or turn them over to the Spanish authorities. Many of them sought sanctuary in the embassies. Others, like Antonio Casal, the former Gerundian Socialist leader, tired of having to flee so often, voluntarily reported to the Germans; but for the most part, after making futile efforts to board a ship in Bordeaux for England or America, they sought salvation by settling in the "unoccupied" French zone. That was the case with Gorki and José Alvear, both of whom, after being badly frightened, settled down more or less comfortably in Perpignan, although always in fear that a sudden German order would set them down on the Spanish frontier where they could expect to see Captains Arias and Sandoval, plus numerous Civil Guards—again.

Meanwhile, the world was in a state of growing bewilderment. The people of England were promised blood, sweat, and tears; in Spain, salutary doses of an enthusiasm for "vengeance." "Now it's our turn!" Those words, uttered by so many people during the outbreak of hostilities stemming from the war in Poland, were repeated to the point of satiety. The humbling of the democracies, and especially of the French Popular Front, brought inner consolation to the many who had suffered from the Front's lacks of understanding during the Spanish War. As if that were not enough, the historic role of the new Spain was thrown into high relief by everything that had happened, precisely because the victors were the despised Axis forces, which had aided "Nationalist" Spain. This triumph surpassed anyone's expectations, and all sorts of prophecies were made by the militants in the blue shirts. "Our turn has come," Comrade Rosselló said. "French Morocco will be ours." Mateo was more inclined to hope Spain would be able to chew off a piece of Algeria. For the present, two significant and encouraging things happened: acts, not mere words. Franco occupied Tangier, using forces from Jalifa, "to assure neutrality and guarantee order," while he was "studying an international plan to limit the scope of the war."

Meanwhile, many people with cooler heads watched with deep sadness the turn the conflict had taken. They were willing to dispense with the advantages that Spain might gain from it. Matías Alvear was one of them. He was desolated; each telegram that came through his office signified to him a bleeding wound. How could anyone possibly relish talk of bombs, naval battles, the "annihilating force of the Stukas"? How could his own daughter possibly say again and again as she sat embroidering her wedding trousseau: "That'll teach them!" How were the English people to blame for what might happen? What about the prisoners of war? What about the dead in Holland? And in Belgium? What about the Germans who lost their lives in battle?

Marcos, the apprehensive Galician, also took it all very hard. In the office they shared in the Telegraph building, Marcos said: "I'm sick to death of war.

If it weren't for my darling Adela, I'd look for a job as a lighthouse keeper, any lighthouse, the lonelier and the more isolated the better."

Manolo and Esther were sitting on the anxious seat. Esther remembered her days as a student at Oxford, and her imagination faltered at the thought of German boots treading those historic classrooms of culture. If only they had someone with whom they could share their worries! But except for Professor Civil and Dr. Andújar, they found little support in the city. Even Ignacio kept vacillating. "This is a catastrophe, Ignacio," they said to the young man. "You don't know what the Germans are capable of doing in the flush of victory. The Aryan race carries something monstrous inside it." Ignacio accepted their statements, but added that England had committed countless outrages throughout her history and that her empire had become the great power it was precisely because of such abuses. Esther threw up her hands in despair. "Please, Ignacio, don't compare them," she said. But she could not rally enough valid arguments to convince him.

Naturally, there was no lack either of persons whose remarks could raise gooseflesh because they were dictated by icy materialism. For example, the administrator for the Constructora Gerundense, Inc., bewailed the fact that the Costa brothers had not had time to set up an insurance company which would monopolize the marine transport business. "We could collect enormous premiums for covering the ships carrying war materiel. Or reverse the operation and simulate sinkings. I don't know what all we could do!" In Barcelona, Ana María's father, Don Rosendo Sarró, was in his glory, for he had established himself in a similar line of business. In his opinion, everything that was happening spelled just one thing: that the hour for Spain to get rich had struck. "Now our raw materials can be sold for any price we ask, starting with wolfram. Besides, the Jewish refugees who are coming into our country can give our economy a big boost. If it were up to me, I wouldn't let them move on to Portugal."

Perhaps the best-balanced person, the man who once more inspired the greatest confidence in all he met, was Comrade Dávila, the Governor, the man who believed in taking a deep breath. He dominated the situation as the Bishop had dominated the Way of the Cross and the General the victory parade. He followed the Madrid line by treating the refugees—French, Belgian, Jewish, and all the rest who entered through the Gerona area—"like gentlemen," not "enemies," even though it might cost him an effort to have another head-on collision with Colonel Triguero. He saw to it that they were escorted courteously to Barcelona, where they became the responsibility of the Governor there. He tried to keep the press and radio under his control from getting out of hand, for he knew full well that if the media were left exclusively in the hands of the fanatical Mateo, it would be a different story.

He gave Commissioner Diéguez the instructions needed to prevent the molestation of several English diplomats who had settled in Gerona, in the Peninsular Hotel. He wanted to avoid anything like what had happened to Dr. Relken when the Falangists had entered his room, beaten him up, and forced castor oil down his throat. Of course the Governor ardently hoped for a German victory, but he prayed to God that the victory would not exact new bloodshed. The one thing he could not prevent was the organization by the Falange in Gerona, and everywhere else in Spain, of constant mass demonstrations demanding the return of Gibraltar. The old, old story. Now England was vulnerable and the time would never be more opportune. Several hundred people, most of them youths and small boys—El Niño de Jaén was always one of them—met almost every day and ran through the streets shouting, "Gibral-ta-a-a-r! Gibral-ta-a-a-r!" Pilar felt sure that the fruit would fall. "How can it help but happen?" she said. "It's at the mercy of our big guns."

Miguel Rosselló, the Governor's chauffeur and secretary, admired his chief and comrade more each day. He could not imagine how that man could stay so serene with such a great weight on his shoulders.

"What's your secret?" he asked the Governor. "How do you manage it, may I ask? If I were told that the Rothschilds would be passing through here and that I would have all those detainees in the Seminary besides, plus English and German diplomats in the Peninsular Hotel, while I was still having to prosecute black-marketeers and arguing with my wife at home, I think I'd go crazy."

Comrade Dávila took off his dark glasses and smiled.

"It's my years, friend Rosselló, my years. The years have taught me not to mix one kind of business with another and to make a coherent summary of them all. That's what my secret amounts to."

"A coherent summary? You don't say!"

"Why, of course. Don't you see that everything that's happening goes to prove just one thing: that we were right? Forget the black marketeers and the nightly fears of my dear wife, María del Mar. Then what? That while Europe is burning, Spain is moving steadily on her own course, which is rebuilding on a national scale. From now on, who would have the nerve to throw the Uprising in our face? Can you imagine what it would be like if the Popular Front had gone on, or if the Reds had won? Hitler wouldn't have stopped where he did, in the South of France; he would have crossed the Pyrenees, and our country would be a battlefield again. Instead of that, see what happened: Spain is a non-belligerent, respected by everyone. The hand that rules keeps the same steady pulse now as all during the Crusade. Read, read today's *Amanecer* and you'll be convinced."

True enough, the day's newspaper did not carry a single item underlined by Jaime's red pencil; he was minding his own business. But the paper carried such news items as that the bourses of Madrid, Barcelona, and Bilbao had been officially reopened. And that Spain had sent a brilliant industrial exhibit to the Milan Fair: thirteen booths, including one with an outstanding display of cork products made right there in the province of Gerona. Also that the National Delegation of Syndicates had set up an "Education and Rest" organization that would offer its affiliates, the working people, facilities for sports, for the enjoyment of vacations, and other benefits of that kind. Furthermore, the first stone had been laid for the reconstruction of Guernica. The Feminine Section's choral group had held its first rehearsal under the direction of the maestro, Quintana.

"You see, Comrade Rosselló? These are the important things. There's one person here who sees it all quite clearly: Field Marshal Pétain. Last night, Pétain said over the radio that 'Franco has the cleanest sword in the world.'"

I agree, I agree, Comrade Rosselló said, "but you haven't answered my question. How do you manage to keep so calm and correct? I can get nervous over anything, like losing at poker or hearing a strange noise in the car. Your argument about your years wouldn't help me; I see people older than you drown themselves in a glass of water."

"Well, I don't know what else to tell you. It must be a matter of temperament. Or because I used to live in the country, or because I love problems. I can't stand to have everything come out right for me. The day that Commissioner Diéguez makes me angry, or my daughter Cristina does, is the day when I come to the office most eager to work."

"Well, then, I envy you. Couldn't it be a question of health?"

"Of course! That's basic. That's why I do setting-up exercises every morning and walk for at least an hour every day."

"Do you mean you wouldn't be what you are if your health should fail?"

"I couldn't guarantee it. Maybe I could rise above it. But I'm not sure."

"Well, just suppose you came down with the grippe. I'd like to see how you'd behave with a fever of a hundred and one."

The Governor smiled again. "I'm sure I'd be like a bear with a sore head, and delirious to boot. I'd have delusions, like lots of others. Like Comrade Núñez Maza, for instance, who thinks it's going to be possible to reforest Spain in five years. Like General de Gaulle, who has founded a 'Free France' no less, in London. Or like those German diplomats in the hotel who think I'm going to hand over to them all the irrelevant reports they ask me for."

THIRTY-FOUR

SPRING was playing chess with nature and man. It seemed to ignore the existence of the war, paratroopers, the Führer's dreams, and the piles of cadavers. Instead it was busy with the restoration of life. With giving back life to the leaves on the trees, to certain sorrows and many yearnings that had been sleeping. Spring was playing with the looks, the age, and the sex of all who felt it glide gently over their skin.

In the prison, where many pardons had been granted at Easter and the anniversary of the Victory, the rumor was circulating that a full amnesty would come by Christmas and that the prison population would be cut in half. The Costa brothers felt confident that they would be the first to benefit by it. Oh, for the day when they could walk the streets! When stone hammers seemed to sing in the quarries, and for the first time they shook hands with Colonel Triguero and Captain Sánchez Bravo.

Carmen Elgazu was getting better. She had recuperated to the point at which she ventured to go to Mass and do some shopping in the neighborhood stores, where she was received like a queen. But she still walked with difficulty; she could not carry anything heavy; and certain movements were forbidden her. She could still feel keenly the shock of the operation. Her gray hairs had multiplied, and she had deeper circles under her eyes. She looked older. "The mirror doesn't lie," she said to Pilar. Knowing that complete recovery would take months, she arranged for Claudia, the cleaning woman, to come every day instead of only two days a week. "After all," Carmen Elgazu reasoned, "it's to be hoped that Ignacio will be making more money before long. And the truth is that I'm not what I used to be."

Jorge de Batlle was sinking deeper into the depression that beset him; he was growing alarmingly worse, suffering much more severe attacks than ever before. Chelo Rosselló, his sweetheart, went to his house after not hearing from him and learning that he had not gone to work in the Veterans' Administration.

She found him sitting in his chair, motionless, staring vacantly at nothing. The maid said to Chelo: "The young gentleman has been like this for forty-eight hours now, and he's hardly eaten a thing." Chelo called Dr. Andújar, who took one glance at Jorge's stony and expressionless face and said: "Something must be done immediately." He brought the patient to his office and within a half hour gave him his first injection of cardiazol. Jorge suffered great distress for a few minutes before falling into a deep sleep. Dr. Andújar told Chelo Rosselló that Jorge's withdrawal was serious, and that he would have to be given the cardiazol treatment at least seven or eight times. When Jorge awoke, he did not recognize anyone. Chelo said to him, "Jorge, darling. It's me, Chelo!" Jorge babbled some unintelligible words. Dr. Andújar was standing by, his face reflecting his concern. But his words were optimistic. "It's a depressive reaction," he told Chelo. "If you'll help me, your fiancé will make progress and perhaps go into an elated phase."

But not everyone was reacting so unhappily to spring as the "resentful orphan," Señor Grote's nickname for Jorge. Happiness also came often quite intimately. The keynote was love. Those affected in turn were: first, Pablito; then Paz; and finally, Ignacio.

From the moment Pablito first saw Gracia Andújar as she played the role of the adolescent Virgin in the Annunciation scene, he felt so shaken that, even though the time of his examinations was drawing near, he began to follow the girl everywhere, with the dogged persistence of extreme youth. He dreamed about her eyes and her single braid of hair, which caressed her neck like a beautiful serpent. Pablito knew all too well that he was only fifteen years old and that Gracia was seventeen. But he thought he could make up for his youth by putting on a somewhat more sober suit, parting his hair on the side, and drawing the knot of his tie more tightly.

He plotted a line of attack worthy of a general. It started with sending her notes, first unsigned, later signed. Some of them were madrigals showing the influence of Rabindranath Tagore. The girl felt flattered, but could not take him seriously. Pablito then wrote her a long letter begging her to answer him. Gracia Andújar elected to remain silent.

Pablito felt like a fool, but something very deep inside him said that a man could not stop loving because he sensed that he was making himself ridiculous. To him Gracia Andújar meant springtime; she meant textbooks and the definitive discovery of woman. When would he be able to talk to her easily, when would he hear her voice, read in her face whether or not he could cherish some hope?

His chance came with the fiesta of San Fernando, the patron saint of engineers. An official reception was held in the garrison, with a well-planned buffet supper, and Gracia Andújar and Pablito both happened to be there. At last Pablito was able to approach his heart's delight.

"I'm so glad you could come," he said.

Gracia, who was wearing a charming light-pink dress, replied with a laugh: "I guessed that."

"You're laughing at me, aren't you?"

"Why, no, not at all. What do you want me to do?"

"Well, your papa has invited me to visit the Insane Asylum. The men's pavilion," Pablito said. "One of these days I'll be there."

"That's good. You ought to see things like that."

Pablito could not pull himself together. He who could show an astonishing facility for words at the Instituto whenever he took the notion; he, the boy with the brain so powerful that sometimes it made his head ache; he, who was strong in Greek, Latin, and all the other subjects in the fifth form, felt like a boor next to Gracia with her single braid.

"Do you mind my writing to you?"

"Well, to tell the truth I do, a little. It doesn't make sense."

"It doesn't make sense?"

"No, Pablito. Surely you realize that."

"Call me Pablo."

"I can't do that. You're only a kid!"

"Would you like a ham sandwich?"

"Never mind. I'll get one for myself."

Gracia Andújar walked away, to the other side of the room where she chanced to meet Alfonso Estrada.

Pablito felt that his world was sinking beneath his feet. A discouragement like none he had ever felt before overpowered him. He left the party and walked toward the Dehesa almost like a somnambulist, his arms dangling at his sides.

ANOTHER kind of amour was Paz Alvear's. Spring had knocked at the door of her heart. Pachín, the center forward of the Gerona Football Club, the blond athlete to whom the cafe waiters always said: "It's already paid for," had finally turned the head of Matías's niece.

They had been going out together for some time, but the innate seriousness of Paz always put a damper on Pachín's desire. Then, lo and behold, the situation suddenly shattered. It happened one evening as the football star was waiting for the girl at the exit from the Diana Perfumery. He was just out of the shower after an exhausting game at the stadium. Contrary to custom, the couple walked and kept walking that day, making a tour of the section behind the Cathedral where the Stations of the Cross had been restored and where the landscape was a constant reminder of the olive trees and topography of the Garden of Gethsemane. The two young people leaned against the railing of the belvedere, from which they could watch the meanderings of the Ter River as it described an elegant curve on its way to the sea, the campanile of San Pedro de Galligans, and the fertile valley of San Daniel to the right.

The scene was reaching deep inside them, as resentment or an unknown illness will do sometimes. Suddenly, the sky began to darken and they were surprised to find themselves alone, for the days had been lengthening.

Without knowing how it happened, they suddenly kissed with almost desperate ardor and yet at the same time with great sweetness. They held their embrace for a long time, until Pachín murmured in the girl's ear: "Let's go up a little higher."

They turned to their right in search of a grassy spot and found one at the foot of the walls, between blocks of stone that had crumbled with age.

Paz had completely lost control of herself, and Pachín was swept away by a violent force. In no time at all Ignacio's cousin, the daughter of the common Conchi, knew fully and definitively the pleasure and pain of love for the first time. It was like finding a treasure or discovering that Father Christmas does not come from the other world.

Hardly a word was spoken; there were no sobs, no cries. Had it not been for the majestic walls, everything would have transpired with an almost primitive simplicity. The only sound was Pachín's deep breathing. He felt like a hero, this time without the plaudits of the multitude cheering him in the stadium.

Paz was too overcome to speak a single syllable afterward. Pachín, however, the victor of many a joust like that, commented: "I'd never have believed you were a virgin."

For some reason she could not define, Paz was not angered by his words. She felt even happier.

"Well, now you know. I was keeping myself for you."

A few minutes later, they got up. The athlete put his arm around the girl and they started back to the Plaza de los Apóstoles, fused together as one being, then headed toward the quarter where the girl lived. Pachín was smoking, blowing out each mouthful several yards.

They were both aware of being united by a secret. And they knew, too, that the attraction between them was so strong that they would do again what they had done as often as they wanted to and as spring would let them.

When they reached the Calle de la Barca, Paz, who was enjoying an increasing and childish sense of well-being, began to laugh at everything she saw, which was quite unlike her. She laughed at a sheepfold, at the gypsy hawking *The Crime of Cuenca*, and at the decalcomanias covering the window panes of the Crocodile Bar, where her mother worked.

Finally, they saw a little gray cat huddled in a doorway, obviously without an owner. Paz detached herself from Pachín and went up to the kitten, picking it up in motherly hands. The little creature made no protest. The hands of Paz seemed to it like another treasure from Father Christmas.

"I'm going to keep it. It's mine," Paz said. "I'll name it Goal!"

"Goal, Goal," Pachín repeated with a hearty laugh. He was still smoking, and he blew a mouthful of smoke into the face of the little gray animal.

"Don't be so mean. You'll make it afraid of you."

"Afraid of me? All the little creatures love me."

This time it was Paz who laughed. She gave her man a tender glance and said: "So they do."

THE last one to be smitten with a violent springtime love was Ignacio. The expert and astute Adela had finally stolen away his brains, as Pachín had bewitched Paz. Ignacio's youth, his intelligence, and his manner of speaking, which contrasted so sharply with the monotones of Marcos, her bored husband, who collected stamps and was constantly examining his tongue in a mirror, all spelled the stimulation for which she had been yearning. Adela was thirty-five years old, overflowing with passion. Ignacio went up to see her every Saturday without fail, although the fear of discovery prompted them to talk about finding some safer place for their meetings. Adela had acquired such an accurate understanding of Ignacio's sensitivity that she was able to occupy his thoughts beyond all reason.

The consequence of that enthrallment was that Ignacio felt still more detached from Marta. Nevertheless, Adela, with considerable malice, refrained from talking about the girl and pretended not to know of her existence. It did not suit her to wound Ignacio's susceptibilities in that regard. She went no farther than saying in moments of intimacy: "Do you realize that you need a very affectionate woman, a very affectionate one? A girl who will know how to treat you as I do and will whisper sweet nothings in your ear?"

The allusion did not escape Ignacio. For a moment he was put on the defensive, and even felt a measure of resentment toward Adela. But her words produced the desired effect, especially because Marta, against her will, was excessively reserved.

In reality, however, the young man saw that he must come to a decision that spring. The approach of Pilar's wedding was forcing him to it, and so was

Marta's unhappiness. She said to him again and again; "You worry me, Ignacio. You've never been the same since you came back from the Ski Troopers. What's the matter with you? Please tell me. You don't even carry the watch with the blue dial that I gave you with so many allusions."

Ignacio excused himself, citing his preoccupation with his examinations and the pile of work loaded on him in Manolo's office. But Marta felt that he was distant. Of course, there were moments when that was not true. Suddenly, Ignacio would feel free of Adela's spell, and at such times, as he thought of Marta's integrity, he might have set the date for their wedding too on October 12. Yes, he and Marta, Pilar and Mateo could have a double wedding. But that change did not last long. He would go right back to a feeling of detachment. Any trifle was enough to cause that: for example, just seeing Marta march along the Rambla at the head of the "little girls" in the Feminine Section.

Ignacio was perturbed enough to resolve that he would make his final decision before going to Barcelona to take his examinations at the University. He had an impulse to consult Professor Civil on his problem, for the professor had known them both for years. But suddenly, he changed his mind and decided to talk it over with Esther, who always prided herself on understanding women very well. "Yes, Esther knows women. And she'll be able to help me."

His interview with Manolo's wife marked the turning point. Esther was flattered that Ignacio, "who was worth his weight in gold, and more," had consulted her on such a serious matter. Wearing a very snug yellow sweater for the occasion, she asked the maid to serve them tea. "Remember, Ignacio, the first day you came here? You didn't like tea at all, but you didn't dare say so."

"Please, Esther, answer my question."

At first, Manolo's wife took a cautious position. "Why are you consulting me about a thing like that, Ignacio? You're a grown man now, aren't you? You've been through the war."

"Yes, but I've never been married."

Esther played with the little bamboo stick that belonged to Manolo. Finally, she decided to speak out. Actually, she detested ambiguous situations.

"All right, I'll be frank with you. I admire Marta a great deal. I consider her a fine woman. A woman capable of making a man happy, of course. Now, then," she said, pulled her legs up and tucked them under her as she curled up in a corner of her armchair, "your doubts seem reasonable to me. No, I'm not at all sure that your marriage would be a success."

Ignacio did not know whether to be happy at these words or to refuse to listen to them. He waited expectantly. "Please explain yourself a little more."

"Marta strikes me as a trifle dramatic," Esther went on. "I don't know whether I'm expressing myself well. She has a closed mind; she has her ideas and she considers them transcendental. Too much so. And I feel that she'll grow more so every day. If that happens, the whole thing is a risk. Of course, Marta might change. When I first met Manolo he was a fanatic, too, but he's changed. But, Marta—can Marta change? God forbid I should say she can't. When a woman marries, and children come, sometimes she puts everything else second to love."

At this point, Esther stopped. Again she seemed to find it distasteful to have to delve that deeply into the subject. Ignacio, who had let his tea grow cold, urged her to continue.

"Go on, Esther, I beg you."

Esther prolonged her silence for several seconds, but finally shook her head and shrugged her shoulders.

"All right," she said. "I think I've spoken plainly enough. Really, you'd be running the risk that in time an abyss would open between you. Because it's obvious that you don't care a rap about the return of Gibraltar. Marta, on the other hand is right there at all the demonstrations, screaming as if she'd like to swallow the British Isles and Mr. Churchill in one gulp."

Ignacio was thoughtful. After a while, he said: "Would you consider all you've said, which seems to me true, a real impediment regardless of everything else?"

Esther's eyes widened as if in a movie close-up.

"Not at all!" Her tone changed. "Dear Ignacio, we've left out the question that's the real key to everything. The key is this: do you or don't you love Marta? If you love her, all my theories are worthless."

Ignacio bit his lower lip. That query posed the eternal dilemma.

"Please, Esther—is there any way of knowing whether a man loves a woman enough to be sure that he can forgive her for all her defects?"

Esther dropped the little bamboo stick on the floor.

"I'm going to be frank with you, Ignacio. It's always seemed to me that the whole thing breaks down right there—on the fact that you have to be constantly 'forgiving' Marta. That means you have to make an effort to love her and that really you're not managing to do it at all. Think of Pilar. Is Pilar worrying because Mateo is a fanatic or because he has a vocation for politics?"

Ignacio threw up his arms. "Mateo is a man! That makes a difference, doesn't it?"

Esther shook her head. "Only up to a certain point."

Ignacio sat motionless. Suddenly, he fancied he had a toothache. He lighted a cigarette. Esther's words had struck home. "It seems to me that the whole thing breaks down right there..." How long had he been in a state of doubt? Since before the war. And the truth was that he had not moved ahead an inch. On the contrary, things had grown worse lately. Adela was not alone to blame for that; Ana María was, too, through her letters which she was now signing "Rattlebrain."

Esther read the young man's mind and had something more to say.

"Ignacio, please—I don't want to be responsible for your decision. I agreed to talk to you because you asked me to. But I repeat what I said at the beginning: it's your problem, no one else's. Marta really does love you, and for that reason you have no right to let this situation run on indefinitely."

Ignacio agreed with a nod. Suddenly, he rose to his feet with an inner conviction that he had just taken a long step toward the end.

EVERYTHING that followed this conversation came like an irresistible chain reaction. Marta found out what had happened, and as she was willing to keep Ignacio at any price, she made the unheard-of decision to go with him to Barcelona to take his examinations. This entailed incredible complications for her because the Feminine Section had agreed to open a Youth Shelter in Pálamos that summer. Marta was to be in charge of it, which meant making all the preparations now and being away later, through the months of July, August, and September.

"I want to be with you. That's all there is to it."

Ignacio was taken aback. But he realized then how firmly he had made up his mind and spontaneously he forced her to abandon her plan.

"I appreciate what you've just said very much, Marta. But don't you think it might be a bit too much to ask? You're the head of the Feminine Section. What excuse can you give?"

"That's my problem." Marta felt a wrench of desire. "I love you so much!"

That disturbed Ignacio, but it also demonstrated to him that the shell he had grown was hard.

"Listen, darling. You've done enough by just making the gesture you made. I won't deny that I've kept hoping that you'd do something like this for me some day. But stay here this time—and do your duty."

"Would my being there bother you?"

"Don't say that, for God's sake!" Ignacio barely managed to hide his true feelings. "But chances are the examinations will last longer than we've figured. And besides, I'll need to concentrate as hard as I possibly can."

Marta sensed that she was defeated. Her eyes filled with tears and her expression bore no resemblance to the one she wore during the demonstrations for Gibraltar when she screamed as if she were about to swallow the British Isles and Mr. Churchill in one gulp.

"All right, Ignacio. But don't forget that I wanted to be with you..."

Ignacio squeezed her hand. As he did so, he was struck by the thought that he was saying goodbye to the girl. She left him, and her silhouette and the blue shirt faded into the darkness beneath the colonnade of the Rambla. Ignacio sighed. A little later he noticed that he felt absolutely cold. He remembered Esther's words: "The problem is yours and no one else's." Of course it was!

On the fourteenth he took the train to Barcelona. Like Pablito, he had drawn up a plan. The only difference was that Pablito's plan had failed, whereas Ignacio's worked out perfectly.

When he arrived in Barcelona, he headed for Ezequiel's house, where he was to stay as long as the examinations lasted. Ezequiel, happy as ever, exclaimed when he saw Ignacio: "Here comes the great man!" Rosa, the photographer's wife, first warmed a cupful of milk for him, then assigned him the bed in which Marta had slept while hiding there at the beginning of the war.

Ignacio telephoned Ana María from their house. She came at once to see him and refused to leave him until the examinations were over. But her presence would not keep him from studying. She went with him to the University every morning and afternoon and, if necessary, waited for him hour after hour, sitting in a nearby bar. Ana María worried every moment about the outcome of the courses. Ignacio had reported alone, for Mateo had decided to postpone his examinations until December because of the pressure of his work. Ignacio had presented himself and his veteran's papers, but he soon realized that the questions were going to be too much for him. In spite of Professor Civil's efforts, he was still a long way from ready. If he had not been sure that "those examinations were patriotic, too," he would have been mortified. But the atmosphere around him was roundly optimistic. That was true particularly of a boy from Tarragona who always sat beside him during the tests, and who said to him: "What's the point in worrying? You won some medals, didn't you? Well, just write '*¡Arriba, España!*' at the bottom of your paper the same as last October, and everything will be okay."

Ignacio followed his advice and made a bull's eye.

He passed. In one of the happiest moments of his life, Ignacio read his name and patronymic—Ignacio Alvear Elgazu—shortly after he had turned in his papers, for the grades were given out with vertiginous speed. He was on the list of the victors which the beadle of the University posted on the bulletin board in the entrance hall.

A lawyer! He was a lawyer! Ana María threw her arms around him. She flung herself at his neck, reminding him a little of Goering, Dr. Chaos's dog, standing on his hind legs when he saw his master come home in a good mood. Ignacio hardly knew what had happened. What would David and Olga have said? What would Julio García have said? And why was he thinking about them at a time like this? He stood in University Square surrounded by streetcars, almost crying. Ana María, on the other hand, was jumping up and down, and Ignacio said to himself as he watched her: "She really *is* a rattlebrain."

They went to the nearby Telegraph Office, where Ignacio sent a wire to his father, estimating, from the time, that Matías himself would receive it, and picturing him as he read the news. Undoubtedly he would toss into the air the pencil he always wore like a cigarette behind his car. Ignacio sent another telegram to Manolo and Esther, one to Professor Civil, and another to Marta. Then he and Ana María headed straight for their favorite bar, the Frontón Chique Bar, where they sat down and gazed long into each other's eyes, which kept changing color every moment, thus confirming Dr. Andújar's theory that happiness is anything but static.

"Ana María!"

"Ignacio!"

In the back of the café, two old men were smoking as they played a silent game of checkers. The espresso machine was hissing, but Ignacio and Ana María felt as much alone as if they had been shipwrecked in a world predating the first sin.

Until then they had talked about nothing but the examinations. Now that was all behind them. Ignacio felt something stirring within him, and Ana María did too. Memories of the sea and of blue beach balls flitted through their minds. Before they knew it, they discovered they were holding hands.

Ignacio felt so full of Ana María that he knew he must clarify the situation once and for all. That was not easy to do. He made several false starts. He even mentioned his mother's operation, and of course he talked about Manolo, in whose office his professional career would get off to a good beginning. Finally, he made up his mind.

"Ana María," he said, "this is a great day. I have another piece of news for you besides the fact that I passed. I've fully decided to break off with Marta."

Ana María jerked her hand away. The summer before this she had felt sure in herself that this would happen, that some day Ignacio would speak those words. And the young man's behavior since his arrival in Barcelona had confirmed her opinion. Yet when she heard them spoken aloud, syllable by syllable, she felt a thrill of something like fear. Could a man pass like that from one woman to another over a café table?

Ignacio sensed the girl's misgivings and gave her all kinds of explanations.

"I understand your reservations, Ana María. You don't have to say a word. But I have no other recourse. I could no more make Marta happy than she could make me happy. If you knew her, you'd realize I'm right. We both made a terrible mistake." Then he added: "The thing is that I was a fool to let things go on as long as they did."

Ana María was happy then. She realized that Ignacio was not lying to her, that this time it was final. But she could not help thinking: "If that happened to me, I'd go crazy!"

By good luck, Ignacio found the right phrases. He needed a gay, affectionate woman, one who would not have to make an effort to rank him just below José Antonio or the youth hostels or the documentary movies of the Third Reich. (In marriage a whole lifetime was at stake.) Sooner or later, Marta would find another man; probably an Army man. As soon as some scar tissue formed over her wound. As for him, he had realized ever since meeting Esther that he needed a woman like her. Ana María could be the one. Ana María would be capable of playing tennis, sending out Christmas cards, and doing a thousand other things of that sort. And she was feminine from head to toe, even to the point of preserving the wrapping papers from the two lumps of sugar they had taken in their coffee, as she just had done.

Ana María finally lowered her head—with a smile. And she declared herself vanquished—or the vanquisher—in view of his misgivings, which, on the other hand, did honor to his sensitivity. Then she was seized by a burst of gaiety. She leaned over to Ignacio and gave him a sound kiss on the cheek, as if to seal the pact they just had made.

"I love you, Ignacio. I've loved you since the day we met. But that other matter had to be cleared up. Now I believe it is. Lord, what a joy! Do you realize I've passed my examinations, too? Please order another cup of coffee for me."

Ignacio and Ana María lost themselves in each other again, and love, a cloudless love now, lent beauty to their faces. They spent an hour delighting in thoughts of the future that awaited them, while there in the back, the two old men were still smoking and playing checkers.

"Ignacio!"

"Ana María!"

Ana María put her head on Ignacio's shoulder.

"I'll write to you every day," she whispered.

"And I'll answer."

"Do you know something? We're going to be in San Felíu again in July. How often will you come to see me?"

"Every week. Every Sunday."

"We shall see if you do."

Ignacio suddenly pretended to be frightened.

"Do you suppose there'll still be Civil Guards on the beach?"

Ana María made a face. "Oh, that! I guess that won't have changed."

"Okay," Ignacio accepted it with a shrug of the shoulders. "I'll have to be content, as usual, with being able to look at you as much as I like under the water."

Apart from the unforeseeable reaction of Ana María's father, "the ever more powerful Don Rosendo Sarró," to their news, the future held only one problem to solve. When and how was Ignacio going to tell Marta that it was all over between them? He would have to hurt her as little as possible. He said: "I'll go back to Gerona and wait for my chance. Too bad I can't count on Pilar. She's so fond of Marta that she's going to be furious."

Ana María said: "I'm leaving it to you. And I hope with all my heart that Marta will be able to get over it."

Their interlude ended then because Ignacio wanted to take the train home that same afternoon. They left the Frontón Chiqui Bar and took a taxi to Ezequiel's house to pick up Ignacio's bag. Ana María's head rested on his shoulder all the way, and it seemed to her that the taxi was decked with flowers and white ribbons like those carried in church by a bride.

Ezequiel congratulated Ignacio on passing his examinations.

"So now you're a lawyer, eh? Let's see you slap down the black-marketeers then."

Ignacio said: "I'm already doing that."

The same taxi carried them to the station. When they got there, they had only a few minutes before the departure of the last train. A final loving embrace on the platform as the locomotives belched thick black smoke, which dissipated in the huge trainshed. Ignacio thought that doubt had vanished like smoke and that at long last his heart was free—and it was high time.

GERONA welcomed Ignacio with everything but a brass band. "Some telegram!" Matías cried. "The best I've ever had since I started to work in that office."

At the Alvear house a bottle of champagne was uncorked. To every one's surprise, the champagne made Eloy feel as tipsy as Aunt Conchi had at Christmas. "Whoopee!" he shouted, doing handsprings down the hallway and passing out big smacking kisses all around. Marta was a part of the rejoicing—indeed, she outdid them all by appearing at the apartment with a gift for Ignacio almost as stunning as a blow on the head. She handed him a brass name plate identical with the one on Manolo's door except that it said: "Ignacio Alvear, Attorney at Law."

Ignacio turned pale. The best he could do was to stammer: "Thank you, Marta. This was—very thoughtful."

He did not know what to do with the gift. Everyone noticed his discomfort, and Marta realized she had used her last bullet in vain. Pilar stared at Ignacio with open disgust.

An hour later, Ignacio paid his two inevitable calls: on Manolo and Esther and on Professor Civil. More toasts. Manolo said: "Tomorrow we'll talk business. We'll be able to go to work in earnest now." Professor Civil embraced him. "Good for you, Ignacio. I was sure it would all turn out well."

That night in bed, Ignacio decided to wait until Marta had left for Pálamos and the youth hostel before going to see her to tell her of the decision he had made, painful and irrevocable as it was.

THIRTY-FIVE

FATHER Forteza had been visiting the Alvears for more than two hours. He had come to carry out the enjoyable mission of collecting data regarding César as his share of the negotiations for the beatification of Ignacio's brother.

The negotiations had entered their legal phase, and the Bishop had appointed Father Forteza to act as the vice-postulator, that is, to take on the duty of seeking the witnesses and proofs that might eventuate in a "favorable" decision. Later he would reveal the result of his investigations before the ecclesiastical tribunal and would also act as counsel for the defense against the "devil's advocate," in this case Mosén Alberto, who would set forth the pertinent objections. After hearing both sides, the tribunal would decide whether or not it was worthwhile to continue the proceedings and send the findings on to Rome.

The Jesuit's visit lighted up the flat on the Rambla.

"You must forgive me," he said with his open smile, "for making this call in a professional capacity."

Carmen Elgazu had exclaimed: "Holy Mother!" when she had seen Father Forteza, and then had run to the bathroom to tidy her hair and take off her apron, all in the twinkling of an eye.

Meanwhile, Matías and Pilar had escorted Father Forteza into the dining room and offered him a cup of coffee.

"Thank you, but if you don't mind I'd rather have a sweet liqueur."

"Anisette? Calisay?"

"Calisay, please."

"All right, Father. Just a moment."

The bottle of Calisay and the proper small glasses quickly appeared on the table, around which everyone sat down. The family was on tenterhooks. A professional call? What could it be about?

Father Forteza seemed to want to play a little game with the individuals who sat staring at him, half pleased, half wary. With the greatest leisureliness he took out a notebook and pencil as if preparing to take notes. Then, looking at the balcony that offered a view of the river, he remarked: "I suppose it smells bad at times, doesn't it?" Next he inquired about Ignacio. "Do you know whether he'll be home soon?"

Matías shrugged and said, "No, I don't know, Father. Sometimes he comes home from work very late."

Finally, Father Forteza decided to talk. He explained to them what he had come for, and the whole family breathed more easily. He wanted them to know from the beginning what they could expect with regard to the steps that had been taken. "The proceedings are long. They may run on even for years. The Church is very cautious about these matters." He added: "The reasons for initiating the case for beatification were two: first and most important, César really had died for Christ. This in itself would be sufficient if it can be proved." The other, secondary reason was based on the boy's conduct during his few years of life. "Everyone agrees that he possessed supernal virtues, those proper to a holy child."

"Now, then," Father Forteza said in conclusion, "this strange title of vice-postulator means this: I'm here in the capacity of your son's defense counsel."

Carmen Elgazu was so excited that her hand shook ridiculously as she raised the little glass of Calisay to her lips. Matías did not know what to say. He felt obscurely flattered, although he failed to understand why his son should need a "defense counsel." Pilar thought, as she stared at the Jesuit: "If I were a vice-postulator, or whatever it's called, I'd beatify Father Forteza, too."

Matías was the first to collect his forces. He lighted a cigarette with extreme dilatoriness and, as he pulled the ashtray toward him, said: "All right, Father, what can we do to help you?"

"The first thing I'd like to ask," Father Forteza said, "is to see some photographs of César."

Carmen Elgazu turned pale. Since her operation that often happened with or without cause. Pilar, however, was already on her feet and heading for her room.

"I'll get the album."

In those few seconds of waiting, Father Forteza began to use his pencil and paper. Not "to take notes" as they all thought, but simply because he liked to lighten his work, especially when he had to deal with a serious subject, by drawing little houses and trees, with a sheep or two somewhere among them.

Pilar returned promptly. "Here it is," she said, putting the album on the table within the Jesuit's reach.

Everyone was silent. Father Forteza opened the book and started to turn the pages.

Most of the photographs in which César appeared were old and blurred. But that did not matter. The vice-postulator paused at each and studied it. The boy's face made a deep impression on him: those wide-open eyes, those conspicuous ears, that air of meekness. Always his trousers were too long for him. In one of the snapshots he was shown in the Collell, on the tennis court, picking up a ball. In another he was in the Bernat workshop, where images were made; he was painting the wound in Christ's side with pious care. César's expression was like an angel's, an angel perhaps sticking out the tip of its tongue.

Father Forteza did not speak a word, and this only added to the tension. Finally, Carmen Elgazu could not stand any more.

"He was a saint, Father," she cried, putting her hands over her face with a sob. "Lord, and that scum took him away and killed him."

Matías gently pressed his wife's arm. Father Forteza gave her a sympathetic glance. He was anything but a cold creature, but on this occasion he wanted to keep everyone's emotions within bounds.

Finally, he closed the album. "Good, this is enough," he said. "Now I know your son."

Father Forteza took a sip of water before going on to tell them immediately that he was obliged to follow a certain method "in accordance with the rules." He asked their pardon in advance for assuming the air of an interrogator. "But it has to be done. You see?" In beatification cases, many things had to be taken into account: acts of charity, formulas of devotion, mortifications, purity. And a seemingly insignificant detail might be more revealing than a heroic or spectacular deed.

"Quite so, Father. We're at your disposal."

Father Forteza began by saying that everything pertaining to what he might call César's "external" charity was already well known.

"I know he used to go to the Calle de la Barca with a shaving kit under his arm and that he shaved the old men and men too sick to get out of bed. I know he used to sit in the vestibule of some house and teach the little children he found along the street." Father Forteza paused. "I know they called him '4 times 4 equals 16.'"

"Yes, that's true," Carmen Elgazu confirmed. She was calmer now, and kept trying to blow her nose without a sound.

Father Forteza added: "On the other hand, I have no information at all concerning his devotions or his piety. What was it about him that stood out most strongly in that regard?"

The Jesuit's question released a stream of memories in everyone's mind. Carmen Elgazu and, more particularly, Pilar, were careful to sort them out and choose among them so as to inform the priest as best they could. Of course, it turned out to be a little hard to give specific instances. César had prayed continuously. He would utter short, sudden prayers or recite the Credo; he read the Bible often and felt a predilection for the image of St. Ignatius in his room.

"Perhaps," Pilar said, "more than anything else he loved the Virgin. He always carried a lot of printed images and medals, especially of the Virgin of Carmen, and he used to pass them out. When he finished saying the Rosary, he would stay on his knees because he liked saying the Salve Regina, too, with his arms crossed on his chest."

The Jesuit nodded. Just then Carmen Elgazu, suddenly inspired, declared they had forgotten the most important thing: communion. César considered communion the greatest of acts. "He wouldn't have been able to live without taking communion, Father. Do you understand?" The woman explained that each morning after the boy came back from church, he disliked even to ask for his breakfast "out of respect for Jesus who had just entered him."

At those words, Father Forteza looked at Matías, who thus far had contributed nothing.

"Matías," the priest said, "do you remember anything significant about your son's love for the Eucharist?"

The word "Eucharist" always sounded a trifle strange to Matías. He hesitated a moment, then said: "There's one fact that will sum up everything, I imagine. The militiamen arrested him because he had gone out of the house to rescue the sacred vessels in the churches."

Although the priest knew this, he looked thoughtful. He sketched a tree on his pad of paper. Pilar kept thinking: "I wonder if Father can remember all this? Why doesn't he put it all down instead of drawing sheep and trees?"

Father Forteza indicated that he had enough on the subject of piety for the moment and they could go on to another chapter: the one on the mortification of the flesh. He guessed that would prove more difficult to keep in memory, for César must have imposed many penances on himself without letting anyone know of them. But the priest had no choice but to proceed.

Pilar mentioned more specific instances than he had expected. She told of César's austerity about food and games, about his care never to sit in a truly comfortable position, about his biting his tongue whenever anyone was criticized in his presence.

"He mortified himself constantly," the girl said in conclusion. "But he was so used to doing it that it seemed almost as though he didn't feel any pain."

Again Father Forteza addressed Matías directly. "Is it true, Matías, that you forbade him to wear a hair shirt?"

Matías confirmed this. "Of course. I did forbid it." He went on in a mildly ironical tone, "Although I'm afraid he didn't pay the slightest attention to me."

"Why did you forbid it?" the priest asked.

Matías shrugged. "How do I know? César was never a strong child. And I didn't like him to do such things."

Carmen Elgazu was racking her brains lest she forget a detail. How vividly she remembered the moment when Matías angrily threw the hair shirt into the river! Now she spoke again to say that César had mortified himself most frequently during the season of Lent.

"He went all through Lent with hardly a smile. He got thinner, too, because we couldn't get him to eat what he needed. And naturally, he wouldn't even think of whistling."

This brought back to Pilar a happy memory. "But when Holy Saturday came and he heard the bells start to ring with a loud crash, he would jump up and down and throw his arms around all of us. Especially Ignacio."

"Why especially Ignacio?" the Jesuit asked.

"I don't know."

At this point, Father Forteza formulated an odd question, perhaps stemming from what he had said about some insignificant detail proving most revelatory. He asked whether it was true that César frequently visited the cemetery.

The word sounded loud in the room. This time Matías volunteered to answer.

"It's true. That was the first thing he did when he came home from the Collell."

"What do you think prompted him to that, Matías?"

Matías crushed out his cigarette in the ashtray.

"That? No one could imagine why. All I can say is that he used to visit the niches of the young children especially."

Father Forteza opened the photograph album again at this statement. Once more he studied the snapshot showing César painting the wound in Christ's side in the image-maker's shop. Closing the album again, he changed his tone.

"César was a sad child, wasn't he?"

Opinion on this point was contradictory. Carmen Elgazu denied it with much assurance: "Not at all! He was the happiest child in the world. Sometimes he breathed a gaiety I've never seen in anyone else."

Matías looked doubtful but said nothing. Pilar, on the other hand, disagreed.

"Well, it seems to me that Father is right. Basically he was sad. I often used to ask him: 'What's the matter, César? Are you sick?'"

"Ah, yes?" Father Forteza said, staring at the girl.

"Yes, César was discontented with himself. He always considered himself a sinner!"

"A sinner?"

"That's it. He used to say he was a sinner. And he claimed that was why he never was able to convert the men on the Calle de la Barca."

Father Forteza threw up his hands, making it plain that Pilar's remarks had pleased him. Another short pause fell, then the priest addressed Matías again.

"Could you imagine, Matías, that César could ever have been guilty of impure acts?"

Carmen Elgazu stared at Matías as though wishing to suborn him.

"No," Matías said. "Absolutely out of the question." He added after a moment: "He wouldn't even know what that was."

The response was so sure that Father Forteza struck the table with his pencil, then ran his hand over his head, and, as if preparing to shorten the interview, asked them what, after all, had been the boy's chief virtue.

This time they all looked puzzled. What could they say in answer? Perhaps obedience; perhaps humility—César grew nervous if they praised him. Matías recalled that the boy once had succeeded in catching a fish in the Ter River and had been as perturbed as if he had done something bad.

Carmen Elgazu spoke. "May I give my opinion, Father?"

"Certainly you may."

"I think César's greatest virtue was hope. Yes, my son was full of hope. Of a great trust in God."

Father Forteza straightened his back. This was the first time through the interview that the word God had been spoken—how curious! The Jesuit's expression told them that they had reached a particularly difficult point.

"Señora, did your son ever speak to you about supernatural visions?"

Carmen Elgazu bit her lip. She looked as though it worried her to enter this terrain.

"Speak up please, Señora..."

"It's just..." Carmen Elgazu made up her mind. "Once he said to me that he had seen rays of light around the image of St. Francis of Assisi."

Father Forteza seemed surprised.

"St. Francis of Assisi? Was César a great animal lover?"

Carmen Elgazu hesitated. "No, I don't think he loved them in any special way."

The Jesuit noticed that Matías started to light another cigarette.

"Matías, do you believe that it was possible for César really to have seen those rays?"

"To tell the truth, I don't know. But in any case, César never told a lie."

Father Forteza turned to Pilar.

"Did he ever tell you about that?"

The girl shook her head in denial.

"No. But one Christmas day he told me he believed that the Infant Jesus had smiled at him."

Father Forteza's expression was impenetrable; it was evident that he did not wish to pursue that line of thought. Once more he spoke to Carmen Elgazu.

"Carmen, you said earlier that César often breathed a gaiety like none you've ever seen in anyone else. How could he have felt gay at that time when there was so much scoffing and so much persecution?"

Carmen Elgazu said without hesitation: "Because he knew that Jesus would triumph, you see, Father. That was the best thing about César: he believed with all his strength in the promises of Jesus."

The promises of Jesus—Father Forteza instantly called up within himself several maxims addressed to the Apostles: "Your sadness will turn into joy... In a little while, you will not see me, and again in a little while, you will see me."

The word "apostles" turned the Jesuit's thoughts in another direction and focused them on an aspect of the question which held a special interest for him.

"Do you consider, Carmen, that César's greatest aspiration was to be a priest?"

Carmen Elgazu then said something utterly unexpected. "To tell you the truth," she said, "I don't consider that César's greatest aspiration was to be a priest."

General surprise.

"What do you mean?"

Carmen Elgazu assumed great dignity. "I believe that César's greatest aspiration was something else: it was to die. Yes, that was his vocation. He used to say that for the very reason that we were living through a period of scoffing, someone must expiate our sins. Months before the war that thought had sunk very deep in him, and he talked about nothing but that. He used to say we were sinning and that he wanted to die."

Father Forteza stopped drawing trees. He noticed the circles under her eyes. But a few seconds later, he went on.

"Who was the last person to see him?"

Matías answered. "Mosén Francisco. He disguised himself in a blue coverall, and was hiding in the cemetery. When the militiamen got tired of shooting and went away, Mosén Francisco went to the victims and he managed to give César absolution."

Silence dominated the dining room. This time it was broken by Carmen Elgazu, who suddenly put her handkerchief to her nose, saying: "Did you know, Father, that there are still many people in Gerona who pray to my son, as if he were on the altar? They ask him for favors. You could talk with some of them if you are interested."

Father Forteza made a gesture that meant: "That will have to come later."

Just then they heard a key turn in the lock, and Ignacio came in.

Everyone was glad to see him. He was the missing piece. In a way, Ignacio had known César better than anyone, and it would have been a pity if Father Forteza had gone without even having spoken to him.

Ignacio could not conceal his astonishment at seeing Father Forteza from the hallway. He had come home looking somewhat strange, for some reason. Perhaps owing to the excessive amount of work he did at Manolo's house.

In two strides, he went into the dining room. "Father! What an honor! I certainly didn't expect..."

The Jesuit got up to shake hands with him. "Now you see, son, you came just at the right moment."

"Really?"

Somewhat disconcerted, Ignacio kissed his mother on the forehead and sat down beside her in a chair that Pilar pulled up. And it was Pilar also who took it upon herself to explain the reason for Father Forteza's presence there.

As Ignacio listened to her, he kept moving his head rapidly. Evidently, it cost him an effort to adapt himself to the subject, which had been far from his mind. That intensified the change in the atmosphere which Ignacio's arrival had brought to the dining room. He had noticed at once the photograph album lying on the table, however, and that brought him into the situation at once.

"César, sure..." he murmured as if talking to himself while his eyes were on the album.

Father Forteza said to him: "They've been telling me some very interesting things which I can use for my task. I'm very much impressed."

Ignacio finally raised his eyes and fixed them on the Jesuit. And in a tone very characteristic of him, one of longing and discontent, he replied: "What would impress us all most would be to see César still sitting here among us in his usual chair."

Carmen Elgazu turned pale again. Matías changed countenance.

Father Forteza understood the young man. "Of course," he said, "You're quite right. From the human point of view, it would be best to have him sitting here." Choosing his words carefully, he went on: "Nevertheless, on the—shall we say transcendental?—plane, the recognition of César's saintliness might serve as a consolation, mightn't it?"

Ignacio felt the old rebelliousness stir inside him. It was obvious that he was struggling with himself. Finally, he answered.

"You must realize this, Father. It's difficult to speak of consolation in cases like this."

Ignacio's tone had hardened. Carmen Elgazu stared at her son in expectant fear. The play of feeling was complex and the empty glasses of Calisay struck a frivolous note. The people gathered there could not know that Ignacio had not come from Manolo's house, but from Adela's. Hence his discomfort, which affected them all. A quarter of an hour ago, Ignacio had been saying to Adela: "This is awful. I'm beginning to realize that I can't live without you."

A tense silence had fallen. Father Forteza pointed out: "Nonetheless, I insist that the thought that César is already an angel and that he's looking down on us from above at this very moment has its own beauty."

Ignacio grimaced. He recalled the doubts about heaven which he had expressed in Manolo and Esther's house. He even thought: "Why does Father say this, since he knows that the angels and saints are happy alone in their contemplation of God?" But he gave ground. Why? Because there was his mother, Carmen Elgazu, staring at him with the dramatic expression she had worn years earlier when he had stood up against Mosén Alberto.

With a titanic effort, Ignacio succeeded in making his face look brighter and in speaking in a tone of great conviction.

"You're right, Father. Yes, surely César is in heaven—and he's looking down at us right now..."

Carmen Elgazu nearly burst with happiness. "Son!" she exclaimed, taking his hands tenderly. "Thank God for hearing you talk like that."

The situation reversed itself. Ignacio's words fell like a life-giving rain into the dining room. The Jesuit looked at the young man with gratitude, although he did not conceal from himself that Ignacio's reaction had come in obedience to an emotional impulse. But Ignacio was so glad to have conquered himself—and to see his father also looking at him with gratitude—that he decided to put a final gloss on his good deed.

"César!" he exclaimed as though to make it clear that he could go on talking about his brother forever. "Alongside of him I was—I don't know what! A coward." He smiled before adding: "And as you've all seen, I still am one!"

The Jesuit protested: "Don't say that, boy. At your age it's natural for you to ask questions. Besides"—here he made an expressive gesture—"if you didn't do that, you wouldn't be Ignacio, would you?"

Pilar felt like clapping her hands. "I like that!"

Father Forteza picked up his note pad, a definite clue that he was about to end "the interrogation." Just then Ignacio's eye happened to fall on the bottle of Calisay and he said, "Hmm!" poured himself a glass, and held the liqueur in his mouth.

"Bad cess to anything that's a vice," he cried. "It means one's own will doesn't count."

Now determined to change joy into euphoria, Ignacio said to the Jesuit: "Has anyone told you this is a red-letter day in this house?"

Father Forteza shook his head. "I don't know what you mean."

Ignacio informed him that they were celebrating his father's birthday.

The Jesuit was also ready to clap his hands at this news. He turned to the interested party and said: "Your birthday! Many happy returns!" He stretched himself a little to be able to take both of Matías's hands in his. "How old are you, Matías? Which birthday is it?"

"Exactly fifty-five."

"A mere boy."

"I'll say I am. I'm going to enroll in the Youth Organizations tomorrow."

The meeting, now pleasant for everyone, went on for the space of another quarter of an hour. Father Forteza told several anecdotes about his days as a postulant and talked about the evangelical work his older brother was doing as a missionary in Nagasaki, Japan.

Carmen Elgazu asked: "But isn't it dangerous for your brother in those countries?"

"No, no!" Father Forteza replied. "It's much more dangerous to be wearing a cassock right here."

Finally, the gathering broke up. Father Forteza had to go to the convent to hear the women's confessions.

"There must be a long line of them waiting for me in the church."

Pilar asked him: "Are you still handing out such tough penances?"

"Tougher, daughter, tougher! But they come back. There's nothing I can do about it."

The whole family escorted the priest to the door. Pilar tried to kiss his hand, but he quickly pulled it back.

"May César bless you all," the Jesuit said. "And may he help to bring this mission to a good outcome, for today I've only made a start."

So saying, he was off like a hare, running down the stairs two at a time.

Left alone, the family went back to the dining room. Ignacio shut himself up in the bathroom. Pilar picked up the album and took it back to her room. Matías headed for the balcony facing the river, which reflected the lights in its water. Soon he noticed beside him the warm and happy presence of Carmen Elgazu.

THIRTY-SIX

"AREN'T there enough hells here on earth?" This phrase, attributed to Dr. Chaos, was not without justification. The war was like a poison spreading through the world, infecting all its members. Russia had taken possession of the three Baltic states of Latvia, Estonia, and Lithuania, and was gnawing on Romanian territory in the regions of Bessarabia and Bukovina. Meanwhile, Italy, absolute lord of the central Mediterranean, was getting ready to extend the war into Africa by attacking British Somaliland with the intention of crossing Libya into Egypt with the dual purpose of nullifying the mutual aid pact signed by Egypt and England and of seizing the Suez Canal. An event of greater importance, however, was the start of the "air and naval battle of the English Channel." This was to be the prelude to a German invasion of England, which the whole world believed imminent.

Germany already had her grip on two thousand miles of seacoast from Narvik to Bidasoa. She had occupied the two Channel islands of Jersey and Guernsey, which belonged to England, and her air force had begun to trace swastikas in the sky above the island. "Germany, the land of aviators!" This was the phrase used by the Germanophile magazine *Aspa*, published in Spain. General Sánchez Bravo, still sticking flag pins in the huge map that Nebulosa had hung on the wall, estimated that the German air force enjoyed a superiority of eight to one over the English. The Stukas were especially successful; they had dropped bombs with an explosive force so great that they could blow the defenders ten or twelve centimeters off the ground, and were starting to deal mortal blows to the English cities and industrial centers. First, four hundred planes had flown over Portland, then five hundred, then a thousand. Who could clip the "miraculous wings" of Field Marshal Goering? England was fighting the war in the air with greatly inferior forces: anti-aircraft, barrage balloons, some of which got lost in space and were seen along the coasts of Galicia. In his most recent speech, the Führer had pronounced a sentence beyond appeal:

Delenda est Britannia! England must be annihilated. "And all because of the stubbornness of a single man, Mr. Churchill," Matías explained, "a man who won't accept the facts."

General Sánchez Bravo realized that the "invasion" of England would have to be attempted by air, in any case, because the Führer lacked a navy strong enough to cross the Channel and make a landing on the island. Germany had submarines and torpedo boats, but not warships of great tonnage, although it seemed the construction of those was being rushed. England still ruled the sea, the Channel, in spite of the threat from the sky. The British had acquired several battleships, supported by fifty destroyers that President Roosevelt had sold them, an act that meant that the United States virtually had abandoned neutrality and moved to a nonbelligerent status.

As Professor Civil read the papers, which assumed as a matter of course that the city of London, embracing about the same area as the province of Álava in the Cantabrian Mountains, would be wiped out, he felt more and more disturbed. "I don't know what will finally happen in the English Channel," the Professor said. "But for the time being, the men in both air forces, the seamen, and the British civilian population who are dying and losing their homes—the whole thing adds up to an irreparable catastrophe. What madness rules the world, what madness!"

Strangely enough, the hard-core Germanophiles, one of whose chief spokesmen was Mateo, never felt the slightest regret over what was happening. On the contrary, the cartoons that appeared in the press depicting the terrible period the English were passing through merely put them in a good humor. One cartoon, published in *Amanecer*, showed an Englishman so goaded by the shortage of food, by hunger, that he was preparing to eat another Englishman. "Don't worry," the first man said to his victim. "Give me your ration card and I'll tell your family about it." Mateo burst out laughing when he read the caption.

This attitude was so prevalent that most of the people who opposed the Axis did not dare to express an opinion. They were afraid and they kept silent. But there were others more firmly resolved each day to make public their convictions. Agustín Lago was one of those. Indeed, at a meeting called by the Falange to consider the organization of the next summer's youth camps, he challenged Mateo, who had made a joke concerning the fate that the Germans would deal out to the British royal family. Agustín Lago had one concrete objection to the Axis: he considered both Nazism and Fascism anti-Christian movements. That was enough for him, as it was for Mosén Alberto. "I am a member of the Church," he declared, "and the Church can by no means approve of the doctrines of Germany and Italy or the brutal means of conquest they employ."

This came as a surprise to Mateo. Little by little he had become better acquainted with Agustín Lago and had come to feel a certain respect for him. "I'm glad," he said, "that you've spoken so frankly. Now I know what to look out for. But whatever you may think, you'll see the British royal family in Canada before long, or in Berlin sweeping the Führer's office."

Agustín Lago seemed quite unruffled. The great change in the Inspector of Elementary Education since his arrival in Gerona was plainly evident. In spite of his somewhat aseptic manners and his bifocals, he was obviously much more sure of himself. No one knew what had caused the change. The Governor attributed it to a truce granted the educator in his cloistered student days and to the present balance that he had struck, which showed him a more flattering picture of himself than he had once thought possible. On the whole, the students and teachers were working in earnest. Mateo believed the change stemmed from something else: Agustín Lago's success in mastering the complex caused in the beginning by the loss of his arm. The day the city traffic policeman appeared on the Puente de Piedra with his wooden leg, Lago felt that he was in good company. He was no longer the only amputee in the city. "That's when he started to hold his head up."

Agustín Lago could have told them, however: "That's all true, but it's not the whole truth." In spite of the heat beating down on Gerona, Agustín Lago was as conventionally dressed as ever. He realized that he owed his present serenity in great part to a visit from a comrade in Opus Dei, a man named Carlos Godo from Barcelona. The two men had never met before, but Carlos Godo, an architect by profession, knew of the educator and had taken the train to call on him. The meeting between them was so cordial that Agustín Lago was able to forget for several hours the deep pain that the war and the ultra-rigid attitudes of men like Mateo had caused him. He reveled in the ineffable comfort brought him by the sudden discovery of a kindred soul, in itself a rare occurrence.

Carlos Godo! He and Agustín Lago agreed on everything. They agreed that people who were exhilarated by the damage done to others were guilty of conduct contrary to the teachings of the Bible; that a follower of Luther could be redeemed more easily by the truth than could a follower of Rosenberg's creed: that the founder of Opus Dei, Father Escrivá, was one of the "Lord's anointed"; that his *Obra*, which admitted non-Catholics and members of all races, was destined to spread all over the world and rejuvenate the now somewhat spavined Church from within—who could tell? Once in a while, Agustín Lago and Carlos Godo had to laugh at themselves for making such prophecies, for at the moment the Opus Dei consisted of only a few boys scattered across the Spanish landscape, with no basic training and almost no contact with one another. But that did not matter. They felt within themselves an instinctive strength that assured them that the Idea, the idea of living out in the world according to the Bible while pursuing their own calling, unaffiliated with any priesthood, in absolute independence, would ultimately bear fruit. They thought of themselves as in a sense like "early Christians" in their purity and integrity; like perpetuators of that Church which, thanks to the vision of St. Paul, had been able to penetrate to the heart of the Roman Empire by making use of a handful of fishermen and the Holy Spirit.

Well, now it was happening. The world was being ruled off into squares, as Professor Civil so aptly put it. Just as the waves of bombing planes attacking England flew in rigid formation, the men who felt the claws of Catholicism in their flesh and those who watched from afar but espoused one side or the other had formed ideological clans from which the adversary, whoever or whatever he might be, was impossible to reach. Something of the sort always happened when an earthquake destroyed cities and consciences; the consciences were forced to make a choice. And those who chose the same side hugged one another with enthusiasm and raised their voices to shout or whisper the same song.

That was why Mateo and José Luis Martínez de Soria laughed at the same thing, and why the photographs, books, and slogans they kept in their offices were the same as those to be found in the office of any other Falangist in any other region of Spain. That was also why the room occupied by Carlos Godo in his parents' house in Barcelona was very similar to Agustín Lago's room. Both were austere rooms with a Crucifix and an image of the Virgin on the wall. How could it be otherwise? Their objectives were parallel, like those of David and Olga—another clan, another tribe—and those of El Responsable and José Alvear. Carlos Godo and Agustín Lago shared the same mental repertory down to the subtlest details, following the line of *Camino*'s thinking: "So act that by thy comportment and thy conversation all who see and hear thee may be able to say, 'This man reads the life of Jesus Christ.'" The rule that led them to say "the Lord" when referring to Christ; to display no habit or distinctive trait so as to look as much alike as possible outwardly; to commit themselves totally to God while sharing the strictest intimacy; to take for granted that they would be misunderstood for a long time, even by many religious institutions... An archetypal example of all that was Dr. Gregorio Lascasas, who had several times narrowed his eyes to two black horizontal slits as he listened to Agustín Lago.

"Aren't there enough hells here on earth?" After Agustín Lago had talked for five consecutive hours with Carlos Godo, an architect from Barcelona whom he regarded as a brother, he admitted that there were, for he had learned of the Russian advances in the Baltic and Romania, of the massive air attacks on England, and of the existence of men like Mateo who granted an absolute value to questionable creeds. But he also thought that there were pieces of Heaven "here below"—sometimes in the room of a poor pension at a very late hour of the night.

THIRTY-SEVEN

JULY and August. The second summer following the end of the Spanish war had come, and the Gerundians were scattered in much greater numbers than the year before. The vacation fever began to climb, as it always had climbed until 1936. The workingmen, the "producers," had to be content to enjoy their holidays in the city, being lazy, sleeping until all hours, and perhaps walking along the banks of the Ter or through the valley of San Daniel on Sunday with their families. The middle class, too, both civilians and those in active service, could not find a cottage to rent on the coast or in the mountains, but the number of the "privileged few" had grown considerably, and now included the black-marketeers in the city who had managed to escape running the gauntlet of the authorities: most of the aldermen, Comrade Arjona, the Syndicate Delegate, the Chief of Public Works, and others.

Mateo went away to his youth camp, known that year as the Haro Camp in memory of the Falangist Eduardo Haro, who had been shot by the Reds. This camp was not set up in San Telmo, but in the idyllic region of Arbucias in the interior, "for it was good for the boys to change locales and become acquainted with the oxygen-giving diversity of the province." Mateo left with an easy mind, but Pilar stayed in Gerona, working and sewing on her trousseau as usual—October was not far off—and looking after Don Emilio Santos.

Marta also left to prepare her scheduled youth hostel in Pálamos, among the pines. A hundred and twenty young girls, most of them from the villages, chosen on the recommendation of the local Falange leaders, would take turns living there in tents, swimming, learning, answering the customary questionnaires, and singing patriotic songs while the flag was being raised. Before she left, Marta tried to hold back her tears as she said goodbye to Ignacio.

"Will you come to see me?"

Ignacio replied: "Of course, girl. But you know I'm very busy."

Comrade Rosselló also decided to take a vacation, not to fish or go leaping through the woods, but to visit the Penitentiary of Puerto de Santa María. The Governor sent in the petition required to obtain permission for Dr. Rosselló to see his son, and it was granted. Miguel Rosselló got ready to drive alone across Spain from north to south, as far as Cádiz. He was looking forward to embracing his father, whom he pictured wearing convict garb.

Warning Voice also left the city for a fortnight. He went to Puigcerdá, a fashionable resort in the Cerdaña. The dentist could never have imagined that this trip was to prove decisive for him; that in the hotel where he would be staying and at the golf club adjoining it, he would meet a girl of twenty-eight from Barcelona, an heiress with a title of nobility—the Countess of Rubí—or that he would get along so well with her that he would quite forget his matrimonial advances toward the widow of Don Pedro Oriol. Truly the couple understood each other so marvelously that the girl, whose name was Carlota, fancied that the Mayor of Gerona had meant his "Windows on the World" exclusively for her. For his part, the Mayor sent a postcard to his Pamplona friend, Don Anselmo Ichaso, saying: "I've just met a delightful child who understands more about the monarchy than you or I. The amazing thing is that she's put a picture of me right next to one of Alfonso XIII in the card case that she carries in her handbag."

By and large, however, it was Paz who had the most unexpected vacation. The girl, head over heels in love with Pachín since the night when she had become a woman at the foot of the walls, on the grass, had had a presentiment that something good was going to happen to her, that her life would take a complete turn. She was right. What she could not have imagined, however, was that her good luck would come in the form it did.

As it happened, Damián, the leader and trumpet player of the Gerona Jazz Band, chanced to see a blond girl in a dance hall accompanying the band by singing into a microphone. It occurred to him to use that idea for the Gerona Jazz Band. Ambrosio, who played the bass viol, a chronic asthmatic and a pessimist, said: "That's never going to go over here." But Damián scoffed at him, as usual. He spent a couple of days ruminating and stroking his dashing mustache.

Suddenly, like a flash, he remembered Paz. He had seen the girl during the fairs behind the Diana Perfumery stand set up on the midway, and he recalled her deep, throaty voice. "Diana Perfumery is giving away soap to everyone, regardless of who or what they are." He thought of her good looks, her impudent way with the soldiers, and her green uniform, with its amusing little cap. Wasn't she the very one he was looking for?

No sooner said than done—or sung! Damián showed up at the Diana Perfumery and said to Paz without more ado: "The Fiestas Mayores are about to begin in the villages. I need a vocalist. I promise to make you a super-star after a month of practice, more popular than Pachín."

Paz, tired of scrimping, opened her eyes wide. She agreed to a trial before the microphone in Damián's own house. The result was all that it ought to have been.

"I told you so, kid. You'll knock 'em cold."

Everything worked like a charm, and Pachín showed that he was a decent fellow. "Okay! It's the greatest! Smooth as butter! You and I, we're tops!" Dámaso, the owner of the Diana Perfumery, understood also that he ought to give her her chance. "Go ahead, little one. Don't worry about the store." Of course, the flat on the Rambla became the scene of a great to-do. Matías, amused at his niece's boldness, cut it short by saying: "Where's the harm in it? Don't preachers use microphones?" Even Goal, the cat adopted by Paz, seemed delighted; he jumped into her arms and licked her hand.

More happy prospects, like winning the lottery. "Gerona Jazz Band, with the sensational vocalist PAZ ALVEAR!" In no time the city was plastered with advertisements with her name printed in huge, red letters on signs that took the place of those tattered remnants of Holy Week. Soon afterward, her name was posted here and there all over the province.

Paz had a wonderful summer, going from village to village, from fiesta to fiesta. Darnius, Celrá, Vilajuiga, Llagostera, Agullana, Camprodón, Tossa de Mar... The girl learned how to move her body, and she wore gold high-heeled slippers. Her hair made the boys think of a wheat field. Her bosom was provocative. When she went up to the microphone, took hold of it, and looked around the hall with simulated shyness, bowing her head a little, shouts of "*¡Olé!* Hurray for the mother who bore you," broke out. Then Paz, too, would utter something like a shout, and for a few moments the room was spellbound, while Fermín, the man who worked the lights, rolled his eyes up and showed his teeth. And when Paz made her exit, picking up the maracas and moving her hips in time to them, the couples who filled the pavilion to overflowing let themselves become bewitched by that rhythm and also had their moments of fulfillment.

Paz, for her part, discovered that she liked "that business." She liked the old-fashioned draperies and the boxes in the pavilions, the billboards bearing her name, even the smell and sweat of the dancing human flesh. Every place seemed the same. The same hubbub, the same peddlers, the same peasants in their Sunday best, smoking "*caliqueños*" and drinking rum. But each place had something alike yet always different—love. In Celra, the young men offered their sweethearts ribbons for their hair; in Agullana, they gave a trinket. In

Vilajuiga, boy and girl went outside before long and vanished among the straw-stacks; in Pálamos they used the boats. Depending upon the place, love became a bottle of pop or beer or an earthen jug of red wine. Perhaps the differences were traceable to tradition; perhaps to the winds; perhaps to the way the dogs barked at the moon.

Whatever it was, the life that Paz led that summer, thanks to the lucky chance with the Gerona Jazz Band, took on a new dimension. She enjoyed herself much more than Marta, very much more than Comrade Rosselló, as much as Mateo and Warning Voice and the black-marketeers who had rented comfortable cottages.

"Are you happy?" Damián asked her—Damián, the man with the black mustache, the mocking trumpet, who had become her mentor.

"Very much so."

"Tomorrow, in Hostalrich, when we play the first rhumba, you light a cigarette."

As a rule, the fiestas ended quite late, in the small hours. After everyone had gone and broken serpentines, empty bottles, and paper cones littered the floor, a strange nostalgia invaded the pavilions, as it does at circuses after a performance. The piano lid went "tock" as it came down, like the cover on a coffin.

Not long after that, the Gerona Jazz Band would start on its swing back to Gerona, always in the same eight-passenger taxi, which pulled a trailer in which the musicians carried their instruments and usually brought back next to the instruments, in some collapsible boxes built for the purpose, an occasional kilo of rice or liter of olive oil. Even the bass drum had been equipped for the same service, with a special device for opening and closing it.

More often than not, Paz was so exhausted on the return trip, sometimes around dawn, that she would fall asleep and snore. But sometimes she did not. Sometimes, especially if the night was bright, she stayed awake and looked around, seeing how the trees embraced in the darkness.

Then she would remember the days in Burgos and her failure in Madrid. But the "*Olés*" were still ringing in her ears and the echo of Pachín's voice saying: "You and I, we're tops." Lord, how she was getting her own back, how she was making up for the past and its lacerating humiliations!

When the taxi arrived in Gerona, it dropped off the musicians at their homes, usually. When it came time to drop Paz, the girl would stand up and say good-night to her companions, sending them a kiss from the tips of her fingers. Ambrosio, the bass violist, would say to her: "Goodbye, starlet!"

That was the end of the fiesta. For the stairway to the flat in which El Cojo once had lived always struck her as sinister. So much so that as she climbed the stairs, she tried not to touch the sticky banister with her hand and asked herself: "When will we be able to move to a better place?" Goal, the kitten, generally waited for her, sleeping on the landing. When he heard her footsteps, he would wake up and open one eye to look at her as if to say: "It's about time, little girl."

ALL in all, summer was turning out to be somewhat explosive, as if a psychological Stuka had dropped a few bombs on Gerona and its environs.

But the bomb with the biggest payload fell on the head of Dr. Chaos. That was bound to happen.

Throughout the entire winter, Dr. Chaos had comported himself in grand style at the hospital and the clinic, and with extreme discretion in the pursuit of his peculiar pleasures. He was living in the Citizens Hotel on the Calle de los Ciudadanos, where he received an occasional suspect visitor to be sure, usually a soldier or a boy who looked like a gypsy; but there was no law which forbade him to open the door of his room, Number 42, to anyone asking to see a doctor.

Accordingly, though he was looked upon askance in official circles because of his opinions, and though the Governor and Commissioner Diéguez were waiting for a propitious occasion before dropping on him, he had a good name in the city, especially after he had skillfully won the sympathy of almost all the women who counted, including María del Mar. That fact astonished the inexperienced. But the very sexual anomaly of Dr. Chaos, the elegance of his dog Goering, and the pursed mouth with which he sometimes talked or listened, were most acceptable in the ladies' conversation groups. And, besides, he knew how to flatter them, to tell them witty stories, and to toss off *double-entendres*, all of which brightened the parties as much as a pinch of snuff will enliven the old peoples' cliques in the villages. Doña Cecilia, in particular, adored Dr. Chaos; she was always saying that just to see him took her out of the bad humor into which she was thrown by the everlasting little flags that the General kept sticking in the maps at the garrison.

But when summer came, Dr. Chaos felt constrained to find a hotel for himself—the Hotel Miramar in the beautiful town of Blanes, there to spend his weekends. One of his reasons for doing so was that he needed a rest. His work in the operating room was exacting, not to mention the spread of gonorrhea among the enlisted men, which was like an epidemic.

As it happened, Dr. Chaos, a man of forty-five, drunk on the sun which toasted him on the beach in the mornings and on the good wine served him at table in the hotel in Blanes, lost some of his control over himself. He fell suddenly in love with a beardless young waiter named Rogelio, eighteen years old, who bore a distant resemblance to Alfonso Estrada.

Dr. Chaos, that splendid and elegant specimen of humanity, had worked out in the course of his career an entire program of seduction which had brought him success on previous occasions: large tips, packages of cigarettes, unusual amiability. Young Rogelio, who worked in a brickyard during the winter and who knew the prestige of Dr. Chaos, simply felt a little perturbed at the onset of the siege. The doctor finally told him that perhaps he was wasting his time on such humble tasks as making bricks and waiting on table in a hotel, and that he might aspire to enroll for some courses in something. This idea dazzled the boy, who was of very humble origin but cherished certain aspirations. Then one day, Dr. Chaos, seizing upon the chance that the boy had suddenly lost his voice, adopted a professional air and approached the lad to examine his throat and eyes and listen to his heartbeat through a stethoscope.

When Dr. Chaos finished his examination, he said to Rogelio: "There's something here that I don't like. Take this medicine and we shall see."

The boy regained his voice but did not lose his pallor. A week later, the doctor happened to be listening again to his heart with the stethoscope at his back and chest when he promised to take Rogelio to Gerona to give him a thorough going-over in the Chaos Clinic.

"You notice that you feel tired, don't you? And as if you had no strength."

"Yes, I do, a little."

Perhaps Rogelio was led to believe that by the power of suggestion and could see no other way of showing his gratitude than to go to the doctor's room whenever he was called.

Finally, one afternoon in August, when the Mediterranean sun was shedding oblique rays over the beautiful town of Blanes and filtering kindly through the Venetian blinds in the doctor's room, Dr. Chaos suddenly felt possessed by his evil passion at the sight of Rogelio's bare torso, and having brought with him an unguent, he began to caress the boy's skin as if trying to relax his muscles.

It took Rogelio more than a minute to realize that something abnormal was going on, especially because his initial sensation was one of pleasure, of relief from his imaginary fatigue. But suddenly, he began to grow alarmed. He turned around quickly and stared at Dr. Chaos. He saw the doctor's face aflame as if covered with a mask. The sight horrified Rogelio. He felt an indescribable loathing, although he stood as if paralyzed. Then Dr. Chaos tried to kiss him. The young waiter gave a kind of squeal, pushed the doctor away with unsuspected strength, and fled, although it took everything he had to manage to get the door open. He ran downstairs panting, not knowing what to do, thinking that the doctor was pursuing him. He flung himself into his room, where he burst into angry tears. Suddenly, he pulled himself together, threw the package of cigarettes on the floor, and got up to go and tell his employer, the hotel manager, what had happened. His indignation was so great that he wanted to notify the Civil Guard. He kept constantly rubbing his lips with the back of his hand.

The hotel owner, Victoriano by name, a man of experience after having worked for six years on the Côte d'Azur, calmed young Rogelio as best he could and persuaded the boy to leave the matter in his hands. He realized from the start that it was not to his interest to let the matter become public.

"Go on, take a shower and have a cold drink. I'll deal with that cur."

Much against his will, young Rogelio obeyed. Victoriano, the proprietor of the Hotel Miramar, wasted no time before going to Dr. Chaos's room.

His interview with the doctor, who had already packed his bags, was very brief.

"If you ever show your face around here again, I'll turn you over to the police. For the moment, I'll see to it that the boy keeps his mouth shut."

Dr. Chaos answered: "Very well."

A quarter of an hour later, the distinguished surgeon was driving his car, a second-hand Peugeot, along the road that would take him back to Gerona. It was Sunday. His hands were trembling on the wheel. He felt intensely sad. He felt sorry for himself. He looked around him at the landscape and asked why Nature, so wise in coordinating plant life, had played such a filthy trick on him. He met other cars, a few in which men and women were traveling together. His face still smelled of the eau de cologne and cold cream that he had used in his conscientious preparations for his frustrated plan. And what made it all the worse was that the remembered face of young Rogelio haunted him more than ever. Goering, the dog, also seemed sad; instead of putting his head out the car window, he lay crouched down on the seat next to his master.

When Dr. Chaos arrived in Gerona, he turned toward the hospital. The nuns greeted him with deference. "What are you doing here, Doctor? We didn't expect you until tomorrow." He said: "I had some things to attend to," and locked himself in his office, from which he telephoned Dr. Andújar.

He knew that Dr. Andújar was powerless to change his make-up, but he needed to open his heart to his friend, the only person who could understand what had happened. Dr. Andújar, his intimate friend, had tried before to rechannel his life in the far-off days when they were students together.

Dr. Andújar was at home enjoying a peaceful Sunday afternoon with his family of eight children. They were working on a jigsaw puzzle while Señora Andújar was preparing a snack for all of them.

"I'll leave immediately. I'll be there in not more than ten minutes."

The interview between the two doctors in the hospital office was dramatic.

It was dramatic because Dr. Chaos had spent his life justifying his deviation from every angle, as Dr. Andújar knew very well. Dr. Chaos based his self-exculpation on the manifestations of bisexuality in both men and women; he cited passages in the Talmud, the Greek philosophers, Freud, and Gide, ultimately affirming with Ulrichs that homosexual love was superior to normal amorous relations.

But that August afternoon, none of his arguments was of very much use to Dr. Chaos; the scene with young Rogelio had overwhelmed him with embarrassment amounting almost to desperation.

"My dear friend," he said to Dr. Andújar, "I've just proved Oscar Wilde right in saying: 'I'm a clown with a broken heart.' I've fallen again and I can't even inspire pity, only repugnance or laughter." He told his friend how he had been swept away by passion in the Hotel Miramar.

Dr. Andújar took a very keen interest in the problem of homosexuality, and in addition felt extreme respect for the person of his colleague. Consequently, he felt no repugnance and no desire to laugh. He did, however, feel a deep pity as he saw before him a big man nearly destroyed, his head sunk between his shoulders as he played with the blotter on his desk.

"I've kept hoping you'd call me some day," Dr. Andújar replied, sitting down with great naturalness in an armchair from which he could see his friend's face perfectly. "Ever since the day I arrived in Gerona I've wanted to study this subject seriously with you, but I did not dare to. I was hoping that you'd bring it up, since you told me that you hadn't succeeded in getting yourself straightened out."

"Well, now you see. The moment has come. If the owner of the hotel had denounced me, I'd be making a statement to the Civil Guard this very minute."

Dr. Andújar lighted a cigarette. "The trouble is that I don't know just how to help you," he went on. "A religious faith would be useful, but you've already told me there's nothing to be done in that direction."

Dr. Chaos made a gesture of helplessness: "Nothing, unfortunately. Quite the reverse. Supposing I did believe in God, I'd be cursing Him right now for not having created me like you or most other mortals."

Dr. Andújar's expression did not change.

"Neither can I be sure that what has happened will teach you a lesson that will keep you from backsliding."

Dr. Chaos sighed with great weariness. "I don't believe—I know myself too well. Tonight I'll sleep for ten hours straight, and tomorrow I have two appendectomies and one kidney operation waiting for me in the clinic. Today I loathe myself, but that's happened before. The only possible moral I could draw is that I must give up forever risking my neck with strangers."

"Are you still more inclined to be interested in men from the lower classes?"

"Why, yes... The same as ever. But lately..."

"Lately what?"

"It must be age, but I'm becoming more and more a pederast. Lately I find that young men excite me, especially adolescents. What happened this afternoon is an example of that."

Against his will, Dr. Andújar recalled how Dr. Chaos had stared at Pablito one night in the Governor's house.

"That's much more dangerous—socially, I mean."

"I know that. The best thing I could do would be to shoot myself."

Dr. Andújar was disturbed by those words. "You're a doctor like me," he said. "You know there's no miracle drug."

"Yes, I know."

"I mean," Dr. Andújar amended, "there is one, but you don't believe in it either. That's will power."

Dr. Chaos still played with the blotter. He sighed again. "Will power..." He smiled faintly. "I'm a slave, you know that. You're one, too, because you love your children. Could you stop loving your children?"

"No."

"Then maybe you ought to shoot yourself also."

Dr. Andújar was silent a moment. "If I didn't believe in God, I wouldn't have brought children into the world, and I'd kill myself sooner than you. Do you think I don't have my own problems?"

"What problems? You're the happiest creature I've ever known."

"You're wrong about that. When I finished my training, I went through a very serious crisis. I used to spend my whole day with prostitutes. But I fought and I won."

"Naturally. Because your crisis was a normal one. You got married and you found peace."

"Peace? What psychiatrist can ever talk about peace? He's surrounded by the mentally ill, and he can do nothing. He wants to help men like you, and he can do nothing. He can understand that you may want a pistol, and he hasn't the right to give you one."

Dr. Chaos seemed to be pulling himself together. He had often raised the question of suicide. During the war, a wounded German in the Condor Legion had committed suicide before his eyes because he said he did not feel that he could live with only one leg. Dr. Chaos realized that his friend was provoking him in order to show him that he was a coward and that he talked about shooting himself in order to place himself on the same level as the unhappy man before him.

"It's curious," Dr. Chaos said, turning on the fan beside him because he noticed that he was perspiring. "I called you because I couldn't bear my own suffering. Now all you've done is to tell me that you have problems, too, and that you were rescued by a woman."

Dr. Andújar nodded. "That's how it is with me. That's the road I took. No, please don't get excited. You ought to sleep ten hours tonight—and tomorrow you have to do two appendectomies and a kidney. But my advice to you is to try the last resort. Approach a woman. I'm not talking about marrying, you understand. But I'm turning back now to my theory of my student days. I still believe there are curable cases and that yours is one of them. I'm sure also that a woman could give you pleasure."

Dr. Chaos felt abject again. "Do you think I haven't tried that? During the war, with a nurse, and before that, with a widow in Madrid. I was a terrible failure. I felt as though I were touching a snake."

Dr. Andújar stood up to put out his cigarette in the ashtray, which was not within reach of his hand.

"But you told me that a change had come over you, that you're becoming more and more interested in adolescents."

"Yes. But what does that have to do with anything?"

"Who knows? Adolescents have smooth, soft skins. They look more like women than, say, a railroad section-hand does."

Dr. Chaos challenged his friend with a look. For an instant he seized upon the idea as on a fiery spike.

"Do you mean that?"

"I'd try it if I were you."

Dr. Chaos stared involuntarily at his dog lying at his feet. Its skin was soft, like Rogelio's.

"You're pulling a trick on me," he said abruptly. "My desire isn't satisfied with touching a skin."

"Nevertheless, I insist that you try it," Dr. Andújar said again. "You yourself mentioned the changes that come with age."

"Deviations tempt me more than ever."

"We don't know a thing. You yourself are defending that thesis. Our whole organism is a mystery. Do you want me to tell you something? Seeing you so ashamed of yourself has given me hope. Up to now, an incident like the one today wouldn't have mattered much to you. You'd have said: 'I'll try someone else.' Perhaps you've started to feel repulsed—through shame."

"I didn't say I was ashamed. I said I loathe myself."

"You can't prove that either. And don't tell me again that I'm using a trick. Other men have been cured, especially when they reached your age. That is a clinical fact. And they were less reflective, more instinctual men than you." The fan was blowing Dr. Chaos's abundant hair now. "Imagine that you've met a young woman and that you can demonstrate to yourself, even if it's only once, that you're capable. The whole world would open up for you, wouldn't it?"

Dr. Chaos shook his head in desolation. "The trouble is that I can't even imagine it. And besides, what would one time mean?"

"A great deal! It would be enormously significant. Because then you'd be able to think of the unheard-of thing I mentioned to you once before: you could have a son."

Dr. Chaos almost gave a leap. "Even if I could, I wouldn't ever have a son."

"Why not?"

"Because I share the Nazis' opinion that only selected persons, people without blemish, should have the right to be fathers. And since I've suffered too much..."

Dr. Andújar seemed totally concentrated now.

"Pain is fruitful."

"In that case, I'm fertilizing the whole earth this evening."

"Who knows? It may be that you're purifying yourself."

"Please! Don't use that word right now."

"Why not? I used it advisedly. I know that right this minute you're thinking of yourself as absolutely impure and that you're quite mistaken. Because there's something in you that redeems you: love."

"Love?"

"Yes. Your basic need is for love. This afternoon you needed love. To love with the same intensity as I love my family. You yourself said: 'I couldn't stand my suffering.' You were right. If you didn't have it in you to suffer so much, you'd never have loved anyone. Not even inferior men. Not even your dog. You wouldn't have called me on the telephone."

"I called you through fear, not love. I was afraid to be alone."

"Of course. Because mere flesh is not enough for you. The spirit is what needs company constantly. Autopsies don't reveal that, I know. But coming face to face with death does. We've talked about this before, haven't we?"

"Sure!" Dr. Chaos touched his hair, which was blowing ceaselessly in the breeze from the fan. "And you already know what I think about that."

"I must insist that you're mistaken. Life is a law, but death is one, too."

"Death is no law, except the law meaning that the end has come. Death is the ultimate stupidity."

"You can't possibly talk like that, you who've spent several months as the head of a mental institution."

"I don't know what you mean."

"In every insane asylum there's always one madman who believes he's immortal. That's true even of the asylum you're acquainted with. Doesn't that make you think? You know very well the mad people are the ones who are right in the end."

A glint of irony again shone in the surgeon's eye. "It so happens that the madman you're referring to is a homosexual."

"I know that. But that hasn't destroyed his certainty of immortality. He keeps drawing wings on the walls. And when the sun is high, he feels lucky."

Dr. Chaos gave Dr. Andújar a glance full of sarcasm. "Are you going to try to make him approach a woman, too?"

"Not him. That would be a mistake. His mind will never recover. But that's not the case with you. You really ought to try it. I agree that up to now it's been a failure. But I can see some gray hairs, and I think this time it will probably turn out differently."

Dr. Andújar's words were so full of warmth that his Adam's apple bobbed up and down in the way that amused his younger children. Dr. Chaos managed to take into account his friend's good intentions. He turned off the fan, and his hair settled back on his head. It seemed as though his heart had quieted down a little, too.

The struggle went on for a long time, even though a nun inopportunely interrupted the two men with a knock at the door. Finally, Dr. Chaos felt worn out and made it clear that for him the battle was over.

"Neither of us has moved an inch. But I feel better than when I stepped out of my Peugeot and came into the hospital. I'm very grateful to you for coming."

The surgeon's smile meant victory to Dr. Andújar, who stood up. Suddenly the friends found themselves standing very close together in the middle of the office.

"Don't make me any promises, my friend Chaos. But don't say no either. Why do you feel that you haven't moved an inch? The shocks of childhood aren't the only ones that mark us for life. That can happen in maturity, too."

Dr. Chaos shook his head and started to escort his friend to the door. Dr. Andújar was much paler than he. Goering had awakened and was accompanying them. He looked happy. Dr. Andújar gazed at the animal and said: "Don't you think that's a good sign?"

Dr. Chaos smiled sadly. "You don't miss a trick, do you?" As he held out his hand to his colleague, he said again: "Once more, thank you."

Dr. Andújar left the hospital and started to walk home. He felt in his heart that his words had not fallen upon rock and that young Rogelio had done Dr. Chaos a great favor. Now then, what woman would be able to help his friend? Was the advice he had given morally justified?

People were coming out of the motion-picture theaters. The Sunday afternoon show had ended. It was hot, the summer was explosive. Couples, couples, countless couples were walking arm in arm.

"This is a painful moment, Marta, I'm well aware of that. I don't know what to say to you; words fail me. I've struggled and struggled for weeks on end. I've seized on any detail to convince myself that this was a passing crisis, but I've lost the struggle. I've come to the conclusion that we wouldn't be happy together, that we'd be making an irrevocable mistake. And we're quite young, both of us. I mean we have time to make our lives over in another direction. If you look back, you'll realize that except for some high moments, we've always had to force ourselves, as if something was keeping us from being united as Manolo and Esther are, for example, and Pilar and Mateo. For my part, I've reached the conclusion that the something between us is politics, your passion for politics. I simply can't adjust myself to the idea that my wife would be spending a large part of her life on something other than her home. I know that women, especially women like you, are good for more than having children and talking about clothes, but that extra something ought to be books, or medicine—how do I know? Anything but politics. The idea of women in politics bothers me. I can't help it. It must be that I'm turning into a skeptic. And it's clear to me that you're never going to change in that regard, because this has been going on since before the war. Right now, just as I came here to the hostel and saw this campaign tent, your headquarters, with all those flags and a couple of little girls standing guard, it made me feel a little bit sick, really. Sure, I know what you're thinking. You're thinking that if it's a case of real love, of a whole-souled love, these obstacles would mean very little. Yes. I grant that you may be right. That's why I think that possibly my love for you hasn't been as deep as I thought it was. I'm not saying that's true. I merely admit the possibility. But in any case, we can't go on as we've been up to now. I can't keep on pretending forever. I know I wouldn't be happy. And besides, for another thing, I'm sure you wouldn't be happy with me either. If you compare our families, you must agree that I'm right. You were educated in a different atmosphere. The Martínez de Sorias belong to a definite class—which isn't mine. Your mother, for instance, inspires a great deal of respect in me. I'm very fond of her; I've always liked and admired her, but I've never felt that I could talk with her as plainly and naturally as I'd talk to another woman who hasn't always had the map of Spain presiding over her household, and some medals, too. Marta, there's something, something serious, standing in our way. I'm a lawyer; I listen to everyone, and I notice that my ideas keep evolving along a line that wouldn't bring you much satisfaction, I think. I grant too much importance to things that aren't important to you, and vice versa. I belong to civilian life. Every day more so. Right now the European war makes me sick. And whatever involves thinking like someone else puts me on the defensive. Well, I know I'm not doing much of a job of explaining myself and that I'm talking too much. Please don't think I've been deceiving you. I repeat that I've spent weeks being haunted by this idea, turning it over in my mind. I know you've always loved me a lot and that I've robbed you of your youth. But I've made up my mind at last, and I came here to talk to you as plainly as I can. It's best for us to break our engagement, Marta. Best to do it now, not to go on with a mistake that couldn't be corrected later. We wouldn't even be able to agree on the way we ought to bring up our children. But what depresses me most is that we've gone on like this so long. That's my fault. I ought to have made up my mind in Valladolid that time I went there and found that you were in Germany, dedicated to your work, which is the Feminine Section and your conception of our country. Forgive me, Marta. Don't hold this against me if you can help it. I feel as badly as you do, and your tears hurt me to the quick. But what can I do? Understand me! If you can. But let's make an end to this today; let's not spin it out any longer. I came here expressly to tell you this because the day I came back from Barcelona and you gave me the lawyer's name-plate, I just didn't have the nerve. Let me say I hope that you'll realize all this in time and that you won't hate me. Although you'd have every right to, for as I said, this decision ought to have been made a long time ago."

Marta did not have the courage to answer. She had been standing when Ignacio started, but as he talked she had had to sit down on the stool in her tent, beside her knapsack. She was crying. She was crying disconsolately, but Ignacio did not dare to smooth her hair, much as he would have liked to. Marta had left Gerona convinced that Ignacio would come and tell her exactly what he had just said. She had even promised herself that she would stand up to the blow courageously, that she would not show her despair. But she had failed. She loved that man so dearly. And she sensed that all his words, all his arguments, were merely arguments, that he did not love her, that he had never loved her as she loved him. She was sure that if she promised to give up everything—the youth hostel, the Feminine Section, even the name Martínez de Soria—Ignacio would still say: "No, it's best for us to break it off."

"Please go, Ignacio. Don't say another word. Go away, and if another woman has come between us, I hope you'll be happy."

Ignacio stood quite still. He did not know what to do. It would be ridiculous to prolong the scene. Ridiculous and useless.

"Goodbye, Marta. Forgive me. I hope you'll meet a man worthy of you, and I hope you'll be happy, too."

Ignacio went out of the tent. The little girls in the camp were jumping rope among the pines. Between the tree trunks he could see the water.

The girls at the gate saluted him as he left, screaming: "*¡Arriba España!*"

"Ana María, Ana María! It's all straightened out now. I've broken off with Marta. An hour ago—hardly an hour. I've just come from Pálamos, from the hostel where she's working. It was all quite painful. The poor girl really loves me. It was awful to see her suffer like that. She had to sit down, and she cried and cried. But I couldn't do anything else except face up to the situation, take the bull by the horns. I had thought I ought to speak to Pilar first. Or go and see her mother. But no. It was my duty to do what I did, tell her plainly myself. The worst of it is that she never lost control of herself for a moment. She just said: 'Go away, and if another woman has come between us, I hope you'll be happy.' That scared me a little. But I don't believe that she could have found out about us. It must have been intuition. Well, Ana María, it's all over now. No more pretending, no more writing to you more or less on the sly. Let's let some time go by and keep on being discreet, the same as now. Until I can tell the whole world that I love you, that we love each other and that you're the woman I need—my rattlebrain. A rattlebrain! Do you realize what that means to me? I've made all sorts of plans, Ana María, a lot of plans. Manolo keeps saying to me: 'If you go on the way you're going, you'll be a first-class professional, a great lawyer.' Pooh! All the same, I think so too, because I like my work. But I've still got a lot of studying to do. Anyhow, what matters most to me right now is that I can tell you that you're my sweetheart, that nothing can come between us. Let me kiss you, Ana María. This is a sad day, but it's a glorious one, too. I feel bad, but what's that! Come here, darling! Close to me. Like this. Now kiss me. Lord, Lord, I feel like a kid with a new pair of shoes!"

"Ignacio! Ignacio! I'm as happy as I can be!"

"I know we're going to be happy."

"Of course, we are!"

"We'll be happy as long as we live!"

"If it weren't for Marta, I'd be completely happy now."

"Please, let's not think about that any more!"

"Yes, you're right."

"Are you thinking of telling your parents about us?"

"My parents? Not right now, no. You know how my father is; all he thinks about is business."

"It's all right! We can wait a while."

"Good! But I'm going to tell Charo. I can tell her because she's spending the summer with me here at San Felíu. I've simply got to let myself go with someone. I've got to!"

"All right, then—tell her."

"Darling!"

"Ana María!"

"I want to do something. I've got to do something!"

"Me, too!"

"Well, could you give me another kiss, for example?"

"Oh, what a naughty girl you are!"

"If I weren't, I wouldn't be here in your arms now."

"That's true, too."

"Ignacio..."

"What?"

"I love you."

Night had come to San Felíu de Guixols, to the Paseo del Mar. The light in the lighthouse was turning slowly. In the distance, lights gleamed from the boats. Stars were being born in the heavens. It was a beautiful summer.

THIRTY-EIGHT

GENERAL Sánchez Bravo still enjoyed reading "Windows on the World," the daily column written for *Amanecer* by Warning Voice. The Mayor's commentaries on the news most germane to Spain and the world often happened to concur with the General's opinion.

In that month of September, as the end of summer drew near, the General's impression was confirmed as he read the Gerona paper, and he did not fail to congratulate the Mayor when he returned from his stay in Puigcerdá, although the latter would rather have exclaimed: "Long live love," meaning "Long live Carlota, the Countess of Rubí" instead of "Long live the King."

The recent "Windows on the World" that gave the General particular satisfaction were on very diverse subjects. The first had to do with the assassination of Trotsky in Mexico on August 20. The assassin, not known as yet, had split Trotsky's skull with a *piolet*, a mountaineer's axe that he had carried hidden in the folds of his trench coat. The former Bolshevik leader had been sitting in his office at that moment, with his head bent over a manuscript. Warning Voice wrote a rapid and incisive sketch of Trotsky and his followers in Spain, the militants of the POUM, and went on to state that the famous Russian exile had characterized Stalin as "the jackal of the Kremlin" on his arrival in Mexico, "Trotsky," wrote Warning Voice, "was a theorist; hence it is logical that he died from having his skull split open. His death has caused the greatest amazement among those who refused to be convinced that each man digs his own grave, and that he who kills with iron, dies by iron."

What neither the General nor Warning Voice knew was that David and Olga, who were living in the Mexican capital, hoping to publish some of Trotsky's works on their brand-new press, were among the people most deeply shocked, and that Cosme Vila, still in Moscow, was equally shocked by the news, for he recalled that the Asturian teacher, Regina Suárez, had told him soon after his arrival in Russia's capital "that several Spanish secret agents had left Russia for Mexico with the special mission of assassinating Trotsky."

Another "Window on the World" of great interest to General Sánchez Bravo was one in which Warning Voice commented favorably on the recent decree by the Spanish Government creating a student officers' training corps that would enable students to do their military service without interrupting their studies and would automatically commission them as reserve officers.

The General was becoming more and more convinced by the way things were going at the moment that the Army must continue to be the keystone if the fruits of victory were not to be allowed to spoil. "The Army! The Army!" he cried again and again to his wife, Doña Cecilia. "Without it, everything would jump the track by midnight tonight." The truth was that a year and a half after the end of the war, the General could not find the guarantees he required in the Falange, or the Requeté, or the Church. The Bishop upset him by apparently attributing all the merits of the war campaign to Divine Providence. As for the Requeté, it seemed to the General to be maneuvering stealthily to shorten as much as possible the Caudillo's stay in office. He and Warning Voice differed on that point. The Falange—well, the Falange simply made him nervous. This had been true always. So much so that on one occasion he asked Mateo point blank why the Falange called itself a "Party" when it wasn't one. "There'd have to be several parties before it could call itself one, wouldn't there?" That claim was the reason for the petty squabbles between the Falangists and the Requetés—it was rumored that some Requetés had charged into a Falange local in Navarre leading a donkey. That amused the General. All in all, however, the General's chief argument, which he brandished to reinforce his attitude, was that the Army had won the war. "Try to imagine that the Falange didn't exist," he said to his officers in his speech to them on July 18. "Franco still would have won. Do away with the Requeté in imagination, and Franco still would have won. Do away with the Army, and the Reds would have won. It's the same now. If we were to retire to our garrisons right now, with no control over what goes on around us, we'd end up in a kind of organized chaos. You mark my words."

Another "Window on the World" that caught the General's interest was one that voiced approval of the official establishment of an agency to set price ceilings in order to cut off at the roots the schemes of the unscrupulous. "That's what we needed," the General commented. "We've got to have a body with absolute powers which can pack the violators off to disciplinary battalions."

But the problem that perhaps irritated the military commander most was the greed the people were displaying, starting with his own son. General Sánchez Bravo was by nature an enemy of the easy way. Ever since he had enrolled in the Military Academy he had believed with his whole heart that the strength of a country radiated from the maintenance of its virtues as a race, not from encouragement of its lusts. Consequently, he was anything but pleased to learn that the recently appointed Minister of Industry and Commerce, Don Demetrio Carcellar, had come out of the Falange and that he kept talking about industrialization *ad nauseam.* In the "Window on the World" that dealt with the establishment of an agency to set price ceilings, Warning Voice reminded the people of Gerona first, that the defenders of Numancia had been reduced to eating human flesh, and second, that at the time of the mutiny of Esquilache, the rulers' faith in the efficacy of material progress had been so great that a minister ordered his speech on popular industry to be read like sacred scripture from the pulpits of the churches. "In the end," Warning Voice said in his column, perhaps thinking of Professor Civil's theories, "material wealth will rot the spirit. We have seen an example of that in prosperous, gourmet France, which has just provided the world with the most abject spectacle of cowardice which modern history records." When the General read those words, he twirled his commander's baton and vowed that Spain must be vaccinated against that virus. He believed that the Caudillo ought to impress on the country its own natural rhythm, as he was unquestionably doing; an instance of that was the harshness of Castile. "We must not be contaminated, especially now, by the democracies' shortcomings; their only aspiration is to fatten the savings banks. We trust that the Office of Price Administration will prevent the great industrialists from drinking champagne in the cabarets side by side with peasants who got rich on the hunger of the citizens."

Of course the General's thesis found many detractors, outstanding among whom were the Governor and Doña Cecilia herself. In spite of the abject spectacle of France, the Governor was aspiring to increase the number of new dwellings needed to house the people of the province. And in spite of what had happened during the mutiny of Esquilache, Doña Cecilia was aspiring to see her son, Captain Sánchez Bravo, married to a rich woman. "You just say yes to your father," she advised the young man. "But let's see if you can't find some millionairess around here who'll let herself be loved."

In a certain sense, then, the General found himself without a shield against the arrows of ambition. Whence his interest in striking up an acquaintance with the head of the price control agency appointed to the province of Gerona, Don Oscar Pinel. Almost as soon as he learned of the official's arrival in the city—on September 23, the day that Marshal Pétain, "a great soldier," announced in Vichy his plan to break up the French Masonic lodges—the General invited the new appointee to have a glass of wine with him at the barracks.

The head of the price control agency accepted, and his meeting with the General could not have been pleasanter. Don Oscar Pinel was a short man of fifty-five with a piercing, authoritative eye. As if that were not enough, he was an old Army man himself. During the war he had been a major in the Quartermaster's Corps, and he could talk about supplies as assuredly as Agustín Lago talked about teachers and pupils.

Pinel was a widower with two daughters. The older girl had entered a cloistered convent as a novice; the second, whose name was Solita, was unmarried, a nurse by profession. "You must meet her, General. She looks like a top sergeant. She's the boss of the household."

She looked like a top sergeant! General Sánchez Bravo congratulated himself on all that the arrival of the Office of Price Administration would mean to Gerona. Oscar Pinel's plans as head of the office could hardly be more suitable. He had brought with him a staff of inspectors, most of them Basques, who would patrol the province incessantly. They were to put into effect on a permanent basis that disagreeable but efficient measure by which informers would be paid forty percent of the fine imposed. And of course, the more serious law-breakers would be sentenced without mercy to a long prison term or forced labor.

The General shook hands effusively with the head of price control, Don Oscar Pinel, whose chin revealed tireless energy.

"You can count on me, Major."

"I'm at your command, General."

A few days later, Warning Voice devoted another "Window on the World" to the new agency, marking the opening of the headquarters on the Plaza del Marques de Camps of the Office of Price Control. "We shall expect the collaboration of every citizen," he said. "We cannot permit someone in Madrid to sing such couplets as the following:

> *If Candelas were still alive.*
> *These bad times would not arrive.*
> *He'd not let black-market profiteers today*
> *Enjoy good names and have their way."*

The opening of the Office of Price Control was sure to be a great relief to the Governor. The agency collaborated closely with the Food Delegation, in which Pilar was working. That took a heavy burden of responsibility off the Governor's shoulders and gave him more time to concentrate his energies on other duties more in keeping with his talents and character.

Other people, however, knitted their brows as they studied in *Amanecer* the likeness of the former Major in the Quartermaster's Corps, Don Oscar Pinel. He looked adamant, and as they read his flat statements, they felt uneasy. Among those individuals were Colonel Triguero and Captain Sánchez Bravo. Not to mention Tower of Babel, Padrosa, the attorney Mijares, the owner of the Crocodile, and the manager of Constructora Gerundense, Inc.

To be sure, Captain Sánchez Bravo had not lifted a finger to help the corporation since his father had called him into the Hall of Arms and cautioned him against "dishonoring his uniform" by taking part in questionable business deals. Impressed by the General's integrity, the young man had called a halt. Perhaps that was also because his ideas were not as fixed as Colonel Triguero's. The Captain had many doubts and a deep-seated fear of losing in a moment's time both his peace of mind and his pride in having fought in the war and earned the stars on his sleeve. Consequently, he had worked wholeheartedly during the month of August at his position as president of the Gerona Football Club, which was to play in the Second League next winter. This was a major step, which would require him to recruit new and better players, spruce up the stadium, which undoubtedly would be packed to capacity, and build a tunnel that would enable the players to go directly from the field to the dressing rooms.

Colonel Triguero was another breed of cat. He had a heart-to-heart talk with Captain Sánchez Bravo, a talk that would have delighted Mosén Alberto, who enjoyed delving ever more deeply into problems of conscience.

"Captain, the Corporation is complaining about your inactivity. You're letting matters slide. And you know that's the last thing an Army man should do."

"My father's right, Colonel Triguero. If we're going to spend our time on business, we ought to hang up our uniforms."

"Never! No uniform, no influence. The Costa brothers wouldn't have any more use for us."

"That's the whole point."

"For God's sake! Correct me if I'm wrong. Gasoline's going to be rationed. Do you realize what that means?"

"I realize it. The Corporation could build cracking plants, get extra allotments, and so on. But I'd rather look the situation over calmly."

"For how long, may I ask?"

"Until Christmas. That's when the Costa brothers will be let out of prison, unless my spies have lied to me."

"By Christmas you'll be shedding tears over all that stuff about the Nativities and the Adoration of the Shepherds."

"We shall see. As far as I know, no one has ordered me to be sanctimonious."

"Well, you're not far from it. You've caught the disease. You like army rations. You like chickpeas. And you like to look at your scars."

"Maybe I do, but right now the main reason is my father. You live alone, so you don't care. Besides, I'm scared. Now we've got the Office of Price Control breathing down our necks, and breathing hard just now."

Colonel Triguero twisted his mustache, looking as though his sideburns were growing longer.

"I respect your father's attitude. But you surely don't think everyone's like him. If you just take a walk around Madrid, you'll see."

"I know, I know. But that's Madrid. I'll have to think it over, and at the moment I'm looking for a good right end and a good goalie."

Colonel Triguero clicked his tongue. "Okay! So go on being poor. Enjoy yourself. If you change your mind, you know where I am."

He left.

Colonel Triguero reported all this to the undercover manager of the Constructora Gerundense, Inc.

The manager said: "That's all understood then. We'll wait till Christmas. But that boy's a born fool. Meanwhile, Colonel, see if we can't get a finger on the currency the French and Belgian refugees are bringing across the border."

Nothing doing, the Colonel said. They could never crack that. The people fleeing from the Germans inevitably fell into the Governor's hands, which left them no room to maneuver, either with the jewels the refugees carried or by bribing them with promises to smooth their way to northern Africa or Portugal. Their goods were confiscated and put under the control of the Civil Guard. Then they were deposited legally in the Bank of Spain. Orders from the Government were so strict in that regard that Colonel Trigueros office in Figueras was beginning to look like a jail.

But that was not all. The attitude of many of the refugees gave Colonel Triguero food for thought. They did not seem to think that England and France were going to lose the war, not by a long chalk. Accordingly, they were beginning to organize. Most of them put themselves under the protection of the British consul who had recently come to Gerona, an imperturbable man named Edward Collins who had moved into the Hotel del Centro, a man who smiled almost imperceptibly at the word "Gibraltar." The American Red Cross also had mobilized to help the refugees. As for the Jews, they extricated themselves with great shrewdness, even though some of them had fled directly to Spain from Germany, even from Poland! Perhaps the most stricken of the refugees were the British airmen, who had had to make appalling efforts to get out of Belgium or occupied France. They arrived exhausted; some were wounded.

Colonel Triguero had to provide special care for them. One of the pilots told the Colonel that there were Spanish exiles among the Allied troops fighting the Germans on Belgian soil and even in Narvik, Norway. Colonel Triguero's jaw dropped but he could not help saying: "So what?" The Englishman replied: "Very good fighters."

AT that juncture, Colonel Triguero had an unexpected caller in his office, Gaspar Ley, manager of the Gerona branch of the Arús Bank. The interview was cordial and it opened great prospects for the future.

Gaspar Ley went straight to the point. He introduced himself to the Colonel as the official representative in Gerona of the Barcelona corporation Sarró and Company, which, he said, would like to join forces with the Constructora Gerundense, Inc. "You've heard of Sarró and Company, no doubt, haven't you? It's a corporation that plays to win."

These words inspired Colonel Triguero to call Nati, the beautiful typist, and tell her to fetch a couple of beers from the downstairs bar. But he concealed his enthusiasm and adopted an expectant air.

"Can you tell me who Señor Sarró is?"

Gaspar Ley smiled "No one calls him Señor Sarró. He's Don Rosendo Sarró, a man with plenty of push and a former prisoner to boot. He spent the entire war in the Modelo Prison."

Colonel Triguero bit his lip. "So! Now what can we do for you?"

"Nothing at the moment. Don Rosendo Sarró is planning to come to Gerona to talk things over with you people."

"As I understand it," Colonel Triguero said, "for the time being it wouldn't suit the Constructora Gerundense Corporation's plans to merge with anyone."

"Oh, it's not a question of merger," Gaspar Ley answered. "If that should come up, it could all be settled without anything in writing. You might say it would be all in the family."

"Well, then, we understand each other. I'll pass this on to my colleagues."

"That's the ticket," Gaspar Ley said approvingly. "I'll keep in touch with you."

Gaspar Ley said his farewells and left. He had no sooner gone than Colonel Triguero burst out laughing. He went out of his office and said to Nati: "That's enough work for today! You can go out and flirt with some guy until further orders."

The trouble with Colonel Triguero was that he had lost any feeling of guilt. The war had brutalized him, and he was growing more amoral by the day. So much so that he hoped in his heart that the refugees who were coming in full of optimism were right in believing that the war between the Axis and the democracies would go on for a long time. If it did, the opportunities in Spain—with or without Sarró and Company—would increase by leaps and bounds, and Captain Sánchez Bravo would have to decide once and for all to throw his scruples overboard and rejoin the corporation. Unless he had lost his mind completely.

THIRTY-NINE

MATEO suddenly found himself face to face with a difficult problem. He would have to postpone his wedding, set for October 12, a day that combined the Fiesta of Pilar, the *Día de la Raza* in honor of Columbus, and Hispanidad Day. Three weeks before that date, he received an order from Núñez Maza, the Propaganda Delegate, to be in San Sebastián on that very day to attend a grand convocation of the provincial leaders of the Falange from all over Spain. As usual, the order read: "No excuses or pretexts will be accepted."

Mateo had no choice but to obey. Pilar had been keeping herself busy, putting the final touches on her trousseau and on the flat on the Plaza de la Estación, where she would live with Don Emilio Santos and Mateo, and now she reacted almost hysterically. She cried, she stamped her foot, she bit her fingernails almost to the quick. Mateo could do nothing but show her with a disconsolate air the order he had received from Madrid.

"You've got to understand. All the provincial leaders are going to be there. Núñez Maza even called me on the telephone. It seems that something's up, something serious. I couldn't possibly get out of going. As far as I know, it has to do with the attitude of the Falange with regard to the war."

"The war?" Pilar looked frightened. "What are you talking about?"

"Don't let that scare you, girl. The Germans want to know what we think. Serrano Súñer is going to Berlin, so these preliminary talks are necessary."

This added to Pilar's fear. "What? Is Spain going to be an ally of Germany? Is that what you're hinting at?"

"I'm not hinting at anything, darling. They called me and I've got to go; that's all there is to it. What I want is to marry you, and the sooner the better."

Pilar sank into the rocking chair that was Carmen Elgazu's favorite spot for a rest. She did not know what to say. This was the first "direct" blow she had had to take since she had been going with Mateo. With a superhuman effort, she stopped crying.

"What are we going to do, then? How long is this going to last?"

Mateo put great affection into his next words. He understood very well what this meant to Pilar. All he could suggest was to set another date, as soon after the original one as possible: December 8, for example, the Feast of the Immaculate Conception.

"That's bound to be a good day, isn't it?"

"Yes, of course. Fine."

"That's only two more months."

To add to their dilemma, the Governor intervened in person, pointing out to Mateo that it was his duty to go to San Sebastián. Pilar finally had to give in, but she locked herself in her room and thought for the first time that Hitler was much what Señor Grote, her superior in the Food Delegation, thought he was.

The news dropped like a bombshell into the Alvears' flat. Matías took it hard. He went to see Don Emilio Santos in the flat, where the plasterers and painters no longer needed to rush their work.

"My dear friend," Matías said to him, "these 'grand convocations' are getting to be a nuisance. I don't like that kind of work. One doesn't do that to a woman. At least I would never have dared to."

Don Emilio Santos felt depressed. "What can I say, Matías? It seems the Falange is going through a sort of crisis."

"The one who's going through a sort of crisis is Pilar."

Carmen Elgazu confronted Mateo, but found his attitude so rigid that she was disconcerted.

"Pilar has agreed to it," Mateo argued. "Why make such a fuss?"

Carmen Elgazu was at a loss for words. She muttered several phrases under her breath and finally said, turning to Pilar: "Now you see how it is, dear. You can tell the Campistol sisters there's no hurry about your wedding gown."

Indirectly, the incident worked in Ignacio's favor. He had not yet made up his mind to tell his family that he had broken off with Marta. But he did it then. Of course, it took the family's breath away. They felt much more disgusted with him than with Mateo, for this time it was a definite break. Matías delivered an out-and-out philippic, and so did Carmen Elgazu. They loved Marta; they had loved her for years and they thought it indefensible of him to have broken for no good reason a promise that meant everything to the girl. "What on earth are you thinking of, Ignacio? This is a very serious thing. An engagement like that is sacred. Now we understand, of course, why Marta is down to skin and bones!" They even called up the memory of Major Martínez de Soria. "You ought to think it all over very carefully, and then start over again. Marta really loves you. What has she ever done to you? Tell me that. Didn't she offer to go with you to Barcelona during your examinations?"

Pilar railed at him. She came within an ace of slapping her brother. "This is just what I was afraid would happen. For heaven's sake, why didn't you let Marta know before this?" She called Ignacio "a monster of selfishness" and withered him by telling the whole family that this cur had been ripening his plan for a long time. She knew that he had never stopped writing love letters to a cute little thing in Barcelona named Ana María.

"A cute little trick in good society. See? The kid has aspirations. That's all there is to it."

Ignacio rode out the storm. His only defense was the order that Mateo had received. No, if it were he, he wouldn't care to expose himself to disappointments like that. In the end he said to Pilar: "All I want for you, sister, is that your fanatical Romeo doesn't force you to postpone your wedding five more times. Until Germany wins the war. Or until Spain gets back her empire."

Mateo went to the grand convocation in San Sebastián. Not only had he had to postpone his wedding; he also had had to defer again his examinations at the University on his final year of law. But almost against his will the whole subject of marriage vanished like a lump of sugar melting away as soon as he met his old comrades and some new ones who had come to the meeting in San Sebastián. He spent three intense weeks in the Basque capital with yokes, arrows, and blue shirts. Needless to say, the war was discussed at length in the long-drawn-out sessions. The good weather had gone by without Germany's expected landing in England, and the Falangists believed generally, although not unanimously, that Spain had an obligation to help the Axis militarily. Mateo, all excited by the atmosphere of the meeting, was in favor of that. But the fact remained that the men who met there were not those who would decide the question. Whatever they might decide, Franco and his generals would have the last word; they would arrogate to themselves the right to make any such agreement, and knowing that, the Falangist leaders were thrown into a state of great perplexity.

After the closing of the summer camp, Marta returned to Gerona. Her state of mind was worse than Pilar's. She threw herself into her mother's arms and cried until she was exhausted. Her pain was so great that she felt she could hardly bear it. Her brother, José Luis Martínez de Soria, repeated endlessly Pilar's phrase: "He's a cur." At one point he seemed on the verge of going to have an understanding with Ignacio, but Marta made a gesture of such hopelessness that he refrained.

The girl's mother lacked the moral strength to be able to lift her daughter's spirits, for once Marta's engagement to Ignacio was broken, the widow could see the specter of loneliness hovering over the household. Some day or other, José Luis would marry María Victoria, of course, although the girl had flatly refused to leave the Spanish capital to live in Gerona. But then what? What was there in the city to hold the two women? Nothing except memories, the Dehesa, the river, and the body of Major Martínez de Soria lying in the cemetery.

Marta tried to find relief with her girlfriends, but none of them could help her either. Pilar, her best confidante as always, had finally broken to her the news of Ana María's existence, which added the pangs of jealousy and anger. "What has that girl got? What's she like? Do you know her? Good Lord, isn't this terrible!" Esther feigned ignorance of the news and said nothing about Ignacio's request for her advice. "I'm sorry, Marta. It breaks my heart. I know what this means to you." María del Mar, however, tried to encourage her. "Time heals everything, Marta. I once loved another man. Possibly, Ignacio's right. Maybe your marriage would have been a failure. I know how easy it is to say this. But you must do all you can to take your mind off it, and come and see me whenever you feel like it. See that the Feminine Section takes up your time. And wait and hope."

Hope was a word of hopeless augury. Especially because Gerona was a small city. That meant that Marta would meet Ignacio often on the street or in some other place least expected. How would she react to seeing him? What would she do? Pilar's revelations had humiliated her. "Ana María, Ana María..." She could not push out of her mind José Luis's chant: "He's a rat."

But was Ignacio a rat? Mightn't she have failed him? Marta looked into the mirror and saw that she had deteriorated shockingly.

Her religion was a strong support for her. Marta made a general confession to Mosén Falcó and took communion devoutly, asking God for the strength not to do anything foolish, for some strange thoughts had coursed through her mind. Chelo Rosselló, who was still haunting Dr. Andújar's consultation room with Jorge de Batlle, said to her: "Marta, please get hold of yourself. Don't let yourself fall into the same well as Jorge."

All efforts were in vain. Marta could not manage even to keep up appearances. She could not put up a good front even in her office of the Feminine Section. And what made matters worse just then was that orders from Madrid kept arriving in an endless chain, all phrased with the usual impersonality. One of their requests was for her opinion on the duty of the Falange with respect to the war. Worse, the National Command chanced to send out circulars on the subject of maternity, a problem that had taken first place in Madrid. For another thing, Marta had to organize a big celebration for December 8—the new date set for the wedding of Mateo and Pilar. She had to fill *Amanecer* with slogans heralding that day. One of them said: "After God and Country, a mother is most sacred. She gave you the good fortune to be born in Spain. Honor thy mother, give her a little gift on that day, no matter how small."

Who in Madrid had composed that slogan? María Victoria, perhaps? Yes, of course, María Victoria, the fiancée of José Luis. María Victoria, likable and exuberant, would simply have said to Marta, no doubt: "What can you expect, girl? Men are like that."

Marta could not go to the flat on the Rambla now. Her blue shirt drooped on her. She moved like an automaton, and when the midwife Rosario, queen of the Child Care Section, told her that thirty-eight hundred mothers in Spain died in childbirth every year, she could not squeeze out a tear. When Gracia Andújar reported to her the progress she was making with the Dancing Section, Marta shook her head as though she were hearing about a remote galaxy. "Dancing? Can anyone in the world be spending his time dancing?"

The girl spent hours on end in her room. How strange the medicine kit looked to her now, with the initials C.A.F.É. on it, though this was the kit she had carried as she went through Gerona on the day of the Uprising. How pregnant with feeling all the gifts that Ignacio had returned to her seemed now: the lawyer's plaque; the watch with the blue dial; the stone from the Alcázar of Toledo which she had brought him from her trip to Madrid. That stone had been a mistake. Any stone would always be a mistake.

Her only consolations were her religion and the affection of her mother and Pilar. Her current challenge was the balcony outside Manolo Fontana's office where Ignacio worked. Manolo Fontana! With the arrival of autumn, he began wearing again the little green Tyrolean hat adorned with the small peacock feather.

FORTY

PILAR was suffering; Marta was suffering; Comrade Rosselló was suffering, had been suffering since he had come back from Puerto de Santa María, where he had gone to visit his father in prison. The boy had driven across all of Spain—and in what a state he found the roads, bridges, fields, and villages! He had been permitted a bare quarter of an hour in which to talk through the bars to the prisoner. "Father, how are you?" "What about you, son? And how are the girls?" It was impossible even to start a conversation. Dr. Rosselló was wearing a convict's uniform. The son felt such a lump in his throat that he could hardly utter a word. In Gerona he had often congratulated himself that his heart had been hardened by the war; but in the Puerto de Santa María Penitentiary, he realized that it was not true. "How's the hospital going, son? Who's in charge there?" "What did you say? Chelo is going to marry Jorge de Batlle? No, no, I didn't receive a letter about it. Here—well, you can imagine!"

The wardens were friendly enough, but they had to do their duty, and once the regulation fifteen minutes had passed, they separated the two men. Comrade Rosselló stepped into his car in a fury, with the image of his father in the flesh stamped on his retina, a man broken inside. He returned to Gerona in a state of mind not propitious to driving the Governor's automobile. Comrade Dávila, who had problems of his own, said to him: "Come on, kid! Snap out of it! Cheer up! I give you my word I don't want to run into a tree!"

BUT this October, like the preceding one, proved generous to Mosén Alberto; to Agustín Lago, who had conscientiously laid out the second postwar course of study; and especially to Warning Voice, who was ready to put his whole heart and soul into the task of earning renown for the year's fairs and fiestas.

Mosén Alberto's first reward was his appointment as provincial president of the Commission on Historical Monuments, a post that flattered him beyond measure. All ancient artifacts were becoming more and more attractive to him as well as to Professor Civil, and the province abounded in half-ruined castles, Iberian settlements awaiting excavation, ancient vessels from shipwrecks a few rods off the coast. So much work to be done, and what a pleasure it was! The priest had grown a little tired of hearing people talk about Gerundian archeology exclusively in terms of the ancient Greek colony of Ampurias.

At about that time, as it happened, the many hunters and fishermen of the region requested the Bishop on their own initiative to arrange for a Mass for them every Sunday at four o'clock in the morning. Dr. Gregorio Lascasas chose Mosén Alberto to officiate at that ungodly hour. Mosén Alberto's first reaction was somewhat pompous; he advanced, among other reasons, that he had never felt the slightest inclination for the chase or for angling. But later he thought better of it and rejoiced in the inconvenience because it gave him an opportunity to show his self-abnegation. This assignment also redounded to his favor, for of late he had been seeing in his mind's eye the flagellated shade of Father Forteza, whose sanctity was a constant example.

As another proof of his favored status, Mosén Alberto heard a *sardana.* That was in connection with the celebration put on by "Education and Rest," the sports-syndicate organization, in honor of workmen whose children had won official scholarships for advanced studies. Mosén Alberto had gone for a walk in the Dehesa to contemplate the autumn leaves falling from the trees when suddenly—a *sardana.* He thought he must be dreaming, but he was wide awake. Mosén Alberto was as deeply moved as the members of the Cobla Gerona, who had come back together in a split second. The director of the Feminine Section's choral group, Quintana, was one of the musicians. Someone who happened to be passing that way said to Mosén Alberto: "I don't know whether they're making fun of us or whether it's all a mistake." Neither was true. Mosén Alberto saw it rather as a new demonstration of the tact that characterized the Governor.

The priest's final blessing was in the field of friendship. He had been able to channel the course of little Manuel Alvear. The initial sympathy inspired in him by Matías's nephew, later augmented by the Christmas dinner in the Rambla flat, was translated into something positive, into the practical idea that Carmen Elgazu had had in the beginning but which she had not dared to make known. Now Manuel was to enroll in the Instituto for the first course toward his baccalaureate. And every afternoon when he left school—except on holidays, naturally—he would work in the Diocesan Museum as César had before him; he would be paid something for it, and would also keep the tips given him by visitors.

Obviously, Mosén Alberto would have to clear the hurdle represented by Paz. But as it happened, even though Paz became the singing star of the

Gerona Jazz Band and gave rein to her youth in Pachín's arms, she remained intransigent on political matters; she was still paying dues to the Red Relief and longing to see Germany crushed. But for no known reason, perhaps for her own convenience or in order not to thwart Manuel's inclinations too much, she was beginning to be more tractable on the subject of religion. "I ask only one thing," she said to Mosén Alberto as they were discussing the question. "Don't try to get that baby into the Seminary." Mosén Alberto stroked his shaven cheek and replied: "That is not my duty. In any case, it's something that Manuel will have to decide."

All in all, then, Mosén Alberto was satisfied, and that inspired him to write with more enthusiasm than ever in his column for *Amanecer*, "Praises to the Creator." He had only one worry: the skies over Gerona. Suddenly, such heavy black clouds began to pass over the city, with such a dramatic-looking load, that the priest said: "I shouldn't be surprised if we have a flood this winter." Notary Noguer, who could remember many floods that had scourged the city, objected. "I don't believe so. Last year at about this time we were afraid of the same thing. But then the tramontane came and swept away the threat."

AUTUMN treated Agustín Lago generously, too. But the end of summer brought with it an unpleasant clash that soured for several weeks the consolation brought him by the recent visit of Carlos Godo, his comrade in Opus Dei.

Our pedagogue and Professor Civil clashed head-on in a completely unexpected collision. The Professor had heard the Bishop speak of the Opus Dei, and, drawn by curiosity, he wanted to drink from its headwaters. Accordingly, he asked Agustín Lago to permit him to cast a glance over Father Escriva's *Camino*, which furnished the key for the Inspector's meditations. Agustín Lago was glad to oblige the old professor, sure that *Camino* would impress him favorably. But instead of that, Professor Civil put his hands to his head. He acknowledged that *Camino* contained some beautiful thoughts, but some of its maxims struck him as quite inadmissible. "Do you realize that, my friend Lago? Look what it says here: 'The level of sanctity that the Lord asks of us is determined by three things: holy intransigence, holy compulsion, and holy insolence.' What does that mean? And what about this? 'If you feel an impulse to be a supreme leader, your aspirations must be: with your brothers, the last; with others, the first.' Who are others? And why should you want to be first with them? Then, too, what's the reason for this crudeness, if you'll forgive me the word, friend Lago: 'The most delicate and choice tidbit, if eaten by a pig (that is the creature's name, and no pardon is asked) becomes pork in the end!' I don't understand, I don't understand. Friend Lago, permit me to say to you that this book is unclear, contradictory. And why does the author use the familiar form of address? It's bad enough for the Falange to use it, isn't it? It has never seemed right to me to use the familiar address with anyone and everyone. If you don't mind, I'll go on reading the Bible from time to time—and *The Criterion* by Balmes."

Agustín Lago pondered the Professor's point of view and longed to convince him that *Camino* was worthwhile in context, if only because from its pages emanated a breath of the supernatural. He reminded the old man that Father Escrivá, the founder of Opus Dei, had merely been imitating Christ when he spoke with sternness occasionally, for on some occasions Christ had also wielded the lash. Professor Civil shook his head in denial and said sententiously: "Christ was God, and he had a right to scourge whomever he wished from the Temple; but when Peter drew his sword in the Garden and cut off the car of Malchus, the servant of the procurator, Christ ordered him to sheathe his sword, thereby giving Peter a supreme lesson in tolerance."

Agustín Lago spent several subsequent days feeling unsure of what the Governor and Mateo would think of him. Fortunately, he remembered his conversation with Carlos Godo—"We shall be misunderstood for a long time"—and, what was more important, he found a consoling thought in *Camino* itself: "When you give yourself to God, no difficulty can take away your optimism."

Thus inspired, he tried more seriously than ever to "comport himself with the greatest naturalness out in the world," and after paying his compliments to the image of the Virgin which he kept in his bare pension room, he turned to his own affairs with renewed brio, to his work and his concern over the teachers' situation, which was still crucial.

He met Carlos Godo again. By that time he was corresponding assiduously with his great ally. Godo wrote him, saying: "Don't be discouraged, my dear Agustín. Here in Barcelona, I've had battles like that of my own. We shall move ahead, keep moving ahead, little by little. Remember Chesterton's words? He said the miracle of Christianity is that it's mad; it tries to sell soap that will not wash."

Carlos Godo did more than that. He built the bridge his brother in Opus Dei needed to produce positive results by his efforts in the field of education, in so far as that was possible. Carlos Godo gave Agustín Lago the address of another comrade in Opus Dei who lived in Madrid and worked right in the Ministry of National Education. This man, Victor Camacho, held the position of head of a bureau. "Write to him, using my name. Send him a detailed report on everything you need, and he'll advise you and help you all he can. In my opinion, you ought to bring him up to date on the teachers' problem of tenure, for example, but don't neglect that other one, the 'purified' teachers. I think you ought to concentrate on them because as you know very well, the thing that matters least is anyone's ideological past. The whole question is whether or not they are competent."

Agustín Lago followed his friend's advice to the letter and found it good. When Victor Camacho received the educator's letter, he felt as though a flame had flared up in the midst of the bureaucratic coldness of the Ministry. And he proved that he was efficient in the highest degree. He obtained the necessary permission to enable the teachers of the province of Gerona to collect their pay for overtime in the coming year, that is, for their extra hours outside the classroom. In addition, he managed somehow to get an allowance for purchasing stoves. And for putting panes of glass in the schools that were without them. Not to mention an official promise to build thirty dwellings in the neediest villages within a relatively short time.

"Overtime," stoves, panes of glass, thirty dwellings! Agustín Lago shouted the good news at the top of his voice to the teachers who had come together for a Brotherhood banquet which was held in the Central Hotel of Gerona, where Dr. Chaos and the British consul, Mr. Edward Collins, were staying. The banquet went along with so much healthy gaiety that the schoolmaster from Santa Coloma de Farnes, by nature a mordant man, was moved to compare the dishes he was being served with the menu faithfully followed in the village pension. He got up to offer a toast and said: "I propose that all of those present declare this meeting in permanent session."

Agustín Lago laughed. What was happening to him? Undoubtedly, he had taken a step forward.

But the second part of his program was still to be resolved, and that was no laughing matter. The Inspector reported to Victor Camacho on the course inevitably taken by the teachers who had been expelled from their profession at the end of the war by the Purification Commission over which he had had to preside. Lord, what a problem! Some of them had emigrated to Barcelona; others, fewer in number, had started small businesses; many had found jobs in offices. But most of them, whether male or female, had suffered shameful privations, not to say starvation. They had become demoralized parasites, like many of the war cripples who had fought in the Red army. They were sitting ducks, ready for any illicit adventure. This was confirmed by the fact that some discharged schoolteachers were among the first informers of the Office of Price Administration simply because they wanted to collect the forty percent of the fines imposed. What could be done about it? Victor Camacho supplied several leads. They must try to place these teachers in religious secondary schools, even though that might seem paradoxical. Many schools in that class were operating without a full staff. Another suggestion was to offer them facilities for establishing private academies.

Agustín Lago was successful in both projects. To his boundless joy! There was no shortage of teachers of mature years devoted to their profession heart and soul. They called him their rescuing angel, as grateful to him as the musician Quintana had been to Chelo Rosselló for giving him a chance to direct the choral group of the Feminine Section. "You've saved us! You've saved us!" Agustín Lago was tempted to say to Professor Civil: "See that, Professor? That's holy intransigence." But he refrained because the Brotherhood preferred to act in secret, to shun the always humiliating name of benevolent paternalism which its work might otherwise acquire.

Carlos Godo congratulated Agustín Lago. "Blessings on you, Agustín. Keep up the good work. You have a very great responsibility, for Spain's basic problem is just that: teaching. According to Victor Camacho, more than a third of our population is illiterate. Let's love those illiterates because they are our brothers. Let's try to help them to consecrate themselves by decent labor. Again I say: congratulations. And believe me, I'd like very much to take another trip to Gerona between now and Christmas to embrace you."

Now what about Warning Voice?

Euphoria, euphoria all around! First for being president of the Committee on Entertainment for the fairs. The whole province would move into the city to enjoy them. And the fireworks would be epoch-making! What had happened at the first try, three months after the end of the war, when Gerona had been celebrating the anniversary of the Uprising, would not happen again. The final cascade was not going to fizzle out for lack of revolving frames. This time the crowd would see more than "*¡Viva...Julio!*" Added to that, prizes were being offered for posters and store-window decorations, special prizes for the best-decorated streets. All this was an inspiration to the neighborhoods. Each street already had appointed its committee, and a frantic display of pennants and flower pots burst forth on the balconies. And the finale, at the gala dance in the Casino, the Gerona Jazz Band!

Dearest Carlota:

We're off and running. It must be the result of the inner joy given me by my stay in Puigcerdá and the good luck God sent me by offering me a chance to meet you, but it's all under way. I'm doing everything I can to raise the morale of the city, and I believe I'm succeeding. You told me you'd be interested in learning all the details of my work, so here goes. Of course, I'd rather talk exclusively about our common plans.

I'm enclosing the program for the fairs so you'll know what we're cooking up. As you'll see, an unusual concert of *sardanas* will be played in your honor on the Rambla. Yes, on San Narciso's day the Municipal Government will treat the people to six *sardanas*—six!—right on the Rambla, and they'll be played by the Cobla Gerona. That's a real event! I imagine that even the old people will come out to join in the circles.

The people—not to mention some of the aldermen, who keep asking what's happened to me—are full of enthusiasm because I say yes to everything. I grant all the petitions they send me, whether they're for setting up a newspaper kiosk, a booth for fritters, or a stand for selling chestnuts. This has created a very favorable atmosphere. You'd be surprised at the zeal with which the city police watch out for anyone who tries to shake a carpet over the street or throw garbage in the river, and they see to it that the lights on the stairways are burning at the proper time. The spirit of cooperation is such that untold quantities of lost property are piling up in police headquarters as a token of good will. Today, which is market day, a neighbor went so far as to give me two ducks that she found running loose around there. Can you imagine that? I say that a town where lost ducks are returned is a healthy place. I realize now that in the past I went too far in denying that the masses could possess certain virtues.

Of course, to be honest about it, I must acknowledge that it hasn't been all my doing. The football championship games have started, and the Gerona Football Club won a smashing victory over Málaga—4:0. My fellow citizens went crazy. And as if that weren't enough, a hockey club has been founded in the city. It's a magnificent sport, very elegant. I'm sure it will delight you when you see it.

Another item of good news is the renovation of the radio broadcasting station. It's a powerful station, and the director has drawn up a program that is bound to make itself popular immediately. He's planned to rebroadcast some novels adapted for that express purpose. To put it better, they'll be long, blood-and-thunder novels, full of enamored shepherdesses or orphans of the storm, and bullies. Naturally they'll all end with wedding bells, and naturally I rejoice over that. You can't imagine how successful those "serials" have been. Housewives weep over them. Dressmakers weep. Everyone weeps, including the Governor's wife, María del Mar, and my maid, Montse. In short, thanks to the "soap operas," Gerona weeps—with happiness, which goes to show that the imaginary is more moving than the real.

My dear Carlota, I'm sending you my latest "Window on the World" which I've dedicated to you, as you'll see, because in it I show that the Catalan language, which you know so well, came to be spoken all over the Mediterranean and even in Byzantium. I quote your favorite author: Ramón Llull. There'll be some protests, but what do I care! The Office of Price Control can't stick its nose in that. Nor the Inspector of Elementary Education either, even though he comes from the land of Don Quixote. On the other hand, Mosén Alberto and Professor Civil, of whom I've so often spoken to you, will be delighted. And I'm sure you will, too.

I could go on and on writing to you, but the Bishop is expecting me. It seems some wretches are going from one flat to another offering scapulars that guarantee eternal salvation. His Lordship is in for quite a disappointment because I'm a sinner—as you well know—and I'd be willing to buy one of those scapulars.

I hope the mail will bring me a letter from you. I'll write you again tomorrow. Meanwhile, receive whatever you wish from one who goes through an attack of insomnia every night because of you.

Warning Voice

FORTY-ONE

A few days before the opening of the fairs, Mosén Alberto's presentiment about those heavily laden clouds which had been floating above the city was confirmed by a catastrophe. For once, Notary Noguer had sinned on the side of optimism. The tramontane refused to come at his command. Instead, a flood came and washed away Warning Voice's euphoria, the magic spell of the fair, the triumphal arches above the decorated streets, some bridges, some houses, and some human lives.

It had to happen sooner or later. Water had been a part of Gerona's history, long, long before the day of Cosme Vila and the Governor, even before General Alvarez de Castro, the hero of the War of Independence.

Rain began to fall on Saturday afternoon and did not stop until Monday at dawn. After water had poured down for several hours, there came a moment when the sky was the color of mud. A dark, dramatic sky, so black that it was reminiscent of some passages in the Bible, or so Señor Grote said. How it rained! It was frightening. The faces of the buildings, the trees, the business signs were all streaming water. The lights failed and the gas lamps went out. The water fell on a slant, obliquely. Gusts of wind twisted the telegraph wires and stopped the public clocks. Neighbors congregated in strategic spots to watch the spectacle. The main streets, the Plaza Municipal, the La Barca quarter, all were rampaging rivers.

By Sunday morning, the news could not have been worse. Since it was raining also in the Pyrenees, the Ter came down with an angry roar, which meant that the Oñar could not discharge its waters and that it, too, would overflow. That happened. In spite of neighborhood emergency measures to stop up the entrances to the buildings in haste, the water began to flow into the places of business as if determined to climb onto the counters and shelves. The Gran Vía, where the Dodgems and merry-go-rounds had already been installed, was a canal. The Café Nacional was violently invaded by the water, which came up to the level of the mirrors. The Diana Perfumery, Raimundo's barbershop, the government stores, and the dry-cleaning shop recently opened by the Widow Corbera were all deeply awash.

Nothing could be done about it. The flood was a fact. Any attempt to curb it would mean being swept away by the current. People were praying in their homes. The Alvears, safe because of the height of their flat, were saying the Rosary. La Andaluza was burning candles to Santa Barbara, and El Niño de Jaén was crossing himself constantly in unison with her girls.

The bridge in front of the artillery barracks had been washed out. Two dilapidated buildings on the Calle de Pedret collapsed. The prisoners in the Seminary, huddled behind barred windows, were thinking: "Maybe we can make a break." The terrified patients in the hospital wanted to leave their beds, and a blind old man asked: "What's happening?" The nun on duty told him, as she pulled a blanket over him: "A flood." The sepulchers in the cemetery were under water, and inside the common grave, which had become a mudhole, the old and the recent bones intermingled in total anonymity. There was talk of people cut off on some roof or other. Cats chose unheard of places in which to safeguard themselves. The horses in the stables on the Calle de la Rutlla were neighing in their stalls. But the worst thing happened behind the swimming pool on the banks of the Ter, where two Andalusian families had built their huts. They were carried off, ultimately to be swept out to the infinite sea. No one was aware of their tragedy. Their only farewell was a clap of thunder, born in the belly of the Apocalypse.

Everyone helplessly gnawed his fingers as the rain continued to fall relentlessly. Only a few unsung heroes defied the calamity at the risk of their lives. One was Mosén Falcó, the young religious adviser of the Falange. He jumped from his own balcony to the next house to rescue the paralyzed old woman who lived on the mezzanine. His flying leap was so unlikely that it might well have ended in the great beyond. Another hero was Aunt Conchi. All by herself she went out like a shot with a sack over her in lieu of a cape and managed to carry to safety two small children whom she discovered sitting perilously in the embrasure of a small window in front of the Crocodile Bar.

The rain did not stop until dawn on Monday. At that moment the clouds acknowledged their fatigue and some spots of clear sky appeared. Rescue squads were able to go to work at last. Their members were wearing the most absurd articles of clothing, as strange as those worn by the Anarchists on their way to the Aragón front. The Governor, in a helmet and raincoat that he had worn during the war, looked like a Russian commissar. Alfonso Estrada was lost in a hunting jacket that had belonged to his father, and had no leggings. The fire trucks moved ahead against the current, their sirens shrieking and their wheels sending out fans of water, on their way to the lower sections of Gerona: the Calle de la Barca and the Pedret quarter. Fishermen from San Felíu de Guixols and Pálamos, equipped with ropes and ladders, rowed their boats through the streets. They had orders to remove the injured to the hospital, where Dr. Chaos had arranged everything to take care of them.

The water level was very slow to fall. But finally, it subsided and the railings of the bridges began to emerge again. By the middle of the morning the sun had come out. Gerona was a distressing sight and its walls smelled like a swamp. The colors hurt the eyes, as if they had come out, too, after a long stay in a dark place.

All the Gerundians turned to the work of unblocking the drains to let the water run off. Piles of rubbish stood everywhere, and here and there furniture, plumbing fixtures, and dead sheep began to show. The work in the shops and basements was feverish. Some men, accustomed to digging trenches, swung their shovels with great mastery. The women, with handkerchiefs covering their heads and tied beneath their chins, looked a little like those Cosme Vila had seen shoveling snow in the streets of Moscow. Leaders stepped forth to order the clearing of each piece of property. The town streetcleaners' brigade was increased. Marta went out at the head of the girls in the Feminine Section with her famous medicine kit that said C.A.F.É. Amateur photographers climbed up on the train tracks to contemplate the impressive panorama of the Dehesa under water and to watch the Ter, which was engaged in going down, and trying to look important. Félix Reyes was making rapid sketches from a rooftop with pencil and paper in hand.

The troops had been called out, and Captains Arias and Sandoval were going around the perimeter of the bull ring in a boat painted red, helping to string catwalks and inspiring courage in the people injured by the flood by their presence. Captain Sánchez Bravo went to the football stadium and found it a calm lake, although the recently installed benches had vanished as well as Esther's beloved tennis courts.

The nightmare was over, but Gerona was a mudhole and would be one for a long time to come. The building that had once been the Costa brothers' foundry had come down. And now it was common knowledge that the flood had done damage not only to Gerona, but also to extensive areas throughout the province, especially those through which the Ter ran. Undoubtedly, the sum of the losses would be terrifying.

Flood, the autumn's mourning brooch for the city and province. It would be remembered for years, and Mosén Alberto took ample notes for the Municipal

Archives. The victims were many, and a large part of the herds that the Army had turned over to the peasants had been lost.

Amanecer would fill its pages for many days with data on the catastrophe. But in the midst of it all, a consoling note was struck. All Spain rang with the news, and once more the efficacy of the existing cohesion among all the regions of the country was manifest. Indeed, the Civil Government began to receive food, clothing, and money, in addition to innumerable telegrams of condolence. A nationwide subscription was established "for damages caused by the floods in Gerona." A generous donation from the Caudillo himself headed the list.

Mateo saw the extent of the disaster on his return from San Sebastián. He was put in charge of entering the contributions on the books and said repeatedly to Comrade Rosselló as the list kept growing; "This is marvelous! Can anyone doubt now that Spain is united?"

Comrade Rosselló would agree with a nod and say: "Yes, it sure is…"

THE man most affected psychologically by the catastrophe, aside from the flood victims and their families, was the Governor, Comrade Dávila, no question about that. After making a tour of the province and the city from one end to the other, he commented: "This is calamitous. All in all, the one thing that has remained intact is the Soler factory. We'll have to start all over again."

The water had demolished the fields like an armored tank. The people endured a November as black as the cassock of Mosén Obiols, the priest with the big feet and the thundering voice. The Governor saw immediately that the situation was made to order for unscrupulous men; it would give them their greatest chance to batten, like birds of prey, on the needy. Reports were coming in to him from everywhere confirming that, and not infrequently the leading actors were the local authorities themselves: the mayors and the Party or syndicate leaders and secretaries whom he himself had appointed. Such acts recalled the entrance of the Moors into a ruined village after a hard battle, to seize the reward their chiefs had promised, which was the right to loot.

The Governor underwent a crisis of demoralization. The war had never crushed him, but now water had annihilated him as it had the Italians in the offensive at Guadalajara.

He realized that a lack of discipline would undermine the foundations of the structure of patriotism and honesty that he had tried to build ever since his arrival in Gerona. He knew, too, that José Antonio's phrase "impermeable to discouragement" proved beyond the strength of one man at times.

Once again he confided in Mateo, who, in spite of the fact that the meetings in San Sebastián had made it patent that the Falange had less power than the man in the street imagined, still gave proof of enviable integrity. Mateo was the one who advised him to move in all directions. The first was to do the impossible by putting the situation to rights; the second, to demonstrate that he could be implacable in his punishments. "Besides," Mateo added, "you know we'll all help you. We're all on your side, from the head of the Office of Price Control down to the janitor in my office."

The Governor, who was sitting at his desk, could not summon up a smile. "Yes, I know. I know your good intentions very well. Nevertheless, I'm the one who has to direct the orchestra. I'm the Governor, the one who'll be held responsible for everything that happens. And all in the name of what? In the name of whom? No one presents arms before me, because this isn't a barracks. No one kisses my ring or asks me to bless him, because I'm not the Bishop. I'm not even the head of the Falange; you are. This office is not a comfortable spot to fill, I assure you. Look at this desk! And that telephone never stops ringing. 'We'll tell the Governor about it. The Governor will settle it.' What if I make a mistake? The General will put me in jail or he'll invite me kindly to retire to Santander, thanking me 'for services rendered.'"

Mateo understood his boss and friend. The problems really made bedlam. And it was obvious that what most repelled the Governor was the use of violence.

"I realize all that, Comrade Dávila. Nevertheless, I don't believe that any of this comes as news to you. After all, the marrow of the question is the same as ever, the one you've just mentioned: responsibility. The responsibility of authority. But after all, doesn't a general have to cross himself three times before he decides whether to attack on the right or on the left? And if he makes a mistake, and a hundred men, or two thousand men, lose their lives through his fault, then what? That's worse than having to retire to your own land. Come on, get out your tube of inhalant and take a deep breath. And read today's newspaper. The Japanese have definitely joined the Axis. Now it's the Berlin-Rome-Tokyo Axis. Doesn't that comfort you some? All right, I know it has a far-away ring to you just now. Do something else, then—look at your children's photographs. Luckily, the flood has respected Pablito and Cristina."

Comrade Dávila still could not call up a smile. His dark glasses looked like two black, impenetrable discs. Photographs of Pablito and Cristina seemed to him as remote as Tokyo just then. Reality had obliterated them. People were in need; they could not wait until the end of the month, whether they were officials, workers, or widows. The head of Price Control, whom Mateo had quoted, had informed the Governor only a short time before that several factories had decided to close their doors—owing to lack of raw materials, they said. It seemed an honest claim. Professor Civil had called him to say that a swarm of families had gathered at the Social Auxiliary. Public Works suggested that he take a trip to Madrid to find out the impassable state of the roads. By the nails of Christ, couldn't he hear any good news?

"Come on, tell me about your wedding. Maybe that will pep me up a little. Or tell Manolo to come here and tell me a joke..."

Mateo took out his lighter. "You seem to have forgotten what Don John of Austria said after the victory of Lepanto. He said he was in the same state as every other Spaniard on his most glorious day—without food, money, or medicine."

"Do I look like Don John of Austria? And what Lepanto have I won? Tell me that. And if you call this my most glorious day..." The Governor waved a paper that listed the villages left virtually incommunicado by the flood.

"When you go on like that, it makes me want to laugh," Mateo said. "First, because it shows your self-confidence. And second, because I know you're more sure of yourself than ever. The four Dávila brothers! You were famous, weren't you? I can't get it through my head that one of that four can sit there and say he's licked because a few extra drops of rain fell on his fief. Okay! I'll leave you to your own devices. Probably that's best. At times like this it does some good to meditate a little and look out the window. You'll see that the bell towers are still there; the women are still sewing at home; and the sky is going to be as blue as it was on the day the war ended." Mateo added: "Any time you need me, let me know," and left.

"Mateo's a strange fellow," Comrade Dávila said to himself. "He doesn't talk for the sake of hearing his voice. He's the one who should be holding down this chair. On the verge of getting married, and yet he voted in favor of Spain entering the war."

The Governor was left quite alone. He said to Comrade Rosselló, who was waiting outside: "I'm no good for anyone. Not even myself."

He started to think, and spent several minutes in intense concentration not unlike those thoughtful moments of Dr. Gregorio Lascasas at the beginning of Lent. He pulled in the muscles of his abdomen, got up, and looked out the window. And a refrain he had heard from a Moorish sentinel of La Mehalla during the battle of the Ebro came back to his mind: "When the moon is but a swatch, that's the time to be on watch." The new State, like a new moon, would need watching over.

He could do nothing but go on, and now he felt a renewal of strength. The allusion to the four Dávila brothers had been like a touch of the spur. So had Mateo's integrity. And Marta's. She was conquering her deep sadness—what a dirty trick Ignacio had played on her! She was traveling through the valley of the Ter in the cabin of a truck, distributing everything she could wangle out of the Food Delegation. He turned around and saw the newspaper on his desk. The headlines about the Berlin-Rome-Tokyo Axis hardly caught his attention. Instead of studying them, he read attentively an announcement by the Agencia Gerunda addressed to all the citizens which said: "We will solve all your problems. Trust us with your business. Agencia Gerunda can settle everything." The founder of that concern was a poor boy from the UGT whom people called Tower of Babel.

The word "discipline" hammered at his head, now lucid. He picked up the telephone and called the Commissioner of Investigation and Vigilance, Diéguez, a man with whom he had had as little contact as possible. The Commissioner's office was in Police Headquarters on the ground floor. He came up the stairs four at a time.

"Did you wish to speak to me?"

"Yes, please sit down."

The Governor's orders came as a surprise to the Commissioner. "Send your men up here and we'll give them a lesson. We're going to impose fines all over town. I hate to do it, but I have no choice."

"If you could tell me the specific objectives..."

"Whatever you like, Commissioner. Fines for defeatism, for spreading false rumors, for not keeping Sunday a day of rest, for not raising an arm when the national anthem is sung, for hunting without a license, for not carrying a light on a bicycle, for resisting authority, for not recognizing the emblem of the Social Auxiliary. Anything you like! The only thing you must avoid is inventing an infraction, of course. The infraction must be a real one. Do you understand?"

"I understand."

"Whenever the violator is a local leader, a mayor in short, or any authority—whoever he may be, you must let me know about it by making some special notation on the report."

"Three red crosses, if that suits you."

The Governor was like a machine gunner trying to sweep the widest possible field covered by his authority. His final phrase was: "I want to be in control of everything."

Commissioner Diéguez had listened without batting an eye. But when the Governor came to this, his final point, the policeman stared down at the white carnation in his lapel for a moment. He had had the same idea all along, not so much for political as for psychological reasons, and had felt sure that the Governor, "so liberal and humane," would put a foot in his field some day. Well, he had done it now.

"I believe I understand you, Governor. But may I ask one question?"

"Ask it."

"What is the reason for this change of attitude?"

"Sausages are the reason."

"Pardon me? What did you say?"

"The Health Department has found out that sausages adulterated with all kinds of filth are being sold here, and they notified me. I could hardly ask for a more graphic example!"

Commissioner Diéguez got up, satisfied.

"With your permission, I'll get right on the job."

"You'll find me here, me or someone who represents me, all around the clock."

"So long, then…"

"*¡Arriba España!*"

Up, Spain! The Governor took off his glasses at last and wiped the sweat from his face. It was hard for him to fight his own temperament. He rubbed the finger that had worn a bandage; it was aching. He thought about Colonel Triguero. He did not want him and the many others like him to have things all their own way. He thought of the General; he did not want him to be proved right in his affirmation that the only clean, loyal body in existence was the Army. The Falange, which had struck a realistic balance regarding the situation at the San Sebastián meeting, would have to save the sheep from the shearing pen. He thought of the Bishop and decided to follow him, to swim with his current in order to keep the Church on his side. Religion was an awful, a decisive force. But, Lord, how ridiculous it made itself sometimes! With all that had happened, the only thing that had occurred to His Lordship had been to set a Youth Week for the little virgins in Catholic Action and to publish still another pastoral letter on the lack of purity and modesty.

Now the Governor felt that he was on his way. He called Warning Voice and ordered him to publish for a month in *Amanecer* every day the following communiqué: "It is your duty to join the Falange. Laggards will be judged indifferent now and later considered opponents of the New State." A few second after that he was asking himself: "Have I gone too far?" No. He noticed the paper lying on his desk, and it came to his aid again. Really, it was absurd for Boisson Blanche to say in its daily advertisement: "Watch your breathing! Clean out your digestive tract and sanitize it!" Too bad he could not advertise something like that to put an end to indifference and the revival of selfishness.

One flaw was evident in his procedure. What could he give the people in exchange for those hundred eyes which would control their everyday movements? With the whole world reeling and the word "peace" damaged, the sweet word that the people had been savoring since April 1, 1939, what could he do but ensure public order? And give people the certainty that everything was being done for the commonweal in order to keep alive the principle of authority, whose decline had brought Spain to its cataclysm. But how far should rationing go? The Reds had lost the war largely because they had been hungry, as he had said a hundred times. And now smokers were soon to be issued ration cards, which Don Emilio Santos in the Government Tobacco Monopoly already had sitting on his desk. Why couldn't he give the men all the tobacco they wanted? And why couldn't the women buy as many sheets, handkerchiefs, and silk blouses as their hearts desired, even if only so they could continue to sew inside their houses?

The Governor brought his fist down on the useless yellow telephone and went to the window again. He saw some seagulls wheeling above the Ter, their favorite spot, where they clustered by the dozen. Winter was on its way. Why did there have to be winters in the life of the villages? Churchill had promised the English people "blood, sweat, and tears." But the English were rich and they had provoked and exploited half the world. Now they were reaping what they had sown. Spain, which had not incensed anyone, was undone, to adopt the phrase used by Comrade Rosselló on his return from Puerto de Santa María.

The Governor was tired. He thought of his wife, María del Mar, who said to him when she saw him go out in helmet and raincoat during the flood: "Lots of luck, darling!"

He felt a wave of tenderness sweep over him and forgot everything in the sudden desire to see his wife, to put his arms around her. They had shared their lives for so many years.

No sooner said than done. He left the office and went down the long hallway—saying to the porter as he went: "You may go now. See you tomorrow"—and entered the portion of the building which was used as his residence.

"María del Mar!" he called from the door.

She did not answer immediately. Where on earth was she? Finally, she appeared. "Has anything happened?" she asked.

The Governor gave her a long, sweet look. "No, nothing. I just wanted to see you."

María del Mar was surprised. Her husband usually did not come home so early, much less look at her that way and speak to her in that tone. What a hard time the poor man was having!

She gave no sign of what she was thinking, but, noticing all at once that she had her knitting in her hands, she laid it down on the first handy piece of furniture she came to, and asked him: "Do my ears deceive me? Did you say you wanted to see me?"

"Yes, that's what I said."

Her eyes lighted up, expressing her joy and showing her that the Governor was tired.

"Is there something you want from me?"

"Yes, I want a kiss."

María del Mar was touched. She moved a pace forward and they met as he stepped toward her. They merged in an embrace and kissed with unusual ardor. The Governor had not kissed her like that in months.

As they separated, her cheeks were flushed and her heart was beating as it had beaten during the war when he had told her that he would have a day's leave and could come to see her.

"Juan Antonio! You don't know how happy you've made me feel. This is such a surprise!"

"Yes, I imagine it is. This life we lead—it's hard on you. Sometimes I forget I have a wife."

That made her feel capable of anything. "Don't worry. You see how things are…" She glanced at the piece of furniture beside her. "I was knitting."

"So I see. But how do I know what you were thinking?"

María del Mar's expression was somewhat coy as she said: "What do you expect me to be thinking of? You, of course. And the children."

The children! Mateo's recommendation concerning Pablito and Cristina came back to the Governor's mind. He felt a need to round out his emotional complement.

"Where are they?" he asked.

María del Mar almost felt jealous. She did not care to have him interrupt their scene.

"They must be around, in their own rooms."

The Governor gazed at his wife again. He gave her another kiss, this time on the forehead, and said: "If you don't mind, I'd like to see them, too."

María del Mar made no move to follow him. She turned, remembering that she looked less than tidy and went to look at herself in the mirror.

The Governor started toward Cristina's room. The thought of the child suddenly made him happy. Mateo was right after all, his children—and María del Mar—were not among "the few too many drops that had fallen."

The door of Cristina's room was open. The Governor went in on tiptoe, approaching her from the rear until he could surprise her by putting his hands over her eyes.

"Who am I?"

"The Governor!"

The Governor! He smiled, pinched the little girl, and pulled her hair.

"What are you doing?"

"As you can see, I'm dressing my dolls. The nuns told us to, for Christmas."

"For Christmas?"

"Yes, for the poor kids."

The poor kids... Cristina said that word *poor* as though it were something far, far away from her.

"Are you happy, Cristina?"

"Yes, Papa. Why?"

"What would you like the Three Magi to bring you this year?"

"Oh, I don't know. It's coming pretty soon, isn't it? Well, a bicycle! To ride in the Dehesa."

"Good Lord! In all that mud?"

"It'll be dried up by then, won't it?"

"Surely."

Cristina had seated herself on the Governor's lap. Suddenly, she said: "I like you better without glasses."

"I don't wear them for fun, you know. My eyes hurt."

"Pooh! You're strong. Nothing hurts you."

What an odd little girl! She felt safe from any mishap, and she honestly believed that her father was all-powerful.

They chatted a while longer until the Governor heard a faint sound in the room next door, Pablito's room. He felt an urge then to finish his itinerary. Gently setting the little girl on the floor, he kissed her on the forehead.

"All right, I'm going now. The bicycle is a sure thing."

"Thank you, Papa."

He rose to his feet, said goodbye to his daughter, and went out of her room toward Pablito's. The door was closed; he knocked and heard a "Come in."

He went in. Pablito was sitting hunched over his desk, studying. The temperature of the house was high enough to let him wear his favorite garments, his pajamas. He was almost a man.

"Am I bothering you?"

"No."

Pablito turned around. He, too, was surprised to see his father home at that hour and looking affectionate.

A brief silence ensued while Pablito waited expectantly, not venturing to ask whether "anything had happened."

The Governor went to the sofa beside the desk where Pablito was studying and sat down with an air of fatigue.

"Are you tired?"

"A little." Pablito swung around in his swivel chair. "What are you studying?"

"Chemistry. What a headache!"

The Governor did not want his son to suspect that he had come to see him because he needed to. Pablito was a man now.

"Are you sure I'm not bothering you?"

"No, really you're not."

"Chemistry is a hard subject."

"Hard? I said it before: it's a headache."

The Governor smiled. "You like your other subjects better, don't you? History, literature..."

"Of course."

Pablito felt pleased. Why was his father showing such an interest in him? He was very fond of the Governor, even though he was a "viceroy."

"You're like me, son. I used to hate science, too." Hastily he added, "I don't remember a thing about it now."

Pablito said lightly: "Okay, but you don't have to take a test."

The Governor smiled faintly and took a eucalyptus tablet out of his pocket.

"Care for one?"

"No, no. Please!"

The Governor sighed. "You've no idea," he went on, resting his back against the sofa, "how many things I've forgotten. My diploma! I wonder where it is."

"Maybe something's wrong with your memory," Pablito said.

"No!" the Governor protested. "You lose what you don't use."

Pablito tugged at his ear. His father's visit was beginning to excite him. He reflected for a second or two, then a vagrant idea occurred to him.

"Have you really forgotten a lot of the things you studied for your diploma?"

"Well, you can imagine... What with the war on top of everything else."

"It would be fun," Pablito suggested, "to find out."

"How?"

"I don't know. I'll play I'm asking you questions."

"Questions?"

"Yes. As if I were on the examining board."

"I refuse!" his father exclaimed. "I won't play that game."

"Why not?"

"Because I don't want you to lose your respect for me."

"I couldn't do that."

"Truly, Pablito. I'm not fooling. One forgets a lot of things."

Pablito was so carried away with his idea that he was reluctant to give it up. He picked up the paper knife on his desk and put it in his mouth. Then he asked point blank: "Just let me see. I promise I won't ask you anything about chemistry. Take this, for example: what year was Michelangelo born?"

"Do you mean the exact year?"

"Yes."

The Governor shook his head. "I don't know."

Pablito nibbled the paper knife. "How many bishops were at the meeting of the Council of Trent?"

The Governor burst out laughing. "Lots, a whole gang of them, I'd say."

Pablito was relentless, firing like a rocket. "Who was Nobai?"

The Governor stared at the ceiling with the expression of a sleepwalker.

"Nobai? That rings a bell. It seems to me he's in the Old Testament."

"Can you draw a polygonal prism?"

The Governor retreated again into laughter. "Please, son, don't give me such big words."

Pablito started to laugh, too. But clearly he felt a little uneasy. He suspected that if he were to ask his father for the first verse of the *Aeneid* he would fail that, too. Neither would he be able to give the distance from the earth to Mars.

He put down the paper knife and started to play with the fountain pen his father had given him when he started the school year.

"Have you forgotten all those things, Papa?"

Pablito spoke in an enigmatic tone. The Governor was afraid Pablito would draw some extreme conclusions from their game.

"Look, son, I warned you. All those data eventually lose their importance. Depending, that is, on the profession you follow later in life. But if you should have to know them some fine day, you'd look them up in an encyclopedia."

Pablito frowned. "I don't see quite what you mean."

"Let me see if I can explain it," the Governor went on. "It's one thing to learn certain subjects, which is what you have to do while you're in high school—and another thing to be an educated man. To be an educated and cultivated man means to have a feeling about the world, to have lived, to know people at a glance. Education has nothing to do with dates or polygonal prisms."

Pablito was silent. Finally, he asked: "Why don't you give me an example that will explain the difference?"

At that moment the Governor wished he had a pipe with smoke rising from it in a spiral. "Well, that's easy. You asked me what year Michelangelo was born. An educated man feels as he studies a statue by the artist that he understands what Michelangelo wanted to say, what the work means, even though he may not know the year Michelangelo was born."

"But the ideal thing would be to know both, wouldn't it, Papa?"

The Governor was about to answer, "Oh, of course!" but then modified his answer to suit himself.

"Well, I'll tell you. It's pretty hard for the two things to come together. People who know facts usually wind up by giving examinations in an institute. Or working in a laboratory. Or in an office. Educated people go much farther. They create things; they move the world. And the artists, too, of course," he added.

Pablito was still keenly interested. "Take Gerona for example," he said. "Whom would you call a person who knows facts and who do you think is an educated man?"

The Governor thought a moment. "A person who knows facts? I don't know. I suppose your history teacher is one. And our dear Mayor, of course! An educated person? Well, Dr. Andújar. And Dr. Chaos, for another, and Professor Civil. Even Mateo!"

"Mateo?"

"Yes. Why are you looking at me like that? Mateo is educated. I suppose he's forgotten the number of bishops at the Council of Trent, like me. But he's formed a concept of life. Understand?"

Pablito frowned again and objected to those words. "A concept of life? I suppose there are educated men with very different opinions then. I'm thinking about religion now. Dr. Chaos—you said he's an educated man, but he's an atheist. Dr. Andújar and Professor Civil are both very religious."

"Well," the Governor explained, "that's only natural. I didn't say an educated man has a corner on truth. All I said is that he has a concept of it. So you're right. Not only can people and concepts be different, but they can be opposites, even."

Pablito seemed to be growing restless. He kept shrinking down in his chair, making himself smaller.

"Then being educated doesn't guarantee being right, does it?"

"No."

"So what good is it?"

"It's good to make you move ahead a little, to keep sloughing off mistakes. It's useful because it shows you how to correct your mistakes." The Governor wished he had a cup of coffee. "To know who was right, for example, when this war is over—whether it will be the Anglophiles or the others; or us, who believe in Germany. Then we'll have taken a short step forward."

"But you've already made up your mind. And you've taught me to think the same as you."

"Of course."

"Then would you be willing to correct your mistake?"

The Governor wished he could put on his glasses. "I feel sure I won't have to."

A thousand objections occurred to Pablito, especially as he thought of Manolo and Esther. Manolo must be an educated man, too, yet he wanted the English to win. He was on the point of saying something to that effect, but suddenly noted the loving look his father was turning on him, full of a love so intense that he laid aside his objections and seemed to understand in a flash that a love like that was a great truth. A truth that would last all his life.

He was happy. How long had it been since they had had a conversation like this?

"Do you want to know something?" Pablito went on. "I like the artists best of all. I think they're the ones who go ahead the most quickly."

"Are you saying that because you write poetry?" the Governor asked ironically.

"No, that's not it at all."

Pablito eyed his father with equal irony. He loved his father, yet the Governor's statement raised a serious problem that had disturbed the boy for a long time. If nothing was certain *a priori*, then the act of governing, of being a "viceroy," let alone of imposing a certain predetermined doctrine—and punishing infractions with fines or prison—was a very risky undertaking.

He went so far as to think that a truly educated man never would dare to give an order to anyone. Pablito felt a little confused, and once more his own reflections tortured him.

"Papa, do you mind if I ask you a question?"

"Of course not, son. That's why I'm sitting here talking to you."

"Take a kid my age. What am I supposed to think about you and grownups in general? About Mateo, about the General, even about you. Am I supposed to think you've always acted like educated people?"

"I don't know what you're talking about."

"I'm talking about the fact that you fought a war, and that there's another one on now. And about war being a terrible thing, even if one side is fighting for something that's right."

The Governor turned serious. "There's no easy answer to that, Pablito. I understand your objections very well. But you must realize that life forces us to do some concrete things. If you believe a thing is unjust, you have to fight it. And there are always unjust things in the world." The Governor suddenly noticed that his son, sitting there in his pajamas, looked like a child still, and that made him feel tender. "Besides, didn't you write a sort of anthem to José Antonio at the time his body was transferred to the Escorial? What made you do that? José Antonio used to talk about pistols and shooting."

Pablito was disconcerted, but he also felt a stir of admiration for his father.

"I think that what impresses me about José Antonio is that he was a poet," he finally said.

"Nonsense!" the Governor replied. "He expressed himself poetically, but he was a thinker. He was defending a doctrine. History will say I'm right. And it will demonstrate, too, that he was an educated man."

That marked the end of the dialogue, for at that moment María del Mar came in, looking burnished and carrying her husband's slippers and a cup of coffee!

"Well," she asked sweetly, "are father and son in agreement?"

"Of course."

Pablito straightened himself in his chair with an air of greater assurance and responded to his mother's sweetness with a look as he said: "Well, I can tell you this: it seems to me that the only thing that's clear is that chemistry is still a headache."

"Is that all?" María del Mar protested as she knelt at her husband's feet to take off his shoes.

The Governor said: "Pablito would like life to be a multiplication table—two times two is four, and that's that."

María del Mar shook her head. "Then that young man is in for a lot of disappointment."

Pablito stared at his mother. "I didn't say I'd like life to be like that. What's worrying me is that I'm finding out that no one knows what it's really like."

María del Mar got up and stared back at her son.

"Your mother knows," she said with conviction.

"You do, eh? All right, tell me!"

"Life is love. Life is making people love you."

"You see," said the Governor, addressing his son. "You win. Your mother is an artist, too."

Pablito stared at the floor. No one spoke. Finally, he said: "It's too bad you're not one, too."

CHAPTER FORTY-TWO

THE Alvears received a letter from Julio García dated in New York, to their surprise. The letterhead read: "Hotel Lincoln, Fifth Avenue." The letter was fairly long. Julio explained to his friends, in a much more serious vein than usual, that London had become an *awful hell* owing to the bombings, and that for that reason he "and his beloved wife, Doña Amparo Campo, had decided to cross the pond and settle in the United States." Julio García ended his letter by begging Matías to mail him a copy of *Amanecer* from time to time, if that could be done. Doña Amparo Campo confessed to them in a postscript that she personally missed Paris a great deal; it was a city "that had captured her heart."

Matías and Ignacio, who had had no news of José Alvear for months, or of David and Olga, were glad to know that Julio García and Doña Amparo were safe and sound. Ignacio ventured to say as a joke that possibly Julio would quickly perfect his English, and that, being flanked by other important exiles who, so it was said, were hanging around the White House, "he would end up by making friends with Roosevelt himself."

London a terrible inferno! The expression fitted exactly the picture of the war given by the Spanish press correspondents in Berlin and Rome. Manolo and Esther read their dispatches with sinking hearts. Yes, it did seem that things were going well for Hitler and Mussolini, especially since the alliance with Tokyo. True, the British Air Force was showing signs of increasing activity and the anti-aircraft defenses, the barrage balloons, and the fighter squadrons were growing in size and strength; but England had not been able yet to prevent the systematic destruction of key cities on her island fiefdom. The city of Coventry had been razed. The factories of Bristol were in ashes. Even the royal palace, Buckingham Palace, had been bombed, although the royal family escaped harm. All in all, the machine of destruction set in motion by Marshal Goering was taking on an apocalyptic quality.

It seemed logical enough, then, that Julio García should be writing from New York. He always followed the gold trail. Day after day, gold reserves were pouring into New York, not only from England, but also from the other countries that Germany had invaded. The one thing that the people of Gerona could not fathom was how the English people could stand fast, for, according to statements by the German Führer, that inferno was not going to end, quite the contrary.

On the sea, however, events were taking another course because of the power of the British fleet, which was fighting even in the Mediterranean between Sicily and Malta. Seemingly, it was all that stood in the way of a German landing in England. As Manolo kept saying: "Crossing the English Channel by air is by no means the same thing as crossing it by sea." He was seizing on every encouraging detail. "Churchill has battleships; he has sowed the English coast with magnetic mines, and his seamen are highly skilled. Possibly, it's Hitler's plan not to risk his navy and to force a surrender on the basis of air attacks." Father Forteza, who was following the course of the war with as much fervor as he was devoting to César's beatification and to consoling Marta, told Esther that while he had been in Germany he had heard again and again that Hitler had an almost superstitious fear of water. That he never immersed his entire body in the sea, and that he had even gone so far as to confess: "On dry land, I'm a hero; on the sea, a coward." Father Forteza speculated on the possibility that this fear might have had something to do with the repeated postponements of the announced invasion.

But in spite of everything, the German submarines were still prowling the oceans, sinking such a large number of British ships that *Amanecer* was beginning to become known to the Gerundians as "The Tonnage" because its headlines kept proclaiming with typographical ostentation the tonnage that the submarines sent to the bottom of the sea every day according to Berlin. Some people kept a running account of the sinkings and arrived at the conclusion that the German command was padding the figures considerably.

In Gerona the general impression was, "This can't go on." Now Italy was collaborating strongly, not only by attacking Egypt from Libya, but also by demanding that Greece hand over several strategic spots in order to advance the war against England. "It would be curious," Professor Civil remarked, "if Mussolini, the great admirer of the architects of the Roman Empire, were to destroy the Athenian Acropolis."

José Luis Martínez de Soria and other young officers, including Captain Sánchez Bravo, believed that Hitler would finally achieve a landing in England. "Napoleon didn't dare to do it," he said, "but Hitler has what Napoleon lacked."

Marta's brother had followed closely the German style of combat, and his admiration was boundless. He kept telling everyone in the casino how each of Hitler's soldiers carried in his knapsack a copy of the so-called "Ten Commandments for Deportment in the War," forbidding the men at the front to use dum-dum bullets, to maltreat prisoners, to loot, and so on, and so on. The first commandment said: "The German soldier will fight in a chivalrous manner for the victory of the people." José Luis declared that, in addition, the German flyers who attacked England were introducing brilliant innovations in their behavior in the air. For example, a plane would simulate being hit and falling so that the English anti-aircraft guns would turn their sights away from it. But as the plane approached the ground, it would drop its lethal charge and calmly climb aloft while another plane repeated the same maneuver in another spot.

General Sánchez Bravo displayed a little more caution than the young officers. He believed in his heart that England had lost the war, but he could not see the invasion as a sure thing. He, too, admired extravagantly Hitler's decisions concerning the war and believed a report that Hitler was getting ready to flood England with enormous quantities of counterfeit pounds sterling so perfectly forged that they would be sure to cause great confusion among the British people. He also praised the scientific idea of distributing candy containing vitamin C on the German home front in order to provide the people with an adequate diet. "That candy would be a good thing for us," the General told the Governor and Don Oscar Pinel, the food ration chief.

Manolo and Esther clung to two threads that still connected them with hope: the ever-serene face of the British consul in Gerona, Mr. Edward Collins, and the dispatches of some of the Spanish correspondents in London. They read the reports aloud and commented on them with Ignacio, who often merely frowned, like Pablito, before asking an important question. The correspondents in question, especially the one for *La Vanguardia* of Barcelona, agreed with Julio García's summary: London, Coventry, Bristol, and all the other cities were indeed infernos, especially on moonlit nights, which gave Goering's bomber pilots good visibility. Nevertheless, the English people were showing such courage and steadfastness that the writers believed it was highly improbable that the bombing could demoralize them. The English women had enlisted in the struggle for the duration and were behaving with unimaginable valor, not alone in the Red Cross and as fire wardens, but also in the heavy work of transport and manufacturing, and they were ready to bear arms, too. Furthermore, the great number of cellars in the London buildings provided shelters for the people and enabled them to continue numerous activities, including the publication of newspapers. Best of all, the English had not lost their sense of humor. While bombs were falling like rain, the chorus girls in the capital went on strike because the owners of the "cellars" in which they put on their light-hearted performances were threatening to demand that the girls should appear on stage "more scantily clad than formerly" in honor of the fighting men. The trade unions objected to giving up their weekly day of rest, which the workingman needed. The people were still betting on the dog races, which had not been suspended; private cars lined up ready to transport the public wherever needed; many men had traded their derbies for helmets—often a German type of helmet—and the innumerable wounded men who appeared in public with bandaged legs or arms in casts were nicknamed "the army in white." People rescued the dogs and cats roaming lost and terrified among the ruins. All of which was summed up in a cartoon that appeared in the newspapers and became famous. It showed an enormous German tank driven by Hitler and his generals, on the point of entering London until it was halted at a barricade in front of which a London policeman stood demanding a penny toll.

Aside from getting back into shape the tennis courts that had been destroyed by the flood and sitting on the board of the recently founded roller-skate hockey club, Manolo's and Esther's dearest wish would, of course, have been to establish contact with Mr. Edward Collins, the British consul, but they had no entrée. He always contrived to avoid any engagement not related to his work. Finally they found out, thanks to an indiscretion on Mateo's part, that in his obligatory conversations with the Governor, Mr. Collins always gave assurances to the Spanish authorities of the British Government's readiness to keep Spain afloat economically. "Just think of that," Manolo commented. "England is under the tightest blockade ever recorded in history, yet she is promising to supply raw materials to Spain to the value of millions of pounds, and on long credit terms. Meanwhile, Hitler is conferring the Grand Cross of the German Eagle on Franco. And Mateo and his comrades in Madrid are doing their best to get us into the war. I swear that if I were wearing a derby instead of a Tyrolean hat, I'd take it off as I went by the Central Hotel, where Mr. Edward Collins is staying."

The possibility that Spain might enter the war on the side of the Axis kept Manolo and Esther awake nights. According to María Victoria, the great exponent of that step was the Minister of Foreign Affairs, Ramón Serrano Súñer, a friend of Germany who was convinced that she would win the war, and who, like Miguel Rosselló, was dreaming of recovering territory in Africa and the Mediterranean "which would restore Spain to her past grandeur." María Victoria attributed to Serrano Súñer some lapidary phrases in praise of Germany and in contempt of the United States, and she declared that on the Spanish minister's recent visit to Berlin, he had virtually obligated his government to back Hitler's plans to close the Mediterranean at both ends: Suez and Gibraltar. "We shall occupy Suez," the Führer had told him, "and you, the Spaniards, Gibraltar, with honor and dignity." Mateo, for his part, believed that he knew that Serrano Súñer had acceded to that plan in principle.

Manolo was openly furious. "Do you know what that means, Ignacio? It means we'll be cannon fodder. First of all, though, I don't see that it would be so easy to occupy Gibraltar as long as a part of the English fleet is there. Next, England would seize the Canary Islands in reprisal. And all things considered, if the United States should grasp the nettle and make up its mind to intervene, Spain would become the main battlefield."

Ignacio did not know what to say. He felt toward England, but not toward France, an instinctive repulsion in spite of the chorus girls' strike and the cartoon of the tank and the penny. He could not forget the Red Zone, where Esther had never spent a single day. César had been shot to death in the cemetery, but that had not prevented Mr. Attlee, the representative of the British Government at the time, from making a later voyage to Barcelona, or from giving the Communist salute, or from going back to England to state more or less that "everything is calm in Republican Spain." Ignacio was beginning to accumulate some serious reservations with regard to the totalitarian doctrines, but the formulas that might lead to a Popular Front gave him gooseflesh. As usual, he stood at a crossroad, and at times he felt jealous of people who could take a wholehearted militant stand on one side or the other. But that was not all—Manolo was a Catalan, from the land of business and finance, and when Ignacio heard him speaking Catalan inside or outside the office, he saw Manolo as another person, a man much readier than he, the son of a Madrilenian, to make contact with Mr. Edward Collins.

"I can't go along with Serrano Súñer or Mateo," Ignacio replied to Manolo, "and the mere words 'empire' and 'Gibraltar' leave me cold. But neither can I go along with you and Esther. I once said about our war that both sides had lost; and I believe that is becoming clearer every day. The Reds defended free love; now the Nationalists post Civil Guards on the beaches, and the Bishop is scandalized if couples walk arm in arm. Well, I'm beginning to suspect that the same thing is going to happen on a much larger scale after this terrible war that's going on now; everyone is going to lose. If Hitler wins, as it seems now he will, God help us—agreed. He'll cut up Europe to suit himself; he'll erase the word 'freedom' from the dictionary, and when Ana María and I get married, perhaps in the Hermitage of Los Angeles, we'll have to say *ja* instead of *sí.* But supposing your wish comes true, supposing the war reverses itself by some miracle and England wins. I'm afraid that Julio García, who has written us from New York, will reclaim this apartment of yours and that we'll even see El Responsable sitting again in the chair that Warning Voice is now holding down in City Hall. And the worst of it is that as you know, I find Warning Voice pretty hard to take. I'd like to lay off this subject, if you don't mind, and hear you explain to me, dear Manolo, why you think we've lost the eviction suit against that poor workman in the Soler factory. I've been scanning the Code, and it seems to me…"

Manolo admired Ignacio more every day. He was pleased that his assistant never flattered him, that he weighed the pros and cons of everything, and that he took such a great interest in professional problems and in learning. Furthermore, he was coming to the conclusion that Ignacio's frequent silences and eternal doubts were not signs of sterility: he had demonstrated his strength of mind in the Marta affair by finally coming to an irrevocable decision, and he was also demonstrating it in the office every day in a thousand details. When the time came to draw up a contract or the by-laws of a corporation, he was slow but sure. In the end, he left nothing to chance, no loose ends. Ignacio had also shown that he had a keen and active bent for the law in some of the business connected with the inheritance entrusted to them by the widow of Don Pedro Oriol. Best of all, he was courageous. The more notable the person or entity whom he had to stand up to in the office, the more he enjoyed defending what he considered right. At the moment he was insisting to the point of boring everyone that they ought to lock horns with the Office of Price Control, no less, because its inspectors frequently imposed fines not on the basis of the importance of the violation, but on that of the economic situation of the guilty person.

"That's illegal," Ignacio kept protesting. "It's contrary to the administration of justice. That's the sort of thing Hitler would do. And what the English have always done when they've applied the law to their enemies. I'm certain that if Mr. Churchill is now granting navicerts to Spanish ships, he's not doing it to save us from bankruptcy, but to promote some dark design that he'll keep to himself."

Esther was also very fond of Ignacio, even though, half in fun, half in earnest, he ferociously attacked the rich Andalusians—like her, they might be from Jérez de la Frontera—who had been educated at Oxford.

"I'm not against bridge, my dear Esther, or golf, or the dog races. I like those cognacs with English names which you concoct in your part of the country. They make me feel a comforting warmth in my stomach. Sure, I'll thank you if you serve me a glass of González Byass. All the same, a friend of mine whose name is Moncho, someone I hope you'll meet someday, told me that the Andalusians have a caste system that prevails from top to bottom. He said it made him sick. In the railroad station in Seville, he brought out a gold duro and three hundred porters, almost all of them Anarchists, got down on their knees and called him Lord. That's what worries me. Sometimes I ask myself, Esther, if you might not have the caste spirit too. You see? You're just like Mr. Edward Collins, who seemingly never moves out of the main section for fear of getting his shoes dirty. Forgive me for speaking like this. I always say what I feel, you know. I believe that the caste system is wrong, for one reason because one always comes up against a higher caste, and that forces one to get down on his knees before someone else some fine day. I don't want to get down on my knees to anyone, I give you my word for that, and social differences have mattered so little to me that if Mr. Churchill were to come in here, I'd say to him: 'Hi, Mr. Churchill, how's it going?' So all told—thank you, Esther, this González Byass is excellent—I know that in spite of appearances, I'm the best democrat here. Oh, no, please don't look at me like that! Don't look so offended and surprised. I owe all these theories to my father, to the way my father has of settling his hat on his head."

Esther finally laughed. Ignacio could go on like that, but the first day he had entered their house he had been openmouthed at his discovery of "good taste." And good taste was a matter of caste.

"You're right about that," Ignacio admitted. "I'm learning a lot from being with you. You don't know how glad I am to find that Ana María dresses more or less like you. She has a sweater almost exactly like the one you're wearing right now. But there's a great gap between that and wishing that the king and queen of England would grant me an audience some day."

SUCH conversations among Manolo, Esther, and Ignacio were very interesting, but they could do nothing to check the march of events, which soon debouched into a totally unexpected event of a nature almost to shake even the furniture in that house and to fill many hearts with fear for a few days. What had happened was that the German Führer and the Spanish Caudillo had held an interview at Hendaye, each accompanied by his respective minister of foreign affairs and surrounded by an ample retinue.

The joint communique, released the following day, said that the conversations "had taken place in the atmosphere of camaraderie and cordiality existing between both nations," and the newspaper correspondents, for their part, gave their readers to understand that it was merely an act of friendship, the handshake proper to those who had had and still had common interests. But people asked one another: "Would Hitler have traveled from Berlin in a special train to Hendaye for a mere handshake, and would Franco have crossed the Spanish frontier in another special train for that?"

The guesses were tailored to every taste. Everyone speculated on the most minute details released concerning the interview. "Why did Franco go to the meeting wearing a military uniform while Hitler had on the campaign uniform of the Nationalist Socialist Party?" The Governor said to Mateo: "And why did the Führer treat the Caudillo and his suite to a dinner in the dining car of his special train? And why didn't the Führer sit at Franco's right during the dinner? Is that according to protocol? And why did three companies of German soldiers, infantry to be exact, receive Franco on the platform of the station to pay him honor?"

Warning Voice was also struck by the fact that as soon as Franco returned to Spain, Hitler went off to hold a meeting with Marshal Pétain "in a little railroad station in occupied France." Was he trying to force Vichy France to join Spain in declaring war on England?

General Sánchez Bravo would have given anything except his sash of office or his telescope to learn the truth. "But how can I find out anything here in this corner of the world?" He complained to his wife, Doña Cecilia. "Of course, if they had arrived at some military agreement, Madrid would have told me something—I guess."

Apparently, however, if any agreement had been reached, it was not to be implemented immediately. A couple of weeks went by and nothing happened. Better still, news began to leak out to the effect that the Führer actually had asked Franco to enter the war and occupy Gibraltar; or at least to permit the passage of German troops so that they could occupy it. Those crumbs of news, confirmed from Figueras by Colonel Triguero, were augmented by the statement that Franco had not refused, but that he had laid down certain conditions that the Führer not only could not accept but that also had sent him off "with an expression of uncontrollable anger on his face." The Governor told Mateo that his colleague, the Civil Governor of San Sebastián, had confirmed this detail by telephone.

Mateo, José Luis Martínez de Soria, Núñez Maza, Salazar, and everyone who thought as they did were indignant. They believed the reports were true, and in that case that the negotiations of Serrano Súñer in Berlin had come to naught. "Franco commands. The Supreme Command gives its orders. We'll have to put up with it. They must know." Goodbye, Gibraltar—until further orders. Goodbye, world prestige. Goodbye, participation in the spoils of victory.

Manolo and Esther had a respite from their fears. They celebrated it with champagne that they invited Ignacio to share—and María del Mar, who said to them: "When are you going to learn that the Caudillo is the very embodiment of discretion? Haven't I told you that a thousand times? But you never pay any attention to me!"

General Sánchez Bravo also rejoiced. He knew his profession and believed that Spain was in no condition to intervene or to take the risks involved. Nebulosa, his aide, purposely got drunk, but only because he was disgusted. As he said to Captain Sánchez Bravo, he had decided to stay in the Army, and that being the case, a war would offer him the best chance for promotion.

While all that was going on, Italy entered Greek territory, only to come up immediately against desperate resistance. Her army was powerless to advance. Señor Grote remarked: "Another version of Guadalajara."

Hitler, on the other hand, had invaded Romania successfully in search of petroleum. The fugitive King Carol, "a collector of Greeks," according to Warning Voice, passed through Barcelona on his way to Portugal, and the German ambassador in Madrid inserted in the newspapers a want-ad for Spanish laborers who might like to go to work in his country. The wages were tempting. *Amanecer* published a similar offer, which aroused loud comment in the Gerona factories. The workers said to one another: "Shall we go, or what? You can see how it is here: a lot of talk, but we're still poor." The decision to accept would exact a high price—their families, their country, the Dehesa, the bell towers. And Christmas was coming. "We'll see. We'll have to think it over."

Paz, in the Diana Perfumery, remarked: "If they're looking for workers from the outside, it's because they've already accepted the fact that the war is going to be a long one."

FORTY-THREE

IN their references to the decisions finally taken by the Bishop, the Governor and Ignacio were correct. Furthermore, Dr. Gregorio Lascasas had balanced out the results of the pastoral visits he had paid throughout the diocese and the reports sent him by the parish priests, and had arrived at the conclusion that within a few months, owing to the relaxation that summer brought and the spirit of "every man for himself" awakened by the flood, the collective inclination to piety which had marked the period immediately following the war and had been quite manifest during the past Lent had suffered a collapse. Not in vain had Saint Paul said repeatedly how hard it is to persevere.

Accordingly, after a close analysis of conditions, the Bishop decided to follow in his field a line similar to the one that the Governor had pursued in his. Was civil discipline perchance more important than moral discipline?

But, alas, in the opinion of many he went too far. Certainly, it was a good thing for him to organize a "Youth Week" and to busy himself with public decency. But it was something else to insult sweethearts and fiancées by applying to them the word "companions"—the very word that the Reds had given their women—only because they permitted a man to put his arm around them or across their shoulders. And then to launch a tremendous diatribe against the songs favored by the girls in the Feminine Section:

Whoever falls in love, look out, look out.
Don't throw away health and small change,
Don't throw them away.

Or the other one that went:

On you I'll bestow
A thing that I alone know: ¡CAFÉ!

Naturally, the Bishop knew very well that those songs were sung by the soldiers at the front. "All the same," he mused, "what is the meaning of this '*café*,' and what about that allusion to small change?"

Mosén Iguacén, who constantly shared the spiritual and physical ups and downs of Dr. Gregorio Lascasas, was privy to the fact that numerous factors had played their part in the prelate's reactions. First, there was the pat on the back given him by none other than the under-secretary of the interior, who had issued an order from Madrid saying: "From this date forward, there must be just enough illumination in the motion-pictures so that the film can be seen without difficulty by the spectators; but the distribution of lights and spot-lights must be such as to prevent couples from committing acts contrary to Christian morality." Another pat on the back from Dr. Andújar. With the contagious sincerity that characterized all his actions, Dr. Andújar had organized the Congregation of Knights of the Pilar in Gerona, and they had decided to make their first public demonstration by a pilgrimage in a body to the Basilica of the Excelsa Patrona in Zaragoza, there to take a vow on the Holy Bible to defend their devout belief in the Assumption and Meditation of Mary before the dogma then being considered by the Vatican was adopted. "That a man of science like Dr. Andújar," the Bishop said, "has taken this step again demonstrates not only that minds will often bend before the faith, but also obliges me to see to it that his example spreads among the rest of the faithful."

On the other hand, the Bishop had suffered a disappointment, had received serious warnings about his health, and had lost an intimate friend—all at the same time. This tended to darken his inner religious world and did nothing to make him realize fully that perhaps the people would not march in time with what was happening to him.

The disappointment came to him through *Amanecer.* Suddenly, some local painters, one of whom was Cefe, the man who had tried to exhibit nudes in the Municipal Library, published advertisements for models. Everyone knew what a model signified in a painter's studio, and it did not escape the Bishop that it did not lie within his power to forbid it. Furthermore, the painters in question were the very ones whom Dr. Gregorio Lascasas had commissioned to paint the murals in the rebuilt churches, and that had meant a considerable fee for them. The disappointment therefore arose from what he considered a flagrant act of ingratitude or spiritual asepsis which denoted that it was all the same to them whether they used their brushes to paint the figure of the Eternal Father on the altar or to depict "sinful flesh" in a gallery.

The warning about his health came to him in the form of a tumor of the throat which at first seemed to be a malignancy. For several days the prelate had to live with the conviction that he was going to die; his resignation edified everyone around him. Luckily, Dr. Chaos eventually was able to bring him the good news that it was a false alarm and that he could be treated successfully by X-ray therapy.

Finally, the intimate friend whom he had lost was Cardinal Gomá, who died in Madrid. He was the Primate of Spain, and the strong defender of the use of the word "Crusade" in connection with the civil war. He and Dr. Lascasas had met often, and the Bishop venerated the Cardinal. Like churchmen all over Spain, the Bishop arranged for solemn funeral ceremonies and all kinds of honors to be dedicated to the soul of the man who was being called the "Fallen Athlete"; but Dr. Gregorio Lascasas wanted to do more than that in homage to his friend. He set about doing it, and it served to intensify his natural obstinacy. Therefore he arranged to have whole chapters of doctrine taken from the Cardinal's written work and read from the pulpit. He had no doubt that some of those dicta would provide food for any amount of discussion, revolving, for example, around the work in which the Cardinal had gone so far as to state that there were no martyrs outside the Catholic Church because the word "martyr" meant witness and only Catholics were admissible as witnesses of Christ. "Then what about the Protestant missionaries?" asked Señor Grote, who had dealt with Nordic people in the Canary Islands. Marcos, ever a fervent admirer of courage, asked: "What about the Communists? Aren't they martyrs to their faith?" Galindo, the bachelor member of the gathering in the Café Nacional, said: "What about the Anarchists whom I saw marching to the front with their chests bared?" Dr. Gregorio Lascasas, following Cardinal Gomá's doctrinal line, would have answered that the Communists and Anarchists were motivated by hate and that love was the indispensable condition for martyrdom. As for the militant non-Catholic religious, the best that could be said was that they were victims of superstition. Matías then spoke up, saying: "Well, as I understand it, there are many kinds of martyrs and no one has an exclusive claim to them. In my opinion, a man who jumps into the water to rescue another man and drowns is a martyr just the same, regardless of whether he's a Catholic, a Buddhist, or an atheist. And a man like Dr. Chaos, to mention the first name that comes to mind, is a martyr, too, burning out his life in the operating room, removing all kinds of tumors."

All in all, then, the Bishop's mood during the months of October and November failed to synchronize as much as might have been desired with the mood of the people. His only popular success had to do with a matter close to the heart: his negotiations to install and bless the big bell in the Cathedral which would replace the one that Cosme Vila had had melted down to be made into a machine gun.

Indeed, when that bell was rung for the first time, it sent a sudden silence all over the city and made the ancient quarter seem more august. Soon afterward, at the advice of Mosén Alberto, the Bishop was pleased to inform all his flock that the name "bell" came from the Italian region of Campania, where in the third century San Paulino had implanted its use throughout Christendom. To be sure there were plenty of music lovers who argued dryly over the sound of the bell. Some said it did not emit the note F, as it should have, but struck the C instead. The profane, however, understood nothing of such niceties and felt satisfied with their venerable acquisition.

Mosén Iguacén was fully aware of all that was going on, and suggested with all due respect that the Aragonese prelate might find it suitable to compensate in some more tangible way for the cool welcome given his inflexible standards. Dr. Gregorio Lascasas recalled the visit paid him by Father Forteza to beg him to intercede for the prisoners whom the War Crimes Tribunal had sentenced to death. Perhaps he was influenced by the fear of death which haunted his days while Dr. Chaos was treating his throat: finally, he decided to take steps in that direction at last by appealing for greater clemency whenever possible.

No one could ever be sure that the change which took place in the tribunal was traceable to this appeal by the Bishop. Perhaps the passage of time was in itself a palliative factor, perhaps inertia, perhaps the tribunal's own attitude. In any case, the sentences began to be more benign. So much so that many people tore their hair at the thought of some relative sentenced a year earlier. "If they'd tried him now, he'd have got off with six months..." "Now they would have simply acquitted him." The Bishop was so encouraged that he even asked for a speeding-up of the cases brought before the Court of Political Responsibility, which functioned with nerve-racking slowness and sentenced even the accused dead to partial or total confiscation of the property that was the concern of their heirs. The Bishop managed to prod them into moving a little faster, but for all the many acquittals and restorations of property—equally unimaginable a year earlier—he could not prevent the exile from the Peninsula to the Spanish possessions in Africa for a relatively long time of landowners large and small, or their debarment in perpetuity from public position, because they had held some post during the Red period.

In any event, the intervention by Dr. Gregorio Lascasas became known to the citizens. Not everyone applauded him, and Paz made a remark that was typical, "Oh, that! It's too late now!" But unquestionably, he reaped much good feeling from it, and on that account many people forgave him, by and large, for his thundering inexorability in the matter of "purity and modesty." That same inexorability prompted him to insert in "The Sunday Leaflet"—a pamphlet that Matías took good care to send to Julio García in New York along with several magazines—an ancient quatrain dedicated to women, which said:

A woman must take all the care she can
When she sets out to trap a man,
To know what charms she should conceal
Instead of what she should reveal.

FORTY-FOUR

OTHER things happened, too, during the month of November. First preparations were being made for two weddings that would take place during the early part of December. One, which was being pushed ahead, involved the union of Warning Voice and Carlota, Countess of Rubí; the other was the long awaited marriage of Mateo and Pilar. Before those events occurred, however, the manager of the broadcasting station conceived the idea of a program similar in popular appeal to the "soap operas" or adaptations of novels which had made a great impact on the city and region.

The manager planned to institute a program of records dedicated to individuals. Any devotee of the radio could request that on the indicated date and hour a record be broadcast in honor of a certain person. Everyone tuned in, not knowing whose name might come over the air at the most unexpected moment; it might be anyone's. "To my sweetheart, Teresa, with all my love, Juan." "To Pili, from you know who." "To our dear grandfather, Ramón, on his birthday. From the entire family gathering."

Comments on the program were enthusiastic, highly favorable. "This is wonderful. It's the sort of thing that should be done." For once, Professor Civil had to admit that "technical gadgets" could be put to poetic use. Needless to say, Eloy spent a peseta to dedicate a tango by Carlos Gardel to Carmen Elgazu because he knew she liked that music best. Pablito also spent his peseta to dedicate a recording of Schubert's *Ave María* to Gracia Andújar, but she was so busy that she did not listen to the radio or even know about Pablito's gesture.

MEANWHILE, Warning Voice wanted no dilly-dallying over his wedding. The letters he received from Carlota proved to him that she possessed a rare intellectual insight, and besides, her handwriting was that of "an expensive private school." Not to mention the quality of the paper she used, pleasing to the eye and the hand. Aside from that, with winter coming, the Mayor dreaded more than ever living in an empty house.

Accordingly, the Mayor made a couple of trips to Barcelona. Carlota accepted his proposal; the request for her hand was drawn up, and the Count and Countess of Rubí gave their blessing.

The wedding, which *Amanecer* called "the nuptial ceremony," was a special event, although out of posthumous respect to Laura, the banquet was omitted.

The Bishop himself officiated in the Cathedral and blessed the contracting parties. The theme of the customary sermon delivered by Dr. Gregorio Lascasas was a large family, a subject that Warning Voice, soon to turn fifty, considered somewhat optimistic. So did Carlota. Her family made a vivid impression on the people attending the ceremony and the onlookers who gathered outside the church. Anyone could see a mile away that the Count and Countess de Rubí belonged to the Catalan aristocracy. They had a distinction based on sobriety—few jewels, but very valuable. The dressmakers waiting at the exit and some of the employees felt a little disappointed. They had expected more pomp, more necklaces, bigger diamonds. The aldermen gave the Mayor the latest model radio-phonograph.

The honeymoon was an idyl. Carlota, a lady with the "caste spirit" who loved Catalonia with her whole soul, suggested an itinerary that Warning Voice accepted without a murmur. They would visit Montserrat, Poblet, and Santa Creus. The three monasteries aroused both sentimental and telluric reactions in the couple. In Poblet they found that the Cistercian Order had taken official charge of the long-abandoned monastery a hundred years after leaving it. The geology of Montserrat struck them both as a miracle of nature, and they endowed La Moreneta, the patron saint of Catalonia, with a votive lamp. In Santa Creus, Carlota, who was not strong physically but was capable of many surprises, owing to her natural vivacity, was so moved that she began to recite under her breath several verses by Antonio Machado, who, she said, was worthy to be a Catalan poet.

The second stage of the honeymoon itinerary was suggested by the bridegroom. He would have liked to go to Italy in remembrance of his flight from the Red Zone, to visit Rome and Florence and there convince himself that he really should have been born at the time of the Renaissance. But Italy's participation in the war deterred him. He decided then to go to Dacharinea, where he had entered Nationalist Spain in 1936, and from there to San Sebastián and Pamplona, where he had sported a red beret during the war.

Carlota fell in love with San Sebastián. They chanced to be there during a couple of days of rough seas, and Carlota was fascinated at the spectacle.

Warning Voice kept making jokes about the "nursing ladies" whom he had gone around with while he was there. Carlota showed that she was jealous and in love. Indeed, Warning Voice was able to enjoy the delights accruing to him from the awakening of a grand passion. Seemingly, the meager body of Carlota enclosed a great desire to be loved. She lacked experience, but that only added to her charm. "The Bishop was right, darling. We must have a lot of children." In his moments of exaltation, the moments when the indomitable Cantabrian Sea could be heard roaring outside their hotel room. Warning Voice agreed with her, but once everything was calm, he thought that it would be quite enough to have one child.

The grand climax came in Pamplona, for Don Anselmo Ichaso lived there. He had already sent his wedding gift of a silver service to Gerona.

"Don Anselmo!"

"My dear friend!"

Don Anselmo was still editing *El Pensamiento Navarro* and still had the same huge paunch. He had changed hardly at all; whereas his son Javier Ichaso, the one with the obsessed eyes too close together and only one leg, had changed. He had aged, although he seemed more talkative, gayer.

Nothing could have delighted Don Anselmo more than the marriage of Warning Voice to a countess, even though she was a Catalan. He laid all of Navarre at the feet of the newlyweds: Navarre and his miniature electric trains, which elicited shrieks of admiration from Carlota.

They talked at great length. Don Anselmo Ichaso still longed to see the Spanish monarchy restored at the earliest possible moment. "It's the natural outcome," he said. "It will happen some day." In referring to Alfonso XIII, who was living in Rome, he assured them that, according to reports, the King was soon to abdicate in favor of his son, Don Juan. "It's a fact," Don Anselmo explained, "that during the war, Don Juan entered Spain under the name of Juan López, donned a Requeté beret, and tried to get to the front. And I didn't know a thing about it. But as it happened, he was recognized in Aranda de Duero, and General Mola, who didn't want any political squabbles, ordered him detained and sent him back to the border."

"Do you honestly believe that the restoration of the monarchy can be presumed?" Carlota asked Don Anselmo.

"That depends on circumstances," he replied with his characteristic assurance, "on the progress of the present war and on whether we can win the support of certain generals."

Don Anselmo went on to tell Warning Voice that the construction business, which he was still engaged in—"You know, my dear friend, that my metier is building"—was booming. He had just founded a corporation, Duarte and Company, which had been entrusted with the plans for a large-scale urban development in Pamplona. But his principal objective was to take part in the open bidding on the contract for El Valle de los Caídos, the gigantic project initiated by the Caudillo. "You know what I'm talking about, don't you? Over there in the Guadarramas. That would give Duarte and Company a very big boost. And I personally would feel very proud to do my bit in a patriotic project of that size." Here Don Anselmo changed his tone. "Aside from that, the bones of my son, German, who died at the front, could rest there."

Javier Ichaso, Don Anselmo's only surviving son, rode with the couple in the car that took them to Javier for a visit to the castle.

"When I get married," he said to them, "I promise to return your visit; I'll come and see you in Gerona."

"We'll be counting on that," Carlota replied. "We can tour the Roman ruins there."

Everything was perfect. Warning Voice and Carlota returned to Gerona, where they found a sparkling apartment. Montse the maid had worked like a dog. During the absence of the "señores" a final gift that touched Warning Voice had arrived: a carved and polished cane, the work of many hours by the old men in the Refuge, who were still the Mayor's favorite protégés.

On entering the bedroom, Carlota threw her arms around her husband and put her head on his shoulder.

"I'm happy," she said, "completely happy."

Warning Voice stroked her hair. "You don't know how glad I am to hear you say that."

On the following day, in honor of his bride, but on the pretense of commemorating the second anniversary of the break-up of the Catalan front by the "Nationalist" forces, he offered the Gerundians, with the Governor's permission, the performance planned at the time of the fair but canceled because of the flood: *sardanas* on the Rambla.

The people turned out en masse. Enthusiasm overflowed. At least ten circles formed, reaching as far as the Montaña Bar, the football players' hangout. The musicians of the Cobla Gerona, led by Maestro Quintana, played to their hearts' content, as though they had been waiting centuries for that moment. And at the end of each *sardana* they started all over again. Commissioner Diéguez thought it a bit too much, a tacit provocation; but knowing that the Cobla Gerona had the Governor's permission to play, he could not interfere.

"You see what good guys we are," he stammered as he sat inside the Café Nacional.

In the barracks, the General heard about what was going on on the Rambla and remarked: "That little Barcelona countess is going to cause complications for us."

THE preparations for the wedding of Mateo and Pilar were somewhat more laborious. To collect all the necessary documents, from Mateo's birth certificate on down the list, Mateo had to keep calling for at least three weeks on Tower of Babel, of the Agencia Gerunda. Mateo was top brass, and he had to be accommodated.

The Campistol sisters had to be seen and requested to make Pilar's wedding dress to her entire satisfaction. She proved very demanding; she brought the dressmakers to the edge of distraction. "Whatever is the matter with you, Pilar? It fits you marvelously!" Pilar looked into the mirror, turning slowly. "It dips a little here. Don't you realize that? ... And that veil! How do you think I could possibly show myself looking like that?"

Pilar wished she could count on Marta's help during those days. But after what had happened between her and Ignacio, that was out of the question, to Pilar's great disappointment. "Marta knows my tastes. Why can't I have her with me now? I can't even invite her to the wedding. Of course not." Gracia Andújar and Asunción did their best to act as substitutes for Marta.

Pilar stopped working—Alfonso Estrada in Safe-Conducts and Señor Grote in the Food Delegation both missed her. In addition to everything else, she had to turn the flat on the Plaza de la Estación into a home. She needed dishes, rugs, the thousand items indispensable to creating a family setting. The selection of the bedroom furniture, the only pieces lacking, caused a great stir in the family. Pilar had taken it into her head that she wanted an antique bed, a heavy bed, as high as possible. Mateo shrugged his shoulders. "Why do you want it so high? Tell me that." "That's the way I want it, Mateo. Is there anything wrong with that?" "Not as long as the Restoration Service doesn't take it away from you—or the Diocesan Museum."

The gifts poured in. They received many more than Warning Voice had. The outstanding one was from the heads of the Falange, who had taken up a collection; it was a gold tray from Toledo engraved with the yoke and arrows. They were very pleased, too, with a Bible bound in parchment which Agustín Lago sent them. Mateo said jokingly: "That yoke on the tray seems to mean something. And no doubt the Bible means we're going to learn the Book of Job by heart."

One ticklish job—the premarital briefing of Pilar. Carmen Elgazu balked at that. Matías mentioned the subject to her, but she refused, looking cross.

"What do you want, then?" Matías said. "Do you want Mosén Alberto to be the one to advise the girl?" Ignacio sensed that the subject did violence to his mother. Why should she feel like that after having borne three children? One fine day, the very day on which Warning Voice was married, he went into Pilar's room and broached the question without more ado.

Pilar suddenly grew nervous. Her relationship with Mateo had been more passionate than Ignacio could have imagined, and on more than one occasion. In any case, it was obvious that she would have to confront "the unknown" on her wedding night. That being so, Ignacio's gesture was justified. Nevertheless, Pilar was confident that Mateo would behave in the expected manner, and in the meantime, explanations were quite unnecessary.

"I can see why you're reacting like that, Pilar. But you've got to listen to me; I'm not going to preach you a sermon. The only thing I want to tell you is that this matter is more important than you think. And it seems that sometimes things don't turn out to be so easy for the woman. Of course, I'm talking only about the beginning. I guess you know what I mean, after all. Luckily, Mateo is a healthy kid. But let me tell you again, sometimes it's pretty hard to adapt yourself— Please now, someone's got to say this to you, right?" Ignacio raised his voice. "Actually, it's absurd that we still keep these things under wraps. By now you must have read half a dozen books that deal with this question. But we're surrounded by taboos all our lives. All right, I'll leave you alone. Come on, calm down, and please understand I came to see you with the best of intentions."

Pilar was struggling with herself. She understood her brother perfectly, but remembered that she had not forgiven him for what he had done to Marta and as a result was always on the defensive with him. In any event, before Ignacio had crossed the threshold of her room she managed to control herself and say to him in all sincerity: "All right, Ignacio, I understand. Thank you very much."

Why was it that when Pilar saw the back of a person she loved, she suddenly felt moved? On this occasion the same thing happened. The words she had spoken had risen spontaneously at the moment when she had seen Ignacio from the back.

The eighth of December came. A number of the balconies throughout the city were decorated in honor of the Immaculate Conception. The hanging on the Alvears' balcony, like all the others, said: "*Ave María Purísima.*" Marta awoke thinking of Mateo and Pilar and gave vent to a flood of tears. Fortunately, she would be very busy all day with the festivals organized by the Feminine Section, for the feast day had been declared "Mother's Day."

The wedding was held in the parish of the Virgin of Carmen. Of course Mosén Alberto performed the ceremony—at last he was playing a role that was agreeable to him. Pilar entered the church on her father's arm—Matías holding the proper pair of gloves in his left hand—and at that moment the Wedding March began to peal and to stir all the congregation. Carmen Elgazu was wearing a big hat, which became her very well in the opinion of Joséfa and Mirentxu, her two sisters, who had come from Bilbao for the occasion. As Carmen Elgazu looked from beneath the wide brim of her hat and saw Pilar dressed in white, she caught back a sob. "Lord, what a beautiful daughter I have!" The guests, who filled the church, were a heterogeneous lot, ranging from the Governor and Dr. Chaos to the head of the Telegraph Office and the beautiful Adela, not to mention Claudia, the Alvears' cleaning woman.

Paz, Aunt Conchi, and Manuel had been given a special invitation by Matías. Pilar hoped that her cousin would come down with the grippe that day and have to stay home. But she did not. Consequently, the "sensational vocalist," who could not remember ever having entered a church before, was present, although she made Aunt Conchi and Manuel sit in the last bench reserved for the family, unlike Eloy, who was kneeling on the first bench and really would have liked to be serving at the altar.

During the Mass, the national anthem was played at the moment of the Elevation. Then a choir of angels began to sing, for in spite of the day's festival, Marta had arranged to send the Feminine Section's choral group to the church. Pilar recognized the voices of her friends and felt tears come to her eyes. Mosén Alberto's eyes were damp, too, as he uttered the solemn words: "I pronounce you man and wife."

The wedding banquet was held in the La Barca restaurant, beneath which the now gentle Tel River ran. There was a barrage of toasts, and Matías and Don Emilio Santos passed out Havana cigars to all the men and kept saying to each other: "Grandfathers inside a year." Adela, who could hardly keep her eyes off Ignacio, had one too many glasses of champagne, which loosened her tongue. She told her neighbors at the table, among them Dr. Chaos, the story of her honeymoon with Marcos, which turned out to be a failure because poor Marcos caught cold on the train and spent the whole two weeks coughing and taking his temperature.

Finally, Mateo and Pilar slipped away from the party. A taxi took them to the cemetery, where Pilar laid her wedding bouquet on César's tomb. Then their honeymoon trip began on the train.

Theirs was a trip half of love, half of patriotism. Pilar would have settled for love, but... They spent the night in Barcelona, where "the unknown" proved painful to Pilar and reminded her of Ignacio's warnings. The next day they went on to Madrid.

They found that it had been snowing heavily in Madrid. Snow had fallen all over Castile, and the metamorphosis of the earth, also wearing a wedding gown, was an apt reminder to them. Luckily, the central heating came on after sunset and they warmed themselves by it as if under a good blanket.

"Mateo, so many years we've waited for this moment."

"That's true, Pilar. But it's here now. And forever."

"Will you always love me very much? Did you hear Mosén Alberto say 'for better or for worse'?"

"Of course. I'll always love you, darling."

"I like to hear you say it."

"Well, then I'll say it again—forever, and for better or for worse."

The better at the moment was the outpouring of themselves, the fusion, which would soon be perfect, of two in one, into a single being. The "worse" was the cold. Mateo wanted to visit the ruins of the Alcázar in Toledo. Pilar had some trouble conjuring up any feeling about it because the thermometer was below the freezing mark and the snow had transformed the venerable stones into whimsical, outlandish forms.

"Let's get out of here, Mateo. Please. I can't take any more."

"Look. There's where a Communist mine exploded."

"Yes, I see it. But let's go, please."

"There's where Moscardó printed his paper."

"How did he keep himself warm? Could they light fires?"

Back in Madrid, another outpouring of love.

"I love you, Mateo."

"And I love you."

"I'll take as much care of your father as if he were my own."

"I hope so. He deserves everything we can do for him."

Mateo showed Pilar through the University City area, the scene of so many battles, where the International Brigades had dug in and fought desperately, and where Durruti had died. "Hundreds of men died here. It was a terrible thing. But now it's going to be rebuilt. Donations are coming in from all over Spain. A model University City where maybe our children will study some day..."

"Would you want to send them so far away?"

"Well, I'm only talking."

They went to the Alto del León. But the snow prevented them from reaching the top. Mateo was biting his nails. He had dreamed of that visit. Of how much he had enjoyed and suffered there, in the huts.

"You should have seen me. I let my beard grow."

"How dreadful! Beards prickle. I like you better this way."

"How do you know that unless you've tried it?"

Once more in Madrid, and duty visits to Núñez Maza in Propaganda and Salazar in Trade Unions; to María Victoria in the Feminine Section.

"Congratulations, turtledoves!"

"I hope it'll last forever."

"Which would you rather have, a girl or a boy?"

Mateo talked with his comrades on the subjects that interested them. About Azaña's death, which had occurred on November 2 at Montauban in France. Salazar assured him that Azaña had made his confession on his deathbed after asking for a priest to be in attendance on him. "The confession lasted five hours. So you see. The moment of truth!"

Núñez Maza was satisfied because he had just set up the Council of the Spanish Nation, with a view to extending it to South America. "However," he said, "the exiles exert a tremendous influence there. Many intellectuals have risen to the top in important positions, and not only in Mexico; in Peru, too, and Uruguay and even Argentina. The Communists have formed several cells in Havana, disguised under the names of cultural organizations, and the same is true in Santo Domingo. Also in the United States; they're getting their nose under the tent everywhere. The universities have opened their doors to them. That Roosevelt! I hope he gets struck by lightning. He's a Mason, and he'll give us plenty to do. The Anarchists have dropped anchor in Venezuela, and especially in Colombia. In short, the Council of the Spanish Nation has a hard bone to gnaw on. Particularly because when Spaniards go abroad, they work. And they have behind them the experience of our civil war."

Pilar interrupted. "When are you going to get married, Núñez Maza? It's about time you did, isn't it?"

"I don't know, kid. I've got so much to do."

"All the more reason you should. Your wife could help you."

"Tchah! You never know. What if she's crazy about clothes?"

Mateo put his arm around Pilar. "Look for one like mine. Feminine on all four sides, and she's studying Karl Marx, too."

Pilar made a face. "Karl Marx? He's worse than Roosevelt."

María Victoria behaved somewhat unpleasantly. After the proper congratulations, she began to speak ill of the Catalans. "I've already told José Luis not to even talk to me about Gerona. I'd die. If he wants to marry me, we'll live here, in Madrid."

Pilar stood up to her. "Well, I like Gerona. It's a good place to live. We've just hung a new bell in the Cathedral."

Mateo added: "And they're playing *sardanas* again. You can be sure José Luis was dancing on the Rambla."

"Go on! What do you mean?" María Victoria said shortly. "So it's come to that."

Mateo wished they could visit many other places. But of course there was one that was sacred to him: the Escorial. He saved it for the last. They went there as the colophon to their trip. Núñez Maza drove them in his car, very slowly. They got out in front of José Antonio's tomb with much more reverence than Heinrich Himmler, the Supreme Chief of the German Secret Police, had shown on his visit several weeks earlier. Mateo shed a tear or two at the foot of the cold slab covering José Antonio. Pilar did, too. "Help us, José Antonio. Help us to be loyal to your mandate."

As they were leaving the Escorial, Mateo asked Núñez Maza whether it would be possible to see the work that had been started on the Valle de los Caídos, which was within a few miles of them, near the village of Guadarrama.

"I don't think there'd be any problem," Núñez Maza said, "although there won't be anything to see. They're only working on the access road to the spot where the basilica will be built. The roads are rocky and the drills are going full blast."

"I'd like to see it, anyhow."

The car, equipped with chains, headed for the spot. The guards saluted when they saw the little flag, and after inspecting Núñez Maza's identification, let them pass. Soon they heard an explosion. Then another.

Suddenly, they could see men working there, wearing the most bizarre garments to protect themselves from the cold. How many were there? Probably more than a thousand. The temperature must have fallen very far below freezing. Some wooden shelters sent up smoke, doubtless from stoves.

"Half these men are hired by a construction company; the others are prisoners who are working off their sentences."

Mateo asked: "Wouldn't it be easy for them to escape?"

"Escape? Oh, sure! But where would they escape to?"

Mateo looked at the snow all around them. "Oh, of course. They wouldn't get very far."

They got out of the car. Civil Guards were patrolling in pairs among the workers with pick and shovel. That was hard work. Very hard work.

"How tall is the cross going to be?"

"I don't know exactly. About a hundred and twenty meters, I think. There'll be places to stay, too, and some barracks."

The view was desolate, like a frozen desert. The stones seemed inimical to man, even though the snow had caressed them. A great deal of dynamite would be needed.

Pilar felt a thrill of fear. The place looked bleak and forbidding to her. She would have preferred something green and lush, like the Valley of San Daniel.

"Don't be silly. Its greatness lies precisely in this, in the fact that it's a lunar landscape. Spain isn't Versailles. We'd be copying from them! Spain is in part what you see here."

Pilar nodded. "Of course."

Mateo approached the prisoners and stared at their faces. They all had a frozen drop hanging from their noses. He recalled the Battle of Teruel and Teo.

Núñez Maza asked him if he was looking for someone, and Mateo said: "Yes, I am… For a certain Reyes, from Gerona. He ought to be here. He was in Alcalá de Henares, but I heard that he asked to be transferred, perhaps to shorten his term."

"Do you want to talk to him?"

"No, no. I just want to see him."

Núñez Maza turned to a foreman, who consulted a list.

"Alfonso Reyes? Yes, he's working over there. I'll go with you."

They walked about six hundred feet, until Mateo and Pilar recognized the former cashier of the Arús Bank within a stone's throw of where they were standing. He had a pick in his hand, but did not look at all tired. A cigarette was dangling from his lips; it seemed to have gone out.

Pilar felt far more touched than she would have believed. She remembered how that man had helped Ignacio in the Red Zone when the other employees of the bank were picking on him. And she thought of his son Félix, whom Professor Civil was taking care of in the Social Auxiliary, the boy who was spending all his time drawing now.

Everyone was silent. Then they heard the ring of the picks, as in the quarries which lay above the cemetery, the Costa brothers' quarries. Some trucks had arrived with food. The Civil Guards stood quietly in their capes, occasionally staring at the smoke that rose from the improvised wooden shelters.

"Thank you very much, foreman." They went back to the car and started on their way to Madrid.

Mateo and Pilar had no desire to talk, but Núñez Maza had.

"It's going to be a magnificent monument. The new Escorial. The Caudillo will direct the work in person."

He went on to tell them that Spain had re-established diplomatic relations with Chile and that Argentina had sent a shipload of wheat. "That's a great help and we must be thankful for it." By that time they were far from the valley, but Pilar fancied that she could still intermittently hear the explosions coming from there.

That visit to the Valle de los Caídos had made a deep impression on the girl.

"I'm afraid," she said to Mateo, "that they might transfer César's body here."

"The things you think about! César is all right where he is."

"That's what I think."

They stayed two more days in Madrid and went to a theater and a night club. Pilar had a wonderful time; the violet lights excited her so much that she hung around Mateo's neck while she was dancing with him.

"If your mother could see you now, she'd have a fit."

"Why? I'm a married woman, am I not?"

"Boy! You surely are!"

The orchestra was called the Columbia Jazz Band. And the vocalist, also sensational, also with long blond hair, was Dorita.

FINALLY, they sent a telegram to Gerona: "Arriving tomorrow."

And so they did. They reached Gerona in mid-afternoon, tired—all the women on the train were carrying baskets and bundles—and although the train was late, they found all the family waiting for them at the station.

Seeing Pilar, Carmen Elgazu thought that her daughter had changed markedly in those twelve days. She seemed much older, much more a woman.

Embraces and laughter greeted them.

"Only a postcard, eh? Were you that busy?"

Mateo said jokingly: "It's all Pilar's fault. She wouldn't let go of me for a minute."

The newlyweds headed for home, the flat on the Plaza de la Estación. Everything was in order. A great peace reigned over it. The bed was high, very high: Pilar had won her point.

Don Emilio Santos said: "Well, so long. I'm going out for a walk."

"At this hour? Why?"

"I've got some work to do at the tobacco shop. People want to smoke, you know. When it's cold, people like to smoke."

As soon as they were alone, Pilar turned to Mateo's office. A stuffed bird on a pedestal! And the walls lined with books.

"It looks like a church, doesn't it?"

Mateo came up to Pilar from behind her and put his arms around her. "A church, that's it. And you're going to be the altar girl."

PILAR'S marriage left a great vacancy in the flat on the Rambla. Pilar had her little faults, like everyone else, but the house had been full of her. Particularly when she felt gay and in a laughing mood. Everyone remembered her sallies when she was very small, like the one she came forth with one day while they were having lunch: "Papa, is it true that the Russians pursue the nuns and touch them?"

Her absence was hard to adjust to. Carmen Elgazu kept thinking: "If only we had a telephone!" Sometimes when Matías came home, he would walk around the house as if he missed something and did not know what to do. One of those times he sat down at the dining-room table and wrote a long letter to Julio García, addressed to the Hotel Lincoln in New York. He gave the details of the wedding. When the letter reached him, Julio García said to Doña Amparo Campo: "We'll have to send them something. A little copy of the Statue of Liberty, for example..."

In a sense, Ignacio gained, for at last he had a room of his own. Without consulting anyone, Eloy moved into Pilar's room, where he thumbtacked to the wall photographs of the great aces of football, although just then he felt a little downcast, for in spite of the fact that the president of the club was named Bravo, the Gerona team was losing all the games played off the home field, so that its standing was halfway down the list.

Yes, at last, Ignacio would have his independent corner in the house. He kept César's bed and gave the extra one to little Manuel, who had been sleeping on a pallet until then.

Ignacio bought an easy chair in a second-hand furniture store and changed the small bookcase for a much larger one, although he did not have enough books to fill it. He called on Jaime, the part-time bookseller, whose small business was prospering. Ignacio wanted to buy out the store, but he compromised on the complete works of Freud, a cheap edition in five volumes. What a time he had finding them!

"If you'll sell them to me on the installment plan, I'll take them," he said to Jaime.

"What's the matter with you? Take them and pay for them whenever you wish."

"Okay. Look, here's fifty pesetas down. The first installment."

"You've made a good buy. Freud is very interesting."

Ignacio went home glowing with pleasure. As he was showing the books to his father, he lifted his index finger, and Matías answered with their usual slogan: "Potax Soup."

"What are those books?" Carmen Elgazu asked.

"They talk about the libido, Mother. I don't think you'd be interested."

"The libido? What on earth is that?"

Carmen Elgazu supposed the books had something to do with Ignacio's work in the law office.

"That's what I like to see, son, that you're studying. Honestly, isn't your boss going to raise your salary? Pilar's wedding was ruinous. Did I tell you what my hat cost me?"

Ignacio smiled. "Don't worry, Mama. I think by the first of the year I'll be earning two hundred pesetas more."

"Well, that'll be a blessing. Now, without Pilar, I'll need Claudia to help me at least four hours a day."

Ignacio arranged Freud's works, all five volumes, in the recently acquired bookcase that Matías had already given a coat of walnut stain which made it look like new. Ignacio pulled out one of the volumes at random and leafed through it. He found these statements: "When amorous relations with a certain object are broken off, it is not unusual to see hate come to replace them." "Hate in relation with the object is older than love." As Ignacio thought of the two sentences, he could not help seeing in his mind the picture of Adela during the banquet on Pilar's wedding day, making herself as odious to him as to Dr. Chaos. He read also: "The crowd reacts only to very strong stimuli. In order to gain an influence over it, logical argumentation is useless. On the contrary, it will be necessary to present to them bright-colored images and to repeat the same things again and again." He fancied he was listening to the Governor—and Mateo.

In the end, however, what he wanted to study especially in Freud was the subject he had mentioned to his mother: the influence of the libido and everything referring to the collective soul and the power of suggestion. Ignacio had lately held several conversations with Dr. Chaos, whose personality was becoming more and more interesting to him, and he wanted to equip himself to discuss these questions with the doctor.

Another "innovation" that Ignacio brought to the room he had begun to call "mine" was several reproductions of Picasso's paintings which he had cut out of a magazine and tacked on the wall. Distorted figures seen simultaneously from several different angles. They were not a joy to the eye, and he did not feel that he was prepared to understand their compositions fully, for they were the complete antithesis of the concept once expressed to him by Mosén Francisco. Yet Picasso interested him. No doubt he was a rebel and a doubter of everything. Who could ask for more than that?

Carmen Elgazu, already horrified by Eloy's football players, was speechless at the sight of those "daubs" put up by Ignacio, especially as they seemed to turn, to pursue relentlessly everywhere the image of St. Ignatius that her son kept on his night table.

"Just what is the meaning of this, if I may ask?"

"Nothing, Mama. That's modern painting. You wouldn't understand it."

"Modern? Why do you call it modern?"

"I don't know. The world moves on."

Carmen Elgazu put on her glasses, which, depending on circumstances, gave her the air of a bluestocking, and planted herself in front of one of the Picasso reproductions: the face of a boy with only one eye.

"Do you mean to tell me that we're going to look like that some day?"

Ignacio laughed. "To a certain extent, we do already, sometimes."

"Go on, son! I trust my grandchildren will come out otherwise, as God meant them to."

"Oh, no doubt they will. Especially if they look like Pilar—and you."

Ignacio gave his mother a kiss, and she left him alone. He sat down at his desk and lighted a cigarette. Why did he miss Pilar so much, so intensely? He got out paper and a pen.

Dearest Ana María:

I'm so sorry you couldn't be at Pilar's wedding, even incognito. It was really beautiful. I still am not used to the idea that mv sister is married. I hope politics won't spoil her honeymoon and her future life. I say that because, according to Freud, hate is older than love.

I intend to tell my parents "our news" soon. Perhaps on Christmas day. Of course they already know. But not officially.

I feel very good here at my desk, thinking about you. Send me a large photograph of yourself soon, because I haven't a magnifying glass to look through at the one Ezequiel took of you. I want a photograph that shows both your eyes. Not just one, as in those very intellectualized paintings by Picasso.

Things are happening constantly. Yesterday was an exhausting day. Not only in the office, but at home, too. First I asked to have a record dedicated to my father. They played it at dinnertime and a great hullabaloo broke out at the table. Then, in the evening, there came a knock at the door and it turned out that a pal of mine in the war had come to see me. I don't know whether I ever told you about him. We used to call him Cacerola; he was our cook. A romantic boy, even more romantic than I am. He had a job as an inspector for the Office of Price Control and asked to be sent to Gerona. Actually, I can't imagine him denouncing

> anyone. Later I went out with him to a coffee shop and we talked about old times in the Ski outfit.
>
> I love you, Ana María… Pilar's wedding aroused the logical reaction in me (if I'm capable of reacting logically, meaning that I don't belong to the multitude, but to myself). It made me dream about the day when you'll be the bride and I'll be in Mateo's shoes.
>
> When will that be? I don't know. I'll have to work hard. I have a great deal to learn. Each day that passes convinces me more than ever that Manolo is right; nothing can compare with the pleasure of making mental associations. Extracting magical conclusions from minimal data. Do you remember what Eugenio d'Ors said: that the anecdote must be raised to an important status?
>
> Have you said anything to your parents yet? Especially to your father, "Don Rosendo Sarró"? I need to see you, Ana María. I need to see you very soon. By Christmas at the latest. Either you must come here, or I'll run down to Barcelona. We've had enough of letters, haven't we? Not that writing doesn't have its charms… Right now I'm having such a fine time that I'm even burning my fingers on my cigarette… But receiving the other's (the other being you) envelope has much greater charm. Does that seem strange?

And so on.

The repercussions from Pilar's wedding. And from the nuptials of Warning Voice. Ignacio was envious. He would have liked to be married, too, immediately. Although the question was, what would his parents do in the flat when he married? Only Eloy would be left. A law of life, to be sure.

What about Marta? *Amanecer* kept mentioning her and her activities.

She had received a succession of "juveniles" into the Feminine Section with an initiation ceremony that was very moving, and she was organizing a cortège of lantern-carriers for the cavalcade on Twelfth Night. Would that those Three Wise Men would bring Marta the remedy needed to heal her solitude!

FORTY-FIVE

PREPARATIONS for Christmas were much like those of the preceding year, perhaps because He who was about to be born was That One who is always equal to himself. More theatrical presentations of the Little Shepherds were put on, and the city, more predisposed than ever to believe in chance, won more in the lottery. On the other hand, champagne, nougat, and all the delicacies in general were rationed, and only moneyed people managed to obtain all they wanted.

Some new things had been added, however. Dámaso, the owner of the Diana Perfumery, wanted to break a lance on behalf of his deluxe barbershop on the mezzanine floor facing the Rambla. Accordingly, he bought an electric hair dryer and ordered his clerks to wear blue smocks. His next move was to hire a manicurist, Silvia by name, who went to work on the very day that Mateo and Pilar came back from their honeymoon.

Raimundo, the barber in the La Barca quarter, his hole-and-corner shop plastered with bullfighting posters and advertisements for Anís del Mono, burst out laughing when he heard about "Dámaso's idea," and the other barbers in the city joined him. "An electric hair dryer! A blue smock for the clerks! How nice! And a manicurist, too! Manicures in Gerona! Don't give me that! Of course, there are one or two 'wrong 'uns' like that doctor with the dog. But not that many!"

Dámaso was right again, however. Ignacio himself went to the Dámaso Barbershop, which had a mirror facing the customers and covering the entire wall, and all kinds of magazines for reading matter. He had taken a great liking to one of the barbers, a man from Madrid named Herreros, who knew more jokes than Señor Grote, although he was not famous for them. But the main attraction was Silvia. True, in the beginning no one had the courage to use her services. Then one fine day Captain Sánchez Bravo screwed up his courage. "Why not?" he said. And Silvia, sitting on a stool, very close to his legs, trimmed his fingernails beautifully. "Please, sir, will you let me have your other hand?" Lord! When had such a thing ever been seen or heard of in Gerona? Soon the city's male *crème de la crème* were following the leader, and that did not exclude Dr. Andújar. Silvia was so quiet, she smiled so nearly imperceptibly, she had such long eyelashes. The first time Ignacio went to have his fingernails done he felt like an important man, and after he went home he stared at his father's nails and exclaimed: "What a sight! You ought to go, too."

In the Café Nacional, Galindo said: "Gerona is making progress. Last year at this time, it was the lawyer, Manolo Fontana's, Christmas cards. This year it's the manicurist in the Dámaso Perfumery. So, we're getting civilized."

Another novelty that surprised the people came from Solita, daughter of the administrator of price controls, the girl whom that official had described as a "top sergeant" when he had talked to General Sánchez Bravo.

Solita was a nurse in the Chaos Clinic. She was a venturesome girl with a desire to learn. After attending a lecture by the doctor which he entitled, "The Importance of Anesthesia," she introduced herself to him the next day and offered to work in his clinic. She soon demonstrated her knowledge, especially of surgical instruments, and Dr. Chaos, who desired discipline in the operating room above everything, accepted her.

And it happened that they got along very well together from the beginning. Although Solita did not know the Madrilenian Herreros or Señor Grote, she had heard a great deal about Dr. Chaos. But she said it did not matter in the least to her, because Dr. Chaos was a competent surgeon and a well-educated man; his private life was no business of hers. She told her father, the price administrator: "Besides, it's all the better for me. He'll leave me alone."

Of course Solita was the source of many surprises to Dr. Chaos. The first was that she showed him she had heard of a Scottish doctor, a bacteriologist named Fleming, who had announced that he had discovered a substance created by a mold which was much more effective than the sulfanilamides for destroying disease bacteria without attacking the cells of the sick person.

"How did you know that, Solita?"

"I get the American medical journals regularly."

"Can you read English?"

"Perfectly well."

"Tell me, what else do you know about that substance?"

"Well, not much more. That Dr. Fleming calls it penicillin. That up to now he has obtained it only in raw form. That he began to test it during the First World War. I only hope that the discovery will prove valuable, and that some day we can have a lot of bottles of it in the clinic. I'd assume that it would be marvelous during the post-operative period."

Dr. Chaos smiled. "I like to hear you talk like that, Solita. I've never before had anyone in the clinic with whom I could talk about those matters. Yes, what you've just said is true. Dr. Fleming has discovered the drug you mention. And there was one detail that struck me particularly. I read that before the doctor found this mold, he made the tests that you referred to with very different media: nasal mucus, saliva, white of egg. And that tears were what produced the best results. Isn't that curious? Ah, yes. For years Dr. Fleming induced tears by giving out dozens of lemons to make people cry." Dr. Chaos went on in a different tone: "Seemingly, he was as convinced as I am that tears can cure many ailments."

Solita stared at Dr. Chaos. They had met in the central corridor of the clinic. "Why do you say that, Doctor?"

Dr. Chaos threw up his long arms; his hands were gloved in preparation for entering the operating room. "For no reason, Solita," he said. "Pay no attention to me."

Solita refused to do that. She reflected on the remarks for the duration of the operation, a routine appendectomy. Later she continued to ponder it. And at suppertime she said to her father, Don Oscar Pinel: "I feel sorry for Dr. Chaos."

"Why, my dear?"

"Because he has a lot of class, but he isn't happy."

"How could he be? But that's not our fault, is it?"

"No, of course not."

CAME December 25, Christmas. A dinner like that of the preceding year in the Alvears' flat, except that Mateo and Don Emilio Santos were at the table, which had to be extended as far as it would go. Fortunately, there was no difficulty whatever over Paz, thanks to Mateo's very tactful manner toward her, and because Mosén Alberto stayed at the Diocesan Museum. His maid was ill, and he believed it was only decent not to leave her alone on such an important day. Manuel again recited his poem to the Infant Jesus, and Eloy again got up to kick an imaginary football high into the air. Aunt Conchi got a bit intoxicated again and belched.

In the Civil Governor's house the holiday was something special. The Governor had dreamed of having his whole family meet in Gerona for that day: the "four Dávila brothers" of whom Mateo had spoken. But as it turned out, the two brothers who lived in Santander looking after the farms and the cattle business had a great many children and could not go away. Only the first-born brother visited them, a cavalry colonel in Madrid who brought gifts for Pablito and Cristina. At the table, the Colonel talked with such precision and authority about a succession of matters relating to Spain and the war that when the time came to propose a toast, Cristina nudged her brother and said to him in a low voice: "Listen, which is the bigger boss, Uncle or Papa?" One of the affirmations made by Colonel Dávila, upon whom María del Mar was showering attentions, was that Franco had arrived at the railroad station an hour late for his interview with Hitler in Hendaye. He had made the Führer wait one long hour. The Colonel went on at great length about the huge Nativity set up in the Parque del Retiro in Madrid. "It has more than four hundred figures: Herod's palace, Rachel's sepulcher, the Sealed Fountain, the Gates of Glory. It's a marvel. I doubt that anything like it has ever been seen in Catalonia."

Yet it was a strange Christmas in Gerona and all over the world. The war, the battles in the air, on the sea, and on land weighed on people's minds. More prayers were said for peace than for anything else. The Pope held a reception for the College of Cardinals as he did every year. They gathered to felicitate him. One of his messages to them was that the condition indispensable for the "new European order" was "peace with justice." He announced that the Church would undertake to deliver news of the wounded, the prisoners, the refugees over the Vatican radio so that their families would know that it was reliable. This plan sincerely moved Mosén Falcó, the religious adviser of the Falange. "As always, the Church is doing its job," he said to the Martínez de Sorias, who had invited him to their house. "Still, that could have its drawbacks from the military point of view," José Luis commented.

Official sources were to announce later that "activities had been minimal" on that day, doubtless in homage to the birth of Jesus. Goebbels, however, said over the Berlin radio: "The entire world admires Hitler. We Germans are privileged to love him." It became known also that in the little town of Bethlehem, in the Holy Land, Christmas Eve had been celebrated in total darkness for the first time in two thousand years. The British authorities had forbidden even the traditional shepherds' bonfire in front of the Temple. The processions and the pilgrims' parade had been put on in the dark, watched over by patrolling British airplanes.

Agustín Lago had wanted to share that day with his friend Carlos Godo from Barcelona, but instead he had dinner with the owners of the modest pension in which he lived. Over the coffee and liqueurs he told them a number of witty anecdotes about the war, with a flippancy that astonished everyone who knew that a shell had torn off his left arm. But that was not all. The Inspector of

Elementary Education could not take his eyes off a newly acquired maid with a full bosom and a wicked way of walking. "How about it? That's a cute little girl, isn't she, Inspector?" the proprietor ventured to say. Agustín blushed, but managed to answer: "I wouldn't mind at all teaching her to read!" The militant of the Opus Dei bit his lip at the sound of his own remark, but thought: "Nothing new has happened. Things are the way they are."

Asunción celebrated the feast day in a more churchly spirit. In the middle of the afternoon she went to the Episcopal Palace, where the Bishop was expecting her. The object of her visit was to deliver to the prelate the so-called "Boxes of the Little Grain of Wheat" which the pupils in the Grupo Escolar had been filling ever since school had opened. The idea had come from the directress of the group and was to be applied practically during that quarter of the school year. Every Saturday the pupils put a grain of wheat into the appropriate box for each good deed they had done during the week. To no one's surprise, the boxes were filled to the top. The ultimate destination of the wheat contained in them was to become Sacred Hosts, which were made by cloistered nuns. Those Hosts were to be reserved for the priests who officiated at Mass. Dr. Gregorio Lascasas said to the girl as he received this surprising and virginal offering: "I believe nothing could please the Infant Jesus more than these boxes you've just given me. I often ask myself whether you're not truly one of the Lord's elect."

A strange Christmas in Gerona and all over the world. And what happened in the lottery? Everywhere it was a resounding success, but this year it was as capricious as ever; the big prize went to Madrid; second prize to a number of poor neighbors in the Gracia quarter of Barcelona; third to some women cigar-makers in Seville. A Civil Guard won a million pesetas. railroad section hand, half a million. Matías said: "That's what I like to see. I like it when the lottery favors humble families." Eloy remarked: "We're a humble family. Why haven't we won anything?"

To Gerona, only chickenfeed. Among the lucky were the members of the Gerona Jazz Band, thanks to the electrician Fermín, who had bought one tenth of a ticket in Barcelona. Paz would collect a few pesetas, which she would divide into four parts. One, for the Red Relief, to which she had been appointed cashier recently at Jaime's suggestion; another for a new dress for Aunt Conchi and a shampoo; another to buy a woolen muffler for Manuel because the Diocesan Museum was always freezing; and the last, to buy three green ties, all alike, for Pachín. "Doesn't Commissioner Diéguez always wear a white carnation in his buttonhole?" Paz said to the football star. "Well, now you'll always wear something distinctive, too: a green tie." Pachín smiled and as usual blew a mouthful of smoke into the eyes of the girl's cat-mascot, Goal.

ONE fact was beyond question: the gayest of the Christmas dinners took place in the homes of the Costa brothers. The brothers had been set free on December 24. The expected pardon had gone through. They left the prison in the company of many other prisoners, also beneficiaries of the decree.

The liberation of the Costa brothers constituted a kind of catastrophe for the other inmates of the Seminary. The prisoners who had to remain there felt as though they had been orphaned; that was the measure of the strength and encouragement lent by the two former deputies of the Republican Left. But what could they do?

The Costas emerged at eleven o'clock on Christmas Eve. They were like shadows passing the faithful heading for the Cathedral to hear Midnight Mass. They devoted the whole of Christmas day to their wives, who, during the preceding weeks, had been doing everything necessary to get their houses—the same properties on the Calle de Ciudadanos—ready for the event.

Christmas dinner was celebrated in the upper flat; the Costas felt ready to fly.

One word dominated all the toasts proposed: freedom. Free at last! A conditioned freedom, to be sure—they would not be permitted to leave Gerona—but freedom all the same. Wasn't that a beautiful thing? To sleep in a bed with a soft mattress! To take a bath in warm water! To smell a woman! "The hardest thing about being in jail was that it always smelled of men. Do you know what I mean, girls?"

The Costas also stayed at home the next day, the Feast of Saint Stephen. On the one hand, they were longing to go out into the street for a breath of air; but on the other hand, it was so cozy indoors, walking on carpets, using an ashtray, turning on a lamp, looking into mirrors! They had spent nine months without being able to see themselves full length. Now they could study their bodies at will in a pier glass. Each of them thought he had aged a great deal, and that was true.

"Yes, there are no two ways about it. We've both got a lot of gray hairs."

"The odd thing is that we're fatter."

"It would be a good thing to have a doctor go over you from head to foot."

"Perhaps."

They went out on the twenty-seventh. Everything was in readiness for New Year's and Twelfth Night. Dazzling store windows. And severe cold. A big letter box on the Rambla into which the children would drop their letters to the Three Kings from the Orient.

The whole city recognized them immediately. The reactions were varied, which surprised them, for the Costas had been dreaming of unanimous demonstrations of affection. That was not the case. Once they were out of prison, many people greeted them with "Congratulations," spoken while passing without stopping to shake hands with them. Worse yet, there were many attitudes of reproach, even of scorn. The Red workers considered them traitors, owing to their activities in France on behalf of the "Nationalists," and the dyed-in-the-wool "Nationalists" would not look them in the face because they considered that by any lights the pardon was unmerited.

Their reception was a lesson to the Costas. They attributed the general indifference "to the fact that people are afraid." Their wives admitted: "That's possible. In any case—when they hear about your plans!"

Nevertheless, it was obvious that they must make their moves with caution. Any exhibitionistic acts would prove untimely. They did not even dare to go to the La Barca Restaurant to eat frogs' legs. But in spite of everything, there were a couple of visits they could not escape. The first was to the tomb of their sister Laura. They hired a taxi to take them to the cemetery. The stone said: "Laura Costa, who died for God and Spain." They crossed themselves. The second duty call was on Notary Noguer, to thank him for all he had done for them at the time of their trial. "You know where we are. You can count on us." They had no sooner left than Notary Noguer said to his wife: "Did you notice? For a moment there it looked as though they had to get a guarantee from me, that they were as wary of me as if I were guilty of something." Before visiting Warning Voice they considered it best to think it all over, for, among other reasons, they felt reproachful toward their brother-in-law for having let such a short time go by before marrying again after Laura's death.

On the thirtieth, they felt less uneasy as they went out. They took a walk around the city, more or less at random. How many changes there were! A great number of small things to which their wives and the Gerundians in general had grown accustomed struck their eyes. What quantities of signs, of posters, of slogans! Hardly a hand's-breadth of wall was clear. Some of the slogans astonished them. "The final outcome of the Youth Front is Empire." "Each child who dies is a citizen lost to his country." "People of Gerona! God is watching you." And those portraits of Franco and José Antonio against a black background, done on the sly.

They were surprised, too, at the human stream going into and out of the churches. Suddenly, they would recognize a certain person with his missal under his arm and would stare at each other, saying: "That fellow too?"

They paused in front of the bookshops. Aside from children's books, appropriate to the season, there was a great predominance of prayer books, catechisms, lives of the saints, of Thomas à Kempis. Only one book on history: *General Sanjurjo, His Life and Works*, by The Daring Knight. Where were Baroja and those pamphlets by Gorki on "The Little Miracles" of Lourdes?

They felt deeply moved in the Dehesa. "This is always the same. This is eternal." They recalled the day when the volunteers had left there for the Aragón front in heavily loaded trucks. "Do you remember Porvenir with his speaking trumpet? He was whistling." "Do you remember Santi, with the placard that said: 'We're the Second Coming'?" Their wives cautioned them. "You'd better not talk about that. You could get yourselves into a lot of hot water."

Everything looked dilapidated to them: the aftermath of the war. They carried vividly in memory the picture of a flourishing France, the France before the German invasion: Marseilles, the Côte d'Azur. Now, in Gerona, not only had the Costa foundry collapsed during the flood, but also there were empty lots; buildings started but not finished because the work on them had stopped; the remains of air raid shelters; a kind of monotony, a single expression on all the faces. "What could be the reason for that?"

The Vista Alegre Stadium. Their beloved football field. That pleased them. The green turf, rectangular and perfect, and that little underground passage for the players. "That Pachín. Is he as good as they say he is?" The Costa brothers suddenly felt sad in the stadium. It did not matter to them that they could not leave Gerona and that they knew they were being watched constantly. But not to be able to be on the board of the Gerona Football Club…

Well, of course, in spite of their plans and their checkbooks, they would have to let some time go by before they could adapt themselves to a changed situation. They decided that the idea of a medical check-up was sound. They went to the Chaos Clinic, where the doctor examined them solicitously: blood analysis, urine analysis, X rays, listening to their hearts.

"A little anemic. Who would have thought it? All right, if you take vitamins and keep to a reasonable diet, everything will be fine."

Their wives took them to the tailor, too, a tailor who had come there recently from a village, but who had learned his trade in Lyon.

"What can I show you?"

"The gentlemen would like several suits."

"Several? One moment, please. Sit down, please."

On the first of January they ventured to go into the Café Nacional for a glass of cognac. There they received the first spontaneous show of loyalty. Ramón, the waiter, went to meet them as soon as he saw them and said in an undertone: "Long live the Republic!"

That encouraged them. The next day they went to the Dámaso Barbershop and were astonished at the installation. In their respective chairs, they discovered Silvia's presence, and the two brothers exchanged winks. "Please do my fingernails." Each of them gave her a five-duro tip when she had finished. Silvia was so overcome that for a moment, contrary to custom, she permitted her legs to separate a little.

On the fifth, they watched the Cavalcade of the Three Magi. The spectacle fascinated them. They thought how sad it was that they never had had any children. They would have liked to see them parading with their little lanterns. "Of course, those traditions are charming," they remarked. "They are one reason why the war was lost. Cosme Vila and his lot did not respect such customs."

Cosme Vila and his lot—they were obsessed by thoughts of them. What had become of the exiles? Of the men with whom they had made common cause during the Republic and at the outbreak of the civil war? Now, since the Germans were in France…

The manager of Constructora Gerundense, Inc., gave them full information of the whereabouts of each—except Antonio Casal, who had remained in Paris—adding a piece of news that made them feel desolate: in October, three months before, Companys, the former president of the Generalidad de Cataluña had been turned over to the Spanish authorities by the Germans. "They tried him in Barcelona and shot him immediately, in Montjuich."

"How could that be possible? Could the Vichy Government possibly have delivered him up?"

"Yes, that's how it was. But that's not all. Companys asked for a priest and made his confession before he died, like Azaña."

"A priest? But Companys was a spiritualist!"

"That's just it; he believed in another world."

The Costas shook their heads. "Who'd have believed it? Who'd have believed it?"

After that they began to be interested in the "conquered" who were at large in Gerona, and the manager also gave them detailed reports on their fate. Of course, the intention to provide jobs for all the prisoners who had been freed on the day they were had entered their plans. They had promised, and they would keep their promise.

They felt particularly upset over the fate that had befallen Alfonso Reyes, the former cashier of the Arús Bank, who had always been a dedicated, honorable, and loyal man of the Republican Left. "So, he's actually working off his sentence in weather that's below freezing, is he?"

They felt guilty. The feeling that they were to blame came over them. "He's out there, and we're having manicures." They had been rendered completely powerless to help Reyes, but they turned their attention to his son, Félix. They sent for him, and when the boy responded, seeming somewhat intimidated, they asked: "What would you like to do?"

"To draw."

Félix made an impression on them. He was very thin, but a fire was smoldering inside him. After a brief conversation they agreed to pay for his studies and to help him and his mother with a monthly stipend.

"And whenever you want to go to the School of Fine Arts, you know..."

"Thank you! Thank you very much!"

Félix felt convinced that the Costa brothers were not two, but three men: Caspar, Melchior, and Balthazar.

THE people interested in the activities of the Constructora Gerundense, Inc., could find no explanation for the fact that two weeks after leaving prison, the Costa brothers still had not set foot in the offices of the corporation, on the Calle Platería. The supposition was that they had not had time to settle into the office marked with a plaque reading "Management," but that they would call a general meeting. Instead, the Costa brothers were still taking romantic strolls around the city and viewing everything with a coolness that got on the nerves. Especially Colonel Triguero's nerves, as he had received a visit from Gaspar Ley with an offer to put them in touch with the Barcelona corporation of Sarró and Company. He was on edge. "What on earth are they waiting for? They've been pardoned. They can't hold public office. But who's to stop them from carrying on their business affairs?"

The Costas tried to soothe their collaborators. "Just be patient. It will all get done." They knew that the Governor had said: "They'd better watch their step. I think more of someone in the FAI than of those opportunists who always come out on top." They knew also that the regional administrator of price controls had the power to send violators to disciplinary battalions, even— "Don't be impatient with us, please. Just let us do things our way. In any case, we're not wasting our time. The important thing right now is to observe the whole panorama."

In line with this plan, the Costas were devoting most of their time to informing themselves about something that they judged an essential preliminary to deciding what would finally become the focus of their future action: the progress of the war. Whatever news had reached them in prison had been so one-sided that they had come there believing that Mr. Churchill was a louse and Hitler an elephant. During their two weeks of freedom, however, they realized from reading between the lines of *La Prensa*, and especially from listening to the nightly broadcast of the BBC of London, that the conflict was not that simple. Their astonishment was great, but there it was. "Do you realize that it's not so clear? Actually, it's still all up in the air."

Before saying that, they had formed their judgment on the basis of what had happened in the preceding few weeks. While the Italians were suffering serious reverses on the Greek-Albanian front, the United States, pressured by the re-election of President Roosevelt, was consistently increasing American aid to the British cause and voting enormous sums for rearming. In the Libyan-Egyptian desert, Mussolini was coming up against unexpected enemy resistance. The commander-in-chief of his forces, General Graziani, had had to fall back before the joint action of the British troops and their reinforcements, this time consisting of several companies of New Zealanders, several Australian companies, units of the Camel Corps, and an Indian division. That was an indication that England was beginning to bring about a coalescence of the resources of her Empire. Meanwhile General De Gaulle, temporarily in London, after Pétain had repudiated him, was claiming more loudly every day that he was the absolute leader of Free France, and was trying to attract to himself the citizens of the French overseas possessions.

The Costas realized that they must not overrate what was happening, for "the Italians can't be counted on," and Hitler was still ahead and perhaps preparing to strike a decisive blow at any moment. Nevertheless, for the time being, the ball was in the air, and never mind who was a louse, who an elephant. The more widely the conflict spread and the more complicated it became, the better the chances for England and the better the prospects for the Constructora Gerundense, Inc.

Another matter was absorbing the attention of the Costas. This was obtaining the legal counsel they needed to get them an official clearance. They really wanted to place their business in the hands of Manolo Fontana, whose performance in the War Crimes Tribunal had seemed to them beyond praise; but they wrote Manolo off precisely because of that, because of the "professional integrity" being displayed in private practice by the former judge advocate's lieutenant. On the other hand, they considered that the Agencia Gerona's manner of proceeding would suit their purpose, not only because its advertisement in *Amanecer* was still assuring the world that "we will take care of everything for you," but also because its legal counsel, Mijares, was a shark who had demonstrated ample experience and the will to prosper. That was the unanimous opinion. "If the lawyer Mijares can bring himself to give up the post of advisor to the CNS," the Costas said to their manager, "and if he will handle our business exclusively, through the good offices of the Agencia Gerunda, we shall make him an offer, a special one."

The manager smiled. The trolley was getting back on the track. Colonel Triguero also smiled, although he was still asking himself day after day: "Why don't they call me? When shall I be able to shake hands with them?" He had a talk with the manager.

"Please," the Colonel said to him, "tell them for me that I'm of age. That the Governor and the General have been sending reports and more reports to Madrid for at least four months with the intention of papering me fast to the wall, but they haven't done it yet. That's because I have a fairy godmother watching over me in Madrid. And, God willing, she'll keep on doing it."

The manager nodded and said: "Nevertheless, it would be a good thing, Colonel, if you'd talk to Captain Sánchez Bravo. Do everything you can to convince him. We need him. He promised to make up his mind when the Costa brothers came out of jail. So now they're out, but he hasn't said a word up to now."

FORTY-SIX

THE newborn year 1941 had come in prodigal with events of every description. The people were waiting on tenterhooks for whatever might happen at any moment.

In the interim, the news of those days which Jaime underlined was as follows:

"The Wagner festivals are about to start in Barcelona, under the auspices of the National Company of Frankfurt. At the same time the German book exhibit will open to the public with an abundant display of National-Socialist literature."

"In Valencia the girls in the Feminine Section have been given a number of roosters for breeding in order that the Sisterhood of City and Country may undertake to improve poultry raising in the region."

"The daughter of the Caudillo, Carmencita Franco, visited an exposition of toys, where she was given a little doll and a toy cat dressed as a musketeer."

"The Moorish Guard of the Chief of State celebrated the Moslem New Year in the Pardo. The wife of His Excellency, Doña Carmen Polo, lent her presence to the ceremony and partook of the dinner."

"In the Comic Theater of Barcelona, a revue opened with a fanfare of guitars; its title is *The Stukas.*"

"Merchant ships have unloaded frozen meat from the Argentine in several Spanish ports. The meat will be rationed out to the people immediately."

"In England, the members of the British Fascist Party have been placed under mass arrest, with Sir Oswald Mosley, their leader, at the head of the list."

"A plan is under way to turn the bedroom of the proto-martyr Calvo Sotelo into a sanctuary."

"A plan is under way to give images of the Virgin of the Pilar to all the offices of the official banks."

And so on.

The inscrutable year 1941—what was going to happen? Every man knew that his life was not a lake but a sea. That he might be served frozen meat one moment and be arrested like Sir Oswald Mosley the next. That sleeping appetites were awakening and others vanishing forever. No wonder, then, that Solita, Dr. Chaos's nurse, had begun to realize that she felt such admiration for this man that she was becoming alarmed. And Pablito, more than ever enamored of Gracia Andújar, was going to the Municipal Library every day after leaving the Instituto to read the stories of Paul and Virginia, and Romeo and Juliet. The good Cacerola, Ignacio's friend, had been working as an inspector for the Office of Price Control three weeks now and had not yet sworn out a single complaint; nor had he felt impelled to impose a single sanction.

Aunt Conchi turned out to be the best proof that at any second the appetites may vanish forever. Aunt Conchi died. Ah, Jaime might indeed have underlined that news item too. For Aunt Conchi died in a stupid train accident near the village of Sils, on the Gerona-Barcelona line; it was one of the many accidents that happened daily and which had forced the military authorities to say publicly that they would investigate the causes of them, in case they might be traceable to sabotage. Aunt Conchi had left at dawn in obedience to the request of the owner of the Crocodile. She went in search of olive oil to be sold on the gray market. And it happened that several cars jumped the track on a curve, turned over, and caught fire. Aunt Conchi was taken to the hospital in an ambulance, but died on the way.

The news came like the slash of a kid-skinner's knife. Mourning the accident, the family went to the hospital in a body. But Aunt Conchi already had been sent to the morgue, and some of her relatives lacked the courage to go there to see her.

Paz and little Manuel were crying in each other's arms, still unable to accept at all that such a thing had really happened. Everything in Aunt Conchi's room looked the same as always, poor and dirty, as though waiting for the woman's return; the bedclothes scrambled and a couple of hairpins lying on the pillow, turned sidewise on the edge of the mattress.

Carmen Elgazu covered her mouth with her hands at the thought that her sister-in-law had not had time to make her confession. Matías was deeply moved. He was the one who had got along best with Aunt Conchi because she was the wife of his brother. He had known how to handle her and to make her smile occasionally. Only on the past Twelfth Night he had given her a modest wrist watch without telling anyone about it.

The crucial problem arose of where she was to be buried. The common grave was out of the question, but no niches were available in the cemetery.

The Municipal Government kept enlarging the structures, but deaths occurred more frequently in winter and all the available room was taken, as during the big fair.

Only one place was possible: César's niche. The idea came—like a gunshot, it seemed. A shiver ran through the flat on the Rambla. César! Wouldn't there be something sacrilegious about that intimacy, that intermingling?

But who would dare to say such a thing aloud? Matías stated the matter with so much authority that not even Pilar ventured to voice an objection.

The funeral was held. The women stayed at home, sitting in a semicircle, scarcely speaking. The men accompanied the hearse. Little Manuel led the cortege in a suit that had been dyed black in a matter of hours. Matías, Ignacio, and Eloy bought themselves black ties and wore mourning bands on their sleeves. Mateo, Pachín, the owner of the Diana Perfumery, and the proprietor of the Crocodile, some friends of Matías, and all the members of the Gerona Jazz Band, comrades of Paz, walked in the mourning procession.

The uncovering of the niche in which César's remains rested was especially dramatic. Once more the masons went into action. Finally, the stone yielded to them. Manuel stared at his cousin's coffin with bulging eyes. Matías and Ignacio were biting their lips until they almost bled. Aunt Conchi's coffin was placed on top of César's and the niche was closed again. It was cold in the cemetery. All the surrounding wreaths had withered, and the cypresses towered as ever, dimly silhouetted against the gray sky. Mosén Alberto said the prayer: "Our Father, Who art in heaven…" They all responded in unison, in quiet voices. The masons had withdrawn, pushing their cart before them.

The ceremony was over. How quickly eternal things were disposed of! There, joined forever, lay César and Aunt Conchi. Life and death were striking against each other and rebounding fantastically.

The men went back to the city in two cars. Those who were not members of the family went their separate ways at the Calle de la Barca. The others met in the damp flat that belonged to Paz. Pachín went with them, for the first time. There were not enough chairs, so the football player stood beside the girl and put his hand on her shoulder as if to protect her. But suddenly he felt shy, said goodbye to everyone, and left.

No one knew what to say. The expression on the face of Paz, also dressed in black, was indefinable. A mixture of furious anger and sorrow. From time to time she said: "This is absurd. Life is absurd." Carmen Elgazu did not dare to suggest that they say the Rosary aloud.

Pilar felt sorry for her cousin, dressed in black and without any makeup. She saw her as an orphan, particularly after the moment when Pachín left. She reacted so nobly to family feeling that she offered to make coffee for Paz. Paz stared at Pilar in surprise and said: "Yes, thank you, I'd like a cup."

Matías and Ignacio wanted to console Manuel, but Eloy undertook to do that. He sat quietly beside his friend, his hands on his knees. In any case, Manuel looked hypnotized. Doubtless he was reflecting deeply. His suit, hastily dyed, had shrunk, and under other circumstances would have made him look laughable.

Suddenly, something like a groan was heard, coming from the room that had been Aunt Conchi's. There was the cat, Goal, huddled in a lump. Ignacio went to it and handed it to Paz, who took the little animal from him, set it down in her lap, and began to caress it.

Silence fell again. Everyone was looking at Goal as if he were the real protagonist of the tragedy.

FORTY-SEVEN

IGNACIO'S and Ana María's fears proved well grounded; the girl's father opposed his daughter's relations with Ignacio. Don Rosendo Sarró, the founder of Sarró and Company, a former war prisoner and a man "of huge appetites" who "constantly made trips to Madrid," aspired to see his daughter married to a moneyed man. From Barcelona, if possible, and with a social position equal to his own.

For a long time now, Don Rosendo Sarró had sensed that his daughter was keeping "her" own secret; but he had not paid as much attention to the subject as he should have. Finally, as a result of Ignacio's letter, the girl confessed to her mother her love affair with "a boy living in Gerona, a fledgling lawyer, the son of an official in the Telegraph Office." "Please help me, Mama! This isn't a whim at all. I won't change my mind."

Within two days, the father heard the news from his wife. Don Rosendo Sarró reacted according to a principle of his which warned him not to make any decision without first having all the pertinent data in hand. Nothing could have been easier for him, in this case, because his friend and colleague, Gaspar Ley, was in Gerona. He asked Ley to give him a complete report on Ignacio.

The report was impartial and unequivocal. "I know Ignacio personally. A healthy, sound, intelligent boy. A little unstable and confused, but brilliant and well endowed for his profession. He has good connections. Ambitious. He can be assured of a comfortable future, but, of course, always within the boundaries of the middle class."

That was enough for Don Rosendo Sarró. His final word was, "No." A "no" as resounding as the voice of Mosén Obiols, the teacher in the Seminary.

He called in Ana María. At first he tried to dissuade her by soft words, but in the face of his daughter's persistence, Don Rosendo Sarró, a man not accustomed to being crossed, decided to resort to stern measures.

"Very well, then. I forbid you to go on with this affair for a single day. You write to that boy and tell him it's all over, and that's the end of the matter. Give him any excuse you want to. Tell him you're going to Japan to live—something like that..."

Ana María answered him with almost majestic serenity. "That wouldn't settle it at all, Father. If I were to go to Japan, Ignacio would keep on loving me just the same. And I'd keep on loving him."

Don Rosendo almost had a stroke. "You know now what I've decided. It's up to you to come up with a solution. Don't let me find out that you've paid no attention to me! Right now, you'll go with me on a trip. I have to be in Málaga until after Twelfth Night. Your mother and you are going with me."

Ana María, who knew her father like the palm of her hand, understood from the first moment that he would do all he could to prevent Ignacio from coming to Barcelona to see her. A trip to Málaga. That was where Ignacio had been born. The girl smiled inwardly and even lighted a cigarette, something which her father had also forbidden.

"Father, I know what you're trying to do, and I warn you that it won't work. I'll wait as long as I have to, but nothing will make me change my mind. I'll go with you. All right. But that won't solve a thing. As soon as I come back, I'll call Ignacio and start seeing him again."

Don Rosendo Sarró moved toward her as if he felt ready to strike her, but his daughter's attitude was so dignified that he did not dare to. Ana María seized the moment to add, without moving from her seat: "I'm sorry to upset you, Papa. I realize that Ignacio isn't the man you'd choose for me; but my mind is made up. Why hasn't it occurred to you that the man you might choose for me would be someone I couldn't stand for five minutes?" Then softening her tone, Ana María added: "Do please try to understand one thing: I'm not looking for money, only for happiness."

This was a knotty problem. The founder of Sarró and Company felt disconcerted. He was so used to believing that money and power were the keys to life that he could not comprehend how anyone, least of all his own daughter, could cling to another standard. "I'm not looking for money, only for happiness." Where did she get such nonsense? With money, he had succeeded in recovering his health completely after it had been somewhat impaired by his stay in the Modelo Prison. He had submerged his wife's personality under money, and had formed innumerable friendships. Sometimes it seemed to him that he had managed even to add a little to his stature lately—with money. Yes, in the Palace Hotel in Madrid, the center of his operations, he felt tall and growing taller. The crowd of hotel servants who came to meet him looked to him like pygmies who had emerged from the carpets. How could it ever enter the head of his daughter, a girl with a noble bearing, grace, and naturalness, to renounce all this and be set aflame by "that Ignacio," who smoked black tobacco, it seemed, went around with his shoes dirty, and now dedicated himself to defending penny-ante cases. Oh, no! If need be, he would use every expedient.

Don Rosendo Sarró pretended he had not heard the last words spoken by his daughter.

"Get going," he ordered. "You can pack your bags."

Dearest Ignacio:
As I told you on the telephone, we left Barcelona the day before yesterday. And now we're here. We won't be able to see each other during the holidays as we had planned, but we'll get together when I'm home again, which will be about the 10th of January, I think.

I've spent the whole day thinking about you. Write to me in care of General Delivery as soon as you get this and give me the exact address of the house where you were born. I'm planning to go and see the street and the balconies. I'll spend hours sitting in the doorway...

Don't worry, Ignacio. I won't back down. I love you. I love you with my whole soul. No one and nothing will be able to stand up against our love. My father is living on the moon, obsessed with money. He can talk of nothing but that; and Mama listens to him...and buys jewelry and ivory elephants. It seems that's what she's going to do here, collect ivory elephants. Can you imagine that?

But what I want is love. My own father will serve me as an example. He never has a moment's peace; he's always hanging on the state of the stock market, news from the office, telegrams. At home—and here in the hotel it's the same—he paces the floor like a caged bear. It's strange to watch him. He walks with his arms behind his back, measuring off the tiles as though he were still in the Modelo Prison.

I love you, Ignacio, but you must realize that we'll have a fight on our hands.

So pay attention to what I'm going to tell you; don't trust Gaspar Ley too much. He's changed a great deal. He's not the man he was during the war. Papa has thrown him a chance to make a lot of money, because seemingly Papa's going to be the owner of the Arús Bank. Last night he bored us to death with that. My father, the owner of the Arús Bank! Isn't that funny? A few years ago, you'd have been my father's office boy...

On the other hand, you can count on Gaspar's wife, Charo. Charo is on our side. She's a woman and she understands me. Besides, she's had experience of her own... She used to be happy with Gaspar! But now they're living apart, as you know. Gaspar tells her he "can't find an apartment" in Gerona. Catch on?

The letter you wrote me before I left was beautiful. I loved your telling me you'd almost burned your fingers on a cigarette while you were writing to me... Write to me again. Every day! I need to know whether you do or don't love me more than ever. I love you. And I'll keep on loving you more every minute. This is no story; it's the absolute truth.

I'm enclosing the photograph you asked me for. Do you like it? I'm very ugly...but I'm me. But am I really ugly?

You asked me if I were studying English. Yes, and I'm getting along very well. On our wedding day, I'll know how to say "yes" perfectly.

Of course I'd have loved to be at Pilar's wedding. And I hope, like you, that they'll be happy...in spite of politics. That problem won't arise between you and me, will it?

I'm delighted that you decided to dedicate a record to your father... Surely you've told him about us. I suppose that what happened in my house won't happen in yours...

But I say again, don't worry. It will all work itself out.

When I go back home, ask for time off and come to Barcelona. The Jai-Alai Café is waiting for us!

Meanwhile, I'm sending you a good, big kiss. One of those kisses that oblige a girl to go to confession...

Your Rattlebrain

Ignacio answered Ana María immediately in care of General Delivery. Nevertheless, he felt irritated. By the nails of Christ! Why did the same thing always have to happen to him? Why couldn't he manage to carry on a normal courtship?

His first impulse was to go to the Arús Bank and give Gaspar Ley a tongue lashing. Ley was gambling with two decks of cards, it seemed, for whenever they met he was more than friendly. But Ignacio gave up the idea. Where would that get him? Gaspar Ley was in the pay of the important Señor Sarró.

Nevertheless, he did not fail to indulge in the time-honored reflections. In spite of Ana María's promises, might not difficulties come up later? Would Ana María be reconciled to living modestly in Gerona? And what if the caste spirit that he had discussed with Esther should come out in her—from her "unconscious," as Freud would say? He recalled Pilar's words: "A cute little thing from Barcelona, in good society. Oh, sure, the kid has aspirations!"

Suddenly, Ignacio felt horrified at the possibility of playing the role of "poor relation" without a sailboat, a car, or an ivory elephant.

While he was waiting for Ana María to return, he spent some days that he would not have wished on anyone. As if that were not enough, he had seen Marta several times with Lieutenant Montero, the man of the witty remarks. Why had he felt jealous? Why? The last time, he had spied on them because it seemed to him that Montero was holding the girl's arm. It turned out that he was wrong. But why should it matter to him? Jealousy was a purely idiotic emotion indeed, or so he had always said.

As usual when he was passing through a crisis, Ignacio thought of Adela. Adela, passion and flesh, whispering words in his ear. He felt an imperious need to see her, to rid himself of his mood immediately. But Adela already had told him she could not have him in her house because she was afraid. She had discovered that Marcos suspected something. "Not about you, exactly. But he suspects something. We'll have to find another place where we can meet. It mustn't be here at home."

Ignacio had been aghast. "Some other place? Where?"

Adela had replied, "Excuse me. We can't talk about that right now. I have to hang up."

He had heard a click and had stood with the receiver in his hand, looking foolish.

Now that it was all over, he went back over the scene as if it had happened today. He had left the telephone booth more confused than ever. He had sat down in the Café Nacional and ordered a glass of cognac from Ramón, the waiter. He had run his eyes over the mirrors in the depths of which Julio García's ironical hat always had appeared. And Doña Amparo Campo's bracelets.

A mortal tedium seeped through him. As if the world had caved in beneath him. As if everything were going to turn out badly for him.

Then the door opened and his friend Cacerola came into the café. Good Cacerola, who well deserved a smile and a pat on the back.

"What's the matter with you, boy? You've got a very long face."

"You think so?"

Cacerola laughed. Whenever he met someone he was fond of, he would laugh at anything.

"I know what's the matter with you. You've been cooped up too long. You don't remember the mountains any more. I bet you never go on an excursion. See? You do miss the pure air we used to breathe up there."

Ignacio nodded his agreement. "That's possible."

"Possible? Certain. Listen…why don't we go out together some Sunday? To La Molina, to ski, just like in the days at Panticosa."

Skiing, the mountains, what had happened to all that? He had given Moncho the same advice every time he wrote.

"Maybe you're right, Cacerola. We must go some day. Yes, I'll call you some day."

"Don't forget now, Ignacio. Call me at the Price Control Office. You'll surely find me there during the first hour in the morning."

OOF, what a time he had been having! But at last Ana María came back. On January 12, two days later than she had expected to. Ignacio talked to Manolo, then took the train for Barcelona. The two lovers met as usual, in the Frontón Chiqui Café, and for a while they were paralyzed with happiness. "Don't you think it's a good thing to have to fight?" "Yes, you enjoy things more if you do." A billiard table had been set up in the back of the café; the balls glided across the green felt cover, as Ana María's eyes had glided across the face of the house in which Ignacio had been born.

Then they went to see Charo, who received them with great affection. But she began by warning them that the struggle they would have to make would be hard indeed.

"I don't think you realize, Ana María, what your father is like. As long as you're under age he can do whatever he likes with you. Send you abroad, to some school—who knows what!" Charo paused a moment. "Don Rosendo Sarró—who would have thought it? Do you know what they're saying about him in financial circles in Barcelona? That he's a power."

Ignacio burst out laughing. At about that time he had chanced to read in his renovated bedroom library the chapter that Freud had dedicated to "those who collapse upon winning." According to Freud, many men fall ill, lose their balance when they have achieved their deepest, longest-cherished desire. "As if then such people could not stand their triumph." They fall into a state of anxiety, not infrequently related to the guilt feelings hidden in the Ego. Ignacio had no doubt whatever that Ana María's father, and perhaps Gaspar Ley, Charo's husband, too, would end in that situation one fine day.

But Charo had struck the key to the situation: "As long as you're a minor…" Well, and after she came of age? Then Ana María would be free to make her own decision. And that time was only a year away.

"It's nothing, Charo. Let's not let it frighten us. Love conquers all."

"Yes, I know. Of course, it does."

Ana María interrupted her. "Besides, you'll help us, won't you? You have some influence with my father."

"I?" Now it was Charo's turn to laugh. "Is there anyone with any influence over Don Rosendo Sarró?" Their friend spoke to Ignacio: "It comes down to this, Ignacio. You're the one who has to win your prize the hard way. You've got to get ahead in that office where you're working! Try to make a good showing in court. After all, an able lawyer is a far cry from a hod carrier."

Ignacio nodded.

"That's what I say."

They talked on lightly, although Ignacio had to force himself, for he knew full well that if the Constructora Gerundense, Inc., kept on as it was going, he might very well make his debut in court as an opponent of Sarró and Company's interests.

Ana María sensed that something was worrying him, and she pinched his cheek.

"What are you thinking about? Tell me."

Ignacio blinked and managed to hide his thoughts. "I was thinking about what Charo said. Being a lawyer really isn't the same thing as being a hod carrier."

Ana María stared at him.

"Don't tell me you're scared."

The young man reacted to that. "Scared? Me? Talk to my boss! He thinks that before ten years are up I'll be appointed Minister of Justice by acclamation."

"You don't say! Your modesty overwhelms me."

Ignacio laughed and threw out his chest like an athlete.

"Don't you want me to toot my own horn once in a while? Would you rather have a perfect man for a husband?"

"Good Heavens, perfect! You don't need anyone to say it!"

Charo saw how closely the two were wrapped up in each other, and her eyes filled with tears. She had lived like that with Gaspar Ley for many years. Then money suddenly had come between them, and the whole thing had gone up in smoke. Might not the same virus eventually consume Ignacio? If for no other reason than to show Señor Sarró that he did not need him for anything?

The young couple were oblivious to Charo's feelings. They were gazing into each other's eyes, lost to the world. Ana María was saying to Ignacio: "One of these days I'll run away to Gerona."

"You haven't got the nerve…"

"How little you know about me!"

"I'll know you some day, all of you."

"Don't be so brash."

"Brash? Me? Never! There's someone in Gerona who gives me lessons in manners. Someone who studied at Oxford."

Ana María pretended to be angry.

"Yes, and I know who it is. You better watch your step with that la-di-da lady."

"Ana María—please! She's a lady, a married lady, very properly married."

"Yes, but she's named Esther. And Esther's a name that scares me for some reason."

"Well, I'm crazy about it."

They laughed. And Charo, who was very fond of them and missed the point of what they were saying, finally laughed, too.

"Well, now," she said, picking up the idea that Ana María had mentioned earlier, "let's do go to Gerona some day! I'll go with you."

"When? Tell me when."

"Well, some day when your father's in Switzerland or Lisbon selling the same wolfram to both the Germans and the English."

"What?"

Seeing the expression on the young couple's faces, Charo exclaimed: "Lord, how little you know about business! Don't you know that's the thing to do now?"

The trip to Barcelona had been perfect; it erased all the discouragement that had filled Ignacio while Ana María had been in Málaga. He went back to Gerona bubbling over with joy. When he entered his house, he shouted "Eureka!" which made his mother think she was back in Bilbao. And at the office the next morning, he said to Manolo: "Know something? Ana María is a living doll!"

Manolo stroked his little beard. "Is she now? I'm glad to hear it." Then he added, enigmatically: "Some day we'll go into the subject of living dolls at great length."

Ignacio stared at his boss and was thoughtful. That night when he closed the door to his "den," he studied the Picasso reproductions and told himself that Picasso was right: everything could be viewed from many different angles.

FORTY-EIGHT

FOR all his wisdom, for all the moral authority he had acquired among the Gerundians, Dr. Andújar could not easily meet the family budget.

He worked hard in the Insane Asylum, but had very little to do in his private office. The forecasts of Dr. Chaos had proved correct: people were not ready to grant the validity of a psychiatrist. To a great degree they would accept any kind of diagnosis—tuberculosis, hepatitis, rheumatism, lack of red corpuscles—but if they heard such terms as "nervous and emotional mechanism," they became defensive. The words "anguish," "anxiety," "compensation," "psyche," aroused some remarkable, strange reactions. "Doctor, would you please tell me what you're talking about?" "Look, you don't think I'm crazy, do you?" One time Mateo said to Dr. Andújar: "In my opinion the thing is clear: it's a problem of education." "Nonsense!" the psychiatrist answered. "I'd say that's like discovering the Mediterranean."

The common attitude was all the more unjust because Dr. Andújar had had some successes by that time in spite of everything. He had restored the spirits of the widow of Don Pedro Oriol, for one. The Widow Oriol had been so lifeless since the wedding of Warning Voice, after all the attentions and the many bouquets of flowers he had lavished on her, that she thought she was going to die. Dr. Andújar managed to console her by finding work for her, in her case designing figurines. After an exhaustive test given her by Dr. Andújar, the Widow Oriol found out that she had a talent for such things, and now she was spending all day modeling figurines, none of which resembled Warning Voice.

Another success was with Lieutenant Montero, Marta's occasional escort. This young man had been obliged for a long time to issue orders to firing squads with the automatism of a subaltern. But suddenly, he began to feel nauseated in the cemetery and afterwards to have nightmares almost every night. In a matter of a few weeks he sank into a deep depression. He talked to Dr. Andújar, who said to him: "Your only recourse is to put in for a discharge from the Army and start a new life that will gradually erase those images from your subconscious." The Lieutenant followed his advice. And as soon as he saw himself wearing civilian clothes and starting to work at something completely removed from the War Trials and garrison life, he began to smile again and to frequent the casino and La Andaluza's house. And because he had a great liking for literature, he was given a temporary appointment in the City Library.

The doctor was successful with Marta, too. Gracia Andújar was instrumental in sending the girl to her father's office. "It's good to go to communion; we all need it. But you need some medicine also to help you. And some new orientation, something concrete." Dr. Andújar gave Marta both. A tranquilizer that had shown evidence of being very effective—the girl noticed that it made her less sensitive, that she did not suffer so much—and at the same time he convinced her that she should submerge herself more deeply than ever in her chosen work. That is, in her job with the Feminine Section. "What you need is to escape from yourself, and there's no better escape than work. Besides, there's so much work to be done! The Feminine Section would go under without you. And no one would forgive you for that. Neither the Governor, nor Mateo, nor my daughter Gracia, nor I."

Dr. Andújar had discovered some fine qualities in Marta, but he suspected, of course, that she was not the ideal woman for Ignacio, whom he had met several times. The doctor was so persuasive that, to the girl's own great surprise, she found herself once more taking seriously the orders sent her from Madrid by María Victoria. She was sad, but that was her normal condition, especially since her father's death.

But Dr. Andújar's major triumph, the only one that became widely known among the people in the city, was with Jorge de Batlle.

The doctor discharged Jorge de Batlle on January 18, the very day when, according to *Amanecer*, the remains of Luis Moscardó, the son sacrificed by the hero of the Alcázar, were identified in Toledo.

Jorge left the sanitarium still with many inhibitions, still with anxiety. But he loved life again, and, above all, he loved Chelo Rosselló, who had been his guardian angel, living proof of the thaumaturgic power of a soul capable of sharing another's pain.

Jorge de Batlle sang Dr. Andújar's praises from morning to night. "He's a wise man. He has won me over. I want to live. And I'll never denounce another person, never again. I'm going to marry Chelo as soon as I'm completely well and as soon as we can find a flat we like."

Jorge de Batlle vowing that he would never denounce anyone again! That was the talk of the conversation circles, of Raimundo's and Dámaso's barbershops, and everywhere else. What had happened to him? What had brought about that change of heart? Was there some substance, some injection of a liquid that could convert anger into gentleness? Well, then, Dr. Chaos had not been completely off the track when he had cast doubt on man's freedom in that lecture of his which had aroused such a furor.

That was another of Dr. Andújar's problems: people immediately confused his terms. If he did not cure the sick, he was a quack, a pedant who mouthed strange words and liked to ask a person if there were any precedents in the family or if he had retained some disagreeable memory from childhood. If he cured them, that showed that the spirit was so much rubbish, and that what was lacking was the proper biochemistry.

Gracia Andújar, her father's familiar spirit, kept encouraging him. "Couldn't you give a series of lectures explaining what it's all about? Or give talks on the radio. Why don't you try it? Would you like me to see to it?"

The doctor looked skeptical as he stroked his daughter's fair hair.

"No one would come to the lectures. Just you and the Widow Oriol. As for the radio, people would rather listen to soap operas and records dedicated to someone or other."

Dr. Andújar knew that there were certain people in Gerona who would have been able to collaborate effectively with him—the priests. But he could see no easy entree to their field. The only "purveyor," as he put it, was Father Forteza. Indeed, the Jesuit was the only religious in the city capable of saying to a penitent who came to him in his cell or in the confessional: "I'm going to be frank with you. The absolution I can give you is not going to solve your problem for you. We would need the collaboration of a doctor, for example Dr. Andújar."

Except for Father Forteza, there was no one to help the psychiatrist. The Bishop, whom Dr. Andújar had approached on the subject through the good offices of Notary Noguer and Agustín Lago, had decided not to take his side. Dr. Gregorio Lascasas argued, in spite of the esteem in which he held psychiatry, that the problem was extremely delicate, and that a minister of God would have to think twice before deciding to "abandon a soul" by handing it over to medical science. He even quoted a text from Saint Mark: "And he gave unto the twelve the power to cure sicknesses..." That did not keep the Bishop, however, from meditating on the subject. In the first place, he did not think for an instant that the doctor was motivated by ambition. In the second place, the doctor's contention that a priest ought to distinguish between a religious or moral conflict and a psychic disturbance was correct and in line with reality. The Bishop himself had often been worried sincerely to discover that many nuns lived a life submerged in a world of sickly qualms and speculations or went into hysterics when he deigned to visit their convent. He had not been unaware either that many a priest had passed, without realizing it, from hating the sin to hating the sinner, and that many another took such an aggressive attitude toward evil that he became incapacitated to reach the sublime plane of his mission, which was love. In such cases, it was obvious that the consciences of the faithful who made their confessions to priests like that would be exposed to noxious influences.

All those considerations notwithstanding, the Bishop thought it would be imprudent to try to modify the mental posture of priests who already had spent years in the exercise of their calling. On the other hand, he granted the possibility that steps should be taken in the seminaries to train the priests of the future along new lines.

The Bishop's attitude, which implied postponement *sine die*, was a disappointment to Dr. Andújar, particularly because, in his opinion, the first man in need of help was the Bishop himself. Certainly, that was the root of the problem and the reason why Dr. Andújar had not ventured to confront the prelate directly. He did not want to put the Bishop on his guard or to offend him. But he felt certain that Dr. Gregorio Lascasas ought to undergo treatment. An anxiety neurosis? The aggressiveness that he attributed to others? An obsession with detail, with his metal filing cabinets, with the Sixth Commandment? No, no. Something worse: loneliness.

Dr. Andújar believed that the Bishop was suffering from loneliness. His authoritarian temperament isolated him pitiably. He saved himself by action, by his daily work, and his unquenchable apostolic zeal; but Dr. Andújar had read in the prelate's eyes traces of a deep sadness. In his opinion, the Bishop was making a great mistake by not seeking wider counsel. He listened to the canons and certain other persons, but when the moment came to make a decision, he broke away from others and acted according to his most rigid innermost persona. He wanted to carry the cross alone. He had taken too much to heart his role as shepherd of his flock, whence his exaggerated reactions to the Moralization Campaign, his repeated reading of the Apocalypse, his colds—Yes, Dr. Andújar would take his oath that the Bishop's sneezes were psychological in origin.

"If only Mosén Alberto would lend me a hand!" Dr. Andújar thought. For Mosén Alberto was the Bishop's confessor, and had been since the day the prelate had entered Gerona to take charge of the diocese. But Mosén Alberto was more interested in archeology than in neurology. At the moment he was happy because the members of the institution called "The Friends of Ampurias," established in Barcelona, had supported his old theory that the Apostle James had landed on that spot to start his evangelical work through Spain.

Dr. Andújar saw Dr. Chaos frequently, for ever since his summer episode, the surgeon had put himself in his friend's hands with entire good will. "I'm desolated, friend Chaos," he said. "I have to admit you were right. It's very hard to do my work here. As hard as, or harder than, in Santiago de Compostela. Yes, I go along with the people who believe that the new bell in the Cathedral sends off too somber a sound."

Dr. Andújar's worst fault was that he wanted to heal the whole world. His mind almost never rested, for whenever he met other people face to face, he could see into them, mainly through their eyes and their individual nervous mannerisms, and that tired him. Fortunately for him, people often surprised him greatly, especially by their evolution, their conduct. That was true of Paz and Manuel Alvear, to cite two recent examples. A week after her mother's death, Paz had decided that she would put off her mourning after only a month. She appeared at the Agencia Gerunda and asked Tower of Babel to find them a better and more central apartment. Manuel, on the other hand, much less able to shake off the weight on his spirit, had not opened a book in the Instituto. He walked through the halls of the Diocesan Museum like a soul in torment, pausing from time to time in front of the skull that Mosén Alberto had given him.

Fortunately, Dr. Andújar knew himself, and he was more adept even than the Governor at using the necessary means to keep himself in trim, with all his faculties alert, and at not letting himself be overly affected by anything. It helped him a great deal to listen to Gregorian chant. Besides, he was an optimist by nature. He was convinced that, in spite of everything, in spite of his difficulties and the somber sound of the bell, he would eventually persuade the Gerundians to surrender to his zeal for service. Then he would be able to educate his children properly and keep them laughing at him when his Adam's apple moved up and down with irresistible comic effect.

"Dr. Chaos, I grow more convinced every day that in order to achieve the proper balance, man needs to give himself, to give himself to others. To put it another way, man needs companionship. I assure you I'm not talking about you now, or your problem. But a person must open up, he must open up. Open his heart as you open the abdomen of a patient in the operating room."

Dr. Chaos could not help asking himself whom Dr. Andújar opened up to, unless it was his daughter Gracia. For he could not imagine that his friend could conceivably share his professional worries with his wife, the ineffable Doña Elisa, or confide to her his partial failures. Of course, she would make "her" response to Dr. Andújar. She would tell him it was enough for him that love reigned over their marriage. Certainly he had nothing to complain of in that area. Doña Elisa loved him to the bottom of her soul, and in sweetness and solicitude she was the perfect mother. That was palpable from the moment one entered their house. The furniture was always unmarred, the clothing always clean; flowers decorated the waiting room, the children spoke in low voices and enjoyed a snack of toast and hot chocolate every Sunday in the family gathering.

"Yes, I understand, friend Andújar. But there are people who open up to others without necessarily becoming well balanced or finding the needed compensation in that way. If your theory were right, every charlatan would be happy."

"That objection is unworthy of you, friend Chaos. Opening up doesn't mean just talking. You know very well what I'm saying. Sometimes simply to put one's head on a beloved shoulder is enough to make one feel comforted. I'm talking about yielding one's self inwardly. Sometimes a look is enough, or merely the feeling that another person is near."

Dr. Andújar had succeeded perfectly in that. He loved his wife and children as naturally and deeply as the roots love the growing tree. He believed firmly that a large family was a gift from God unless it was a product of poverty, or promiscuity, or even of boredom. He loved his patients, too. And even those who, though ill, would not seek him because his degree in psychiatry frightened them or because they were afraid that he might ask them if they had retained some unpleasant memory from childhood.

Furthermore, it was such a wonderful feeling to pull someone out of the black well. Marta, the Widow Oriol, Lieutenant Montero, Jorge de Batlle...

But what about the Insane Asylum, Lord? And when was he going to be able to pull Commissioner Diéguez out of the well—the well of aggressiveness?

FORTY-NINE

FEBRUARY, 1941. On the fourth of the month, Gerona celebrated the second anniversary of its liberation by the "Nationalist" troops. The day before, on the third, coincidentally, Marta received a postcard from Salvatore, the Italian legionnaire, dated "Somewhere in Albania." Seemingly, Salvatore was one of the thousands of the Duce's "Black Shirts" fighting against the English on the Mediterranean coast or the Greek front. Salvatore said only, "*Ciào*," and signed his name. If "*Ciào*," meant "Goodbye" did that also mean that Salvatore was saying farewell forever? Mightn't he be in some hospital mortally wounded? Marta stammered: "Lord, why must there be wars?"

According to *Amanecer*, the fiesta of the "liberation" was a day of "unusual splendor." Religious and military ceremonies. Ending with a showing of the patriotic film *All Quiet in the Alcázar*, which was roundly applauded. In the course of the day it was agreed that the city would confer its gold medal on the Caudillo. At the moment when Warning Voice signed the appropriate document, Carlota was at his side. She said to him: "On the day when the monarchy is restored, you must remember to confer that medal on the King. But I hope it'll be a little larger." A week later, Warning Voice learned that His Majesty Alfonso XIII had just abdicated in Rome in favor of his son, Don Juan, thereby confirming word to that effect which had been circulating for some time.

The month of February was full of surprises, like every other month. Life was still a sea, not a lake. In Paris, the philosopher Henri Bergson died. Notary Noguer and Professor Civil always had felt a special predilection for him because he had defended the primacy of the spirit over matter. On the same day, Lord Baden-Powell, founder of the Boy Scouts, died in England at the age of eighty-three. The event passed almost unnoticed. But when Mateo read it, he said that the Youth Front and all the boys in the world ought to wear a mourning band on their sleeves for a week.

The feast of San Antonio Abad provided grounds for another celebration. The orders of knighthood were blessed and small loaves and twists of bread were passed out. The Plaza de la Catedral was turned into an assembly of horses, conspicuous among them the mounts that had taken part in the horse show organized by Captain Sánchez Bravo. The Bishop blessed them, thinking as he did so that those noble animals presented fewer problems than human beings. They let themselves be caparisoned without preening themselves on their appearance; they accepted the Holy Water without either blaspheming or considering themselves saints; they were always willing to obey their riders; and they did not suffer—"they merely endured"—for they had no souls. With only a little exaggeration they might be called martyrs to man, for at one time in this very city they had been sacrificed in the slaughterhouses to supply the emptied butcher shops.

In that month of February, the anniversary of the Liberation, the person who had won enough merit to be given a special blessing was the man whom Dr. Andújar had been thinking of: Commissioner Diéguez. He was singled out for the simple reason that he had carried out the Civil Governor's instructions of a few weeks earlier. With praiseworthy zeal he had tried to counteract in so far as possible the insane greed for money that had seized the province.

Commissioner Diéguez had done his duty so well that many of the "undisciplined" had called a truce and backtracked. He did not give some of them time enough for that. For example he jailed the members of Tejero, Inc., who were convicted and admittedly guilty of a succession of smuggling crimes. Their president, one Pedro Riuró, an old stock-exchange agent, was sent to a disciplinary battalion, and at that moment he was boring a tunnel near Garrapinillos, in the province of Guadalajara.

"Send those men there to teach them a lesson and as a warning to others," the Governor said, "an objective lesson, or any kind of lesson you wish. If the guilty man holds an important position, if he's one of the top men, make that known in your report."

In line with those orders, a succession of persons fell into the clutches of Commissioner Diéguez for infractions of every description.

Ambrosio, the bass violist of the Gerona Jazz Band, was accused of swindling the electric company. He had invented an ingenious device for preventing the current from going through the meter. He was found out and punished.

One of the junk dealers in the La Barca quarter was put in jail along with the members of Tejero, Inc.; thus they took the places of the prisoners who had been pardoned at Christmas. The authorities had found out that he had a number of old crones working for him, going from house to house offering potatoes on condition that first they be given a sack in which to transport them. The man had collected five hundred sacks since the first of the year, and had sold them at a good price, for jute was in short supply.

Galindo was fined for refusing to recognize the badge of the Social Auxiliary, which was required for entrance to the motion-picture theater. El Niño de Jaén, known as a "dancer," was surprised while stealing a tire from a transport truck. He was held in the police station for forty hours, until La Andaluza told Mateo about his predicament and Mateo got him out. Herreros, the Madrilenian employed by the Dámaso Barbershop, was fined in turn for spreading false rumors that in spite of the national food scarcity, Spain was sending supplies to Germany.

Another of the persons caught was the young waiter of the Hotel Miramar in Blanes, Rogelio himself. The boy had turned out to be a downright rascal. At the end of the hotel's summer season, he had settled in Gerona, disposed to adopt some plan that would enable him to live without turning a hand. He got in with the servant girls, made them fall in love with him, and then urged them to steal silverware from the "señores"; but one of the girls was caught and when she was interrogated by Commissioner Diéguez, she "sang." Rogelio also was hustled off to jail. And when he found himself behind bars, the boy, who had never before been guilty of anything illegal, thought it all over and came to the conclusion that Dr. Chaos was the man responsible for his changed state of mind and his corruption. The incident with the surgeon had left its mark, perhaps by showing him the twisted face of life. "He'll pay for it," Rogelio said to himself. "He'll pay for it."

All in all, however, the most important service rendered by Commissioner Diéguez was in the matter of abortions. The scapegoat in that case was Rosario, the midwife in charge of child care for the Feminine Section. Rosario, a complicated woman with hidden ambitions, had become the replacement for Dr. Rosselló with the help of a druggist and for a very cheap clientele: the prostitutes and some of the "Andalusians" living in the Montjuich caves. Who could have foreseen that? Marta did not bother to lift a finger to help Rosario when she learned of her plight, for the actions of her comrade in the Feminine Section disgusted her.

In sum, the activities of Commissioner Diéguez imposed the discipline desired by the Civil Governor and caused a panic among unscrupulous mayors, especially in the villages.

To be sure, there was one phase of the question that seemed somewhat ambiguous: the "well of aggressiveness" in which the commissioner seemed permanently stuck. What was it that impelled him to smile with great satisfaction every time he did his duty? Was his performance an homage to justice for the common good or was it an act of secret revenge?

In vain had Eusebio Ferrándiz, the Chief of Police, a man who had preferred to study causes than register effects since the brutal loss of his daughter, tried to pry into the mind of Commissioner Diéguez in an effort to rationalize his behavior, but he came up against a stone wall.

"Commissioner Diéguez, how do you feel when you find a person guilty?"

"How do I feel? Well—what shall I say? I know it's my duty to swear out a warrant. To get out of him everything I can."

"But Commissioner Diéguez, how about when you begin to question him while there's still the chance that you might be making a mistake? How do you feel then?"

"Well, I want to get to the truth of the matter. I'm a cop, am I not?"

"What if it turns out later that the person is innocent?"

"Oh, well, those things happen, don't they? If the suspect turns out to be innocent, then you beg his pardon. You don't lose any sleep over it."

In the opinion of Don Eusebio Ferrándiz, that was the key to the Commissioner's psychology. At his most spontaneous moments, he used the word "individual," not "person." A professional distortion. Commissioner Diéguez could be forgiven for that. He behaved as naturally and self-sufficiently as a field that grows grass.

A dangerous mentality? Perhaps, but in any event, he was the best officer on the force, beyond any argument. He had a nose for crime and he acted speedily. Without his collaboration, the network of vigilance established by Don Eusebio Ferrándiz in the province would wither at the root. Consequently, he was the unthanked but inevitable chessman, more or less like the hangman or the dog-catchers whom the city government mobilized whenever a rabid dog was found in the city.

Don Eusebio Ferrándiz was cut from another kind of cloth. Twenty years on the police force, and he was still asking himself frequently: "What right have I to allow people to be threatened or beaten to make them 'sing'?" The answer was categorical: his job demanded it. He must ensure the safety of the people—in short, as Commissioner Diéguez argued: "I'm a cop, am I not?" A complicated world!

FINALLY, the Costas decided to make their move, and they took possession of the director's office at Constructora Gerundense, Inc., on the Calle Platería. The simple investiture took place on the thirteenth; the day on which Franco went to Bordighera for a meeting with the Duce. The Chiefs of State ended their interview with a joint communique that was made public the next day. In substance it resembled the one published at the time of the Franco-Hitler meeting in Hendaye. *Amanecer* added that the Caudillo stopped in Montpellier on his way back to Spain for a long and friendly conversation with General Pétain, his "teacher," one of the men whom he admired.

From the first moment, the Costas gave the impression that they would go their own way, but with discretion. The head of the Office of Price Control, the Civil Governor, and Commissioner Diéguez made them uneasy. The Commissioner, especially, was the arrow they must dodge in any way they could.

They tried, then, to avoid any ostentation. No question of improvements on their premises, which were somewhat dilapidated. They bought two cars second-hand. They kept the promise they had made to Félix; thanks to them, he was able to enroll in the School of Fine Arts, which had opened its doors in the city under the management of Cefe, the painter of nudes. The one somewhat showy gesture they made, apart from sitting in the front pew at Mass, was to donate a substantial sum to the Civil Government, to be used for the reconstruction of University City in Madrid.

Their first step in regard to the internal reorganization of the corporation was to appoint a secretary. They chose Leopoldo, the young man working in the Spanish Consulate in Perpignan, Ignacio's friend, whom the Costas had met in connection with their negotiations to come back from France. "He's a capable man. He doesn't aspire to become a millionaire in two months, like the manager. We'll be able to discuss policy with him and the maneuvers of De Gaulle, who's turning out to be a chap that needs watching."

The second arrangement was to bring together Tower of Babel, Padrosa, and the attorney Mijares in their office. The meeting proved most satisfactory to them. Not only did they persuade Mijares—the checkbook did the trick—to leave the syndicates, but they also bought fifty-one percent of the shares of the Agencia Gerunda. By that act, Tower of Babel and Padrosa became partners of the Costas, minority partners to be sure, as a reward for their boldness.

Immediately afterward, the brothers called in the city architect and gave him the instructions needed for rebuilding a new Costa foundry from the ground up. "Actually," the brothers said, "what interests us professionally is this: metallurgy. Everything else is peripheral."

At the same time they began to pay the going wage to the prisoners who had come out of the Seminary with them, in fulfillment of their promise to give them work. "You're working for us from now on. You're workers—excuse me, producers—for the foundry."

Some of the so-called "producers" had worked there before the war. The foundry manager commented: "I think that was a practical idea. This means they won't have to go to work in Germany, like so many others."

Meanwhile, the Costas made the acquaintance of Colonel Triguero. At long last he was able to shake the hands of the two former deputies. The interview was shorter, however, than the Colonel could have wished. They gave him no chance to talk about past operations, in which the head of the Frontier Service had played a masterly role. The future was all that counted with them. In other words, it was necessary to get the contract for work on the new prison scheduled to be built in the neighboring village of Salt—the Bishop was demanding the return of the Seminary to the Church, and with reason—and more especially for work on the new barracks, for which the General had obtained authorization from the Ministry of the Army. "This job on the barracks is important. We assume, Colonel, that it will be easy for you to get it."

The Colonel gave them a very knowing wink.

"Well, I'm sorry, but you're mistaken about that," he objected. "You're sticking your hand in the wolf's mouth when you talk about barracks."

The Costas stared at him.

"What about Captain Sánchez Bravo?"

"There's no way to convince him. I talked to him this very day before I came here. He keeps saying: 'I'm scared of Papa.' He's not making up his mind to collaborate."

The Costa brothers sat in silence, confining themselves to several shakes of the head.

"Offer him a hundred thousand pesetas if he can get the barracks for us. Just this one thing. He doesn't have to see us or be a part of the corporation. A hundred thousand pesetas in cash, in old bills."

Colonel Triguero was awestruck. He felt like asking: "What about me? What do I get out of it?"

"All right, I'll try."

"Thank you very much," the Costas replied and rose to their feet.

The Colonel, speechless before the forcefulness of his interlocutors, also stood. He was about to say something, but the Costas anticipated him.

"Colonel Triguero, we are trusting that miraculous fairy godmother who watches over your interests in Madrid, according to you."

The Colonel, still not fully recovered, replied: "You can trust her."

"One request: stay in Figueras. Come to Gerona as seldom as possible."

"I'll do that."

At the door the Costa brothers said to him: "And, please, always wear civilian clothes when you come here."

The Colonel glanced down at his uniform. "Oh, of course! I'm sorry."

THE next day the Costa brothers interviewed Gaspar Ley, the Gerona representative of Sarró and Company. They chose to visit him in his own bailiwick, the Arús Bank.

That meeting was also brief, but it left Gaspar Ley with an excellent impression of the two former deputies. For no reason, he had pictured them as somewhat common, as lacking facility and finesse in their speech. Not so. They made a very good appearance in their well-cut suits, and they expressed themselves straightforwardly and with precision. Physically, they looked soft, but that could be attributed to their stay in prison. Aside from that, they were not without a sense of humor, always an engaging quality.

Gaspar Ley cut short the brief preamble by verifying that Sarró and Company, officially engaged in an import-export business, would like to broaden its scope. "Don Rosendo Sarró takes a modern view of production and transportation. He'd rather be a grasshopper than an ant, see? To put it another way, he has a mind like the Americans in the field of finance."

The Costas nodded.

"How much available capital has the corporation, if one may ask?"

Gaspar Ley touched his hearing aid.

"It would be hard for me to give you an estimate."

When the Costas heard that, they both turned up the toes of their shoes.

"There's one point it would be well to clear up. Why, if Sarró and Company are so important, do they want to connect with us?"

"Geography's the reason," Gaspar Ley explained. "Gerona is near the border. And it has the use of the port of San Felíu de Guixols, which is small and not well guarded."

A silence ensued.

"Could you be more explicit?"

"I'm sorry. Don Rosendo Sarró would rather explain the secondary details in person."

The Costas were silent again for a time. "You realize that we can't leave Gerona?"

"That doesn't matter. Don Rosendo Sarró is prepared to move."

"When?"

"He's spoken to me about that. He's set the date for Saint Joseph's day. He says the saints' days always bring him good luck."

The Costas smiled. "We agree. They've brought us luck, too."

Gaspar Ley smiled in his turn.

"Is there anything else?"

The eyes of the Costas moved around their host's office.

"Yes, one more question. The Arús Bank—does it have a hand in this?"

Gaspar Ley threw out his arms. "You might say the Arús Bank belongs to Sarró and Company."

The reply seemed to satisfy the Costa brothers, who rose and shook hands with Gaspar Ley. Before leaving, one of them left a box of Havana cigars on the Manager's desk.

Once outside, the two former deputies looked at each other and made a face which meant: "We're on our way." For his part, Gaspar Ley could not help thinking that the Costas, like Don Rosendo Sarró, were the classic Catalan industrialists who stamped a progressive rhythm for the country. As long as types like that existed, Catalonia would keep moving ahead, even though there were signs forbidding people to speak Catalan. Even though General Sánchez Bravo might rejoice inwardly each time he read in the newspaper that the Government intended to establish a factory in the province of Málaga or the province of Segovia.

By the first of March, the Costa brothers had the situation well in hand. Among other things, they realized that the methods of labor imposed at the moment had nothing to do with those used before the civil war. True sleight-of-hand artists had emerged, the kind of whom it was said that "they must have learned their trade in the professional chair of Don Juan March." For example, they learned that some textile factories were not manufacturing. They obtained from Madrid their quota of wool, cotton, or whatever the fiber might be, and automatically proceeded to sell it without bothering even to have it brought to the mill. They found out also that a titanic struggle was going on to get permission to manufacture gazogenes, which the Government had declared to be in the national interest.

All in all, the Costas were happy. The sufferings they had undergone had left no scar, and their prospects were most pleasing. Everything was standing on a firm foundation. Captain Sánchez Bravo was said to have changed color and sworn at the figure of a hundred thousand, a pardonable oath by any lights. The personnel surrounding the brothers was given to swearing—Leopoldo was the most fluent—and he outdid himself when he learned that the former deputies planned to reward all their employees with an annual bonus from their profits. Furthermore, on another scale of values, they were beginning to see spontaneous demonstrations of affection in the way they were greeted on the street.

Tower of Babel, who came often to see the Costas, was also showing a contagious euphoria. "Just think!" he said to them from his unattainable height,

"There are times when I don't know whether I lost the war or won it!" The same was true of Padrosa, his partner, whose dream was to possess a car of his own and thus be able to inveigle Silvia, the manicurist in the Dámaso Barbershop, into climbing into bed with him. Or marrying him—it was all the same to him.

The Costa brothers were more cautious. They knew that in spite of appearances, they had lost the war, and consequently they kept harking back to the same old problem: that the authorities could make life hell for them with one stroke of the pen; they could even send them to Garrapinillos in the province of Guadalajara to bore a tunnel—there were precedents for that.

Always conscious of such an eventuality, they adopted an outwardly circumspect attitude. They had been known of old for their exuberance and their bursts of stentorian laughter; now they were known for their sobriety. Very rarely did they go out except with their respective wives. Ramón, the waiter in the Café Nacional, did not conceal his disenchantment with them. "While you were in France didn't you hear a single story unsuitable for young cars? It can't be true that you've never left Marseille. This is boredom itself."

The Costas unshackled their impulses only in the Vista Alegre Stadium—that is, at the football and roller-skate hockey games.

Hockey on roller skates, which was almost completely strange to them, aroused their enthusiasm. It was a feline, passionate sport, and the Gerona team was unquestionably the best, the leader in the list of championship matches.

As for football, the brothers yelled themselves hoarse at all the games. Thanks to Captain Sánchez Bravo, they obtained seasonal grandstand seats and cheered with all their might, first because they put their whole hearts into the game—Pachín made some record-breaking goals—and second because anything went there and no one was bothering about them. Of course, football was the great safety valve that the authorities had thought up, the substitute for political struggle, meetings, and strikes. "Out, out!" "I hope he breaks a leg!" "Criminal!"

The only thing that pained them, really pained them, was their brother-in-law's attitude. They had finally decided to send Warning Voice a note saying: "We'd like to see you." The answer was a refusal. "I did what I could for you when you were being tried. Now I see no reason to continue our relationship."

The Costas did not know that Warning Voice might have been willing to meet them for Laura's sake. But Carlota, the Countess of Rubí, opposed it with all her strength. "You would displease me very much if you were to shake the hands of that pair of rascals." Ah, whenever the Countess of Rubí said, "You would displease me very much," her husband would suddenly let his staff of office fall clattering to the floor.

FIFTY

COINCIDENTALLY with the Costa brothers' strategic integration into the life of the city, winds of hurricane force lashed wide areas of Spain, Portugal, and the Straits of Gibraltar, causing a chain of catastrophes.

The city most heavily struck was Santander, the home of the Civil Governor and María del Mar. As everyone would talk for a long time about the flood in Gerona, it was foreseeable that for years to come, and with better reason, people would talk about the "fire in Santander," which started on February 17 as a consequence, it seemed, of a short-circuit in the Cathedral, which caused a high-tension cable to part. The wind took possession of the initial fire and carried it everywhere in flying tongues of flame. The first news to reach Gerona told of the destruction of the Cathedral, the Episcopal Palace, the two local newspaper plants—the *Diario Montañés* and *Alerta*—and of a large part of the business section of the city. It reported, too, that the hurricane had caused many deaths in Vigo and along the Portuguese coast, and that the Bilbao electric train had been swept into the Urola River.

Santander, the small fatherland of the Civil Governor and María del Mar. Needless to say, the Governor got ready immediately to go to the mountain capital, where almost all his own and his wife's relatives were living. Unfortunately, she could not go with him because she was in bed with the grippe. But Miguel Rosselló would drive him there, and José Luis Martínez de Soria, who saw the work of Satan in everything, especially fire, would go along, too.

As the news grew more alarming from hour to hour, the Governor decided not to delay his trip another minute and to leave the province in Mateo's care.

His was a dramatic farewell. María del Mar, in bed, kept saying: "You can see I can't go with you. How are you going to arrange to let me know what's happening?"

"I'll do the best I can, darling. Now please don't keep me any longer. Take care of the children."

Pablito and Cristina threw their arms around him and smothered him with kisses.

"Goodbye, Papa. Call us right away!"

"Of course, I will."

At the last moment the Governor said to his son: "All right, Pablito! Take care of your mother. You're in charge of the house while I'm gone. Don't forget that you're the man."

"Don't worry, Papa."

THE car got off to a fast start. And thanks to the newspapers and radio, their worst fears were confirmed along the road: more than four hundred houses destroyed; the wind had not died down; and the Army, the Falange, the fire departments and dozens of volunteers had arrived from Bilbao, from Burgos, from everywhere to help with the work of putting out the fire and salvaging whatever they could.

The trip was wearing, almost without a rest, the three men spelling one another at the wheel. José Luis Martínez de Soria drove like an angel—or a devil—and experienced such pleasure, particularly on the curves, that no one would have thought that he was on his way to watch the spectacle of a city in flames.

They hardly spoke to one another. Each kilometer took an eternity. Miguel Rosselló was the one best able to drop off to sleep. The Governor could not even begin to nod, but he whistled at times. Whenever the nervous tension became too great, he would suddenly forget the reason for the trip and talk about the most diverse things: the strange personality of Fray Justo Pérez de Urbel, the national spiritual adviser of the Feminine Section; the new five and ten céntimo pieces which had been put into circulation just recently. Until suddenly, he would remember Santander. He compared what was happening in the city with the air raids on London, Berlin, Genoa. According to the radio, Genoa had been the target of a devastating air raid by the British; compared with it, that total of four hundred houses destroyed and thirty thousand persons homeless in Santander was insignificant.

"Yes, indeed," the Governor said. "But after all, I haven't anything to lose in Genoa. In Santander—God, how awful!"

At last they reached the mountain capital. The view of it took their minds back to the war: to Teruel, Brunete, the Casa de Campo, Madrid. But all the Governor's and María del Mar's relatives were safe. Safe! He could have wept with joy. The Dávila family had got off with barely a scratch—a couple of lots on the Calle de la Esperanza.

The Governor and José Luis Martínez de Soria—María Victoria was there from Madrid, of course, with some relief trucks from the Feminine Section—stayed in the capital working with the authorities, while Miguel Rosselló left for Torrelavega to send a telegram that would relieve the minds of María del Mar, Pablito, and Cristina: "Everyone well, happy. Love."

WITHIN the Governor's household his departure was the source of repercussions on the psychological level, especially with regard to Pablito. "Well, Pablito, take care of your mother. You're in charge of the house. Don't forget that you're the man." And Pablito's reply had been: "Don't worry, Papa."

Yet the car had hardly pulled away before Pablito suddenly felt abandoned. Shut in his room, surrounded by textbooks, magazines, and a couple of drawings by his friend Félix tacked on the wall, he thought of his mother, María del Mar, coughing in her bed; about his sister, Cristina, more irresponsible than ever; about that enormous Civil Governor's mansion—and it seemed that the weight of it all was too heavy for his shoulders. As he sat in his student's chair, he felt ridiculous, lacking the courage to light a cigarette, as he had imagined he would. "You're the man..." He fancied that the fire in Santander was pointing a finger at him, that it was sewing notice on him that he had not yet reached the age of sixteen, that he was only a child, a child with many questions in his mind and on the tip of his tongue—questions without an answer.

Pablito tried to pull himself together. He went to the bathroom. He rubbed eau de cologne on his skin, combed his hair, pulled the knot of his tie up tightly, and, looking like a handsome child, turned toward his mother's room as he heard her coughing. "I've got to console her," he said to himself. "I've got to make her feel better." But his legs were trembling more than if he were on his way to an examination.

He came to her bedroom, bathed in a warm twilight.

"Mama..."

"Hello, son. Come in. Why are you standing there?"

Pablito went to her bedside. This boy who thought nothing of asking his father who Noab was and why grownups habitually fought wars had barely enough courage to approach the bed in which his mother was lying with a thermometer in her mouth.

"I'll only stay a minute, Mama. But I'm here."

Pablito went closer, and in the twilight he could see his mother covered up to her chin. She looked beautiful to him. Her eyes were bright with fever and her lips looked dry and very touching. She was pale, but her hair was carefully combed. She was not wearing earrings and she smelled of eau de cologne; no doubt she, too, had just rubbed it on herself. Her hands were showing at the edge of the sheet—white hands, looking astonishingly virginal.

"Is anything the matter, son? Don't be afraid. I'm sure the news will be good."

Pablito could not answer. He felt in his heart such love for that woman who had given him life that he flung himself down beside her neck.

"Be careful, son. Watch out for the thermometer!"

He did not care. Let all the thermometers in the world break, for none of them could measure the fever of love that possessed Pablito that February afternoon.

"I love you, Mama! I love you very much!"

"Son..."

"I love you, Mama, and you're beautiful, very beautiful."

María del Mar swung from astonishment to tenderness. With her right hand she stroked her son's youthful head of hair snuggled close to the maternal bosom.

"Pablito! Son, what's the matter with you? You're frightened."

"No, I'm not scared. But I love you, and Papa's away."

María del Mar surrendered; she understood. She smiled and cried with happiness in spite of the anxiety she felt and her spinning head.

"Calm down, darling. Your father will be back soon." Pablito gave a sob. "Remember how it was during the war. He always came back. He always came back."

The scene went on for five minutes, which seemed like an eternity. Finally, Pablito recovered possession of himself. Then the boy realized that he was hardly letting his mother breathe...

He sat up. "I'm sorry, Mama. I don't know what happened to me. Forgive me."

"Forgive you? Why, I haven't felt so happy in months!"

Pablito sat on the edge of the bed. He studied the back of his hand. He took out his handkerchief and blew his nose. He looked as though he were about to smile, for he, too, felt a great sweetness filling his chest, something that had no relation to the ordeal of Santander.

But just at that moment he became fully aware that the bed he was sitting on was the conjugal bed. Dark images ran through his mind; those pictures which Dr. Andújar called "flashes of intimacy." This was the first time that it had happened to him. As a rule, he reacted badly, almost with hostility toward his father. But this time it was all different. God knew why. It all seemed normal to him. As logical as the appearance of the stars in the sky according to the mysterious logic of Nature, the logic that decreed that he was to be there and Cristina elsewhere getting into mischief.

Perhaps deep within him he noticed a twinge of jealousy, no more than that. But his mother, who was now lovingly squeezing his hand, had become the perfect image of purity to him.

"Honestly, Mama, I'm sorry. I guess I'm acting like a child still. Right?"

"On the contrary, son, it's a good thing for men to cry. You know your father cries, too, sometimes…"

"Everyone well, happy. Love." The telegram sent by Miguel Rosselló helped to hasten María del Mar's recovery, but in spite of it she had to spend a few days in the house, in bed.

The evidences of affection she received during those days almost overwhelmed her. Everyone wanted to know whether the fire had affected the Governor's or her family directly, and how she was feeling. "Fine, fine. We've been very lucky, all in all. Juan Antonio has called me twice already, from Torrelavega. It was a terrible thing, but our families are safe. And now I feel much better."

Her friends—Esther, Doña Cecilia, the Widow Oriol, and Carlota, who had entered that house by the main door—often came to keep María del Mar company. Meanwhile, Mateo arranged through *Amanecer* for the usual subscription for the suffering people of Santander. Everyone in the city contributed, not excluding the German consul recently arrived in Gerona, whose name was Paul Gunther. Nor the British consul, Edward Collins. The list of donors was published in the newspaper, and of course the amounts varied widely. The Bank of Spain contributed five thousand pesetas, the poor a peseta or two.

María del Mar's conversations with her friends were very pleasant.

"Do you know, I'm glad Juan Antonio had to be away for a few days. I needed a chance to do a little thinking. It's pleasant to be alone once in a while, isn't it?"

That sounded strange coming from María del Mar, for she was always complaining that her husband had to travel a great deal. But on this occasion she took it in good part. And it was true that she needed to reflect. Since the scene with Pablito, she had decided to accept the Governor's political vocation with more good will. When he came back, she would try to get more interested in his problems.

Her friends encouraged her in that. "But of course, girl. Men need that."

"Sometimes I have to put up with long speeches by Manolo on such and such an article in this or that code of law."

María del Mar was recuperating—the Governor's absence was going to last a week—and his wife realized that the confidences she voiced to her friends in the living room of the Governor's mansion, while the flames leaped in the fireplace, were doing her good.

Doña Cecilia, for example, possessed the artless virtue of being able to put them all in a good humor by making such a hash of proper names, especially in referring to international matters that they had to laugh. "What's the name of that Chinese general who hates the Japanese so much?" "Chiang Kai-shek," Carlota told her. "Oh, darling, with a name like that, how can he win?"

They talked about everything—their husbands, their children, the priests, the servant problem, and Dr. Chaos. The doctor's name came up frequently, particularly because Solita, his expert nurse, had come to give María del Mar some injections. Finally, the Governor's wife began to realize that Solita was sighing over the doctor.

"Wouldn't it be funny if they were having an office romance? Sometimes when men like that reach a certain age..."

"But," Esther asked, "do you seriously believe that Solita has fallen in love with him?"

"Do I? I'm as sure of it as that Manolo and you smoke light tobacco."

"Well, that's refreshing."

María del Mar found, to her great satisfaction, that tense situations never arose during those visits, not even between Carlota and Esther, the eternal rivals in matters of good taste and elegance. Even when they began to compare their respective places of origin they tried not to collide. Perhaps the more belligerent or more rigid of the two was Carlota. Indeed, she reproached her friends in effect for failing to feel entirely at home in Catalonia and accused them of not bothering to become fully acquainted with it.

"I'd be willing to bet you've never been in Poblet or Santa Creus. And that you've never gone to the Valle de Arán. You see? If you don't, you'll never..."

Esther was lolling in her chair in an indolent pose, as usual.

"Well, have you ever traveled through all of Andalusia? What? You've never been there? Fancy that! And you accuse me—after I married a Catalan."

"But all of Spain is beautiful!" Doña Cecilia exclaimed. "Why draw distinctions?"

They were not drawing distinctions. But each of them was proud of what was hers. Esther, for example, longed to raise range cattle. "You'd love to see a cattle ranch. I'm sure of that." María del Mar, who couldn't stand bulls except for the bison painted on the walls of the Altamira caves, boasted of the great number of choral groups and glee clubs in the Cantabrian region. "From Guipúzcoa to Asturias...you ought to hear them!" Carlota pretended to be shocked. "But for heaven's sake, how can you compare them? In Barcelona we have the opera, the Liceo! Of course right now they're giving an all-Wagner program..." "What about the flamenco?" asked Doña Cecilia, pretending to clap. "*¡Olé!*" "No, not that," the Widow Oriol said, energetically rejecting the flamenco. "It ruins your ears."

No one took it very seriously. And when María del Mar or Esther complained about something, Carlota would suddenly interrupt them, saying: "And to think that if only I had a couple of children, like you, I'd be happy."

María del Mar and Esther looked at her in surprise. "But, dear! You've just been married."

"I know, I know, but I wish that I had already had some, and pretty well grown, too. Just to talk to them. That's my dream."

María del Mar thought of Pablito. "Of course, they make a lot of work. And they're full of surprises. But they bring a lot of happiness, too."

Esther said that she was delighted with her pair also, "They grow more amusing every day."

"Don't worry, Carlota. Everything comes in time."

Doña Cecilia's only complaint was that her son, Captain Sánchez Bravo, was living the life of a butterfly, showing no desire whatsoever for marriage.

"That rascal," she said, "he's going to deprive me of the joys of being a grandmother."

Sometimes they reviewed the beautiful women in the city, recalling the beauty contests before the war. "If we were to put one on now," the Widow Oriol said jokingly, "it would shock the Bishop to death." "But since the Bishop isn't here now, whom would we choose to be Miss Gerona?"

The idea aroused lively controversy. Discounting Esther because she was married—Esther sketched a curtsy—the argument came down to Silvia, the manicurist, or the daughter of the head of Public Works, a real beauty, but seemingly destined to dress the images of saints. One day Carlota came out uncompromisingly for Paz Alvear. The others protested. "She's quite a common girl, isn't she?" Carlota replied: "Perhaps so. But it's certain that she captures all the men in the street, beginning with my husband, believe it or not." Then the Widow Oriol recalled that in 1933 a girl from Gerona had won the title of Miss Europe, no less.

María del Mar enjoyed bringing up the problem of femininity. She was convinced that Spanish women were the most feminine women in the world. Esther objected: "Then how can you explain that in this country, with only a few exceptions, the husbands spend their whole lives in the cafés?" Carlota considered men very much superior in everything, even in generosity. "We're selfish. We have to recognize that. Sometimes I ask myself what we're good for. They're the architects, engineers, lawyers, mayors. They write, they invent. If there were no men, we women would still be living in the Stone Age." The Widow Oriol was strongly of the same opinion. "They seem to have a brain more highly developed than ours; their brains weigh more." Doña Cecilia laughed. "That I believe! They're heavier than the Bishop's sermons."

The afternoons in the Governor's mansion went by on wings. Among those women there was never any acrimony. Sometimes the light refreshments that María del Mar offered them were so succulent that the thought of ration cards pricked their consciences. "I suppose this is being a bit greedy, isn't it? But these cream tarts are so delicious!" Whenever they played cards, they put such passion into the game that Doña Cecilia, always a spectator, made fun of them. "Even the General doesn't make such a face when he's playing at war in front of his maps!"

Not infrequently Cristina came in about halfway through the sessions, wearing one of the amusing pairs of pajamas she usually put on at home. Then everything came to a halt and the little girl became the queen of the meeting.

"Cristina! Darling!"

"Go on, dear. Speak to mama's friends. Give them a kiss."

"Yes, Mama."

Doña Cecilia would smooth the child's hair and think again that Captain Sánchez Bravo was a rascal for not presenting her with a granddaughter like Cristina.

At the end of the gatherings, when María del Mar's friends had left—Carlota drove her own car, a handsome black one, and delivered the others to their respective domiciles—the Governor's wife would sigh with satisfaction. She would sit in her favorite chair and rest. Sometimes she felt envious of Esther's and Carlota's youth, and then she would feel sad. She refused to look in the mirrors, for they would have revealed too many wrinkles. Then, without Pablito's knowledge—almost without her own—she would take out a package of cigarettes which she kept in a drawer and light one, of yellow tobacco. The spirals of smoke traced words in the air: Santander, grippe, femininity; or whole phrases: the glee clubs of Cantabria; masculine brains, which weighed more; the monasteries of Poblet and Santa Creus, which, out of sheer laziness, she had never visited.

FIFTY-ONE

THE least that could be said of Pilar was that she was happy. The flat on the Plaza de la Estación was modest in spite of all the improvements, especially in the kitchen, and in spite of the handsome bedroom with the antique, very high bed, but it was a living testimonial to peace. Pilar and Mateo understood each other beyond words. As Don Emilio Santos put it: "They are two turtledoves." Don Emilio vowed that the one who was best off was himself. "I've gained a daughter who takes care of me as my wife took care of me, may she rest in peace. If there's a trace of a slight, a treat on the table. Clean clothes. Every morning Pilar gives me my injection for my legs, and she fills a hot-water bottle for me before I go to bed. All in all, I've won the lottery."

Perhaps the only discordant note was struck by Teresa, a girl just turned fifteen whom Pilar had taken on as a maid. She was awkward; she did not do what was required of her; and Pilar often was angry with her. But Pilar kept things within bounds, and Teresa, who was very amusing, addressed her as "señorita," telling her to have a little patience and adding that what she wanted most was to learn.

Pilar's great advantage was that she followed to the letter the advice given to her by her mother, Carmen Elgazu. "Men like a clean house. Be clean, above everything. The floor, the lamps, the shirts, especially the shirts. And a varied menu. Luckily for you, Mateo will be able to get you the food you want. Sometimes a dish of cream is worth more than a hundred speeches. Oh, and put ashtrays everywhere."

Pilar obeyed. Almost to excess. The flat shone. Mateo, stricter in such matters than María del Mar, refused to double or triple their rations; but Pilar was careful. Their money was not sufficient to acquire many things on the black market, but she had not worked in the ration card section of the Food Supply Delegation for nothing, and not for nothing had Señor Grote, who was still there, said to her often: "If there's anything you need, you know what to do."

Pilar discovered that having her own home, being the mistress, the "señorita," the "señora," gave her such a feeling of fulfillment that all she needed to do to feel lucky, happy, was to see the sun shine as she opened a window. And if it rained, it was all the same. Lighting the stove which, like the one on the Rambla, burned sawdust, was wonderful, and so was sitting down to sew while the rain fell gently outside. Besides, the sounds she could hear from inside the house became intimately dear to her, especially those made by the passing trains. The chuffing of the locomotives and the train whistles spurred her imagination, reminding her that the world was on the move. And that her heart was beating with the world. Sometimes the smoke from the station filmed the window panes, but then Teresa would go to them quickly with a white cloth and restore them to their original transparency.

Mateo had only one complaint: Pilar telephoned him too often. Suddenly, for no reason, she would dial 1374, the number of the Falange. "Is my husband in? Please put him on." My husband! How good the word sounded. Mateo would pick up the receiver. "What's the matter, darling?" "Nothing. I just wanted to hear your voice." "But don't you realize?" "I don't realize anything. I just wanted to hear your voice." Sometimes she would invent feeble, trifling excuses. "Mateo, don't forget your lighter; if you do, you'll fuss with me about it later." "Mateo, Teresa and I have dusted all your books, one by one. And you should see what I put in your office!"

Everything delighted her. Going shopping with Teresa, who carried the basket. Stopping in front of the shop windows to look for a small treat for Don Emilio Santos or some insoles for Mateo, who sometimes complained that his feet hurt him. Calling her friends on the telephone, trying to keep from revealing by her voice the happiness that overflowed her. Inviting them to lunch or simply to see the new coverlet she had just finished embroidering. Calling Asunción to joke with her about Alfonso Estrada. "You listen to me. Be tough with him. And put on lipstick." Calling Marta. "We must surely see each other, mustn't we? Try to get away for a while this afternoon." Calling Chelo Rosselló to say to her: "But child, haven't you married Jorge yet? Honestly, I don't know what you're waiting for. I swear marriage is the ideal state for a woman."

Less frequently she telephoned Esther. Esther intimidated her a little. She was very "wise," she read a great deal, and Pilar had no time to open a book. Perhaps by making an effort, because she felt it was her duty, she would skim the newspaper so as to be able to comment to Mateo on the progress of the war. It must not happen that Hitler had entered London without her knowing about it. Besides, Mateo's name appeared in *Amanecer* almost every day. At least three times a week—by Pilar's count—his photograph also appeared. Pilar clipped all mentions of him and pasted them into an album that she intended to give him on their first wedding anniversary.

Carmen Elgazu came to see her often in the afternoons. Sometimes they listened together to the current serial on the radio. Mateo had acquired a rocking chair for his mother-in-law, almost exactly like the one in the Rambla flat, so that Carmen Elgazu could sit down in comfort. Matías made fewer visits. Whenever possible, he tried to be there when Don Emilio Santos was at home; they had long talks on varied subjects. Ultimately, they would start to laugh as they told each other adventures of their youth, and it became clear that Matías had lived a much livelier youth than Don Emilio Santos. "Matías, if Carmen knew all this she'd faint." "All right! She's not going to know. That's the advantage we men have. We manage to get married without their knowing anything."

For Pilar it was a glorious day when Mateo happened not to have anything to do, no local leader to appoint, no speech to deliver, and could take her to the movies or the theater. Then Pilar put on her best dress, her best necklace, her best coat, and settled herself in the box "reserved for the authorities" in the row of seats "behind the red rope," feeling like a queen. If she should meet the wife of the Syndicate delegate, so much the better; she was a likeable woman who did not mind talking about clothes. If she met Carlota, the situation was more complicated. Carlota aroused in Pilar as much respect as Esther. And she was much older. Pilar's only weapon was to brandish her few years, her rosy cheeks, and her handsome low neck.

Sometimes they invited Ignacio to dinner. Everything went smoothly. Since Pilar had married, Ignacio had taken his sister more seriously. She had ceased to be for him the little girl who could joke but had few ideas of her own and was given to somewhat impertinent reactions. He saw her now as a woman. Three months of marriage had conferred on her an aura that affected Ignacio deeply. Added to that, those invitations, those dinners served to revive the old connection between Mateo and Ignacio. Lately their different types of work had drawn them apart. But now they were brothers-in-law. To a certain degree, their blood lines seemed closer, mingled, which demonstrated that marriage was a sacrament that sprinkled others, many others. As Mateo and Ignacio drank their coffee together, served by Pilar, they revived their feeling of affection, the course of their thoughts turning back to Mateo's arrival in Gerona, about 1933, ready to found the local cell of the Falange, of the time when he said to Ignacio in Professor Civil's house that "to be Spanish was one of the few serious things one could be in life."

"Mateo, wouldn't you say now that one of the most serious things is being married?"

Ignacio's words arose from his preoccupation with his own problem, the problem raised by Ana María's father. Seeing Mateo and Pilar, so much of the same class, so like each other in their gestures, their way of folding their napkins, even of saying, "Excuse me a moment, I'm going to the washroom," he asked himself whether the same thing would be true of him in his intimate life with Ana María. After all, he and Ana María knew each other only through their feeling for each other. Sometimes it seemed to him that they had seen each other only in bathing suits, under the water. They had drunk coffee together, but they had never eaten a meal together. And neither of them had ever seen the other in bedroom slippers.

And the worst of it was that he could not discuss this subject with Mateo and Pilar because the shadow of Marta always fell between them. So he tried to forget it and watch his sister and Mateo. Oh, yes, they had surrendered to each other: two turtledoves. Mateo melted whenever Pilar rumpled his hair or took his hand and gave it a couple of slaps on the palm as she passed behind the chair he was sitting in. And Pilar went crazy when Mateo suddenly went looking for her in the kitchen and tickled her. "Ooo, how silly you are! Don't you see the olive oil is bubbling in the frying pan?"

By the middle of March, Carmen Elgazu's visits became somewhat more frequent. A certain air of mystery was circulating through Pilar's flat. Matías and Don Emilio Santos looked at each other from time to time and smiled. Until one day the news was confirmed: Pilar was going to have a baby.

"Mateo! It's true! It's true!"

For a moment Mateo stopped thinking about the Falange. He put his arms around Pilar and rested his head on her shoulder; he could not quite repress a sob. He had a feeling that this was going to balance his life definitively. Sometimes he was aware that he was living too much for others, with no time and no tempo for himself. Knowing now that he was to pass himself on through another being, that the creature now cradled inside Pilar was his, an entity beyond slogans and struggle, brought him back to a reality he had almost forgotten: the fact that he was a man. A man first, then a political leader.

"Sit down, Pilar. This is a miracle! My love, my little one!"

"Mateo!"

"Do you know something? You can telephone me as often as you want to. You won't need any excuses."

"Mateo, please! You're hurting me."

"What? Can hugging you hurt you?"

"Well, it seems it can."

"Darling. I don't need any more insoles. I think I'm going to start to fly."

Mateo did indeed fly. He flew toward the realm of dreams. He had wanted always to be a paterfamilias, of a numerous family if possible, like Dr. Andújar. Six, eight, twelve children—it was all the same to him. Sometimes at the summer camps he had felt as though the entire gaggle of boys in blue belonged to him. But on that March afternoon, as the locomotives of the RENFE—the wide-gauge railroad lines just nationalized by the State—were chuffing and the tramontane wind was whistling loudly off the Ampurdán, bouncing off the window panes polished by the amusing Teresa, he realized that the Youth Front was something quite different from fatherhood. The "arrows" were adopted children, children of thought and duty; but the life beginning within Pilar—what strange form had it already taken?—was a real son, the epicenter of mystery, of a mystery which, unlike most mysteries, was fighting every day to unveil itself, to convert itself infallibly into reality; a black, blue, and pink reality, with twenty digits, two eyes, two ears, and a little nose to breathe through.

This was truly an event. An event that made the blood of both families run faster, but at the same time stopped the clocks. From that moment on, the clocks seemed to have ceased to run. As if they were waiting for a new hour to come on earth, which had but one inhabitant: Pilar.

Showers of congratulations. The telephone conversations with girlfriends became more frequent than ever. Jokes in the Café Nacional. Señor Grote, Marcos, Galindo began to call Matías "Grandfather." "Ramón, a cognac for Grandfather." "What did Grandfather say?"

"Grandfather," Matías said, lifting all his domino tiles at once with mastery, "salutes the gathering with the cry of *¡Arriba España!*"

Carmen Elgazu went overboard; she practically moved into the flat on the Plaza de la Estación, and her advice proliferated.

"Eat, daughter, eat a great deal. You have to eat for two."

"Don't ever think of taking a cold shower, dear."

"Be very careful about your whims, dear. You know..."

"Yes, I know, the baby might be born with a birthmark."

Pilar felt so spoiled that she became very demanding. A moment came when Ignacio feared that his sister would turn into a despot. But that did not happen. Pilar enjoyed feeling pampered, but she was fully aware of her responsibilities, too.

From all appearances, what did happen was a turning to religion. She thanked God for the coming event, and each time she went to Dr. Pedro Morell's office and heard him say, "It's all going perfectly," Pilar left there to go into the Church of the Sacred Heart, the place she had turned to when her mother had had to have an operation, and prayed to the Virgin of the Annunciation, the Virgin of that parish, Father Forteza's Virgin, asking for help to carry through her pregnancy and give her the needed strength to behave as a woman should during her labor.

Dr. Morell, what a man! Pilar admired him and his profession. He touched the extremes of life and death. One day he ordered the extirpation of what had made Carmen Elgazu a mother, her sterilization; another day, not far off, he would help her daughter do the opposite, bear a child. A boy or a girl?

Pilar wanted a son. She would name him César. Without a word to anyone, she hired a taxi and went to the cemetery, where she turned to the niche in which César was sleeping. Pilar offered her brother the fruit of her womb and prayed that he would pass on to her child a little of his goodness.

The scene among the dark cypresses was lonely and moving, even though Aunt Conchi's body was there, too, behind the stone, witnessing the whole thing.

Mateo did not care whether she gave him a boy or a girl. "We're going to have a lot more, both kinds."

Esther disagreed with the advice that Carmen Elgazu was giving Pilar.

"Don't be foolish. Those ideas are old-fashioned. You should do the opposite: bathe, take exercise. Don't you know that? And please, not so much eating! Come, Pilar, I had my two babies almost without realizing it."

Pilar listened to everyone, but especially to her own heart. And it was playing her a trick that she did not dare to mention to Mateo: she had grown afraid of war.

Ever since she had become pregnant, she had been unable to think about the war or read the German, English, and other dispatches without feeling a terrible fear. An infinity of words now had another meaning for her, including words very dear to Mateo: "Half monk, half soldier." Why should her son be half monk, half soldier? He would be what he wanted to be, wouldn't he? And what about the slogans of the Feminine Section or the Sisterhood of City and Country? "Each son who dies is a citizen who loses his life for his country." Only for his country? What about his mother? Didn't she lose him?

"For heaven's sake, don't say such things to Mateo!"

The voice that said those words was Pilar's own. And now and then Carmen Elgazu's. Although her mother would add: "Whatever happens, don't worry. Mateo will change, too. When men have a son, everything is different. If you could have known your father! When Ignacio was born, he wouldn't let me open the windows. And yet he was the one who was always talking about airing the rooms."

In spite of all appearances, however, the clocks were running. Especially one clock, the one in the flat on the Plaza de la Estación, installed in the dining room. Tick, tock, tick, tock—March, April. When it reached October, the end of October, what would happen? The great miracle that Mateo talked about. A new César would be born, or a little blue, pink, and black girl with twenty digits, two eyes, two ears, and a little nose to breathe through.

"What did Grandfather say?"

"This time Grandfather comes up with four doubles. The tiles will have to be shuffled again."

THE happiness of Pilar and Mateo made a strong impression on Ignacio. Theirs was not a dream or a plan; it was a fact. A fact that intensified indescribably his own love for Ana María, but upset him again. Sometimes Ignacio would look at himself in the mirror and see himself as common, as if he were being inspected by the schizoid, distorted Picasso faces that hung on the wall of his room. And for all that his latest meeting with Ana María in Barcelona had been enchanting and that the letters the girl wrote to him almost daily could not be more stimulating, it was evident that a long time would have to pass before he would be in a position to equip his own office and be able to offer "the daughter of Don Rosendo Sarró" a standard of living worthy of her.

Added to that, his home on the Rambla complicated things more each day, now that he was intimately acquainted with Manolo and Esther's flat. To be sure, he had possession of the long dreamed-of room of his own—with Freud's works in it—but it was a very humble setting. And what about his parents? That was still worse. For some time he had not been able to keep himself from judging them in this light as from an observatory. Why did his father, Matías, have to make so much noise when he gargled before going to bed? And why did his mother sometimes forget and leave a couple of hairpins in the bathroom, like Aunt Conchi?

Finally, Ignacio reversed himself. To hell with phantasms! After all, Don Rosendo Sarró was not an aristocrat; he was a financier. And a strictly immoral financier at that, especially in whatever stemmed from the war. Who could say how much noise he made when he gargled? And, of course, to judge by what Ana María had told him, her mother was totally lacking in the spiritual distinction of Carmen Elgazu, whose acts always taught a lesson in goodness.

In the midst of all this, Don Rosendo Sarró, the object of Ignacio's nightmares, made his projected visit to Gerona to interview the Costa brothers. Ana María told Ignacio about it well in advance. "He'll arrive on Saint Joseph's day, about half-past eleven."

Ignacio watched for him in the Calle José Antonio Primo de Rivera, which his future father-in-law would have to pass through, and succeeded in seeing him in the flesh. Don Rosendo arrived shortly before twelve and met Gaspar Ley in the Café Savoy. He came in a conspicuous car, with a uniformed chauffeur. His air was that of a conqueror. To Ignacio, who was spying on him from the Puente de Piedra, he seemed taller than when he had seen him in San Felíu de Guixols in the summer with his fishing pole on his shoulder. Now he was wearing a gray hat and a solid double-breasted overcoat. As he held out his right hand to Gaspar Ley, it seemed as though the bones in Ley's hands cracked, like the knuckles of Dr. Chaos.

Shortly afterward, the two men headed for the local office of Constructora Gerundense, Inc., on the Calle Platería. Ignacio felt sure that, as they walked along the Rambla, Gaspar Ley would say to Don Rosendo Sarró: "There, up that dark staircase, is where your daughter's suitor lives."

He thought it would be humiliating to wait until the meeting was over. Accordingly, he went home. He ate without any appetite, asking himself: "How am I going to find out what kind of agreement they've come to? Perhaps Ana María can tell me something in her next letter."

He did not need to wait that long. The next afternoon, Manolo informed him in the office of the outcome of the conversations: positive. Sarró and Company were going to work with the Constructora Gerundense, Inc., without anything written down on paper. Everything would be done through a new corporation that the Costa brothers had thought of—a corporation that would be called Emer—Empresas Españolas Reunidas—which apparently would compete with Constructora Gerundense, Inc., in the market and before the public eye. Indeed, their trick was a common one at that time. The Costas would place at the head of that dummy corporation a strawman, none other than Carlos Civil, Professor Civil's son, who was still in Barcelona, lying low and trying in vain to make his way.

"Do you get it, Ignacio? It's a perfect ruse. Creating their own competition! With the name Civil as a guaranty. Besides, the Professor's son will do what they tell him to."

Ignacio was dumbfounded. The shrewdness of the "birds of prey." Emer would not arouse suspicion, not even in General Sánchez Bravo.

Ana María's letter, dated March 21, confirmed what Manolo had said. "My father came back from Gerona very satisfied with his business deal. His appearance did not lie. But naturally, he used the occasion to take a jab at me. He told me that Gerona is a dirty, dull city with no future."

Fortunately, Ana María added something. She said she had had her way regarding her plan to go to Gerona also. She would be there with Charo during Holy Week, on the pretext of wanting to see the procession. They would spend at least two days in the hotel where Gaspar Ley was staying. "Everything is all arranged. My father hit the ceiling, but he finally decided to give in. He can see that I'm so firm about it all that he knows everything will go worse if he opposes me. So we're going to see each other soon, Ignacio! Do you realize what that means? Charo is a great help to me. In fact, the laying of this plot is largely her work. Oh, I'm sure Gerona won't seem dull or dirty to me! To me, it will be heaven. Because it's heaven to be in love, isn't it, Ignacio?"

Ignacio's joy was indescribable. Ana María was demonstrating that she was ready for anything, and that gave him courage. He drew up a detailed map to follow so that Gerona would make a good impression on her: the ancient quarter, the road to the Calvary, the Dehesa. He would search out the exact historical and archeological data that he would need in order to be able to say to her in the Cathedral or the Arabian baths: "This is from such a century, this is from such another century..." And they would have coffee at the Savoy! If possible at the table at which Don Rosendo Sarró and Gaspar Ley had sat.

Manolo and Esther approved his plan. "Yes, yes, bring her to our house," Esther said with enthusiasm. "I'm dying to know Ana María. We can watch the procession from our balcony."

Later, Manolo and Ignacio had a long conversation in the office on professional matters. Ignacio's need to excel started it. The young man told Manolo that he could never have dreamed that he would learn so much in such a short time. And he was content with the new salary that he had been collecting since the first of the year and, above all, with the fraternal friendship which bound them together. But he knew that Manolo was exaggeratedly honest. That some very important business was slipping through their fingers. He did not dare to mention the Costa brothers and their affairs. But Manolo had refused many offers which, in Ignacio's opinion, were perfectly defensible. A lawyer was not a missionary. Times were as they were, and occasionally a man had to close his eyes. Look at Mijares, for example; in a matter of a few months he had risen like foam. And there was also the post that a son of the incorruptible Professor Civil, no less, had just accepted. Yes, yes they had a great deal of work, he knew that. They could not keep up with it all, and prestige was prestige. Nevertheless, for the most part, their cases did not bring in much. Wasn't it a man's job in life to seize the big chances? Ignacio understood perfectly how much the War Trials had repelled Manolo. But the world of finance was something else again. There it was understood that all kinds of ploys helped and that the left hand did not know what the right hand was doing. Morality was not a question of mathematics. Perhaps they ought to think it all over.

Manolo listened to Ignacio with an enigmatic expression except that at the end his face hardened, until suddenly Ignacio heard a few stern words. "Please, Ignacio, shut up. Don't disappoint me, I beg you."

Ignacio felt as if the cigarette he was smoking had fallen out of his fingers. He was indescribably abashed. Manolo was wearing one of his American sports suits, a cheviot, and playing with a paper clip, although he did not put it in his mouth, as had been Padrosa's habit. Manolo's little Roman beard seemed to tremble and take possession of the office as if passing a summary judgment.

"Don't disappoint me. I thought I'd convinced you that prestige means income."

Manolo's dignity was so great that he hardly needed to add another word. Ignacio suddenly felt ridiculous. Ridiculous and guilty. He had been precipitate. He had been talking like a fool. Now it was going to be hard for him to get himself back on the right track. Manolo was still looking at him, playing with him at his will more than with the paper clip. Ambition had blinded Ignacio for a few minutes. God, how hard it was to forge a definitive personality! Or was it that he would never reach that supreme state?

Manolo saw how greatly Ignacio was abashed, and that annoyed him again for another reason.

"I can read you like a book. And still I'm at a loss to understand you. Since you decided to raise the problem, you might at least defend your stand now."

Ignacio was sunk. He did not know what to say. "I'm just plain stupid. Actually, I wish I could simply fade away."

Manolo stood up then, walked around the office a few times, but said nothing. He had lived too long not to be aware of the reasons that had impelled Ignacio to talk in this fashion. The shadow of Don Rosendo Sarró, the uncertainty—something similar had befallen him when he had begun to go with Esther. She had talked to him about horseback riding over the English moors, and he was merely the son of a reputable lawyer in Barcelona. He had joined a golf club. At that time he would have given anything to be able to make Esther the gift of a pure lineage or to win the Derby.

He stopped in front of Ignacio, who had lighted another cigarette and was waiting for the sermon to start. But he saw something in Manolo which permitted him to try to smile, although he could not do it. Finally, he said: "I'm waiting to be sentenced."

Manolo stroked his little beard with an ironical air, which was a good sign.

"Listen to me, Ignacio! Gauge your own strength. Gauge your selfishness.

Sit down in front of Freud's works and meditate. But do it soon! Decide for yourself what your scale of values is. Decide whether money is going to be for you a means or an end."

"I understand."

"If you're willing to settle for money as a means, and admit that prestige is income-bearing, act accordingly. For myself, I can say that I've made up my mind. Better still, I have evidence on my side: tomorrow the Soler factory, which employs a thousand-odd people, as you know, will appoint me its official legal adviser." Manolo threw out his arms and tossed the paper clip in the air. "If that seems to you like small beer, what can I do about you?"

That was a most important object lesson to Ignacio. The young man was impressed. He rose to his feet and was on the point of going to Manolo and embracing him warmly. But he had no right to do that; he had been too stupid.

He would have liked also to prolong the scene a little to have time enough to make amends to Manolo. "Manolo, listen to me for a minute. Sometimes, it happens that..." Manolo interrupted him somewhat brusquely, giving the excuse that Esther was waiting for him, and started to walk toward the door. Fortunately for Ignacio, he knew his boss and understood that he was not given to dramatics.

"All right! Until tomorrow, Manolo."

"Until tomorrow, Ignacio. That is, unless you'd rather go over to the Agencia Gerona, with Tower of Babel..."

Ignacio ran down the stairs, sure that he would never forget that scene.

When he reached the street, he took a deep breath and went home with his mind at rest. He found his father playing parcheesi with Eloy. When the child saw him, he shouted: "Come on, let's play three-handed. Two-handed is boring."

Carmen Elgazu called from the kitchen: "Wait for me! I'm not going to Pilar's today. Let's play four-handed."

She chose the yellow men. And she won, as usual.

HOLY Week came in due course. The Passion, as adapted by Agustín Lago, was not presented in the Municipal Theater that year. Gracia Andújar would not play the Virgin Mary, nor Father Forteza, in a wig, Jesus. But the procession was promising already to take on the prestige of old; three men's sodalities would take part in it, with that of the Most Pure Blood leading; and there would be three floats with images which, unfortunately, had been sculptured in the studios of Clot. By ten o'clock at night, hundreds of torches again would commemorate the death on Golgotha, and, according to tradition, would light the narrow streets of the city with spectral effect. Everything would be extremely somber. No one would get drunk, as in Seville, and neither would anyone sing *saetas.* All would be respect and silence on the balconies. Respect would reign on the balcony of La Andaluza and her girls as much as on the balcony of the Town Hall, where María del Mar, Doña Cecilia, Carlota, and Pilar had made a date to meet.

Ignacio could not identify himself for one moment with the sadness of Holy Week because Ana María, faithful to her promise, reached Gerona on Wednesday evening, accompanied by Charo. Ignacio waited for them in the station with Gaspar Ley, who treated him with courtesy, although with a somewhat distant air as they stood together. Ignacio did not care. Nothing mattered to him then except Manolo's esteem and Ana María's love.

How kind Charo was from the beginning! She closed the ambitious mouth of her bootlicking husband, Gaspar Ley. As soon as she saw Ana María and Ignacio embracing on the platform, she put on a very complacent face and traced a playful cross over them, to which the young people responded with a smile of gratitude.

Moments after leaving the gloomy station, Ana María exclaimed: "Gerona! The unbearable city!" She glanced around her and added: "Why—you even have a taxi!"

Indeed, a line of taxis was waiting.

Gaspar Ley, who was hearing strange whistles in his hearing aid as he took charge of Charo's luggage, said: "Yes, we're going to take a cab."

When they got into the car, Ana María reprimanded Ignacio, reminding him of the day when she went with him to Ezequiel's house. "This is the second time you've forgotten to tell the chauffeur to put a bouquet of white flowers here in the back."

Ana María's stay in Gerona turned out to be a success. The girl behaved with such ease and showed a joy so deep that all of Ignacio's misgivings were dissipated as if by magic.

They spent two happy days, which went by in the opening and shutting of an eye, and in complete contrast to the sadness of the city. Only occasionally, as they passed the hospital or saw a rachitic child or a homeless dog, would Ana María and Ignacio think: "Christ has died." All the rest of the time, Gerona had reached the Resurrection already.

The strangest thing about it was that they forgot themselves. Both the young people were savoring their honeymoon in anticipation, knowing that they were free in Gerona, without the proximity of Ana María's parents. But the honeymoon was so far removed from the flesh that they wished even that the rest of the world could share their happiness. Who were the rest? The whole world. Of course, Charo had been their guardian angel, and Gaspar Ley, too, who, poor man, trailed behind them, visiting "monuments"; and the Bishop, who presided over all the ceremonies; and El Niño de Jaén, whom they kept meeting everywhere; and Cacerola, who was going crazy in his search for a penitent's hooded cloak; and Manuel Alvear, Ignacio's cousin, who was running his legs off on errands for Mosén Alberto and who turned out to be the only person in the family to whom Ignacio introduced Ana María.

"Manuel, I want you to meet my fiancée, Ana María."

Manuel turned very shy and stammered: "Pleased to meet you, señora."

Señora! How funny! But for heaven's sake don't laugh, for Christ has died.

Everything worked out as well as they could have wished. The stairway to the Rambla flat did not seem forbidding to Ana María, quite the opposite. The mere thought that the postman climbed it to hand her letters to Ignacio's mother moved her so much that she stood still in the middle of the sidewalk and said: "Did you know that the house in Málaga where you were born looks a lot like this one?"

How she stared at the balcony hung with black crepe. How she peered through the half-open Venetian blinds to catch a glimpse of Carmen Elgazu or Matías Alvear!

Ignacio pressed her arm and warned her. "Not at this hour of the day, no. They'll be in the dining room…"

In the dining room— Why couldn't she go up the stairs and embrace them both and say: "You have another daughter"? And why couldn't she do the same with Pilar and Mateo, climb the stairs to their house and say: "You have another sister"?

"You can't do that yet, Ana María, you know that. But I'll arrange things so that you can see them all, at least from a distance."

He found out the exact hour when his parents would be visiting the parish church of the Mercadal to begin their traditional tour in order to gain a plenary indulgence. He took Ana María to the nearby corner to wait for them.

When Ignacio's parents were approaching, the parents whom Ana María knew only from a couple of blurred photographs, she recognized them immediately. It was like a blow to the heart. Carmen Elgazu had "the bearing of a queen" beyond question. Still some distance from the church, she was walking along settling her mantilla. Matías was carrying his hat in his hand and slapping it gently against his right leg.

They were both going to pass so near her that Ana María unconsciously stepped back.

"So there they are."

"Yes."

The girl was extraordinarily moved. "Your parents..." she murmured. And she squeezed Ignacio's hand hard. They were a gentleman and a lady. But they were much more than that: they were man and wife as God ordained.

It took only a few seconds for Carmen Elgazu and Matías to pass by, enter the vestibule of the church, and vanish inside it. It would be impossible to locate them once they were in the church, which was overflowing. In any event, why try?

"You look a lot like your father. Very much! And when you were taking your examinations in Barcelona, you used to tap your leg with a magazine you'd bought just the way he does with his hat."

"I'm glad to hear you say that. I'm really glad."

Ana María also managed to see Mateo and Pilar. Ignacio had told her that they would be present in the Cathedral for the Sermon of the Seven Words, and they went there, too. They saw them sitting in the first pews, reserved for the authorities. Mateo was wearing the dress uniform of the Falange, and Pilar, all in black, had put a tall comb in her hair and a mantilla over it, a detail that surprised Ignacio.

Ana María was touched at seeing them, too. Her eyes followed Mateo involuntarily. "He has a good face," she said. That was true. Pilar seemed to have some difficulty when she stood up, although she was not out of shape. A little full in the figure, and with her lips swollen.

"Of course, the poor girl! She must be feeling very nauseated."

"I don't think so," Ignacio said. "Up to now everything has gone very well."

A question trembled constantly on Ana María's lips, but she did not ask it. Where was Marta? Ever since she had agreed to make the trip to Gerona, her obsession had been to meet Marta, to see the girl who had held a place in Ignacio's heart for years.

Yet she could not make up her mind, among other reasons because she was convinced they would meet her—Gerona was so small—and that Ignacio himself would say, "That is..."

She was not mistaken. On the morning of Holy Thursday they saw some girls in the Feminine Section pass within a few hundred yards of them, walking in formation toward the Cross of the War Dead, which stood directly in front of the Telegraph Office. Marta was at the head of the group. Ana María stared at the girls and especially at their leader, in such a way that Ignacio had no choice but to say: "If you'd like to meet Marta, there she is."

Ana María stared at him, and her spirit shrank. Her feelings were mingled.

Retrospective jealousy, a sense of triumph, a touch of pity. Marta looked distinguished, but physically she was somewhat aseptic. Lacking in expression.

"She's very thin."

"Yes."

She felt a little disappointed. Ana María almost wished that she had had a more dangerous rival. Finally, pity triumphed, and the girl looked at Ignacio with damp eyes: "There's nothing left, is there?" she asked unnecessarily.

"Absolutely nothing. It doesn't seem possible, but that's how it is."

As a guide, Ignacio had learned his lessons well. He was the best cicerone that a stranger to historic Gerona could have wished for. "The Roman walled city was triangular in shape. The vertices are indicated by the Gironella tower, by a corner of the small Plazoleta de San Félix, and finally by the Calle de las Ballesterías. There's the Cathedral. In the tenth century it was a primitive church. But there were so many leaks in the roof that, to the regret of the members of the chapter, it was impossible to hold services on stormy days. Then Bishop Pedro Roger planned to build a new church, and...

That bell tower on San Félix is the most beautiful in Catalonia. You have nothing in Barcelona that can compare with it. The first stone was laid in 1369 by Bishop Iñigo de Valterra, and the French master Pedro Zacoma directed the work. Now we're going to San Pedro de Galligans. The doorway of the church is a jewel of the eleventh century, and so is the central nave. You'll be enchanted with them, I'm sure. I like San Pedro de Galligans very much indeed."

Ana María, who had brought three dresses to wear during those two days, smiled to herself as she watched Ignacio's efforts. She never interrupted him, although she did not retain a single date or manage to discover the meaning of the form of any of the spires. Her only suggestion came after visiting the Arabian Baths. "Why don't you take me to the walls to see the Valley of San Daniel?"

It was cold, and that was a pity; there was fog, too, in that direction. The lush green of spring had died. But it was easy to imagine how beautiful it could be. And she could see the meanderings of the Ter in the distance and the immense bare cupola formed by the leafless trees in the Dehesa.

There, as they leaned their elbows on the ruins of a belvedere, they exchanged their only kiss in those two days, a bare two hundred yards from where Paz and Pachín had frantically come together for the first time on the grass.

Later, as they walked through the avenues of the Dehesa, where there was no one, they enjoyed tramping through the leaves, chasing each other among the bare tree trunks, getting lost in the north part of the swimming pool, where someone, Rufina perhaps, the half-witch of the rag pickers, had lighted a small fire that smelled like incense, but even that did not remind them that lips were made to meet. They embraced, yes. With all the strength of a forest, with all the strength of a love usually constricted by distance.

Ana María saw Charo and Gaspar Ley only at mealtimes in the hotel where Mr. Edward Collins, the British consul, was lodging.

Charo asked her: "How is everything, Ana María?"

"Do I have to tell you?"

"No, you're blooming."

"Would you like to know who Pedro Roger was? A French architect who laid the first stone for the Arabian Baths."

"Come on, what kind of nonsense are you talking?"

"I swear it, Charo. Ignacio is very well informed."

"Have you won your plenary indulgence yet?"

"We've won ten or twelve."

Suddenly, aware that her friend had not asked her about Marta, Ana María said: "Did you know I met Marta?"

"Oh, you did?"

"I saw her at a distance."

"What's she like?"

"Very distinguished."

Then came the hour of the procession. The time came for Ignacio to lay aside the part he was playing and tell his parents that Ana María was in Gerona.

"Manolo and Esther have invited us to their house, to use their balcony. I wanted you to know..."

For a second, Carmen Elgazu covered her mouth with her fingertips. She had felt so sorry for Marta! But what was done was done, and now she was dying to know Ana María. She was about to say something when Matías anticipated her. "All right, son. That seems like a good idea."

An important moment—when Ana María entered Manolo and Esther's flat, Ignacio realized that undoubtedly that was the right environment for the girl. The way she handed her coat to the maid who opened the door to them indicated that she did that habitually. What naturalness! And the same was true as she greeted Manolo, the brilliant legal counsel for the Soler factory and its thousand-odd workers, and Esther, who for the occasion had put on a black dress infinitely more suitable than the dress that Pilar had worn to the Sermon of the Seven Words.

"So this is Ana María! Make yourself at home, my dear."

"Thank you."

"Would you like something to drink?"

"*Café-café*, if there is some."

The inevitable delay in starting the procession, which in spite of the efforts of Mosén Alberto, the master of ceremonies, left the door of the Cathedral at ten-thirty, permitted the two couples to carry on a long conversation. Ana María did not go into ecstasies over the apartment. She merely asked from what century the carving lately acquired by Esther had come; it depicted a San Sebastián pierced by several arrows.

Esther and Ana María got along so well that it was a pleasure to see them together and yet leave them apart. To a degree, they seemed like sisters. They were even wearing almost identical shoes.

Each time Manolo and Ignacio went out on the balcony to see whether the head of the procession had appeared at the corner of the Calle de las Ballesterías—"one of the three vertices of the Roman walled city"—Esther and Ana María talked nineteen to the dozen.

"I've been madly eager to meet you!"

"And I you."

"Do they always call you Ana María, or Ana Marí?"

"Ana María."

"A little long, isn't it?"

"Perhaps."

During one of those low-voiced intervals, Esther sang Ignacio's praises.

"I congratulate you. I really do. He's going places."

"Is Manolo pleased with him?"

"Is he? He likes him better than he does me. Can I say more?"

Ana María asked her: "What about Gerona? Is it really so dull?"

"A little dull, but that's something else again."

"Chances are I'm coming here, and between us we can liven it up."

"Just between us, I trust you will! But whatever happens, don't delay too long."

"That's just it…"

"Tchah! Everything eventually gets straightened out."

"What else can I do?"

Manolo called them: "Esther, get the children. They're coming now."

"Who's coming, what?"

"What? The procession!"

"Oh! Sorry, we were off in another world."

The maid brought in the household's little pair, Jacinto and Clara. Ana María picked them up, one after the other, and kissed them, like Ignacio, who usually made a habit of joking with them. Finally, Jacinto and Clara escaped and ran headlong to the balcony.

Everyone followed them and leaned comfortably over the rail. Ignacio stared at the jutting floor of the balcony and wondered, as often before: "How can it possibly not fall down?"

The Good Friday procession started to file past. It was all very solemn. The torches, the horses, the floats. Manuel Alvear walked beside Mosén Alberto, dressed as an acolyte. On the balcony of the Constructora Gerundense, Inc., on the Calle Platería, the Costa brothers in dark suits stood next to their wives. Manolo was surprised to see them there. He had assumed that they would parade beneath the floats of the Sodality of the Most Pure Blood.

Christ had died. But Ignacio and Ana María were alive. They were alive on that downtown balcony, which by some miracle was not falling, with their arms around each other's waists and saying: "Esther's nice, isn't she?"

"A charmer."

"Do you know whom I thought about while I was watching the procession?"

"No. Who?"

"About Mosén Francisco."

"Mosén Francisco—what a man!"

"Do you love me?"

Ana María's eyes sparkled. "That ought to be forbidden at this moment, but yes."

Jacinto and Clara, clutching the bars and staring as if hypnotized at the huge Christ that Dr. Andújar was holding up with incredible effort, while Agustín Lago and Mijares, who held the ropes that supported it upright, were his escorts.

Soon after that, the jewel of San Félix Church passed: Jesus Descended from the Cross, lying prone in a glass case borne on a litter by soldiers. Then the penitents passed, in chains and with crosses. Like the soldiers, the penitents were anonymous. Probably, they were fulfilling vows made during the war.

Behind them came the authorities. The General's dress sash was like a carnation in the night. The Governor had not taken off his dark glasses. Why not? Warning Voice looked like a count, Notary Noguer like a notary, Mateo like a Roman centurion.

The Bishop, Dr. Gregorio Lascasas, carrying his crozier, seemed to be in deep meditation as he measured off the paving stones and the city's piety and degree of contrition.

"Tomorrow I have to go back to Barcelona. Isn't that awful?"

"Yes, and this will begin to seem like a dream."

"But it wasn't a dream—it was real."

When the procession was over, Ana María and Ignacio said goodbye to Manolo and Esther and the children. They ran down to the street to mingle with the crowd and walked until all hours. Ana María was looking at everything like one who is saying goodbye to something very dear to her. The sodalities were coming back from the Cathedral, carrying their hooded cloaks, which now looked like cast-off garments.

Ana María insisted that she must pass Ignacio's house for the hundredth time, then the Arús Bank, which was almost beside the hotel. In front of the bank she stopped and asked: "How many times did you sweep that vestibule?"

"Lord, too many! And on rainy days I had to sprinkle sawdust over it."

"Do you remember those days very well?"

"Better than you might think. I learned a lot in there."

Ana María looked at Ignacio. And when they arrived at the door of the hotel, she remarked as she kissed him goodbye: "One of the things I like best about you is that you use the word 'learn' so often."

PART FOUR

March 30, 1941, to December 12, 1941

FORTY-TWO

DURING those weeks, the news items published in *Amanecer* that Jaime considered worthy of the honor of being underlined with his red pencil in order to arouse some kind of reaction in the mind of Matías were the following:

"The players on the Barcelona Football Club laid a laurel wreath on the tomb of José Antonio in the Escorial. The captain of the team, Escolá, made the offering. A priest of the Augustinian Community said a responsory, and at the end, the trainer of the Blues led the cheering in the Patio de los Reyes."

"The President of the Argentine Republic, Oswaldo Ortiz, has given the Caudillo a saddle typical of those used by the gauchos on the pampas, who are believed to be descended from the Spanish Cavalier."

"In view of the problem resulting from the increase in beggary in Madrid, shelters for four hundred beggars are being built in the pavilions near the Puente de la Princesa."

"The Spanish writer Pío Baroja will deliver a lecture on April 5. The lecture will be at the clubhouse of the Royal Tennis Club of Barcelona. Evening dress will be worn."

"Former King Carol of Romania, who sought refuge in Spain as a consequence of the German annexation of his country, has fled to Portugal, crossing the frontier on foot at Badajoz. The former king left all his luggage and all his dogs in his hotel in Seville. Some of the dogs are valuable animals; important offers to acquire them have been received."

"The British Ambassador, Sir Samuel Hoare, gave a lecture in Madrid entitled 'Between Two Wars.' At the end of the meeting, the Ambassador stated that, once the present crisis has passed, English ways would still be based on respect for the Crown, the Bible, and the Navy."

"A new corporation, the Fefasa, will manufacture artificial fibers as substitutes for cotton, wool, and silk, using Spanish grains for the purpose."

"The explosion of a powder magazine in Seville has left more than three thousand people homeless. The City Council has suspended the coming fairs as a token of mourning."

THE most important news item published at that time, however, was that Alfonso XIII had died in Rome on February 28, following a heart attack.

The official Government communiqué revealed that the King had been attended during his last moments by Father López, a Jesuit priest, and that he would be buried temporarily in the Italian capital, in the Spanish church of Montserrat, where the remains of the Spanish popes Alexander VI and Calixtus III lay at rest.

The Caudillo decreed a day of national mourning, after which all flags would be flown at half-mast for three days. He announced that the monarch's body would be transferred in due time to the Escorial.

Matías and Don Emilio Santos commented at length on the King's death. Matías had voted for the Republic, but the figure of Alfonso XIII was worthy of respect, for although he had left Spain in 1931, he had done so, according to his own statement "because his country had ceased to love him, because he did not want to reign by terror, and because he believed that his act would prevent bloodshed." According to Matías, he had demonstrated thereby that he was a perfect democrat.

Besides, Matías had always liked Alfonso XIII as a man.

"Do you know what his weakness was, Don Emilio? Women. Is there anything wrong with that? I'd rather he'd been like that than to be called The Impotent like that other king whose name I don't recall."

"Henry IV."

"That's it."

It seemed to Matías that Alfonso XIII had done no wrong in being a ladies' man.

"He had such a poor, dismal childhood! It was only natural for him to want later to amuse himself a bit, wasn't it?"

Don Emilio Santos answered: "Actually, he had bad luck all his life. So puny when he was born; his sisters' early death; the attempt on his life on his wedding day; his children weak or crippled; and, since 1931, exile. Doesn't it almost seem that he drew the number thirteen?"

"That's what I read in a book by 'El Caballero Audaz' which I found in a garret of the Telegraph building before the war," Matías said.

The news also made an impression on the Governor, who gave the appropriate orders to carry out the Government's arrangements and presided over the service in the Cathedral. But the Governor was less indulgent in his comments.

As he talked with Mateo, he said: "He was a weak monarch. And that is something unforgivable in a king."

Those most affected in Gerona were Warning Voice, Carlota, Notary Noguer, the Widow Oriol, and the gypsies.

Warning Voice wrote in "Windows on the World" a moving sketch of Alfonso XIII in which he lamented that while he himself had been in Italy, in flight from the Red Zone, he had not used his chance to call upon the King and pay him homage. In the same sketch, the columnist also recalled that Alfonso XIII was the ruler who had consecrated Spain to the Sacred Heart of Jesus and enthroned His image on the Cerro de los Angeles.

Carlota, monarchist to the core, shed some tears at the memorial services and said as she was leaving: "We'll see now whether Don Anselmo Ichaso's prophecies will be fulfilled and whether a real king, not a general, will reign over Spain."

The gypsies attended the funeral Mass—El Niño de Jaén was among them—lined up in their bright exotic costumes along the side altars of the huge church, the origins of which Ignacio had detailed so minutely to Ana María.

The act of fealty on the part of the gypsies surprised many of the Gerundians. But Notary Noguer, who knew many things, provided the explanation: "It's a well-known fact—the gypsies in Spain are Catholics and monarchists. They adore the Pope, the Virgin of Lourdes, and the King. Don't forget that they consider themselves descendants of the Pharaohs."

"Nevertheless," the Widow Oriol remarked, "it seems strange."

FATHER Forteza was living a life of intense activity those days, although as he read such news items as the construction of shelters for the beggars in Madrid, he often felt a desire to cast aside the religious duties that absorbed him in Gerona and devote himself wholeheartedly to the poor. To move down to the La Barca quarter and surrender his life to the needy there. He feared a Church Triumphant. He feared the very handsome chasubles displayed by Dr. Gregorio Lascasas. He feared that the faithful would put a malicious interpretation on the fact that the religious who had attended the King at his death had been a member of the Company of Jesus.

Meanwhile, however, as he was pondering these matters, he continued to attend the prisoners in the jail. A new director who had just arrived invited the prison inmates to sing anthems with an arm extended, and that created problems. The priest was still busy, too, with the process for the beatification of César, collecting direct testimony, as he had told the Alvears, from people who had benefited by César's charitable work in the Seminary, a greater amount of work than he had expected. In addition, the Jesuit was devoting many hours to the Marian Congregation, as usual, with results that he considered positive. A number of boys, under the leadership of Alfonso Estrada, were doing honor by their exemplary behavior to the blue ribbon that they hung around their necks during the liturgical ceremonies. They were dignified, serious boys, and chaste. Matías, in line with his more or less ironical theory, might stigmatize many of them as lacking virility, at least in appearance and manners. "Why is it that almost none of the members need to shave?" But Father Forteza felt sure that the criticism was without basis and that he was instilling in those little boys a training that would make them men in the strongest sense of the word. He admitted that juvenile chastity, joined with a fervent love of the Virgin, might end in a certain emotional instability, but he realized that the danger would be abundantly compensated for by his use of direct confession, which he was still practicing in his cell, that cell with clothing hung around it to dry, untidy as ever, with the austere Crucifix and the cage holding a little bird.

Indeed, Father Forteza's abhorrence for a "cream puff" religion was increasing by the day, and he was still holding out against having to listen to the confessions of the talkative women. "Saint Francis Xavier, you must model yourself on Saint Francis Xavier," he said to himself again and again, especially when he received a letter from his brother, the missionary in Nagasaki, where the Saint once had preached. "He prayed, but he knew how to endure tidal waves. And hunger. And the Japanese rulers."

The most difficult of the parishioners in his charge was Pablito. The boy was taking his first literary steps, but he dreamed, night after night, day after day, about the roundnesses of a woman, and he was getting pimples on his face. Father Forteza forced him to break the pimples in front of a mirror, saying to him meanwhile: "Get that out, all that pus! Learn to control yourself! Show you're a man!" Pablito thought: "Haven't I already shown that by crying on my mother's bed?" But that other manly act that Father Forteza demanded of him cost the boy such effort that usually he declared himself beaten and dropped back into the same pit. Each week Father Forteza said to him: "All right. See this hair shirt? Tomorrow it will be a little tighter on me. Let's see whether you can manage to control yourself this week." Then Pablito did not know whether to kiss the Jesuit's hand, be angry with him and refuse to see him again, or lock himself in his room and read Salgari's novels.

Lately, Father Forteza had been given another mission to perform. In view of the Jesuit's extensive knowledge of several languages, the Bishop had entrusted to him the task of officiating among the foreign refugees who, after passing through the hands of Colonel Triguero and the Civil Guard in

Figueras, were interned in the Gerona Hospital for reasons of health and were asking for a priest.

This circumstance, which brought Father Forteza into intimate contact with people who had come directly from the theater of war, combined with his profound knowledge of German psychology, necessarily made him, by the very inertia of facts, the most sought-after and incisive "international commentator" in the city. A commentator, of course, who aired his knowledge only in private, who did not write for the newspapers or go anywhere near a microphone.

In fact, his cell began to be known as the "Forteza Information Center," as a number of persons, more of the older ones each day, flocked to his cell to listen to his version of the events occurring in Europe on the war fronts and all over the world. Each of his visitors had his own point of view. For example, Professor Civil, always preoccupied with the Jewish question, which he had discussed often in class with Ignacio and Mateo, knew that no one could tell him more about the Nazi activities in that area than Father Forteza. Notary Noguer demanded, in the name of friendship and the Congress, that the priest comment objectively on the unheard-of changes that Marshal Pétain was imposing on democratic France under pressure from the Germans. Manolo and Esther begged him to tell them the real meaning of the phlegm displayed by Mr. Edward Collins, the British consul—a coolness comparable to that evinced by Sir Samuel Hoare during his lecture in Madrid. Agustín Lago asked the Jesuit's opinion with respect to the attitude of Pope Pius XII, whom the Anglo-Saxon commentators were accusing of Germanophilia. And so on.

Father Forteza saw no reason whatsoever for holding his tongue. Accordingly, always in his parabolic phrasing, he let everyone come, talked, and sent them away satisfied, insofar as he was able to; meanwhile he congratulated himself inwardly that his visitors did not confine themselves to reading the war communiques, but were aware of what the dispatches might mean in the spiritual field.

"Professor Civil, the subject of the Jews, which interests you so much, is a very serious one. In Germany, the Jewish population is close to four million, unless I'm mistaken; ten million in all of Europe. You know all too well the hatred that the Nazis feel toward that race. If you've read *Mein Kampf* by Hitler, that will save me from explaining. Well, then, things are taking on a more and more lamentable aspect. While I was living in Heidelberg, they burned some synagogues from time to time all over Germany; they seized Jewish business firms and stores; they drew up plans for their emigration—to Palestine, to Madagascar—all under the pretext of safeguarding the Nordic race, which

Himmler certainly christened with a fine name: The Order of the Precious Blood. Now, it would seem, there's more to it than that, and the reports of the London BBC seem to be in line with the facts. Ever since the war broke out, much more direct action has been taken, and not in Germany alone, but in all the occupied territories, especially Poland. Yes, it seems that the worst things are happening in Warsaw, where the Germans have confined five hundred thousand Jews to the city's ghetto after first killing off the insane, the old, and the invalids. I'm aware, Professor Civil, that you feel no particular sympathy for that race which, by a trick of fate, is mine. I'm not going to argue with you, although it's perfectly clear to me that a Christian can't permit himself any trace of discrimination. So then, it's my opinion that the thing has only begun. In proportion that the war grows more complicated—and it is growing more complicated, as you must have noticed—the Nazis will carry their persecution to the ultimate extreme. Hitler is convinced that the Jews—and we Jesuits, too—are the incarnation of evil. And unfortunately, he is not a man to consult with God. He consults the stars, which as you well know, are as likely to engender infernal as poetic dreams."

Professor Civil was amazed and frightened. True, he had always placed upon the Jewish people the responsibility for three of the great evils which, in his opinion, afflicted humanity: the deification of money, the psychological breakdown evident in literature and art, and the loss of a sense of individuality. But to go from there to confining half a million men and women in a ghetto, with the ever-present danger of typhus, from there to conceiving of a massive annihilation...

Professor Civil left Father Forteza's cell doubly preoccupied, on account of his son Carlos, who had just come to Gerona to head Emer, a subsidiary of Sarró and Company. Carlos now seemed to have been infected with all the aforementioned evils: he could talk of nothing but almighty gold; he smiled unpleasantly at any mention of the Romanesque art of the Gerundian churches; and he seemed most happy when he was one of a crowd. "He's changed on me," Professor Civil lamented. "Giving him that job has made him change on me. All he has to do now is to hang up the Star of David or the seven-branched candelabrum in his office—or have it presiding over my grandchildren's meals in his house."

Notary Noguer was also astonished and frightened by the word from the "Forteza Information Center." The Jesuit answered his questions, telling him that according to the French refugees whom he had talked with in the hospital, Pétain, at the age of eighty-five, was turning France into a twin of the Nazi state.

"Naturally, my dear Notary Noguer, what may be going on there is what the Bishop would call an alteration of 'the principle of causality.' To be sure, Pétain signs decrees that are surprising from the French point of view, like the one dealing with General de Gaulle, taking his French nationality from him; the enforced religious instruction in official education centers; the prohibition of divorce during the first three years of marriage; harsh warnings to anyone who might circulate anti-German leaflets, and so on. But in my opinion that all adds up to nothing but a proof of the shrewdness of the veteran hero of Verdun. He's trying to keep the Germans content in order to avert worse evils. He's said so himself: 'I'm afraid that the French people will never understand my sacrifice; they'll never forgive me.' But it's true nevertheless, that occupied France is beginning to goosestep, that libraries are being expurgated, and that the *chère liberté* you knew there has become only a memory."

Notary Noguer was frightened at the priest's version; he had never asked himself whether, if he were a Frenchman, he would or would not understand Marshal Pétain. That was a complex subject. Of course, it might be a matter of a saving shrewdness! But to play into the hands of the invader? What limits had the Marshal set himself? How far would he go? Wouldn't it be better to be burned at the stake?

Father Forteza could not help enjoying himself when his visitors were Manolo and Esther. The young couple were begging him with their eyes to give them some reassurance, to assure them that England would finally win, contrary to all appearances. "You're a man of God and you know that the Nazis have killed Catholic priests in Poland and that Himmler has had posted in all the branch offices of the SS Nietzsche's phrase that says: 'Blessed be he who becomes hardened.' Can't you please prophesy that we're right, that this nightmare will pass, and that those girls in the German Feminine Section who are coming to Gerona any minute now, at the Governor's invitation, will soon go back to their own country and leave us in peace?"

But of course, the Jesuit could prophesy absolutely nothing. He was as much up in the air as Manolo and Esther themselves.

"In the first place, in spite of the fact that the Company of Jesus follows a military rule, I'm not a military man, as you well know. In the second place, I imagine that the balance will tip conclusively according to what the United States and Russia decide in the future. In the eyes of a simple Mallorcan priest like me, that's as unforeseeable as what kind of substitute for natural silk will come from straw."

Manolo and Esther stared at each other in despair. They were desolated that Father Forteza could have said what he had, that he had said the only thing that could be said. Because what earthly grounds for blind confidence in the "final victory" could they find in Mr. Edward Collins's little smile? Mr. Edward Collins might very well be the classic English civil servant, trained to revere impassivity.

Everything was unforeseeable. How true that was! Events were proving that daily, and yet they might change radically at any moment. Since the first of the year, so many things had happened to encourage optimism in Manolo and Esther: the British successes in Greece and North Africa, which had brought about the dismissal of Marshal Graziani and had led Churchill to quote in one of his speeches the seventh chapter of the Gospel according to St. Matthew: "Ask, and it shall be given you; seek, and you shall find; knock, and it shall be opened to you"; the development in London of what General de Gaulle called "a Europe in miniature," composed of a nucleus of governments in exile—that of France itself, Poland, Norway, Belgium, Holland, Luxembourg, Czechoslovakia, each of which had sworn to continue the struggle until its country was liberated; the fact that the assault on the British capital had never materialized; and Roosevelt's statement that the United States would aid her sister, England, "completely and unconditionally," together with his order to start building twenty thousand airplanes for that purpose.

But the other face of the coin was there, too, like the presence of La Andaluza and her girls as Jesus Descended from the Cross passed by. Germany had signed another treaty with Russia, effective until August 1942. The Japanese minister, Matsuoka, had announced a forthcoming visit to Europe. But, above all, Hitler, that ubiquitous Hitler, had delivered another speech full of epic rotundities, promising his subjects "coming events of transcendental importance." "When I look at my adversaries in other countries," the Führer had said, "I am not afraid to give my opinion. Who are those poor egotists? Great speculators who live only for the profits they can make out of this war. In such circumstances, there can be no blessing for them. Within a short space of time Germany will teach them a lesson they will never forget."

Of course, such threats were as common as our daily bread. But this time they seemed worth taking as seriously as the campaign of 1939. Indeed, everything indicated that, faced with the failure of the Italian armies, Germany was getting ready to invade the Balkans and to take charge of operations in the African desert. One name was beginning to be bruited about: General Rommel. What would happen if Hitler had his way and could occupy Greece? Egypt and the Suez Canal next? Where would England—where would Mr. Collins—be able to avert the catastrophe hovering over her, unless the enemy should have enemies at his back already, on his own territory?

"My dear Manolo and Esther," Father Forteza said in conclusion, "you have no choice but to keep hoping. And now, if you wish, you can take this stairway that comes out in the Chapel of the Most Blessed, the only one who can do all things."

All in all, perhaps Agustín Lago, who had visited Father Forteza often since his run-in with Professor Civil, was the person who left the Jesuit's consultation room with the greatest tranquility. The preoccupation of the militants of the Opus Dei had nothing to do with racial, national, or military problems—only with religious concerns. In that field, categorical answers could be given.

"Slander, friend Lago, mere calumnies. Pius XII does honor to his office of Pope, that's all. True, he does feel a sympathy for Germany hat is based on his long stay in that country: thirteen years as a papal nuncio. He has never denied it, and it's the only thing he has let shine through his statements. But no one can prove that it has conditioned for one moment his diplomatic activity with respect to the war. First, he tried to prevent it; then he sent messages of consolation to all the countries that became involved in it; now he devotes his efforts to stopping it from spreading and aiding the families of the prisoners and the missing. Why hasn't he officially condemned the territorial invasions of the Nazis? That's not for me to say. Yet I can imagine the reason: there are some forty million Catholics in Germany. If the Pope were to break up the marriage of convenience between the Church and the Third Reich, what would Hitler do in reprisal? It could be something catastrophic. Don't you agree, my son? The Pope would be handing the Führer an excuse for treating the German Church as he treated the Polish priests."

The rationalization sounded convincing to Agustín Lago. But that did not mean that it consoled him. Agustín Lago would have wished the Vatican to be of a mind to condemn openly the occupations by the Nazis, for the New Spain that the Nazis talked about did not engender the slightest illusion in him. He did not believe, like Himmler, that the "Nordic race" was the Order of the Precious Blood. Quite the contrary, with all due respect to *Amanecer*. On that point he agreed with Professor Civil: he put his faith in men born in the Mediterranean region. He preferred the Latin tongues to the German and English languages. He preferred Roman Law to Schopenhauer's philosophy and Bernard Shaw's ironies. And the possibility that the Germans might occupy Athens and pose for their pictures in front of the Acropolis bred great fear in him—as it did in Manolo and Esther and Notary Noguer.

Father Forteza often asked himself when he was left alone, especially after saying Mass: "Well, what earthly reason do they have for consulting me about all this? Might I not be committing the sin of self-sufficiency, of vanity? Of what value is the fact that I've talked with two dozen refugees in the hospital or that I've traveled a little and read Rosenberg's credo? I may be entirely mistaken. I may very well be running the risk of interpreting the facts erroneously."

He would feel again at those times the temptation to devote himself to the poor, to go to some suburb and feed the people, teach them to read and say the multiplication table, as César had done. On the other hand, weren't the people who came to consult him poor too? Didn't their minds need to have their doubts resolved as much as their stomachs needed food?

"All right, then, let's do things in order. First, I'll wash my socks. Then I'll do what I promised Pablito: I'll tighten my hair shirt a little."

APRIL proved Father Forteza right, and Hitler, too, for the situation made a shift of ninety degrees.

In a little more than two weeks, the Führer's troops forced the British to retreat from southeastern Europe. A new Dunkirk. German soldiers, Major Plabb among them, fought their way through the Pass of Thermopylae and poured out onto the Plains of Thessaly, occupied Athens, and planted the swastika on top of Mount Olympus. Meanwhile, at sea, the battleship *Bismarck* sank the British battle cruiser *Hood*, the largest warship in the world.

Then Father Forteza left off commenting and General Sánchez Bravo spoke up. The General said simply: "The German Army has demonstrated one thing: that it's invincible."

He said that to Colonel Romer, Captains Arias and Sandoval, Doña Cecilia, Nebulosa, and, finally, to his own son, Captain Sánchez Bravo, whom the General had had nothing whatsoever to complain about for some time.

Captain Sánchez Bravo nodded. "That's right, Papa."

Noticing then that the General looked euphoric, the Captain asked himself if that might not be the right moment to come out with a question that had been burning his tongue for several weeks. He looked at the General and said: "To change the subject, why are you postponing so long the construction of the new quarters? Don't you think that new corporation, Emer, could be given the contract? Its general director is Professor Civil's son."

General Sánchez Bravo replied: "I've been thinking about it, of course. Emer has given me an estimate. They'll build for a slightly higher price than those leftist deputies you've got yourself tied up with, but I think they'll do an honest job."

"Okay!" the Captain said, raising his shoulders with studied indifference. "I don't know just how far anyone will try to do an honest job today."

"Why shouldn't they?" the General protested. "Do you think all of Spain has been infected with the corruption of the Wall Street bankers?"

"Not all of Spain, no; but you know—In any case, Professor Civil's son has one thing in his favor; he flatly refused to teach English in the Academy of Languages in Barcelona."

"Are you serious?"

"His father, the Professor, told me so."

The General shook his head. "Well, you never know about anyone."

FIFTY-THREE

THE days were growing longer. Daylight was fighting for its own as the Greeks had resisted the German invasion, with such desperation that some soldiers had committed suicide by throwing themselves off the top of a cliff, wrapped in the national flag, preferring death in the sea to surrender.

Spring had come. A spring that announced itself in splendor. The Gerundians rejoiced that after a hard winter, the sun was beginning to show some strength as it glided over their skin. Mosén Alberto reminded his fellow citizens in one of his "Praises to the Creator" that to the Romans the animal that symbolized winter was the wolf, and that when spring came, the shepherds from many of the mountain villages would pretend to enter a cave and kill a wolf in order to make sure that their sheep would be safe.

Mosén Alberto had not written this column for fun. He had noticed that his readers liked best to be regaled with subjects pertaining to history and customs. That was true of his older readers in particular. And, indeed, people of mature years missed many of the things of yesterday which had been lost during the civil war. The phrase, "I remember that before the war," took on a nostalgic ring, often connected with politics.

During that spring, which was accompanied by many events on a world scale, the minute life of every day could not be halted in its course, and Mosén Alberto came to the center of the stage, thanks to *Amanecer.* He used the renewal of family Sunday excursions to the hermitages and the mountains—finally, Cacerola succeeded in persuading Ignacio to leave the city and get some fresh air—as the reason for writing a series of commentaries in his column on the places they visited and Catalonia in general. The success of his plan compensated him partly for the sacrifice he had to make in saying the Hunters' Mass at four o'clock in the morning, an hour that the priest always characterized in a vigorous, humorous tone as "immoral."

Thanks, then, to Mosén Alberto's erudition, Gerona learned that within the walled villages of olden days, it had been the custom to hang a sheet across the gates to the city on the first day of Lent; anyone left outside had been branded a sinner. Women, dressed as witches, with wrinkles drawn on their faces, had stationed themselves at the gates, and as soon as they had seen one of the sinners returning, they had upbraided him harshly and called down curses on him as they had raised the sheet to let him pass through.

Mosén Alberto also told about the ceremony connected with the hermitages that contained an image of the Virgin. If it happened that on a certain feast day the Virgin did not receive a visit, the birds in the region would take the place of men and would make ingenious efforts to enter the chapel and sing sweet canticles to Mary. The Bishop was enthusiastic over that legend. Dr. Gregorio Lascasas said with rare humility: "In Aragón I never heard of anything so charming."

The column heralding Easter Sunday attracted attention, too. The Resurrection had just been celebrated in Gerona without any special fanfare except for the gaiety of the streets and the Easter cakes and Easter eggs in the pastry shops. But seemingly, in addition to those traditional trappings, it had been the custom in days gone by to rock and to swing all day long. According to Mosén Alberto, on the day of the Resurrection of the Lord, it had been the custom to tie ropes to the trees and swing from them. People had lined up before the swings; grandfathers had bounced their grandchildren on their knees; young mothers had rocked their babies in the cradle much more vigorously than during the rest of the year. All this had been done because the shaking and swinging favored and accelerated the germination and growth of plants and fruits.

Spring at sea also had its column in *Amanecer*, thanks to Mosén Alberto. According to him, when the month of May had come around in ancient times, the fishermen along the coast had mended their nets in preparation for the new season and dyed them bright colors as they whistled different melodies, according to the color chosen, for each had its meaning and its virtue. Similarly, at the seamen's picnics of those days, it had been common custom to break a dish or plate that had been used during the open-air meal, then bury it in the hope of being able to find the pieces the following year. This anecdote caught the particular attention of Cacerola, the cook. On the day when he and Ignacio climbed Rocacorba, he broke the crude dish he had brought with him after their lunch and buried it in Ignacio's presence at the foot of a big tree. This gave the good-hearted price control inspector, a romantic man who fell in love easily, his chance to ask Ignacio when the dish was buried: "Do you believe at all that I'll still be here next year?"

Ignacio never failed to clip all those columns from *Amanecer* for Ana María, knowing that the girl would be delighted with them. He was right. Ana María devoured Mosén Alberto's articles and tried her best in her letters always to relate them to her love, a love more potent than the sun, she said, because it did not slide off the skin.

> Yes, Ignacio. I'm glad you went on an excursion with your friend Cacerola. Spring…is just that, spring. Barcelona has been transformed, too. The gardens are in bloom and people walk smiling through the streets. As for me, the way things are, I've spent my time swinging, like the ancient Gerundians. I, too, have felt the desire, the keen desire, to rock a beautiful baby in some beautiful cradle as soon as possible. And to dye the net in which I've caught you pink, as the sailors used to do.

It seemed amazing that those letters of Ana María's and columns of Mosén Alberto should make such an impression on Ignacio. Cacerola said to him: "It's the mountains. Do you realize that? I was right." Perhaps it was. In the city, Ignacio saw that the Catalan people were as subject to the temptations of the flesh as any other people; but on those outings, when he contemplated the hills and meadows sprinkled with hamlets and brooks, he felt that there was a higher truth than Sarró and Company and the schemes concerning wolfram and cotton. And that Carlota was indeed right in telling Esther that the Catalan breed was very old, with a long tradition, the product of a rising culture. Jaime, the book dealer, said to him as he pulled five fat volumes of history out of their hiding place beneath the counter: "You're right, Ignacio. And if you want to be sure of it, take these books. I'll wrap them up for you, just in case you should run into Commissioner Diéguez on one of those days when the guy, as your father would call him, happens to be in a bad humor. You can pay me by installments whenever you wish, as usual."

Love and springtime—Jorge de Batlle and Chelo Rosselló were married, as expected. Dr. Andújar gave the boy the final push by convincing him that in addition to a wife who would take care of him, he needed children to make him feel that not everything had come to an end.

"God has placed Chelo in your path. Besides being an intelligent girl, she's a very good one. Now you listen to me. Believe me."

"Yes, Doctor."

"Go on, then. Get your papers, and then to the altar with you." No sooner said than done. Chelo's brother, Miguel Rosselló, was dumbfounded and raised an absurd objection: "What am I going to do all alone in the apartment?" Chelo told him: "Get married, too."

The girls in the Feminine Section took it upon themselves to make Chelo's wedding dress, a gown that resembled to some degree the one her sister Antonia, now entered upon her novitiate, would wear on the day she took her vows.

The wedding was held in the Church of San Félix. Many lilies and many lights decorated the altar, but there was no wedding banquet in view of Dr. Rosselló's situation and the striped garb he was wearing in the penitentiary.

As they left the church, a moving scene took place, not unlike the one at the wedding of Pilar and Mateo. The bride and groom went to the cemetery to lay the wedding bouquet on the tomb of Jorge's parents and brothers and sisters who had been murdered by Cosme Vila.

The young couple's honeymoon trip was modest. In spite of Jorge's cries of "I want to live," he was in no condition to tour monasteries or go to Pamplona, or even to Javier's Castle. They bought a second-hand Citroën and stopped at some places in the province: the Costa Brava, the Lake of Bañólas, the Baths of Caldas de Malavella.

It turned out that Jorge owned farms and acres of land everywhere. Suddenly, he would stop the car and, pointing out a vegetable patch, a farmhouse, and some trees, would say to Chelo: "This is ours." Or: "Do you see that family? They're our tenant farmers." If the tenants recognized "Don Jorge's son," they would come to greet them, cap in hand.

Chelo kept thinking: "What are we going to do with so much money?" She would rather have been poor and be sure that Jorge would not suffer another crisis like the one he had just passed through.

"Are you happy, Jorge?"

"I am. Thanks to you and Dr. Andújar."

"Think about our children, too. They'll be a great inspiration, won't they?"

"Maybe. But I'm afraid that one of them might be born defective."

"Why do you say that?"

"I've suffered so much!"

"I know that, darling. But we're starting a new life now."

When they came home from their short journey, they settled down in a flat on the Calle de Ciudadanos, and the first thing Jorge did was to decorate it with a reproduction of his family tree, the original of which El Responsable had destroyed one day.

"No suits of armor, please," Chelo begged.

"Of course not, girl."

Dr. Andújar advised Chelo according to his usual therapy to keep Jorge busy with something besides the Veterans' Administration, where he had very little work to do.

Chelo thought she had found a solution to the problem. "He can take care of his farms, Doctor. Maybe that doesn't sound like much, but I've watched Jorge. He seems like another person in the country. He touches the trees, studies the haystacks, takes an interest in the cultivated fields. He seems to feel the earth. And he appears to like animals, too, especially horses. Don't you think we might be able to focus him on those things?"

"Of course! Nothing could be better for him, Chelo. And with a car, it will be easy for you."

Chelo added: "Besides, he himself has said that the living conditions of the tenant farmers must be improved. Actually some of them are having a very hard time. The way they live! It's like the Middle Ages. Just think of hearing Jorge talk like that! It seems like a miracle."

Dr. Andújar never rejected the word "miracle." He accepted it as real. In the practice of his profession he had witnessed so many transformations of one kind or another, upward or downward, that in the end he had inverted the old saying: "Strike with the mace," he would say, "and pray to God."

"Maybe you'll end up by establishing a model farm, Chelo."

Chelo stared at the Doctor. "How strange that you should say that!"

"Why?"

"Because Jorge has mentioned that possibility to Alfonso Estrada."

"To Alfonso Estrada?"

"Yes. Alfonso's father was a veterinarian, although he never worked at it. And it seems it was his aspiration to own a farm."

"Ah, I see." The Doctor went on to say: "All right, Chelo, tell me, has Jorge shown any signs of aggressiveness?"

"Oh! That's history now." Chelo paused. "The only people who still seem to make him nervous are the Costa brothers."

Springtime and love. A new home had taken shape in Gerona. And Marta and her Feminine Section had lost another of their mainstays.

Dr. Chaos and Solita were also feeling the effects of the lengthening days. María del Mar had not been mistaken in saying to her women friends that this was an idyl.

Naturally, Solita had fallen in love with the Doctor. Several factors had entered into that. First, her age. Solita was approaching thirty, and the idea of being a spinster held no appeal for her. Second, the surgeon's professional skill. What had been admiration in the beginning had now become a fervent desire on Solita's part to collaborate. Third, pity. Solita pitied that man from the bottom of her heart because Nature had treated him so capriciously, so shabbily, that he had no consolation but the faithfulness of his dog, Goering.

As for the Doctor, he used auto-suggestion to come to the same conclusion with regard to his feelings for Solita. This was the first time he had ever been able to carry on a long conversation with a woman without getting bored and the first time he did not experience a physical uneasiness and discomfort when he felt a woman's eyes on him, looking at him with love.

The trial period for both had been rather long. The mornings, which Dr. Chaos spent at the hospital, seemed endless to Solita; and like Pilar with Mateo, she found a hundred excuses for telephoning him. Dr. Chaos felt precisely the same when he closed the door of his hotel room at the end of the day. He felt cold to his very bones; he missed the thing that everyone called "home."

Dr. Chaos became aware that he had been cured of his hemorrhoids as if by witchcraft. Dr. Andújar heard about this with a smile, because he believed that the hemorrhoids from which many pederasts suffered were a substitute for the monthly periods of a woman, an experience that such men desired.

Little by little the conversations between the surgeon and the nurse began to take on an intimate character. The course of those colloquies was always the same: a commentary on the latest operation; a rapid review of previous surgery, with more or less philosophical overtones; and finally, a duet on the pleasure that two people could find if they had the good luck to work together so closely, as he and she did.

"I don't know what I'd do without you, Solita."

"I'd be lost without you, Doctor."

"Sometimes while I'm operating you hand me the right instrument without my having to ask you for it."

"I know my trade, doctor."

"Is that all it is?"

"Well, sometimes I can read your mind perhaps. Even though you have your mask on."

Dr. Chaos laughed heartily. When had he ever laughed so often and so heartily? That kind of outburst was something new, and certainly it was thrilling.

Pity, compassion, had played an important role in Solita's attitude. She had realized that the Doctor lacked the crutches he needed to be able to go on with resignation. He never talked about his family. Did he even have a family? He never talked about his friends, except Dr. Andújar. What saved him was his sense of irony and being able to crack his knuckles from time to time. If only he had been a religious man! But on that subject the doctor was like a wall.

"Don't you understand, Solita, that it's man who created God because he felt helpless, not the other way around. To call upon a Supreme Being to intervene in our affairs is like giving oneself an anti-tetanus shot."

This was the point of intellectual friction between them. Divinity was the source of discussions that went on for hours and hours as winter came and went and spring was born. For Solita was a believer. If she had not been, how could she have dreamed for a moment that a woman's love could cure Dr. Chaos of hemorrhoids? She would have acknowledged herself beaten beforehand and would have stayed quietly at home, waiting for the arrival of her father, Don Oscar Pinel, and then would have played the game of naval battles with him, the Administrator of Price Control's favorite game.

"Don't be so sure, doctor. Unless one believes in God, he must believe in the Absurd. And that would prove equally incomprehensible and much less comforting."

"There I agree with you. I said the same thing to Manolo and Esther one time. What wouldn't I give to be able to believe that the little birds go into the lonely hermitages on some feast days to sing songs to the Virgin?"

Poetry. Dr. Chaos maintained that religious feeling was half poetry, half vital need. That was why all religions, from the most primitive to the most civilized, had similar legends, similar liturgies, even similar robes of office. And that was why, in so far as they were able, they had blocked the advance of science: to ward off a feeling that their pillars were crumbling at the base.

"All you need to do is open a history book, Solita. For centuries, the Bible served as the dike against which minds like those of Copernicus or Galileo knocked themselves out. No, no! Anathema! Into the fire with it! It doesn't figure in the Sacred Scriptures."

"Dr. Chaos, would you like me to make you a cup of coffee?"

"Yes. Why not? Solita, where were we? Oh, yes! You know that for years and years the Church was against letting us doctors perform autopsies. If the body was cut up, of course the resurrection of the flesh was bound to be more difficult later."

"How much sugar would you like, Doctor? Two lumps, as usual?"

"Yes, the usual. But why in hell do you keep interrupting me? Are you bored with what I'm saying?"

"No, I'm very much interested. But isn't it possible to talk about autopsies and sugar in the same breath?"

Dr. Chaos took a sip of coffee. "Yes, of course."

Dr. Chaos also liked to dazzle his listener, a woman who abstained from using perfume. The first firm step was taken about the middle of May in connection with an analysis ordered by the police on the corpse of an old man who, it was suspected, had died of poison. The body had been exhumed; it looked nauseating. In contrast, outdoors the sun was shining that afternoon, a sun that seemed to purify the world and justify the simulated death of the wolves.

"My dear friend," the Doctor said to Solita as he was manipulating some test tubes, "do you know what happened to a certain Francisco Redi of Florence in the seventeenth century?"

Solita answered him naturally. "Yes, I think so. He observed under the microscope that some maggots on raw meat had come from eggs deposited by flies. And because the Bible said that it was bees that came out of the body of a dead lion, well, they tried him for heresy."

"Precisely! Do you think that can be forgiven?" Dr. Chaos suddenly changed expression. "But how can a woman possibly know such things?"

"Oh, Doctor! Women—when something interests us, we're capable of studying anything whatsoever. Even such things as raw meat."

Solita had spoken the phrase "when something interests us" with full intent, stressing it with unusual feeling. Dr. Chaos was disconcerted. But he concealed it. And as he asked her for his note pad to write his report on the poor old man, supposedly poisoned, he went on talking. He said that the religion of Islam was the only one which, after a period of intolerance even bloodier than the most bigoted days of Christianity, had come in the end to respect the knowledge acquired by the ancients. The Arabs built astronomical observatories in Cairo, Damascus, and Antioch. And for a long time they were the only people in the field of medicine who made use of the teachings of Hippocrates, Celsus, and Galen. Christianity? Not a flicker! At the height of the Middle Ages, the monks were still drawing outlandish maps on which Jerusalem occupied the center of the earth and the world.

"I believe in evolution, do you understand that, Solita? Nature is in constant evolution. What we don't know is whither it's evolving."

Solita knew that full well. That was why she listened so attentively to Dr. Chaos. That was also why, as soon as he had completed his report for the police—the old man had died of natural causes—she sat down close beside him, closer than usual, and said: "I believe we're evolving, too, Doctor. I'm in complete agreement with you on that. And let me tell you one thing! If we're not evolving more quickly, it's because you don't want to!"

Dr. Chaos was taken aback. He did not know what had happened. Something similar to what occurred at the Hotel Miramar in Blanes the preceding summer. Except that this time the object of his excitement was not a young waiter, but Solita.

He stared at his nurse's lips, then gave her a kiss. A real kiss, into which he put his whole self. The Doctor sensed that many things were at stake at that moment. Perhaps that was why he made an awkward movement of his arm and one of the test tubes lying on the laboratory table fell on the floor.

Solita had also put innumerable hopes into that kiss. Her heart was beating so hard that she thought she would faint.

Congratulations! Dr. Chaos did not feel repelled. He forgot his whole past and lived that moment, a long slow moment, with growing joy. Could it be possible? He felt like giving thanks to God like any other primitive, helpless creature. When he and Solita drew apart, he felt as if he had been dreaming and he seemed to hear Goering's bark coming from the courtyard of the clinic.

That was all for that afternoon. But it was enough, for the moment. Solita stammered: "Oh, Doctor..." He got up like a drunken man, wondering whether Solita had drugged him.

The news flew like dust into Dr. Andújar's consultation room.

"Well, we're getting on, friend Chaos! I congratulate you. We can't shout victory, but we're getting on!"

That was the point of departure. After that, Dr. Chaos contrived to be alone with his nurse every afternoon. She still refrained from using perfume and lipstick. And as soon as his work would permit, and always at the end of a lively conversation that ever seemed to move toward the need for having a companion, the surgeon would pull Solita to himself and kiss her. Now as he kissed her he would bury his hands, the hands of an artist with the scalpel, in Solita's hair, and would even run them over her neck and shoulders. The Doctor discovered that he preferred to kiss her as they were both standing. Solita did not care. Her love for that man, constantly at war with himself, was growing with each caress, and was curing her of many old complexes against which the naval battles she fought with her father had never been of any use. "I must have something," she said to herself, "if I've managed to make a man like Dr. Chaos kiss me and caress my shoulders." Solita wished that her nurse's uniforms had a lower neck, but the Doctor never tried to touch her breasts.

The second step was taken timidly and tentatively. But it, too, was enough to raise a whirlwind of happy auguries in Dr. Andújar's office.

"You must admit that all this used to be unthinkable, dear Chaos. Now you must take these little tablets, too. Meanwhile tell me this. How does Solita rate with you in the spiritual field?"

Dr. Chaos, who looked transfigured, was enjoying a springtime that the brown grass had not yet dreamed of.

"I'm crazy about her," he replied. "I love her. I love her with all my soul."

"Did you say soul? Do my ears deceive me?"

"Well, why shouldn't I? Solita assures me we have souls. So..."

Dr. Andújar glimpsed the far-off possibility that his friend Chaos—how fond he was of the man, how tender he felt toward him—might be led by his passion to become engaged and even marry. "That would be the solution, as I've told you so many times. Probably, you'll still feel shaken up at the sight of another man, Rogelio, for instance. And you may slip. But that's no reason for ceasing to love Solita and being with her. Especially if you should have a son."

The idea of having a son, which Dr. Andújar had put before him from the beginning, now began to haunt Dr. Chaos. Something was happening to him now that had never happened before: he would see a little boy on the street and become absorbed in watching him, thinking that he might be his own. He liked to be present when school let out. Warning Voice would have attributed it to an increase in his perversion, but that was not the case. Chance proved that to him. A girl of nine, the daughter of the Syndicate Delegate, Comrade Arjona, entered the clinic to have her tonsils removed. Dr. Chaos immediately felt drawn to her. He felt impelled to bring her toys and kiss her on the forehead. "When I was a child, I'd have scratched her," he thought.

The situation reached the point where it could not go on much longer as it was. Dr. Chaos thought of Solita day and night, and she of him. In the clinic, the anesthetist Carrera watched them with stupefaction out of the corner of his eye. Unlike Dr. Andújar, the anesthetist did not believe in miracles.

"Solita, why don't we have dinner together one of these days? Saturday, for instance? Shall we?"

"Where, Doctor?"

"In my hotel."

"In your hotel?"

"Yes. I've been thinking about it at great length. Let's celebrate some anniversary or other. Say the day when the big bell was hung in the Cathedral."

Solita thought it over. "All right. Why not?"

The dinner was intimate, unmarred by any untoward event except for the astonishment of the hotel staff at seeing Dr. Chaos with a woman as his guest.

The Doctor started off by talking about surgery. He declared that except for the skull trepanations practiced by the Egyptians long before Christ, surgery had remained stagnant for thousands of years, not taking a definitive step forward until the middle of the nineteenth century, with the discovery first of anesthesia and later of antisepsis. By the second course, however, Dr. Chaos had turned sentimental; he drank a toast to his science or art, thanks to which they had met each other and were sitting opposite each other that night. By the time coffee was served, Solita was completely happy as she picked up the sugar bowl and asked Dr. Chaos: "Two lumps as usual, Doctor?"

Only the definitive step was still to be taken: confronting society. But it was taken, too. That occurred in connection with the first Congress of Spanish Surgery, held in Barcelona early in June. Dr. Chaos was asked to read a paper and give a demonstration. Master and pupil worked almost unceasingly for a week to prepare for that event. And the night before it, Dr. Chaos said to Solita: "You must come to Barcelona with me. I'll need you."

Solita heard the proposal with a shiver along her spine. She passed her hands across her tired eyes and replied: "Very well. I'll speak to my father and I'll go with you."

The trip along the highway in the Doctor's car was harmonious; the two people themselves, their ideas, and the landscape around them were all in tune.

The paper that the Doctor read to the Congress, before more than a hundred colleagues, also struck the right note, as did his performance of a tracheotomy. As Solita handed him his instruments, she was reading his thoughts—in spite of the mask.

Dr. Chaos and Solita were staying at the same hotel, the Majestic on the Paseo de Gracia, where Dr. Relken had stayed in times gone by, where in the hotel dining room he had said to Julio García: "My brain repays me."

As they were having dinner on the third night, after a tense clinical day, this time behind closed doors, Dr. Chaos—what had happened to him?—made no reference at all either to the Inquisition or to the differences between the operating techniques in Madrid and Barcelona. He ate voraciously, as though he had just walked all the way from the ghetto in Warsaw. And he drank red wine from Perelada, because he said its taste reminded him of Gerona and the tramontane wind from the Ampurdán, where the vineyards stretched out in rows.

Solita had rouged her cheeks. Her operating-room pallor had vanished. She was wearing powder, that clever girl, wasn't she? And she was smoking, something unusual for her, and asking for a glass of cognac.

At midnight the elevator carried them to the third floor, where they had their respective rooms. And when they found themselves in the corridor, with huge keys in their hands, they hardly needed to say a word. Dr. Chaos looked into Solita's eyes, which were shining like stars, then the girl started to walk on.

He followed her and they both went into the girl's room.

The change was startling. While Solita was taking off her clothes, Dr. Chaos was following suit while the dim lights in the room seemed to hum a soothing little song. But as soon as the two bodies touched under the sheets,

Dr. Chaos shuddered violently, then went into an ecstatic state which robbed him of the power to move.

The man was concentrating his whole attention, doing the impossible to command his mind, to feel something. To demonstrate to Solita that he was not only a man, but her man, who would love her and with whom he would share the clinic and break bread, then and forever.

All in vain. Dr. Chaos felt a kind of asphyxiation, and his hands, inert on Solita's warm skin, were the picture of anguish and impotence.

Solita turned on her stomach, buried her face in the pillow and pounded it with her fists as she burst into disconsolate tears. Dr. Chaos longed to die. Old contours, of men, lashed his mind. A glacial indifference pervaded him. He loathed himself. He loathed Solita. He loathed the world.

He did not dare to ask forgiveness. He jumped out of the bed intending to take a shower. But he gave up that idea and dressed himself quietly in a state of extreme prostration. He felt utterly exhausted. He was not the man who had performed a tracheotomy the day before in view of a hundred colleagues, with fascinatingly rapid reflexes.

After he was dressed, he managed to stammer: "Forgive…"

He left Solita's room. In the corridor of the hotel there were ashtrays and shoes in front of some of the doors. Men's and women's shoes, lined up neatly. God, what a horrible feeling!

He spent a sleepless night, unable to think coherently. Nothing mattered to him. Why had Dr. Andújar, his friend, talked him into placing himself in such a situation? Why hadn't he left him in peace with his deviation? Some English prints had been hung in his room. They depicted race horses, vigorous animals with stylized lines. Highly bred horses. Goering, sleeping peacefully at the foot of the bed, was a purebred, too.

He thought about castration. Why not? Long ago in Rome the popes had had young boy singers castrated so that they would not lose their childish voices. That would end his torture once and for all. Then he would know what to expect. And Commissioner Diéguez could tear up his record.

He got up at daybreak, composed a note to Solita, a very terse message, and slipped it under the door of her room. Then he went downstairs, paid the desk clerk, and returned to Gerona alone in his car. Goering seemed to feel cold at that hour and refused to put his head out the window. The telegraph poles seemed like fingers pointing angrily at heaven. From time to time he read a slogan: "No hearth without a fire, no Spaniard without bread."

Once in Gerona, Dr. Chaos refrained from telephoning Dr. Andújar or going to see him. He did not want even to go to the hospital. The idea of the nuns greeting him with "Good morning, Doctor" horrified him. He went straight to his hotel and flung himself onto his own bed, which had witnessed so many unconfessable orgies. He slept until lunchtime.

THE next day, after listening lengthily to Dr. Chaos, Dr. Andújar said to him: "Very well, then. It's too soon to draw any conclusions. The only thing I ask of you for the time being is please to give me Solita's home telephone number."

FIFTY-FOUR

PAZ Alvear, Carlota's Miss Gerona, often thought of her dead mother, but not with anguish. Her mother had been a gray creature, as wrinkled as parchment, and she had left few traces behind her, except on little Manuel, who went to the cemetery from time to time. Paz did not want to be cruel, but the times she missed her mother most were when she herself had to cook and clean house. She had given her mother's few clothes to a half-paralyzed neighbor woman and had thrown her comb, her toothbrush, and her other personal articles into the garbage can. Goal, the household mascot, had grown accustomed to sleeping on the bed that had been "Aunt Conchi's."

Paz had two problems: Manuel and Pachín.

Manuel had fallen hopelessly into Mosén Alberto's clutches. Paz did everything she could to break the wall between them, but in vain. She still railed at the Church for permitting her father's death in Burgos. She still pried into and criticized the textbooks her brother brought home in his schoolbag and even showed him an old catechism lent her by Jaime, edited in Gerona during the War of Independence, which said categorically: "Who are the French?" "Ancient Christians and modern heretics." "Is it a sin to kill a Frenchman?" "No, Father; it is a meritorious act to free our country from violent oppressors."

"Do you understand that, you stupid kid? The priests have always been like that. Look at the date: 1808! A century and a half has gone by, and they're still the same."

She could do nothing as long as Mosén Alberto exerted such a decisive influence over Manuel. Furthermore, the boy had begun to ponder certain things in the ever-enriched Diocesan Museum, especially as he studied the pictures that portrayed Christ. Christ's figure had pervaded him, slowly but more and more deeply. Manuel took communion once a week, without the knowledge of Paz. As he communicated, he felt there was something more than bread in the hosts made by the nuns. There were serenity, good thoughts, the desire to love his neighbor and to forgive. That bread was the assurance that everything did not end here below, as his sister claimed. This was the bread on which César was feeding for all eternity. Oh, of course César was another of Manuel's great "spiritual oppressors." He carried always in his schoolbag a photograph of his cousin which Carmen Elgazu had given him. And each time he looked at it, he thought that his sister must be wrong somehow. Or that, at the very least, her convictions were exaggerated. Paz knew that and thought: "Well, this is a fine state of affairs! I said it as a joke but it's going to turn out to be true—they'll end up by sticking the kid in the Seminary."

Pachín was the other problem worrying Paz. Pachín loved her more than ever. He said to her in every imaginable tone: "I couldn't live without you." But two threats to their love had emerged. One, Pachín would complete his military service in August, and his family lived in Asturias. Another, the Barcelona Football Club had stated publicly that it wanted to sign him up for the next season. Owing to his ability to hit the ball strongly with his head, he was the best goal-maker in the Second Division. A manager from the Barcelona club who had been searching the football fields of Spain said: "It's nonsense to say that boy would conk out in the Second Division. He's got the stuff to play in the international matches." International? The word pleased Paz because it was the title of the anthem she kept humming under her breath in the Diana Perfumery. But what would happen if Pachín were to sign up with the Barcelona football team? Either they would be married—although Pachín never mentioned marriage "because she was so young and it would not suit her to get fat"—or she would follow him. Otherwise it would be: "If I ever saw you before, I don't remember."

Pachín kept saying it was too soon to worry about it. "This is only May. I won't be discharged for three months. I won't make any decision that doesn't include you. What more can I say? But I have a right to better myself, haven't I? We'll find some solution."

Paz discovered that she was very jealous, something she could never have imagined. She was jealous not only of Pachín, but also of anything that concerned those she loved. Recently, for example, she had grown jealous of Adela after noticing one day that when Ignacio mentioned her, he showed a particular kind of excitement. "What can you see in that woman? You take off her girdle, but then you've got to leave on the run." Ignacio laughed, but not very hard, for a long time had gone by since he had been able to hold Adela in his arms, owing to the still active suspicions of Marcos.

On the other hand, the problem of the new flat she had been looking for was solved. The Agencia Gerunda, through Tower of Babel, found one for her on the Calle del Carmen; she would take possession of it in August. To be sure, Tower of Babel kept Paz longer than necessary in his office because the mere sight of Ignacio's cousin made him shake from head to foot. He drew out the problem as long as he could. "Come back Saturday—there'll surely be something." "Come by on Tuesday. Will you remember to do that?" Finally, Paz said to him with an impudent look: "That's enough, dear. The apartment is not for you."

She also carried out successfully her plan to increase her income, knowing that in so doing she was moving still farther away from the old slogans of the UGT. Aside from the fact that the Gerona Jazz Band was expanding its activities again with spring—every village was going to celebrate another of its Great Festivals—the girl found herself another job with a salary not to be despised. She became the model for Cefe, the painter of nudes, in response to the advertisements that he, like his colleagues, had had published in *Amanecer*.

"For God's sake!" the painter exclaimed when he saw Paz. "I didn't know a siren of this class existed in Gerona."

"That wouldn't be because I'd kept myself locked up in the house, would it?"

Their accord was complete, among other reasons because Cefe not only paid well, but also worked with only his art in mind. Paz realized that immediately, and grew to like the painter; she chatted with him pleasantly during the long sessions of posing.

Ceferino Borras—that was his full name—turned out to be an odd character. He had grown up in an orphanage. Now he was fifty years old; his wife had gone to France with one of the International Brigades at the end of the war. He had studied in the School of Fine Arts in Barcelona, and was exclusively a figure painter, specializing in women's portraits.

"During the dictatorship of Primo de Rivera," he told Paz, "I took pride in painting ladies with corsages of carnations, but later when your people came in the Popular Front, the business went to hell."

The current period was offering him new prospects. "Yes, yes, let the little countesses come to Gerona. Sooner or later they'll all pass through this studio."

He was working on nudes for the very reason that it was forbidden to exhibit such paintings; consequently, clandestine buyers had emerged, not disposed to haggle over his prices. His agreement with Paz had been binding; he would change the head so that no one would recognize her. "But that body—you have a delightful body, little girl. If only I'd met you twenty-five years ago! You wouldn't have got away from me." Paz laughed: "Cefe, those capers aren't for you!" "Alas, my dear Paz," the painter exclaimed, looking her over from head to foot with one eye closed and a thumb raised to measure her: "How can I deny that? Only one word occurs to me: Amen!"

Ceferino Borras wore a black Windsor tie in a butterfly bow. And his head of hair was worthy of being sculptured. He was an absentminded Bohemian, with a touch of the phony—a walking cliché. He did not like politics. He said that if the people in the garrisons would teach with paintbrushes instead of rifles, there would be no war in the air, on land, or on the sea. "And those Germans! I only hope they don't destroy a single statue in Greece on me! If they do, I'll join up with England and use my secret weapon: nonviolence."

Paz was learning a good deal from Cefe. He never grew tired of assuring her that it was best to hate no one and to keep a virginal vision of the world. "That's how one can live in peace and keep the wrinkles at bay for a long time. I don't like for you to be involved in those Red Relief jamborees, and furthermore I don't like you to classify people at first sight. Why do it? Don't you think everyone is what he is?"

"Don't you hate anyone, Cefe?" Paz asked.

"I? Whom should I hate? Hate is a waste of time. How about letting me see that chest? That's it! Imagine, I don't even hate the Cubists. Actually, I feel sorry for them, and that's all. Because, after all, as long as there are women like you, I'll be academic. Give me the academic any time!"

Sometimes Paz trembled at the thought that Pachín might find out that she was posing for Cefe. That was by no means the same thing as being a vocalist. When she had taken that up, Pachín had said to her: "Go ahead. You and I are our own bosses." But to appear naked in front of another man was something else, even though his name was Ceferino Borras! For the moment, however, there was no danger. Pachín was so sure of himself!

But Ignacio found out about it, she did not know how. And Ignacio got along very well with his cousin, so well that he never passed the Diana Perfumery without stopping to greet her through the window. He reproached her for her conduct.

"Don't you realize that Gerona is a city of Carlists and this could do you a lot of harm?"

"But no one knows!" Paz said in self-defense. "Unless you go around telling everyone."

"Don't be silly! But Gerona is like a small town."

Paz bit her tongue. "Sure, sure," she agreed. Then she thought of herself. "If Pachín finds out!"

This name caused an unexpected reaction in Ignacio. He shook his head in such a way that Paz saw he did not care much for her lover. She had suspected it at times because Ignacio never mentioned him, but now there was no room for doubt.

Ignacio spoke frankly to Paz on the subject. "How shall I put it? I scarcely know him. But I think you could aspire to something better."

Paz was so nettled that she exclaimed: "Better? What do you want? Should I look around for another Jorge Batlle?"

Ignacio tried to soothe her. He was fond of Paz, and it had never been his intention to hurt her. Quite the contrary. He explained himself, saying again what he had said before on innumerable occasions: what Paz ought to do was to associate with people who could raise her level. In other words, she ought to educate herself. Cultivate her intelligence, as she had cultivated her voice and her stage appearance with the Gerona Jazz Band. The girl made dreadful mistakes in spelling and certainly she did not know the name of the President of the United States.

"Do you think Pachín will solve all this for you? I saw him in the Montaña Bar yesterday. Sure, he's an athlete! But what else? Have you ever asked yourself what will become of him on the day he puts away his football shoes?"

Paz flew at him. "Puts away his football shoes? Well, now let me tell you something, dear boy! You didn't know, did you, that Barcelona wants to sign him up for the next season. Get wise to yourself for once! Besides, I love him, see? I love him, and that's all there is to it." After a pause, she added: "Please, Ignacio, let's not talk about changing partners. It's best to leave that subject alone, believe me."

This time Ignacio had to bite his tongue. "All right, dear girl. You win."

FIFTY-FIVE

BOTH the Governor and Mateo had heard rumors during their respective trips to Santander and San Sebastián to the effect that the reformist and revolutionary orientation of the Falange was arousing fears "in the highest circles" in Madrid. Suddenly, the rumors became fact: a readjustment was going on in the bosom of the Government. Changes in ministers, changes in the high command of the Party.

The shift of forces did not catch them unawares. One of the men most keenly alert to it was Comrade Salazar, an outstandingly brilliant member of the old Falange who advocated heart and soul that the trade unions should be a live organism, an authentic defender of the interests of the "producers." But Salazar had always found difficulties placed in his path and had been accused of demagoguery. For example, he had tried several times to replace the lazy Comrade Arjona in Gerona with the ebullient Montesinos of Valladolid. Montesinos was one of the lads who had led the resistance to the decree of Unification in the midst of the war, as a consequence of which he had seen the inside of a jail. Nevertheless, Montesinos had not gone to Gerona. For all the smoke from his outsized pipe, Comrade Salazar had never been given the necessary approval of many of his plans. And when he managed to bring together thousands and thousands of workers in Madrid on April 1, 1940, the anniversary of the end of the civil war, the spectacle was said to have provoked a violent reaction from the Minister of the Army.

In any case, the list of the members making up the new Government added up to great uncertainty for the Governor and Mateo, for if, on the one hand, the names of several men with scant enthusiasm for the social doctrine of the Movement were on it, two important portfolios—Labor and Agriculture—were assigned, on the other hand, to two irreproachable Falangists: José Antonio Girón and Miguel Primo de Rivera, José Antonio's brother.

The prospects looked still darker, or more propitious to the cabal, when

Salazar was dismissed from his post after having taken a trip to Germany some months earlier to study the Hitler labor organization in depth. (He adjudged it a model of its type.) Then to everyone's unbounded astonishment, Comrade Núñez Maza was also discharged, for having made public his disagreement with the shake-up in the cabinet.

Oddly enough, however, Salazar and Núñez Maza remained members of the National Council and each wrote a letter to Mateo in which he said that the only hope for the Party from that moment on, lay in "the good faith which would guide the action of Minister Serrano Súñer, President of the Political Junta" and "in the steps which the new Secretary General of the FET and the JONS, Comrade José Luis Arrese, might take," for "he would enjoy very broad powers through his office." Both of the dismissed Falangists believed that José Luis Arrese deserved their confidence, but they were afraid that in practice the Party's submissiveness to the Government would grow greater by the day "because Arrese felt such great admiration for the Caudillo that it was unimaginable for him to defend the Falangist program if it were to make any kind of attempt against national unity." For the moment, Arrese, a strong Catholic, came out with the following statement: First, "Life must be made spiritual"; second, "Spain must be made more Spanish"; and third, "Social justice must be implanted." Mateo's comment was: "Don't you think, my dear Governor, that the implantation of social justice ought to be rated first?"

In the free moments that Pilar left to Mateo—Pilar and his preparations for the June examinations, now that he had decided to enroll and complete his law course—he felt alarmed by the growing imbalance between the people who were getting rich with astounding ease and the needs of the poor and the lowly. According to reports that came to him, five banking groups controlled seventy percent of the industrial wealth of the country at that moment. Children everywhere made their First Communion with a display of luxury which "was beginning to look like Negrín's orgies." In Mateo's contacts with Ignacio, renewed since his wedding, he had been forced to admit that the economic life of the nation was flowing toward a closed, despotic capitalism, far removed from the first intentions. Manolo's father, Don José María Fontana, was in touch with all this daily. Anyone who could obtain a certain import permit or a monopoly on any product, or who could charter any kind of ship, could sometimes accumulate a fortune in a matter of hours. Furthermore, in view of the fact that by now it was obvious that the international conflict would go on for a long time, the premise might be stated thus: in the provinces it was very easy to imprison small-time black-marketeers or the stockholders of Tejero, Inc. But what about Madrid? Who would jail anyone in the official circles of Madrid?

As Mateo talked to the Governor, he came to the conclusion that it would be extremely naive to be surprised at what was happening. In fact, things could hardly be otherwise. As he had said so often, the Falange had risen too rapidly because of the war. There had not been sufficient time to give a large enough number of men the political training they would need in order to hold the key positions with the essential authority and be able to put on a certain amount of pressure. Neither would it be wise to cast aside those reflections by Professor Civil concerning the extreme youth of certain men in command: "The inevitable has happened: a lack of experience."

The Governor agreed with the thesis of his intimate friend and comrade.

"You're quite right. But what can we do, my dear Mateo? It's easier to turn out a good cavalry colonel like my brother, or a good businessman, than a good provincial leader or a good governor. Politics is an abstract art. How can anyone know whether he's done the right thing? And our people are a difficult breed! Governing them is the work of years and of tradition. For example, when I gave Commissioner Diéguez orders to go all out, I thought I'd hit the bull's eye. Now, frankly, I don't know what to think. Probably, we've made a good many mistakes, and one must suppose that the same thing has happened on the upper levels nationally."

Silence fell between the two men, like the silence of the pupils of the Grupo Escolar San Narciso when Mosén Obiols closed the shutters and ordered them to examine their consciences.

"On the other hand," the Governor went on, "perhaps José Luis Arrese is right and what matters more than anything else under the circumstances is to preserve the 'national unity' that cost us so many lives. Would it be advisable to rupture that in Gerona, for example? Would it be advisable for me, in the name of the yokes and arrows, to confront General Sánchez Bravo openly for failing to share our uneasiness about society? Or for me to challenge the Bishop, Notary Noguer, or our dear Mayor? The Reds fell into that trap, and the result was a catastrophe. If you think it all over, it's no one's fault, not Franco's, nor Serrano Súñer's, nor Salazar's or Núñez Maza's, nor our own that this terrible, endless war broke out so soon after we'd won our war. So all in all, I consider that right now it's our duty to be patient."

Everything the Governor said rang with genuine discouragement. Yet, in a sense, his might be the voice of that prudence which María del Mar always praised in Franco, a trait that might perhaps explain satisfactorily the combination the Caudillo had just put together in the highest circles: to broaden and reinforce the work of the Falange, yet to keep it in a single hand. To permit some people to get rich, but avoid dismemberment. Until the conflict across the world should come to an end, Spain would not have to beg the British on bended knee for navicerts, for certainly they were squeezing the Spanish ships on the Atlantic into a tight circle—not only those carrying combustibles from the Caribbean, but even those bringing food supplies from Brazil or Argentina—lest they fall into enemy hands.

The Governor and Mateo could not look each other in the eye. Mateo's crisp hair seemed to have wilted, and Comrade Dávila's black glasses looked like two mourning rings. The silence grew so heavy that both men realized that it could not go on. Wasn't it their motto to keep up their courage through any adversity? Hadn't they gone through even more difficult moments during the war? "Zamora wasn't won in an hour." But how could something as serious and far-reaching as the national revolution have been won in such a short time? José Antonio had known in advance that it could not.

José Antonio—he was the man they needed, the key man who had left them because the fates and the rapid tempo of the Spanish war machine had willed it so. If José Antonio had survived the war, everything would have followed another course. He was young, too; but he had been tempered from childhood, and he was already a tradition. "His word was reliable. He had moral authority. What a pity there's no telephone to call the dead."

The Governor had used this phrase several times in his speeches, and now it had the virtue of forcing Comrade Dávila to get hold of himself. In any event, it was his duty to do so. He had the advantage of several years over Mateo, and he could not permit the younger man to become discouraged, especially now that his wife was expecting a child.

"Mateo, do you think we might be overdramatizing the situation?"

Mateo sighed and raised his eyes. How strange! He seemed to have tears in them. But he managed an unexpected smile that mingled sadness and sudden hope. In any case, it aroused a wave of affection in Comrade Dávila. The Governor kept talking, moving the conversation into a path apart from the previous one.

"How old are you, Mateo?"

Mateo shrugged. "I'm going on twenty-three."

The Governor stared at the ceiling as though adding figures.

"So, then, you started with the Falange at seventeen."

"About that."

"A mere kid."

The Governor glanced involuntarily at the picture of his wife and children which presided over his desk. Mateo anticipated his next remark. "Yes, I was a little older than Pablito."

The Governor seemed touched. "Do you know this is the first time I ever realized what that must have meant?"

Mateo shrugged his shoulders again. He did not know what to say.

"Honestly," the Governor went on, "you belong to a heroic generation. You gave up everything—I mean you gave up your youth."

Mateo protested: "Yours is the more meritorious. You went to the front a married man and the father of a family."

"Okay, okay, but we'd lived. We'd had the time to do the crazy wonderful things adolescents do."

"Tchah! What crazy things?"

"Everything! Don't you see? At the age when you came to Gerona with a patriotic program and a blue shirt, I was in Santander spending my time buying ice cream and chasing all the servant girls who came within gunshot of me."

Mateo laughed. "To be honest," he admitted, "I can't deny that I envy you a little. Yes, sometimes I'm aware that I needed to have lived a few years like that." Mateo took out his cigarettes and lighter. "Ice cream and servant girls! Not a bad idea!"

The Governor laughed, too. "Anyhow, your sacrifice is none the less fine. Actually, I'm the one who ought to envy you."

"Well, all right!" Mateo lighted his cigarette. "Things are as they are. And if I had it to do all over, I'd do the same thing."

The men looked at each other with a strong feeling of brotherhood. They felt closely united. Changes in ministries, dismissals, seemed far away or had become mere incidents in the mission they had taken on themselves.

"So we agree, then. We'll go on with the struggle?"

"And how!" Mateo exclaimed. "More now than ever! Face to the sun, and the new shirt."

Comrade Dávila rose to his feet. "It's obvious to me that we have no alternative."

Mateo, who remained seated, concluded: "Well, anyhow, it's just too bad we can't call José Antonio on the telephone!"

FIFTY-SIX

SO many things had happened by the time the calendar marked the arrival of summer officially that *Amanecer* would have had to double the number of its pages to cover them adequately. But that was out of the question, for paper was growing scarcer by the day and poorer in quality, so poor that it was difficult to read the daily news. Warning Voice was in despair, for he believed that a poorly printed paper had a negative effect on the reader's morale and gave him an unpleasant feeling of poverty.

Nevertheless, the people of Gerona were informed, in one way or another, of everything that was happening on the local, national, and international scenes. Unless a bolt of lightning were to strike some morning and halt the march of the world, curiosity would remain keen, except in people like the painter Ceferino Borras and the anesthetist Carreras in the Chaos Clinic, both with objectives polarized around either professional concerns or very concrete and circumscribed personal ones.

Gerona learned of the short visit made to the city by the fifty girls of the Hitler Jugend who came to Spain at the special invitation of the Feminine Section. Their strong, healthy look caught the eye and could not fail to evoke remarks of all kinds. Marta did everything possible to wait on them; she treated them to a showing of several documentary films in the Municipal Theater on the rebuilding of roads, followed by a performance of folk dances under the direction of Maestro Quintana, director of the Cobla Gerona. A reception was held in their honor at the Town Hall, and several excursions were organized to spots typical of the region, to the accompaniment of explanations abstracted from Mosén Alberto's columns. The German consul, Paul Gunther, sometimes acted as interpreter, and not infrequently as he was talking, a somewhat scornful smile played around the lips of the German girls.

Of course, Marta could not help feeling displeased by the air of superiority which marked the behavior of her Nazi comrades, the displeasure she had experienced before when she had been in Berlin and expected to salute the statue of the naked German man with upraised arm. Yet it was difficult to shake off the impression of force which emanated from those girls of the Aryan race, which Himmler talked about like a mystic. Later, Marta said to her brother, José Luis: "Really, from the physical point of view, our race is inferior to theirs. Comrade Pascual, from Olot, who goes through the villages preaching hygiene, couldn't help gaping at them." One item was revealing: the first thing the fifty girls asked for when they arrived in Gerona was a shower, and the next thing they did was to squeeze three lemons apiece and drink the juice.

On May 12, the Nordic race surprised the Gerundians again. Rudolf Hess, Hitler's right-hand man, who, according to rumor was slated to be the Führer's successor as supreme head of the Third Reich, fled from Germany by airplane and parachuted down near Glasgow, Scotland. At first no one believed the news, but before long the British authorities confirmed it in full. The airplane was a Messerschmidt 110, which broke up on the ground, and the fugitive was really Rudolf Hess, who, it seemed, wanted his country to reach a détente with England.

The explanations issued from Berlin convinced no one. They were to the effect that for a long time Rudolf Hess had suffered from a mental illness that had been kept secret through inexcusable prudence. The event caused general stupefaction. Manolo and Esther exaggerated its importance. They believed that it meant that something deep-seated and unknown was falling apart inside the German machine. "What if Hess had been sent on a special mission?" Unfortunately, Mr. Edward Collins, the British consul, was still smiling the same unvarying little smile as he left his hotel. So, then, the incident had its own intrinsic importance, but would have no influence at all on the future of the war. It did demonstrate, however, that fissures could open in "the highest circles" of Germany, too. Professor Civil's summary was: "If Hess is in his right mind, he made a serious decision; and if he's really crazy, that's worse yet. What chief of state would choose a madman as his most trusted lieutenant?"

Soon after that, the battleship *Bismarck*, which had recently sunk the British heavy cruiser *Hood*, was surrounded and put out of action as an unexpected act of reprisal on the part of the British fleet. Another blow to Germany's prestige. "So what?" ventured the Madrilenian Herreros in Dámaso's barbershop. "Does that mean that the captain of the *Bismarck* fled to England too and provided the British Navy with the information it needed?" Silvia, the manicurist who always kept her knees together, asked, as she was trimming Padrosa's fingernails: "Have we got a battleship like that *Bismarck* in Spain?"

Padrosa answered: "Not in your wildest dreams, my queen. But if you'll agree to marry me, I'll get one for you."

The course of events was still following a cycle, however. The news unfavorable to Germany stopped there, for the moment. On May 21, the Führer's Army dropped thousands of paratroopers on the island of Crete, like a gigantic magnification of Rudolf Hess's landing, and conquered it within a few weeks, thus forcing the English to seek sanctuary in Africa. The operation was a miracle of strategy with a touch of elegance. At any rate that was General Sánchez Bravo's view of it. "Just think," he said to Captains Arias and Sandoval as they stood in front of a map of the Greek island: "Hitler used his secret weapon, the paratroopers, for the first time in Norway; now in Crete he uses the second: gliders. Each Junker carried three gliders fastened to its tail and dropped the gliders containing the soldiers at the right moment on the previously suggested point. The English stood there with their mouths open. Of course! In short, gentlemen, another Dunkirk for his Majesty the King. And things go in threes."

But no stopping point had been reached yet. On the Mediterranean coast of Africa, Hitler's army astonished the world again, thanks to General Rommel, who was more than justifying the aura beginning to surround his name. Actually, the so-called Afrika Korps under his command had been sent there to salvage the prestige of the *Imperium Romanum*, as in Albania and Greece; however sweetly the name might ring in Count Ciano's ears, however ardently the legionnaire Salvatore might fling himself into the fight, the Italian forces had not succeeded in advancing an inch. The British had won the battle of the desert against the Italians by the audacious use of tanks, which, contrary to the estimate of many technicians, had demonstrated that they could maneuver perfectly in African temperatures. But Rommel paid them back in their own coin. Within a short space of time, his motorized vehicles cut a swath seven hundred kilometers eastward, also riding out repeated sandstorms. He conquered Mara el Bregha and later Agedab and Benghazi. Benghazi! General Wavell's chagrin was boundless, for England had proclaimed him a hero after his victory over the Italians. And the discovery that Rommel had some weak units to work with did nothing to lessen his chagrin. At least half of the German vehicles were ordinary automobiles upon which the General had had some *papier-mâché* superstructures mounted to make them look like tanks. This stratagem deceived the British reconnaissance fliers. General Wavell was humiliated, but he had to retreat again. He withdrew another three hundred kilometers, as far as the Mechilli fort, where Rommel seized an enormous amount of booty which permitted him to encircle Tobruk, take Bardia, and cross the Egyptian frontier through Sollum.

That exploit was so brilliant that the name of Rommel became a legend in the belligerent countries. Even the English radio was ungrudging in its praise of the German general, and the press correspondents reported: "Rommel flew ahead of his troops in a helicopter, landed, and gave the appropriate orders. He could put vehicles that had lost their way back on the right track and force all his mobile units to move as rapidly as possible. When the terrible wind called the *khamsin* was blowing, some of the soldiers protected themselves with gas masks, but even so they vomited. The light in the desert was yellowish, ghostly, a substitute for daylight. But Rommel kept advancing."

During those weeks the pupils in the high schools of Gerona talked about Rommel much as the Russians talked in their schools about El Campesino, "the Spanish hero." Perhaps the allure of the scene of operations had something to do with it—the desert, always a fascinating word that called up in the minds of the little boys visions of camels, dunes, and Bedouins. Miguel Rosselló, who was able to measure the difficulties hampering operations on the terrain over which the motorized vehicles were operating, sang Rommel's praises in *Amanecer.* He felt certain that General Wavell would have to retreat to the Suez Canal, whence the title of his article—"The Flight into Egypt"—which was appreciated for its irony.

MEANWHILE, battles were being won on the national scene too. An accord between the Spanish Government and the Holy See was signed in Madrid on June 8. Ramón Serrano Súñer, the Minister of Foreign Affairs, signed for Spain, and Monsignor Cicognani, as nuncio of His Holiness, for the Vatican. The agreement established, among other things, the procedures to be followed in appointing on a permanent basis archbishops, bishops, apostolic administrators, and so on. The official communique contained the information that further negotiations would lead to the signing of a new concordat, in expectation of which "the exclusive religion of the Spanish nation must be the Catholic, apostolic, and Roman religion."

The Bishop of Gerona, Dr. Gregorio Lascasas, was overjoyed at this agreement; it was one of his major gratifications since the termination of the civil war because it would reinforce to the maximum the authority of the Spanish prelates. He poured out his satisfaction to Agustín Lago, whom he called in at least once a month in order to keep himself abreast of the progress in the schools.

"We're more than lucky, my son. A new concordat is on its way. You know very well that the thing that's most important for Spain is to prevent the introduction of non-Catholic beliefs. And you may be sure that, given the characteristics of the belligerent countries in this war, we're exposing ourselves to an attempt to implant new doctrines here, regardless of who wins. Now the Spanish bishops will be equipped with enough legal power to be able to oppose that! And undoubtedly the Army will support us again. That's important. I may tell you in confidence, dear friend Agustín Lago, that the little nuns in the Palace served me a glass of champagne at lunchtime."

Agustín Lago felt somewhat disconcerted. A monolithic faith like that of Dr. Gregorio Lascasas was a certain guarantee of incorruptibility, but in a sense it was contrary to the basic postulates of ecumenicism and personal liberty that the Opus Dei was defending. He could not doubt, however, that Dr. Gregorio Lascasas would be a willing martyr at any moment to defend his position. That was bound to inspire respect, all misgivings notwithstanding.

"My Lord," Agustín managed to answer with his usual discretion, "I, too, am delighted with the news of the accord. What a pity there are no little nuns in my pension whom I could ask for a small glass of champagne."

Dr. Gregorio Lascasas laughed as he got up and turned toward the window to look out at the marvelous Plaza de los Apóstoles, which gave entrance to the Cathedral.

Suddenly, the Bishop turned back to his guest and said to him in an orotund tone: "May I ask you a question, my friend?"

"By all means!"

"Who is your spiritual adviser?"

Agustín Lago hesitated a moment before replying: "My spiritual adviser is the New Testament."

The Bishop coughed. He still had his chronic bronchitis in spite of the sun streaming into the Plaza de los Apóstoles.

"Not Father Forteza, then?"

"Well—no. Father Forteza is my father confessor."

Dr. Gregorio Lascasas was silent. He seemed a little puzzled.

"But in any case, you're a great admirer of the Company of Jesus, aren't you?"

Agustín Lago looked surprised. "Of course, very much so."

"Then don't you believe," the Bishop went on, "that in the long run the Opus Dei may mean to the Company what Rommel means to General Wavell?"

Agustín Lago's empty sleeve dangled at his left side.

"Forgive me, my Lord, but I don't know what you mean."

The Bishop stared fixedly at his parishioner, but Agustín Lago's eyes did not waver.

"It's simple enough. Since we first met I've informed myself more fully concerning the Opus Dei. Did you know that? We bishops have to have our reconnaissance planes, too. Well, now, I've come up with the impression that you people are trying to do a more modern type of missionary work than the Company of Jesus… Yes, that apostolate which you exercise from the moment of professing—without wearing a cassock—may very well respond to the needs of the times. Do you understand what I mean now?"

Agustín Lago felt uncomfortable sitting on the sofa while Dr. Gregorio Lascasas was standing. He tried to get up, but the Bishop made a sign with his big body, indicating that he was not to move. The militant of the Opus Dei answered him in an assured tone. "If your Lordship will permit me, I'll say there is work enough for everyone. It's true that the plan of our founder, Father Escrivá, differs from that of the Company of Jesus, but that's only natural. And needless to say, we'll never supplant the Jesuits in any number of fields where they've had centuries of experience."

Dr. Gregorio Lascasas smiled. "I'm glad to hear you say that, son. Yes, I'm glad you're not cherishing too many illusions. But If I were in your place now, I wouldn't stop with reading the New Testament; I'd have a spiritual adviser in addition, and he would be that very Father Forteza. Yes, my advice to you would be to sign a concordat with him, a long-term agreement."

ALTHOUGH Hitler made an announcement that would put everything else in the shade for a long time, two significant news items appeared in *Amanecer* that same day. The only reason that Jaime did not underline them was that he had given up his delivery route. His book business was sailing before the wind, and that enabled him to send in his resignation. Matías said to Carman Elgazu: "I'm glad for Jaime's sake, but from now on the paper is going to be more boring."

The first of the items had to do with the Court of Political Responsibility. This tribunal, which was still hearing cases, had pronounced sentence on La Pasionaria. It had fined the accused twenty-five million pesetas, sentenced her to fifteen years of banishment to the Spanish possessions, and taken away her Spanish citizenship. The second item concerned the Falange: the political junta had agreed that the five roses that had adorned the tomb of José Antonio in Alicante, now faded, were to be sent as a gift in an artistic urn to the Casa de las Españas in New York.

THE news that Hitler announced to the world was that Germany had declared war on Russia. With no warning, and in spite of the nonaggression pact signed by the two countries, German troops crossed the Soviet frontiers at dawn on

June 26. Ribbentrop said: "The greatest military machine in history has started to move toward the East." Finnish troops under the command of Marshal Mannerheim and Romanian troops under General Antonescu had joined on the side of the Third Reich and were engaged there.

This time the shift was of such great moment as to shake the earth, it seemed. The teletype machines drummed out their bulletins. The radio stations seemed to have gone mad. Several commentators said: "This is the beginning." Others said: "This is the end."

Hitler issued a startling statement to justify his decision. He claimed that Russia had betrayed the German-Soviet pact. That she had undertaken to issue deliberately subversive programs in the territories occupied by Germany and thus had created disturbances like those which had taken place in Yugoslavia. That everywhere she had used espionage with the concrete object of aggression. That she had attacked Finland without the consent of the German government. That she had been guilty of acts of extreme cruelty in the Baltic states, which she had annexed. "Bolshevism is a threat to the world, and Germany has decided to do away with it."

Do away with Bolshevism? The phrase sounded good. What attitude would the capitalistic democracies take? That soon became known: they breathed a sigh of relief. Hitler, doubtless ill-advised by his astrologers, had fallen into the trap by creating a second front. England lined up solidly behind Russia. One of Lord Marley's phrases defined the stand of the British Empire: "England would unite with the devil in order to fight Germany." The United States would aid the USSR, too. *Amanecer* said: "The struggle staged in Spain in 1936 is being repeated on a worldwide scale."

No one knew what would happen next. Russia's actual potentialities were unknown. No one doubted that the military machine launched by Hitler was the greatest in history. But the question was: would or would it not be great enough to succeed in such a titanic undertaking? The thought of Napoleon came to every mind. The immensity of the Russian land mass, so often mentioned to Cosme Vila in the School for Political Training in Moscow, took precedence in all speculations. And what about the winter, the Russian winter that filled Cosme Vila's wife with fear? Could Hitler deliver a mortal blow to the Red Army before snow buried the roads? June 26...he had chosen the date well. And the initial phase could not have been more promising: the Führer's motorized divisions rolled ahead at full speed. And as if he were seeking a symbol, his first aerial attack set fire to several targets in St. Petersburg, the ancient tsarist city that the revolution had renamed Leningrad, the city in which the Spanish Communists admitted to Russia had first set foot.

The German slogan of the war had changed. It had another name now, based hopefully on what might happen in St. Petersburg: The Crusade Against Soviet Russia. A message quite unlike the statement issued by Lord Marley was read in all the German parishes. It said: "The struggle against the USSR is the struggle for Christianity all over the world." Hungary and the German puppet state of Slovakia declared war on the USSR. France broke off diplomatic relations with Hungary. In Verona the Duce reviewed the first Italian division ready to move to the Russian front. French, Norwegian, Swedish, and Danish volunteers enlisted to join in the fighting. The first impression was that the utmost confusion reigned in Russia. Some persons in Gerona, like Notary Noguer, were thinking: "Now we realize that Hitler's heart is actually capable of something great," though they did not dare say it aloud.

That was the immediate reaction in Spain. Most people's thoughts were galvanized in favor of Germany, and Anglophiles like Manolo and Esther did not know what to think. Patriotic statements burgeoned all over the national map as if by magic. After all, the justification for bombing London was questionable, but who would cavil at bombing Leningrad and Moscow?

The Spanish political hierarchies set the example. Minister Serrano Súñer, speaking before an imposing demonstration in Madrid, shouted: "Russia is guilty! She is to blame for our civil war! Guilty of the death of José Antonio, our founder! The extermination of Russia is demanded by history and for the sake of Europe's future!" José Luis Arrese, Secretary-General of the Movement, reminded all his comrades of the "million dead" who, through the fault of Russia, had made Spain a blood-soaked field.

The collective contagion, that psychological phenomenon of such concern to Dr. Chaos, once more became an epidemic. The Falange announced that it was setting up recruiting stations for men who wanted to go to fight against Russia. In the name of Navarre, the Most Excellent Statutory and Provincial Deputation suggested that all the countries fighting against Communism should pledge their enthusiastic adherence to the cause. Don Anselmo Ichaso wrote the text. "Navarre is united in spirit with the valiant defenders of Christian civilization, and sends its prayers to the All Highest for the total victory in the struggle begun by us in July 1936." Posters appeared everywhere, not excepting the Rambla in Gerona.

"Avenge Spain! Take part in Europe's task. Enlist against Communism at the volunteers' recruiting stations."

"Russia robbed us of six thousand Spanish children, who must be rescued at any cost."

JULY 1, the day on which the great pianist Paderewski died in New York. Since the armistice of 1918, he had been President of the Polish Republic. That same day the press correspondents who had gone to the Russian front began to publish their reports. They revealed that the morale of the Russian troops was unpredictable. In certain sectors they fled in disorder or surrendered at the front with their generals. In others they showed extraordinary courage and "clung to the ground like limpets." Readers did not know what to believe. But all the reports agreed on one point: that the political commissars, so well known in Spain, and Gerona, where the people remembered Goriev and Axelrod—those whom Ignacio had seen in Madrid during his time at the Pasteur Hospital filed through his mind—were behaving ruthlessly. Whenever their men wavered, they gunned them down mercilessly, as they had during the battle of the Ebro. Tower of Babel had witnessed that. At times they decided to herd a section into some shelter, after which they sealed the exit. Sometimes they buried their slain standing in such a way that only their heads showed.

News items of that kind caused waves of indignation heightened by references to the lamentable appearance of the Russian prisoners. According to German reports, some of the men were fighting barefoot because, they explained, they had sold their boots to buy cigarettes. Their sorry state contrasted sharply with the spruce appearance of their officers. Where was the boasted equality? For the sake of recalcitrant readers who suspected that the reports were largely propaganda, there were appropriate photographs. Of course, those could have been falsified, or carefully selected. In any event, it was clear that the truth would come out as time went by. This was all the more likely because people were already trained to read between the lines. At least in that sense, Hitler was to be thanked for his decision. At last the world, and Gerona, would find out whether Russia, virtually isolated from the outside world since 1917, was or was not a paradise.

Pablito could hardly bear to lay down his geography; he could rattle off the names of Russian mountain ranges and rivers again and again. When he heard that the Hungarian troops had gone into action after threading the passes of the Carpathians, he felt that a great secret was about to be revealed to him. Ah, the ring of such words as Carpathian and the Ukraine, Russia's bread basket. Now the Germans were treading that soil. What did the sprouting fields look like? Had Russian scientists produced better, taller wheat?

"This is all very exciting," Dr. Andújar said. "I think my theory is about to be confirmed—that the Russian people are very simple, and that complexity is confined to the governing classes."

"There'll be many surprises," Mosén Alberto mused with strange excitement. "I believe they haven't had time to wipe out religion entirely. Perhaps the young people may be atheists. But not the older ones."

"That Stalin must be a crook," Raimundo the barber remarked. "He's probably sent the weakest into the front lines, people with a cough or something worse. But chances are that Hitler will soon come up against giants."

For the moment it was impossible to know anything with accuracy. The invasion was being played up to such proportions that the news could not be contained in diagrams. The captured Russian materiel looked good, but it could not compare with the German, except perhaps for a forty-two-ton tank. The Russian air force was fighting from a position of inferiority. The German pilots pursued the Soviets and shot them down like trapshooters downing pigeons on Sunday in Gerona. There was talk of inhuman battle practices, such as leaving tins of poisoned food behind in flight. And it was said that many of the wounded committed suicide rather than fall into German hands.

The reports began to be more definite. Since 1917, the Soviets had subjected the Russian people to indescribable tortures in order to force the revolution on them. *Amanecer* published this in big headlines. In the Ukraine, the GPU had dragged whole families to jail and then sprayed them with gasoline. On July 6, Germany published statistics showing that since Lenin's seizure of power, the murders had numbered eleven million, of whom nine million were peasants; one million were workers; seventy-five thousand, officers of the Army; forty-one thousand, intellectuals. "It's evident," the Costa brothers remarked, "that it's always more dangerous to be a peasant than an industrialist." The manager of Constructora Gerundense, Inc., who had a good head for numbers, merely commented dryly: "I don't see who could prove statistics like that in so much detail."

The first great battles were fought in Bialystok and Minsk, where twenty thousand Russian soldiers finally surrendered after murdering their political commissars. The Germans pushed on then to the Dnieper River and headed for the Duna. Pablito followed the course of the rivers on the map with his finger. The Finns and Romanians were advancing in other sectors. And the so-called Stalin Line was about to be breached en route to Kiev.

General Sánchez Bravo paid particular attention to the German side of the war, as was logical for him, but he also followed the reports from London. For a moment the General thought that because Hitler had attacked Russia, the common enemy, England, would want to make peace with Germany. But suddenly he was convinced that it was not going to be like that. On July 15, the British Empire committed itself not to sign a separate peace with Germany. At the same time the British air force intensified its attacks on the Reich's territory and American troops landed in Iceland. No doubt Stalin would start receiving shipments of materiel from the United States through the Arctic. No doubt Churchill would be writing to "Papa Stalin" and ending his letters with a fraternal embrace. A London correspondent wrote that the British alliance with Russia reminded him of the words of a gentleman who married the kitchen wench at an inn. "Of course," the gentleman said, "she's a bit light in the upper story, her manners are bad, and she hates the gentry. But she's so roomy!"

Father Forteza was one of the people in Gerona most deeply chagrined. A crusade against Soviet Russia! That had caught him unawares in spite of his intuition and the latest letter he had received from his brother in Japan, mentioning such a possibility.

The Jesuit called Professor Civil and said: "Get ready now to hear bad news about the fate of the Jews. The Germans won't imprison those who were pro-Bolshevik in any ghetto—they'll wipe them out."

Italy's attitude upset Warning Voice. "Why has the Duce sent only one division to Russia? Has the Axis begun to crack?"

Doña Cecilia, the General's wife, did nothing but cross herself. "Leaving behind tins of poisoned food! Families sprayed with gasoline! Those English are beyond God's forgiveness."

FIFTY-SEVEN

VOLUNTEER recruiting stations opened all over Spain, and the posters appearing everywhere denoted a fact: there were actually many volunteers ready to fight against Russia. Accordingly, the Supreme Command decided to put together a division, the 250th, to be called the Blue Division in homage to the color of the Falange. Enlistments came with great rapidity lest the Spaniards who had suffered the heavy hand of the Soviets on their own flesh might chance to arrive too late.

Amanecer kept a careful count of the progress of enlistment. Cádiz came first. But in fact the movement spread over the entire nation: Valencia, Barcelona, Seville, Madrid, Guipúzcoa. One stirring piece of news followed another. A number of workers from the Navy shipyard, El Ferrol, had enlisted; forty comrades from a small village in Pontevedra had reported to the capital of the province; many officers of all Army ranks also had asked for the honor of enlisting. Field chaplains offered their services, as did nurses and some of the White Russians who sang in the chorus that gave a recital in the Municipal Theater of Gerona.

Consequently, the division would be heterogeneous. Even veterinarians would be in it. And some aviators and engineers and health officers, and a contingent from the Civil Guard. If winter actually should come before the campaign had been concluded, they would need skiers, too.

Of course, Gerona was not going to be left behind. The lightning of patriotism had struck the once-walled city, stinging some consciences. People kept asking one another: "Who's going to enlist?" The schoolmaster Torrus of the Grupo Escolar San Narciso was mentioned. In the Telegraph Office a letter carrier who collected Russian stamps was named. Eloy was afraid that Captain Sánchez Bravo would enlist, and he was president of the Gerona Football Club!

For once, the people's instincts were wrong. None of the men they talked about reported to the recruiting station that had opened on the Plaza de San Agustín.

The first volunteer to enlist from the city was Cacerola. Ignacio's friend had never recovered from his disappointment with the Office of Price Control. As soon as he read that Russia had robbed Spain of six thousand children, who must be rescued at any cost, he decided to answer the call and presented himself at the Plaza de San Agustín, all ready to sign up. "They'll need cooks, won't they?" That was all he said.

He found Captains Arias and Sandoval behind the desk acting like bureaucrats.

"Congratulations, boy. You're at the top of the list."

Cacerola asked, "Can we have girl pen pals this time, too?"

"Certainly you can."

"Well, I'd like to have Gracia Andújar."

"Oh! I'm sure she'll accept."

The second volunteer was Alfonso Estrada. He considered it his duty as president of the Marian Congregation. He went to Father Forteza's cell and left with a special blessing. "I think it's a good thing, son, a good thing. Life is made so that we'll yield to it, little by little or all at once. This is a noble cause. God grant, however, that they don't put you into a German uniform."

Alfonso Estrada thus would quit the office of Safe-Conducts and his books on philosophy. He could no longer tell Pilar frightening tales; now he would live them at the Russian front. Now he would not play the music of Sibelius, descriptive of the wind in Finland; he would have to take shelter against the real wind, as the soldiers of the Afrika Korps had to protect themselves against the *khamsin* of Africa, which made them vomit.

The president of the Marian Congregation enlisted in homage to the Virgin. And he did it with singular wholeheartedness. He felt confident that nothing would harm him. "I don't deserve any credit," he said to Captains Arias and Sandoval. "Nothing's going to happen to me." He was sure that he would come back soon, bringing an icon in his knapsack to show with pride to his children, even his grandchildren, some day.

As Captain Arias handed him the regulation papers, he asked with a smile: "Do you want a girl pen pal, too?"

Alfonso Estrada replied: "I already have one. It's Asunción, the teacher. She's embroidering a scapular of the Virgin of Carmen for me."

The next volunteer was Mosén Falcó, the religious adviser to the Falange. He believed it his duty to set an example and behaved accordingly. His interview with the Bishop was not without emotion.

"See here, son—have you thought it over carefully?"

"Yes, my Lord."

"I congratulate you, I congratulate you! You're a brave man."

Mosén Falcó, knowing that the Bishop had always felt some suspicion of the Falange, said: "I feel sure that some of the boys will want to go to confession from time to time."

"Of course!"

"Will you give me your blessing?"

"With all my heart! Kneel down."

Mosén Falcó knelt. Dr. Gregorio Lascasas threw out his broad Aragonese chest. "*In nomine patris et filii et spiritu sancti...*" At that moment the big bell in the Cathedral rang. They could hear the shouts of children playing in front of the Palace.

"May God watch over you, my son! Write to me when you can."

Five artillerymen also offered themselves as volunteers. They were friends who had never been separated since they had met in the barracks while doing their military service. None of them had fought in the Spanish war, and they thirsted for adventure. They flipped a coin. It came up heads, so they enlisted. "Surely, this will be worth a tail to us."

Captain Arias asked them: "Is it the cognac talking, or have you thought it all over?"

"We don't like cognac. We know what we're doing."

Captain Arias insisted. "War is a serious thing."

"Russia's got to be punished. We want to enlist."

"Okay, boys. *¡Arriba España!*"

¡Arriba!

Another would-be volunteer was José Luis Martínez de Soria, but his mother dissuaded him.

"Son! Your father is dead; your brother is dead. Marta and I are alone. Why do you have to go? Have you talked it over with María Victoria yet?"

"Yes, she's already enlisted. She's going as a nurse."

"José Luis, my son, I forbid it! I don't know whether I have the right to do that, but I forbid you to enlist. Please, José Luis! Don't you see how alone we women are?"

Major Martínez de Soria's widow burst into tears and cried so despairingly that for a moment his mother seemed to José Luis, a judge advocate, to lack dignity. Marta, on the other hand, maintained an almost scornful silence. Since Ignacio had broken off with her, she sometimes behaved like that, and there was no knowing what she thought.

José Luis, who until that moment had acted on instinct, without reflection ("Russia's got to be punished"), suddenly remembered that Russia was enormous and that the waters of the Dnieper, which the war buffs were talking about, must run very turbulent and strong to carry along an infinity of corpses.

He stared impassively at the two women. Their eyes were grieving. Really, why should he expose himself? Hadn't he offered his life a hundred times already? Hadn't enough Martínez de Soria blood soaked the earth already?

Major Martínez de Soria's widow surprised them by suddenly fainting. She turned extremely pale, and her head sagged to her chest. Marta and José Luis rushed to her aid. They dabbed her with eau de cologne. Finally José Luis said tersely: "All right. I won't go." He left the house, slamming the door behind him.

But there was another who did enlist: Rogelio, the waiter. That was a surprise. When Rogelio came out of prison after serving his sentence for having played dirty tricks on the maidservants, he felt aimless, close to despair. He wandered around Gerona, scarcely knowing what he was doing. He had looked for work in a couple of cafés, to no avail. "Not enough customers. You can see that. These messes we serve are enough to scare you!"

Then he read one of the posters. "Spaniard! Enlist!" Why not? Rogelio had never done a worthwhile thing in his life. It had been a gray life, like the winter light of Gerona, like the job done by the men who lit the gaslamps along the Rambla at twilight.

But if he enlisted, he could become a hero. And he would meet new people, other boys who would look upon him with respect. And he would come to know other lands. Because, in order to reach the Russian front, he would have to cross France and Germany. France! And all those nice little French girls. Perhaps he would be allowed to take a walk around Paris. And Germany! With all the nice little German girls. Those fifty who had visited Gerona—Some were taboo, but others. And all of them had taken showers, he had heard, and drunk lemon juice.

"Your name and patronymic?"

"Rogelio Ros Bosch."

"Age?"

"Twenty."

"Trade?"

"Waiter."

"You haven't done your 'mili' of course?"

"I'll do it now."

"Were you in the Falange?"

"No, sir."

"Why are you enlisting?"

"Russia's got to be punished."

Captain Sandoval stared at Rogelio, who had adopted such an air of self-assurance, almost of indifference, that it made the officer's hair stand on end. His cigarette was drooping from the corner of his mouth, giving him an air of cynicism.

"All right, then. But you have to furnish two photographs. *¡Arriba España!*"

"*¡Arriba!*"

Captain Arias called him back at the last moment.

"Did you say you were a waiter?"

"Yes, sir."

"I'm appointing you my orderly."

Rogelio's eyes opened. "What?"

"Yes, I'm Captain Arias. We'll meet in the Dehesa on Friday at ten A.M."

Rogelio bowed his head. "Very well." Suddenly, the boy smiled and donning the manner of a waiter, he added: "Would the gentleman like anything else?"

A few hours later a woman appeared at the recruiting station. She was about thirty years old, somewhat mannish in appearance, although her eyes betrayed her, testifying faithfully to her femininity. Her skin was smooth and unwrinkled, her hair short, and her manner greatly assured. She was carrying an expensive handbag of crocodile skin. High-heeled shoes. She was distinguished and unaffected.

The girl gave the impression of having suffered, of still suffering. That was evident in the twitching of her mouth and a certain skepticism surrounding her whole person. She wanted to enlist, but there was no trace of patriotic enthusiasm in her. Captains Arias and Sandoval rose to their feet when she came in.

It was Solita Pinel, the elder daughter of the Price Administrator and the former surgical assistant in the Chaos Clinic. She wanted to enlist as a nurse. "I imagine that I can be of use. I spent twenty months in Zaragoza during the war, working in various hospitals."

Captains Arias and Sandoval recognized her. They stared at each other in astonishment.

"Señorita, you're to be congratulated. You're a courageous woman."

"Don't you believe it."

"Why not?"

Solita shrugged her shoulders. Her crocodile handbag swung on her arm. "I've brought my photographs, my Falange card. What else do I need?"

Solita had told no one but Dr. Andújar of her decision. She had been in contact with him since the night with Dr. Chaos in the Hotel Majestic. Dr.

Andújar had said to her: "By all means go, Solita. Put some space between you. I can't do a thing. If your father kicks up a fuss, let me know."

Her father gave his consent. And while Captains Arias and Sandoval were taking down the required data, she felt a presentiment unlike Alfonso Estrada's, that she would not come back from that venture. That she would remain forever in Russia, dead in some place near Bialystok or Minsk. Killed in an air raid or by a bullet, or mowed down by the sickle of some young, bold, virile Communist soldier.

"Very well, Solita. Friday at ten A.M. in the Dehesa."

Solita assented. "If you don't mind, I won't wear my nurse's uniform for the time being. I'll wear a blue shirt and a red beret."

Thursday, the day before the volunteers were to gather in the Dehesa—some were beginning to arrive from Barcelona, and gifts were flowing in for the *divisionarios*, from everywhere—Mateo presented himself at the recruiting station. Mateo Santos, Provincial Leader of the FET and the JONS.

Captains Arias and Sandoval rose, stood at attention, and saluted him with outstretched arm.

"I beg your pardon." Mateo said with a smile. "I haven't brought my credentials."

Later *Amanecer* would publish Mateo's photograph on the front page; and still later, very much later, Pilar would paste it in her album marked "Press."

No sooner had Mateo read Serrano Súñer's speech—"Russia must be punished"—and learned that an expedition of volunteers was being recruited than he felt in his heart that it was his duty to go. His recent conversation with the Governor came back to him: "If there were men in politics, we would not find ourselves in this situation." Enlistment represented an effective blow, a political coup. An exemplary act. The local leaders who were not enlisting, on the grounds that they must plant their lands or guard the archives of the Falange, would feel ashamed. And all those who had accused him of seeking political advantage, of getting his own out of the victory, of having the use of an official car, could huddle in a corner, deprived of any excuse for slandering him.

All well and good, but what about his family circumstances? Pilar was expecting a baby. The curve of her abdomen was becoming increasingly noticeable. She was doing exercises, on Esther's advice, and satisfying her little food whims on her mother's advice. Lately, she had decided there could be no doubt that the baby would be a boy and that she would name him César.

Besides, there was Don Emilio Santos. His father was basking in the joy of living after his period of convalescence. Mateo could imagine his astonishment, how his nose would tremble, and he remembered his words at the outbreak of the Russo-Finnish war: "But, son! Can't you live without a rifle in your hand?" Later he would have to deal with Matías, Carmen Elgazu—and Ignacio. Ignacio! Why should his friend be of special concern to him?

Still nothing deterred him. No consideration. He refused to look into a mirror; he was afraid to. He closed himself in his Provincial Leader's office and stared at the Crucifix presiding over it, then at the portrait of José Antonio, whose five withered roses, which once had adorned his tomb, had already arrived in New York.

He did not delay telling his family about his act. Why put off the moment? The sooner the better. That would give them time to adjust to the idea.

He knew that Pilar should be the first to learn of it. He waited for a moment when Don Emilio Santos was not at home. Before bringing up the question he paced the floor while Pilar sat happily knitting. Finally, he sat down in the dining room, with a glass of cognac, and began to talk about Russia, England, the Avila Academy where he had trained to become a temporary lieutenant. He talked about the eleven million murders attributed to the Soviets, of the gliders in Crete—three of them attached to the tail of each Junker—of the words spoken by José Antonio before the tribunal that sentenced him to death: "We believe that a nation is important; that a history of the universe is incarnate in it." Finally, seeing that his whole preamble was accomplishing nothing, that Pilar showed no signs of alarm and had no notion of the climax he was approaching, he grew tired of postponing it, and in the most natural and loving tone he could command, he asked his wife to look at him and said to her: "Pilar, I've decided to enlist. I believe it's my duty."

Pilar made a face when she heard him. But immediately she recovered herself. A smile came to her somewhat puffy lips. She looked at the glass of cognac in Mateo's hand and suspected that he was a little tipsy and consequently that he was playing some sort of joke on her, even though of a kind that might have frightened her.

Yet Mateo did not move. And his expression was indefinable. Then Pilar, still not alarmed, laid down her knitting, wound up her yarn, got up, went slowly to Mateo, and finally sat on his knee. She put her arm around his neck and kissed him several times.

"What a big silly you are," she whispered. "Why do you play jokes like that on me? Don't you know you might scare me?"

Mateo felt as though his wife's kisses were burning him.

"I'm sorry, Pilar, but I'm not joking. I'm enlisting. I repeat that I believe it's my duty."

Pilar got off his lap and drew back, her eyes wide. She opened her mouth and stared at Mateo as if she were about to lose her mind. Mateo, with his soul torn but his mind at ease, thought of the words pronounced by the priest at the altar on their wedding day: "for better or for worse."

"Mateo! You've gone crazy!"

The scream was torn from her. Pilar knew her man. And now that she looked at him from a distance, she realized that he was not drunk and that his decision was firm.

"Please, Pilar, listen to me!"

Pilar paced the floor, then her body folded and she fell. Teresa, the maid, came running. "What the matter with the señorita?" Mateo knelt beside Pilar and settled her in her armchair. He thought that perhaps he should have found some other way to tell her. He should have talked first with Don Emilio. Or with Carmen Elgazu. Or he should have gone, giving some excuse or other, and written to her after he had crossed the frontier. But he realized as soon as he had thought the whole thing over that there was no good way to break the news. The moment would inevitably come when Pilar had to face up to reality.

Her faint was not like that of Major Martínez de Soria's widow. Mateo had a hard time bringing Pilar to. He had to open all the windows and lay her down. She looked deathly pale. And she kept muttering at intervals: "No, no, it's not true."

But it was true. Mateo was standing firm.

"You know I love you, Pilar. If I had known that this was going to happen, I'd have postponed the wedding. But you know what I believe. You've always known. To me our country is sacred."

Pilar was without the strength to reply. She lay like a bloodless patch on the tall bed with the antique lines that she had chosen so lovingly.

"But now it's not just me. I'm expecting a baby. Your baby, Mateo."

"I know that, Pilar. For God's sake, be brave! I love that baby as much as you do. But I have to go. I can't help it. I know I'll come back!"

He spoke with conviction, for Mateo knew what war was. But Pilar did not even hear him. She had closed her eyes softly as if she were going to sleep. Then suddenly she burst into a flood of tears, whereupon Teresa, the maid, realized at last what the matter was and left them.

Later a silence thick enough to cut fell over the bedroom. Pilar moved a foot from time to time. Mateo was thinking of only one thing: whether the shock might have complicated her pregnancy and harmed her or the baby. She was lying on her back with her legs a little apart.

Then they heard a key in the door; it was Don Emilio Santos. He came in feeling happy because he had been able to walk home from the tobacco shop without getting tired. Besides, the sun was glorious. He had been walking toward the sunset, which he had seen for a moment above the roof of the station.

"Tere, will you make me a cup of coffee?"

Mateo went out to meet his father and waited in the dining room, then told him what had happened.

Don Emilio's first impulse was to strike his son a terrible blow. But Mateo had guessed his intention and his look stayed his father's arm.

"Don't do that, Father."

They heard a slight noise in the kitchen, as if a samovar was boiling on the stove.

Don Emilio turned around. He meant to turn his back on his son.

"Where's Pilar?"

"In bed. She's gone to bed."

His father turned toward the bedroom. When Pilar saw him, she made an effort to sit up. Then Don Emilio sat down beside her on the edge of the bed and embraced her tenderly and asked her to lie down again.

"Pilar, my daughter!"

Pilar could not speak. Besides, she had never grown used to calling Don Emilio Santos "father." Sometimes she could, but on a solemn occasion like this, she could not speak the word.

"He's mad! He's gone crazy!" Don Emilio Santos almost shouted, hoping that Mateo, still standing in the dining room near the balcony, would hear him. "He's got to be stopped from doing this terrible thing."

Pilar managed to stammer: "We can do nothing. I'm perfectly sure he's enlisted already."

Mateo heard her, and her clairvoyance almost irritated him. But he let it pass. He realized that he had no right to ask for explanations.

Teresa came in with the cup of coffee for Don Emilio Santos, but he refused it. "Later, later..."

Again there was silence in the house—and sobs.

The silence lasted at least half an hour. Mateo tried to get them to listen to him. All in vain. His words—Russia, the fatherland, duty—all fell into the void. They rang false. It seemed that when a woman was carrying child, words changed their meanings.

Don Emilio Santos said warningly: "There's still time, Mateo. Unless you change your mind, you'll have to take the consequences."

What Don Emilio Santos meant by that was not quite clear. Then something unforeseen occurred. Pilar drew strength from weakness and sat up in bed. She put her feet on the floor and slipped them with unusual ease into the slippers lying there. Next, without saying a word, she went to the telephone and dialed a number: Ignacio's office number.

"Ignacio, this is Pilar. Please come right now! I need you."

She hung up.

Mateo was furious, but he could not protest. He was undecided whether to go out or go to the bathroom and rub the back of his neck with cold water. He chose the latter course. Then he urinated, staring straight ahead at the wall as if the enemy of his ideals were there.

He wished he could stay in the bathroom until Ignacio came, but that was impossible. He had to go out. He saw Pilar sitting in the dining room with an expressibly beaten air. And Don Emilio had finally decided to drink his coffee.

Mateo shut himself up in his office and distracted his mind by running his hand over the backs of his books and by trying to light a cigarette with his lighter.

It took Ignacio about fifteen minutes to get there; it seemed like an eternity to all of them.

When the young man entered the dining room, Mateo was there, too, ready to receive him. Mateo wanted to be the one to tell what was going on, but Pilar anticipated him. She still had not given up the cause for lost. Hope had come to her all in a moment as she lay in bed. Mateo loved her so dearly! He had been dazzled, carried away, that was all, and Ignacio would manage to dissuade him.

"I'm sorry I had to call you like that, Ignacio. But it was because—Mateo wants to enlist in the Blue Division."

A stormy scene followed. After Ignacio had questioned Mateo and realized that he was serious, he argued with Mateo as never before. Mateo's act seemed unworthy of him. The act of a cur. Any man really a man couldn't marry and then go off to war for no particular reason, with no real need to, six months later. Just to play the hero. In the name of the Empire or some such nonsense. A soldier had to do it because it was his profession. But a civilian—What if he did wear a shirt of some special color? War was a horrible thing, and a man would have to be out of his mind to feel attracted to it.

Ignacio challenged Mateo to convince him that such an act was necessary. The Blue Division, that symbolic sacrifice, ought to be for bachelors only. "I could enlist if I didn't prefer the law to a rifle. But you, married and expecting a child, no!" Was Mateo's flesh needed to make the Führer's dreams come true, perchance? Or Pilar's flesh? And all only to pay homage to some romantic anthem. Or perhaps to have his photograph come out in *Amanecer.*

Several times Mateo was on the point of shouting: "That's enough!" Or going up to Ignacio and seizing him by the lapels. But he controlled himself for fear that Pilar might fall to the floor again. In fact, the more Ignacio talked, the more remote from him Mateo felt and the more convinced he was that it was his duty not to compromise and to appear at the recruiting station. After all, the world was as it was, as it always had been. Whenever a man had to set off on some great undertaking, he had always left a woman in tears.

Ignacio read Mateo's mind. Then he tried his last recourse.

"What's happening to you is that you're afraid of life, life as the rest of us live it. It's easier to give orders to an arrow posted at the door than to study, as I do, a division of property case. That's the reason you've never finished your law course, isn't it? Every time examinations came around you had an excuse. And here it's June again, and this time your excuse is that you're going into the Blue Division. Maybe the Russian commissars can lock their men in a shelter and seal the door, just as you're doing to Pilar. You'll seal her up, too. Splendid! It's easier, too, to go there with a star on your chest than to take care of your family, than to put up with the monotony of spending hours watching a woman knit."

As the scene went on, Pilar realized from Mateo's attitude that Ignacio would also lose the battle. Mateo felt hurt, deeply hurt, and it was obvious that he was on the verge of throwing Ignacio out of the house. Don Emilio Santos, for his part, was breathing with so much difficulty that he finally got up, went into his room, and closed the door.

Mateo did not bother to answer Ignacio point by point. He managed to control himself because he realized the showdown was painful to everyone. But he believed still that a man might have higher reasons for leaving everything and giving himself. Besides, Pilar had known what he was like from the very beginning. "She took me as I am. And she knew me. Pilar knows that I've brought other comrades along with me, and that obligates me. Of course, Hitler doesn't need Pilar's flesh! But I have to do my duty. As for seeing my picture in *Amanecer*, I'll forgive you for that because you're Ignacio."

As Mateo finished speaking, Ignacio stared at him with the contempt he had expected. He nodded his head several times. Finally, knowing that the die was cast, he spoke to Pilar: "I'm sorry, sister. The father of your child has been dehumanized. There's nothing you can do about it."

He strode out of the house. And as he walked away, he knew that it was up to him to go home and break the news to his parents. He saw the familiar posters on the walls: "Avenge Spain! Be a part of Europe's task. Enlist for the war against Communism at your recruiting station." As he passed the Diana

Perfumery, he looked in out of habit. Paz had set up a small mirror on the counter and was tidying her hair.

Matías and Carmen Elgazu were speechless as they learned from Ignacio of Mateo's decision. Suddenly, they felt that they had grown old.

"Why—that's awful!"

Carmen Elgazu went to Ignacio and took hold of his arms.

"What does Pilar say? My God, my poor daughter! Isn't there any way to stop him, Ignacio? Should you talk to the Governor?"

Ignacio shrugged his shoulder. "I suspect that the Governor will give him his blessing."

Matías went to the balcony which overlooked the river and mused: "I ought to have foreseen this."

They could not pull themselves together. They thought of a thousand plans in detail. But what could they do? It would do no good for Matías and Carmen Elgazu to see Mateo and upbraid him. They could not interfere. "He's her husband. Pilar married him."

IGNACIO'S prophecies were fulfilled. All the family plots shattered against Mateo's irrevocable decision. He had only one ally: little Eloy. The boy did not dare say it aloud, but he admired Mateo's gesture. In spite of his memories of Guernica. In spite of his love for Pilar.

Ignacio was also right in thinking that the Governor would give Mateo his blessing. Although he did add: "I feel sorry for your wife's sake. Naturally, it's hard for her to swallow."

On the other hand, to his surprise, Mateo found Marta lined up against him. From the start of the enlistment, Marta had ordered her girls in the Feminine Section to make preparations to wait on the volunteers. Yet she said to Mateo: "You're making a mistake. You ought to stay home. My mother and I persuaded José Luis to stay." She pushed back the little arrow above her forehead and added: "I've lost Ignacio for just such things as this. And I assure you it's painful to lose someone you love."

Mateo rejected her argument. "You're wrong, Marta. You lost Ignacio the day you met him. You and he live in separate worlds. I'm surprised that you seem to be reneging on your world now."

Marta looked sad. "What can I say? I'm not reneging on anything. But sometimes when I'm alone I ask myself some questions."

Mateo dropped the subject. "Okay. That's all right for you. You're a woman. But I—I'm surprised that José Luis decided to do an about-face."

Manolo and Esther kept hands off, but they said to Ignacio: "A fine brother-in-law you've got." Esther added: "I realized what Mateo was like at that dance we had in the Anarchists' gymnasium. The time when he broke the record of Red songs that Alfonso Estrada brought."

Aside from that, elation! Beyond that family drama, everything was joy in the city, outwardly at least, on the eve of the departure of the expeditionaries. *Amanecer* published Mateo's photograph, of course, with a caption that said: "The upper echelons set the example." A frieze of pictures accompanied Mateo's, showing Captains Arias and Sandoval, Alfonso Estrada, Cacerola, the five artillerymen, Rogelio, and Solita.

Those men and that woman were heroes to the man in the street from then on. Go to Russia! Especially now that summer was coming and the trees in the woods would cast their shade, and the waves would break peacefully on the beach.

Ramón commented in the Café Nacional: "Some trip!" Commissioner Diéguez thought but did not say: "That's something worthwhile, not like interrogating the little Reds who rejected the Social Auxiliary badge." But perhaps the person most deeply affected was Dr. Chaos. As he studied the faces of Rogelio and Solita, together on the same page of the newspaper, he was speechless, as Matías and Carmen Elgazu had been earlier. He could stand the picture of Rogelio, for he had learned by chance that the boy had been in jail, and that his was an aimless life. But Solita! He felt responsible, immensely responsible. What a terrible blow that woman must have taken to have decided to enlist. Dr. Chaos did not have enough strength even to give Goering the lump of sugar which the dog was begging for with his tongue hanging out.

The General wished that his son, Captain Sánchez Bravo, had enlisted. But the Captain refused with a shake of the head. "Unless that's an order, I'd rather stay home." The General considered making it that. Luckily, however, Doña Cecilia spoke up quickly. "Don't pay any attention to your father, son. Haven't you been wounded three times already?" The General finally said: "I can't order you to do a thing like that."

That settled it. And there was gaiety everywhere in the city. The *divisionarios* who came from outside the city to join the local contingent were fawned upon everywhere they went. They camped in the Dehesa in canvas tents, and all the boys and the small fry in the city, including Pablito, El Niño de Jaén, and the inseparables, Eloy and Manuel Alvear, walked past to see them.

The girls in the Feminine Section took care of the volunteers, who were joined at the last minute by a couple of dozen men who came from the villages in the province. Of course, Gerona was more than the capital; it was the province, too. Each mayor who could offer a volunteer felt somewhat more important in the eyes of the Governor. Comrade Pascual, from Olot, passed out cups of hot coffee. Gracia Andújar distributed medals and lucky badges and talked with Cacerola, her "pen pal," with special solicitude. Asunción was preoccupied exclusively with Alfonso Estrada. She was in love with him. "May God go with you, and the Virgin, too." "I'll write to you, Asunción, if I can see through the gunsmoke." Cacerola looked happy under the trees, surrounded by comrades who said to him when they found out he was a cook: "Say—how about those Russian ingredients? Do you know if they have chickpeas, and if you have to cook them with caviar?"

In no time at all the volunteers shed their mystical rapture and turned to mischief, and from "We're going to raise hell" to riotousness. A Mass was said in the Cathedral, at which they all took communion: another mystical rapture provided for them by Mosén Falcó. But no sooner had they left than they broke into song right on the Plaza de los Apóstoles when they spotted Marta and her followers.

I'm not marching away on account of the girls,
For the girls are beautiful, so beautiful.

Then they went on to a song that shocked the listening ears of the Bishop as it came through the walls of the Episcopal Palace:

A student asked a little girl for something.
What did he ask her for?
He asked her for a pretty thing,
And the little girl gave it to him.

The promise of "raising hell" was kept in the course of a dance given by the Governor in their honor at the swimming pool the night before their departure. Mateo did not attend the dance. He stayed at home trying without success to get Pilar or Don Emilio Santos to speak to him. But all the other *divisionarios* flocked to the festival, which was enhanced by the Gerona Jazz Band. Damián had offered to play gratis that night. His contribution to the New Europe. And when the volunteers saw Paz Alvear grasping the microphone, wearing a dress of silver sequins and one of her provocative green caps, they shouted themselves hoarse. "Long live the mother who bore you!" "If you'll come with us, we'll take Moscow by the eighteenth of July!" "Hey, beautiful! Are you a Cossack or what?"

Paz Alvear was suffering and enjoying herself at the same time, a state that recurred from time to time. Those blue shirts were like daggers to her, but she recognized that there was manliness beneath them. Besides, her father had always spoken very harshly of Russia. So what was she to think? By the third dance, she decided to hate. She hated all that gaggle of girls, perhaps because a lieutenant had taken it upon himself to put on her head a beret with the national flag in place of her green cap. She hated them all so much that she looked still more beautiful. Suddenly she said to Damián: "Let's play the 'Raska-yu.'"

"Anything you say," Damián agreed.

Raska-yu, when you die what'll you do?
Raska-yu, when you die what'll you do?
You'll be dead, you'll be all through.
Raska-yu, when you die what'll you do?

The words, quickly picked up and sung by everyone, could not fail to have an effect on the recruits. Rogelio, for one, started to tremble. The sudden panic that people talked about, and the five artillerymen were shaking, too. Naturally, they preferred the song about the student who asked a girl for some pretty, unmentioned thing. But Paz Alvear was belting out "Raska-yu," and at the words "You'll be dead, you'll be all through," the illuminated swimming pool turned into a cemetery of living men for a few moments, a prophecy of death.

The next day was the Friday set by the recruiting stations for departure. Captains Arias and Sandoval arrived at the Dehesa long before the appointed hour. The final assembling of men had taken place. The two captains reported to Colonel Tejada, just in from Barcelona. Solita arrived, accompanied by her father, Don Oscar Pinel. At the last minute, she had thought better of her decision and was wearing a white nurse's uniform, as she had during the war in the hospitals of Zaragoza.

Half of Gerona went to the Dehesa to escort the volunteers to the railroad station. That was the moment for giving gifts: bottles, cigarettes, chewing gum. "Say! Why gum? Are we allies of the Americans?"

All the authorities were there, from the General and the Governor to the Bishop and Notary Noguer. Doña Cecilia was there, too—in her white gloves, a new hat, and a new necklace—and so were María del Mar and Carlota, Countess of Rubí. Warning Voice shivered. The message sent by Navarre and composed by Don Anselmo Ichaso to the countries fighting against Russia had been so stirring!

Mateo arrived a little late, exactly at nine-thirty. He had waited until the last moment for Pilar, especially Pilar, to understand and change her attitude. He had been sure that ultimately she would give him something—a bag containing a lunch and an orange, a bottle of wine. That at the very least she would have sewed inside his blue shirt an image of his patroness, the Virgin of Pilar.

Not so. Pilar's attitude did not change; it alternated between tears and silence. The last three or four nights had been a nightmare. The two heads on the pillow, separate, even diverging to form a V. They both had tried unsuccessfully to get some sleep. They had kept getting up to go to the bathroom. And when sleep overcame one of the pair, it was worse. If the sleeper was Pilar, Mateo would turn on the amber light on the night stand and study the rosy cheeks of that woman who was flesh of his flesh. And he felt a lump rise in his throat—a lump shaped like a yoke. If it was Mateo who fell asleep, Pilar would listen to his breathing. He breathed normally with the heavy tranquility of a man at peace with his conscience, or else he snored.

Those nights were endless, the first of the month of July. Outdoors the sky was a vast field of stars, lieutenant's stars.

Mateo finally had to go to the Dehesa, holding his shoulders back, without a word of affection from Pilar's lips. And only one kiss, given on the threshold of the door. One kiss and a reminder: "You still have time. Stay home." His father treated him the same way. "Son, stay here." Hours ago he had gone to the flat on the Rambla to say goodbye. Matías, Carmen Elgazu, and Ignacio had received him as if he were a stranger; they had not even invited him to sit down.

But Mateo was the Provincial Leader. As soon as he reached the Dehesa and saw men packing their knapsacks to go to the station, he drew a deep breath. This was his world, the world that suited him, the world to which he had sworn an oath when he had been seventeen years old, "while other boys were thinking of nothing but buying ice cream."

He reported to Colonel Tejada. The Colonel said: "I thought we'd have to go without you."

They lined up two by two.

"Elbow to elbow!"

That brought back the scent of Somosierra, Teruel...

The regimental band accompanied them to the station. The balconies were decorated as for the recent parade of the Corps. The people shouted: "*¡Arriba España!* Long live Franco! Long live Hitler! Death to Russia!"

Death to Russia? Could a nation die?

As they marched through the Plaza de la Estación, Mateo wanted to shout: "Eyes right" so that all the volunteers would look toward his house where Pilar was undoubtedly peering between the slats of the blinds on the balcony.

But he gave no command; he alone looked. And he did see Pilar's shadow, and his father's. But only for a moment. The square was dotted with trees and the formation was moving. Cacerola asked: "When are we going to sing 'Face to the Sun'?"

They sang "Face to the Sun" on the platform. Throats and bodies quivered with emotion. The General would have been glad to get on the train, which was waiting, headed toward Barcelona.

That was a surprise. All the *divisionarios* had supposed they were going directly to France on the Port-Bou line. But now it seemed that the Supreme Command had decided otherwise, perhaps to avoid crossing through that strip of France not occupied by the Germans. They were to travel toward San Sebastián and enter the neighbor nation through Hendaye, where the Führer's soldiers were standing guard.

Death will find me if it comes
And I never see you again.
"*¡Arriba España!*"
"*¡Arriba!*"

They climbed aboard the train, and it started to move jerkily. A huge national flag fluttered above the cars beside another that was red and black.

Alfonso Estrada and Mateo leaned out of the window together. As always before, their last sight of Gerona was of the bells of San Félix and the Cathedral.

"I'll remember San Félix," Alfonso said.

Mateo managed to smile. "Okay, I'll have dibs on the Cathedral. What else?"

All the way to Irún, the train ran between flurries of handkerchiefs. The Feminine Section in Vitoria gave them decks of cards and boxes of cookies. In San Sebastián, the ladies in high society, like those who had once cultivated Warning Voice, handed them huge thermos bottles filled with hot coffee, precisely like that served by Comrade Pascual in the Dehesa. Cookies and coffee—the body demanded both.

As they crossed the international bridge, lined with people who had come to watch "the volunteers" pass by—it seemed this was the third expedition that had come through in four days—the whole train sang:

Goodbye, Spain! My Spain that I love, my Spain!
Goodbye, Spain, when shall I see you again?

At the station in Hendaye, the German guards came to attention and presented arms. This was the spot where the Franco-Hitler interview had been held. The volunteers got off for a few minutes to stretch their legs, and some German girls in uniform came to meet them, looking as though they had just taken a shower, and handed out little bags containing Norwegian sardines, cheese, square loaves of bread with an unpleasant smell, and sausages.

Only a few more miles, then Bordeaux, where Marshal Pétain and de Gaulle had argued whether France should or should not surrender. They had a wait of a couple of hours there, during which the volunteers wandered around the vicinity of the station. Some peasants shook their fists at them or spat. They were French. Or perhaps they were Spanish exiles. The German soldiers looked on with indifference, ignoring the provocation, and the volunteers had orders not to pay any attention. "They're just a bunch of milksops!"

Back at the station, Mateo went to Captain Sandoval as soon as the train began to move again, toward the interior of France now, asking him: "Captain, have you any idea of the route we're going to take?"

Captain Sandoval, who was struggling to open a can of Norwegian sardines, replied: "Well, I can't tell you exactly. But I think we're going to a German camp near Bayreuth called 'Grafemwhor' or something like that. I suppose we'll take some training there, until the day when we take the oath to the flag."

"The oath to the flag?"

"Sure! I'm talking about the German flag. I think we'll have to swear loyalty to Hitler."

Mateo, who was holding the huge thermos bottle given him in San Sebastián, stood motionless.

"Then what?" he finally asked.

"Then on to Russia. To rescue Cosme Vila."

Mateo laughed. "Say, that's an idea!"

FIFTY-EIGHT

COSME Vila, in Moscow, oblivious of the plot by Mateo and Captain Sandoval to arrive in the Soviet capital and rescue him, with the intention, no doubt, of burning him alive on the Rambla in Gerona, did know, however, that a division had been formed in Spain to fight on the Russian front. And he had said to his Catalan comrades, Soldevila and Puigvert, and the Madrilenian Ruano: "I don't like that."

The former Communist leader of Gerona spoke out of the deep chagrin that had overwhelmed him when he had learned that Germany had declared war on Russia. In the School for Political Training, which he was still attending, the slogans in praise of the Third Reich, obligatory after the German-Soviet Non-Aggression Pact, had become almost automatic to Cosme Vila. Unlike his wife, he was beginning to know the Russian language—all the loving nicknames he gave his son were Russian now—and he had become habituated to viewing the Anglo-Saxon democracies as Russia's prime enemies, in addition to Franco. In all the instruction he had received since his arrival in the capital of the USSR, the idea that Russia and Germany would be the countries to impose their will on Europe had been uppermost. England would surrender. Russia would rally her great resources, Germany her technological skills.

Suddenly, everything had changed. Hitler had demonstrated that he would tolerate no competitors and that his aim was to make the resources of the USSR a part of the German hegemony. Ruano, the Madrilenian intellectual, had claimed from the start that the German attack was not "anti-Bolshevik," not "ideological," but "physical and economic." Hitler was aiming to seize the subsoil wealth of Russia, the petroleum of the Caucasus, and so on, to prevent the Soviet Union from actually becoming a great power in the course of time. Oddly enough, that opinion was shared by Warning Voice, Count Ciano, and Mussolini, on the basis of the evidence.

Accordingly, Cosme Vila not only was chagrined, he also was frightened.

His access to information was still virtually nil; neither he nor his comrades knew what was happening "in the highest circles." They knew infinitely less than the Governor and Mateo knew about the same circles in Spain. Since 1939 they had managed to hold brief conversations with La Pasionaria, whose photograph appeared constantly in the newspapers, together with those of Togliatti, the Italian leader, André Marty, the French leader, and Gottwald, the Czech, all of whom had been spending their vacations in Kuntsevo at the moment when the German attack had come. But the Spaniards had always come up against icy indifference on the part of those leaders. They had paid a visit also to the Frunze Academy, where Modesto, Lister, Tagüeña, and others were taking advanced courses in military education, but their alienation from those Spaniards was still greater. As for El Campesino, who might have been the most accessible of them all, he had been expelled early in 1941 for "undisciplined conduct" and for continuing to refuse to become Russified, as well as for proclaiming that the truth was as plain as daylight. Consequently, he was working now on the Pharaoh-like construction of the Moscow subway, built of marble. Since the outbreak of the war the work had been speeded up so that the subway "could be made into the greatest air-raid shelter in the capital."

Cosme Vila therefore had two causes for fear. He was long accustomed to calling Churchill "the first among the stranglers of the movement for the liberation of the people." Then suddenly, he had to name him "Russia's greatest ally," because he had promised Stalin airplanes, shoes, ten thousand tons of rubber, and aluminum. He must avow, too, that Churchill would avert a German attack on Russia through the Arctic by keeping constant aerial and maritime watch over the waters of the North. Furthermore, Roosevelt, "that vile incarnation of the capitalist system, the oppressor of the proletariat," now was ready to lend unlimited aid to the Soviet Union in its struggle against "the cannibals Hitler and Ribbentrop," in the form of all kinds of merchandise, and therefore had become "loyal to the cause of the Russian people."

The first effective German strike had shaken the Kremlin to its foundations, and Cosme Vila knew that. He had tuned in on a radio report announcing that with its first raid the German air force had destroyed three thousand planes on Russian soil, still in the factory or in their hangars on the field. A few days later, Hitler's armored divisions advanced as far as Minsk. He knew that it was true that many Russian units were on the run or had surrendered to the enemy, although, according to Soldevila and Puigvert, who in the school were specializing in the ethnic differences among the Russian people, the divisions that refused to stand fast were made up of Ukrainians, undermined by a longing for independence, or Kalmuck regiments, or mountain units from the Caucasus.

In short, only a minority; the other fighting forces were resisting with all their might.

The question worrying Cosme Vila was: "Will Stalin succeed in controlling the situation?" That was impossible to predict. Cosme Vila trusted him—of course! But Hitler had had so much time to prepare!

Several aspects of Stalin's attitude aroused a certain amount of hope in him, although only time would tell whether or not it was all a mirage. The dictator's behavior was scarcely orthodox from the Communist point of view, but it showed shrewdness and knavery. Indeed, the "father of the Soviet Union" waited ten days after the outbreak of hostilities before addressing the Russian people in person, an indication that he had meditated long over what he would say. His words were: "Comrades, fellow citizens, brothers and sisters, soldiers, and seamen: I'm speaking to all of you, my friends... The attack on our country is an act of perfidy that has no parallel in the history of our country... Death to the invader... Everyone must fight with no thought of retreating. He must say to himself, 'I must not die without first leaving beside me the body of a German.'"

Unheard-of language, indeed. Not a single allusion to Socialism or the Party. Citizens, brothers, sisters, instead of proletarians. Instead of the Soviet Republics, our country. Instead of enemy of Communism, the invader. His words, combined with the parlance adopted by the periodicals, indicated that in order to face up to that war, Stalin was invoking patriotism, not revolution. Ah, Stalin must know very well that he was far from able to count on the loyalty of the two hundred million Russians. On the other hand, if he appealed to the concept of country, he could use that as a catalyst.

"Either I'm very much mistaken," Cosme Vila said, "or we shall soon be reading eulogies to Peter the Great and Catherine II in *Pravda* and we'll be hearing old patriotic tsarist songs everywhere. Yes, this war is going to be a patriotic affair, Russia's war against Germanism, the eternal enemy. The 'old man' knows what he's doing."

Another measure to which Cosme Vila assigned the same motive was Stalin's order to deport all inhabitants of German origin, including Communists, to Siberia, and his announcement that Hitler would attack the Semites by preference—Father Forteza had guessed right, then—and unleash a ferocious campaign against the *Kholkhozy*, the farm cooperatives.

Still another change in the wind was Stalin's reconciliation with the Orthodox Church, which "for centuries had safeguarded national unity against the Mohammedans and Catholic Poland." He received the Metropolitan of Moscow and six archbishops in the Kremlin, if you please.

All that was very stirring from the strategic point of view no doubt, but it did not lessen the seriousness of the current situation. What would happen? What if Hitler should answer these tricks with iron strength and continue moving inward to the heart of Russia? People said that Stalin was having a special shelter built in the Kremlin, but there was also talk of moving the Government to the city of Gorki.

"What will become of the Spaniards? Of those of us who are in Moscow or working in the factories? What will become of Regina Suárez and her pupils? Of all the Spanish children scattered near and far?"

Cosme Vila was afraid that at some critical moment any "foreigner" would be considered dangerous, like the citizens of German origin, and would be deported or used as cannon fodder.

"The most likely thing," Soldevila said, "is that many of our compatriots will volunteer to go to the front. The factories and the mines are so boring!"

"It seems to me," Ruano opined, "that if there's anyone Stalin can trust it's the Spaniards. Who knows but that he may call on us to guard the Kremlin even, in case the situation worsens."

But one thing was certain: Cosme Vila and his comrades in the School for Political Training were not making any voluntary offers to shoulder a rifle. They had begun to think of themselves as an élite; they had become bureaucratized, so to speak. Russian demography, the density of the anonymous population—those one hundred eighty-three races which were the subject of their first professor's, the Lithuanian's, lectures, were the people who would have to bear the full brunt of the battle.

Cosme Vila's wife was always crying. She was afraid of air raids. "There's no shelter near our house. And what if it's true that the Germans are shooting women and children?" That woman's fears were never-ending. The least she could do, if the war went on for a long time—if it lasted until winter—would be to perform miracles in the kitchen with the meager rations assigned to them.

On July 20, Cosme Vila and his friends had in their hands the complete text of the speech that Franco had delivered in Madrid on the 18th, "the anniversary of the Uprising," before the National Council. That speech made a strong impression on them, largely because the Caudillo's oratorical phrases contrasted with his usual moderate language. "The die is cast. The first battles were engaged and fought on our fields. In the various theaters of Europe, other engagements decisive for our continent have taken place. And the destruction of the terrible nightmare of our generation, Russian Communism, is now wholly inevitable. There is no human force capable of turning aside this doom." Farther on, he said: "The war has been badly executed, and the Allies have lost it. France herself has recognized this, as have all the people of Continental Europe. They put their fate in force of arms as a means of resolving their differences, and the result has been adverse to them. Now nothing can be expected from brute effort; the governments themselves have so stated, clearly and definitively. This war that is going on is a new war, a war *between the continents*, which, as their agony continues, may give them an appearance of life, and those of us who love America feel the inquietude of these moments and pray that the evil we foresee will not overtake her... The campaign against the Russia of the Soviets, with which the plutocratic world apparently is now making common cause, cannot change the outcome. Their suffering masses will merely multiply the proportions of the catastrophe... The Crusade undertaken against the Communist dictatorship has destroyed with one blow the artful campaign against the totalitarian countries. Stalin, the criminal Red dictator, is now allied with the democracies. Now our Movement has won an unexpected justification throughout the world. During these moments, while German arms lead the battle for which Europe and Christendom has longed since time immemorial, wherein the blood of our youth will mingle with that of our comrades of the Axis as a living expression of solidarity, let us renew our faith in the destiny of our country, which will see our armies and the Falange closely united."

"It's all quite clear," Cosme Vila commented. "Franco is afraid that the United States will intervene."

Ruano, who missed his Spanish tobacco—the Russian cigarettes made him hoarse—added: "In any event that 'Gallego' knows it all, too. What does he hope to gain with that Blue Division, with the blood of the Spanish youth? This whole thing is nothing but an excuse. He wants to buy the right to a share in the loot with a few Spanish lives."

Soldevila breathed fire and brimstone. "What are you talking about? Are you giving up the war for lost?"

Ruano stared at the roof of the house on Bujanian Street, on which dampness had traced some lines that looked like a map of a battlefield.

"If the United States stops with sending us a few tanks and some canned goods, yes. What we need is what Franco fears—that they'll declare war on Hitler. My own impression is that with only our own means, we'll have nothing to do it with here."

THE Spanish Communists living outside Russia, scattered all over the world, were going through anxious hours, like Cosme Vila. In Spanish America, from Santo Domingo and Cuba to Uruguay, Panama, and the Argentine, a number of organizations had been set up "for the purpose of collecting funds to help the invaded people of Europe," they said, but in reality to be used to extend the reach of the Party's tentacles.

Those organizations went under a variety of names: the National Anti-Fascist Front, the League of Spanish War Wounded, the Committee for Aid to the USSR, and so on. Their members tried to infiltrate the old traditional centers of Spanish emigrants—the Galicians and Asturians—and the universities. Mexico was the nucleus from which they spread widely, the only country maintaining official relations with the Spanish exiles. Its natural beauty and its unique character had finally conquered David and Olga. Aside from the Spanish Communist exiles, the former combatants of the International Brigade were working with their old tenacity, many of them using false passports, especially the members of the Lincoln Brigade from the United States who had fought in the war in Spain.

Gorki, in Perpignan—that is, in Free France—had lost forty-two pounds. He was lost without Cosme Vila and with Marshal Pétain's sword pointing at his belly. He did not dare to set up an undercover radio or compose another pamphlet attacking the Virgin of Lourdes. He wandered through the cafés, where occasionally he met Canela, who was furious because that bigwig of the Republican Left who once had protected her, at the time that Ignacio talked to her, now had abandoned her, and because the public quarrel still going on in exile between Negrín and Prieto—Negrín in Mexico, Prieto in London—about the "monetary funds belonging to the Spanish Republic," was a lamentable spectacle before the whole world.

Added to that, Gorki had lost José Alvear, who had been his good friend in the tragic hours of the German invasion of France. José Alvear stayed with Gorki in Perpignan for several months after that but he missed his Madame Bidot of Toulouse. Suddenly, he learned, however, that embryonic resistance cells were being formed in occupied France, particularly in the north, and were working for De Gaulle's Free France. Without more ado he crossed the dividing line and went first to Lyon and later to Paris, where he met Antonio Casal, half dead with fear and vacillating between hiding in some *chambre de bonne* and going to work in Germany because "they were paying good wages there, enough to feed a family."

"So long," José Alvear said to Gorki as he left. Now, in Paris, he was in touch with other Spanish Anarchists who were planning with a "Frog" or two to blow up trains or stab German sentinels in the back, not in the least restrained by the reprisals promised by Hitler.

José Alvear wished that he could have had some news of El Responsable and his family, but that was impossible in occupied France. His communications had been cut, like Gorki's with Cosme Vila. The latest word from El Responsable had come from Venezuela. He was still in Caracas with his daughters, El Cojo, and others, and had said merely that "all South America is one long spree," that he "would have got along like a house afire with Pizarro or any of those characters." Naturally, he was still ranting against the Communists. "They'd liquidate you at the drop of a hat, when you least expect it, like they did that poor imbecile named Trotsky."

José Alvear buoyed up Antonio Casal's morale. Casal, the former leader of Gerona, the intimate friend of Tower of Babel, had hungered for words of encouragement ever since Julio García had left Paris.

"Come on, don't be a horse's ass," José Alvear said to him. "That son-of-a-bitch Hitler is going to lose. Can't you see what a mess he's got himself into? Russia! Well, even if it was only Andorra! They're going to give him what he's got coming to him. Have you ever heard of anyone taking Russia? Fat chance! Not even Stalin. Besides, can you dig those Teutons? Some jerks! They spend the whole day taking pictures of the Eiffel Tower and playing around with the midinettes. I tell you, Casal, they haven't got what it takes to be a man. No private initiative. They're nothing but arithmetic, I swear they are. You just make Federica Montseny top dog, and she'll swim across the English Channel and go straight to Churchill and bash in that mister's head instead of messing around with Greece or that desert in Africa. And that would be the end of it! If I ever saw you before, I don't remember it. That would be the normal thing to do...and the strategic thing. But now it's Russia—and that's the end of the line."

Antonio Casal smiled skeptically. "That's all very fine, and you put it very well. But I remember Porvenir talking like that when he went to the Aragón front with Durruti's column—'Day after tomorrow, Zaragoza is ours.' And here we all are, including Federica Montseny. And the Virgin of Pilar is in Zaragoza. And the Germans are the top dogs... Even the masters of the midinettes."

WASHINGTON, JULY 1, 1941

Dear Alvears:

Just a few lines to let you know that Amparo and I are well and to give you our new address: Imperial Hotel, Washington, D.C., U.S.A.

How are you all? We received Pilar's wedding announcement. We know she'll be happy, and perhaps is already expecting the stork. I'll bet she is.

We wanted to send a gift—there are lots of wonderful things for sale here—but how could we do it? As you know, for some time the ships have been carrying another kind of gift.

This is a very beautiful city, filled with trees and many old buildings. The Negroes are everywhere, and many refined people, too. You should hear me talking English! It's easy for me. But Amparo, who never learned to say more than *pardon* in France, is the same here; all she knows is "okay."

I haven't received a newspaper or magazine from Gerona. Either they haven't been sent or they were lost in the mail. I miss them. I used to get a lot of fun out of them, especially the "Parochial Leaflets" that Matías used to stick between the pages along with the "Moral Consultant," which I imagine is the work of Mosén Alberto. Did *Amanecer* actually publish my sentence? I'm referring to the open trial held by the Tribunal of Political Responsibility with me as the accused.

Ignacio, how is it going? I know you finished your law course. Congratulations. But tell me, what about Marta? Are you two married yet? Go on, get a move on! Amparo keeps saying it's the ideal state for a man, that the okay status is marriage.

How time flies! We've been away from Gerona for more than two years now. And here it's midsummer again. We imagine that the Costa Brava must be covered with bathing beauties—and Civil Guards.

Well, it's time now to put down the final period. I wonder if this war is ever going to end and if we'll be able to see each other again. Meanwhile, light a candle to San Narciso for our continued prosperity—and yours, too. A brotherly tip of the hat to you all from

Julio García

The address again: Imperial Hotel, Washington, D.C., U.S.A.

FIFTY-NINE

LIFE went on in Gerona. The volunteers had gone to Russia, leaving behind, each according to his circumstances, an aura of romance and drama. But life went on, somewhat slowly because of the heat. Again the city was conquered by heat. Beads of sweat stood like pearls on people's foreheads. They mopped their faces with their handkerchiefs, and Doña Cecilia sighed for the day when women used fans. "Those fans, with such pretty designs, and those lovely ribs, too. A fan was a great ornament to a woman. They ought to make it a law to use them!"

As usual, the heat dispersed the citizens who could indulge in the luxury of a summer vacation. The Syndical Organization dreamed of the day when all the "producers" would be able to enjoy paid vacations in seaside resorts or the mountains; but for the time being there was not much chance of that. The youth camps were open again, however. Not for nothing was it said that the Youth Front was "the regime's favorite project." One of the camps, at Aiguafreda, run by the Feminine Section, was called the "Blue Division Camp" this year.

A number of families left Gerona seeking fresh air, woodland, and water. As he watched them fan out, Notary Noguer thought back to summers before the war, when shutdowns had spelled ruin and the men had sat on the sidewalks, leaning their backs against a wall, with their berets or caps pulled down over their eyes. They had looked like statues—on the point of springing to their feet, however. They had been frightening. One had had the impression that they would get up and start to shoot at any moment, as they finally had.

Now there were few men sitting on the sidewalks. Work stoppages no longer occurred and habits had changed, one must recognize that. Conversation groups gathered at night in the doorways or hallways of houses, especially in the outlying streets. The men did not wear berets or caps that hid their eyes. Their eyes were visible, and that was a blessing.

Warning Voice and Carlota went to Puigcerdá, to the mansion owned by the parents of the "mayoress." Before she left, Carlota went to consult Dr. Morell. She wanted to have a child, and as no child was on its way as yet, she wanted to be examined. Dr. Pedro Morell found nothing abnormal in Countess Carlota's make-up.

"Then what?" she asked.

"Perhaps it might be well for your husband to have an examination," the doctor said. "We mustn't forget that there were no children of his previous marriage."

Carlota nodded. That was true. She talked it over with her husband. But Warning Voice looked displeased. He disliked the idea for reasons unknown to him. In any case, he believed that it was his wife's fault.

"All right, all right! When we come back from Puigcerdá, if nothing's happened I'll go and see Dr. Morell."

In Puigcerdá, they met old friends again, and Warning Voice was well received in the "colony," thanks mainly to his conversational gifts. His ironic wit, combined with his broad culture, had a gratifying effect on people. He gave everyone a nickname and discovered that he was able to make his neighbor laugh, always an ingratiating quality. He called the Governor "The Aspirant" because of his deep inhalations. And Carlota became the "Countess of Rubies" because of her fondness for antique jewelry.

Sometimes he would look at everything around him—golf courses, cricket fields, swimming pools—and as he cleaned his gold-rimmed glasses, he would say: "No matter what Mr. Collins thinks, there's no denying that the standard of living is rising."

Carlota was happy in Puigcerdá in spite of her father, a member of the Catalan nobility, who spent the whole day complaining about the Government's plans to create "a great Madrid."

"Have you seen the paper? They're going to build an Olympic City in Madrid, a covered stadium with a capacity of about eighty thousand people. Parking space for four thousand cars, and so on. Who's going to pay for it? Catalan industry. That's the way it is."

One family that went its separate ways was Manolo and Esther's. Esther had not seen her family since the end of the war. She missed them so much, especially her mother, Katy, that they decided that she should go with the children to Jérez de la Frontera about the middle of September. Manolo would join her later, and would spend a week there—if he could stand it.

"I know you don't like the atmosphere," Esther said to him. "I know the wine cellars and the bullfights make you nervous. But I trust you'll survive, after all..."

Manolo considered Esther's wishes very reasonable. He took care of all the details of the trip. When the day came, he went with them to the station. Esther was wearing a handsome silk scarf knotted around her neck; she seemed to overflow with expectation.

"I'm sorry you have to go by train."

"Why? I love to ride on the train. You know that!"

Jacinto and Clara threw themselves around Manolo's neck.

"Why aren't you coming with us, Papa?"

"I have to work, children."

The three beloved faces stayed at the window until the train was out of sight. Manolo was alone, with Gerona at his back, his office, and his little Balbo beard.

He spent a couple of lonely days, which united him more closely with Ignacio, to whom he talked interminably about Esther, the war, Mateo's "stunt." Ignacio said: "Luckily, Pilar seems to be standing up to the blow."

Manolo said: "Well, no one knows what will happen when the baby is born."

Then suddenly, Manolo began to enjoy being alone in the house. He seemed to breathe an indefinable air of freedom.

"It's strange," he admitted to Ignacio. "It turns out now that this vacation suits me splendidly. How would you like to have frogs' legs at La Barca tonight?"

"All right. Why not?"

The Governor's family dispersed also. Like Esther, María del Mar had not seen her people since the end of the civil war. She was dying to see for herself the state Santander was in since the fire and how quickly it was being rebuilt.

The Governor also considered that reasonable, and María del Mar went to her own little homeland, taking Pablito and Cristina with her. They traveled in the official car, although this time the chauffeur was not Miguel Rosselló because he had to stay in Gerona to fill the vacancy left in the provincial headquarters of the FET and the JONS by Mateo's departure.

No date was set for their return. They arranged to talk on the telephone every day.

"Chances are I'll have to go to Madrid and I'll come by and pick you up," the Governor said.

"All right. Take care of yourself."

Pablito gave his father a warm embrace. He was sorry to be separated from him. It seemed to him like the end of the world.

"Would you like me to stay here with you?"

"By no means, son. Don't you want to go to Santander?"

Pablito made a face. "Well—I want to very much, actually."

"Go on, then. Don't be silly. Go with your mother."

The Governor was not sure whether he was sad or glad. He had a great deal of work to do. Without Mateo, he felt helpless. Helpless himself and helpless for the Falange, in spite of Miguel Rosselló's good will. He spent as little time as possible in his house. Official functions still took a large share of his time. And the major festivals, too. The province had so many of them—that is, there were so many villages in the province, and every one of them was clamoring for his presence as much as for the Gerona Jazz Band.

The trouble was that he could not use the same speech in every place because *Amanecer* printed the full text each time, and its readers would have found him out. Luckily, the subject of the Blue Division was providing him with plenty of new material. In addition, he had come up with a slogan that invariably drew loud applause: "The black bread we're eating these days is far more welcome and comforting than white bread eaten in scorn."

The Costa brothers rented a country house in Pálamos and deposited their wives in it. They came and went in time to the affairs of the Constructora Gerundense, Inc., and Emer. Both corporations made a great deal of work for them, even though Carlos Civil, Professor Civil's son, was showing an unsuspected executive talent. But Emer had promised to take charge of the work on the new prison on September 30—they had won the open bid for the contract without great difficulty. The Costa Foundry building had to be finished by the same date. This company was the brothers' one personal monument. Then there was Don Rosendo Sarró. And Gaspar Ley, his representative in Gerona. They gave the brothers no peace. The Costas had always thought of themselves as miracles of activity. But Don Rosendo could give them cards and spades. He was not satisfied with his exports "to the belligerent countries." Now he had taken it upon himself to administer a push to the conglomerate cork industry, whence his need for the small port of San Felíu de Guixols. And to make connections with the insurance companies. The plans he laid before the Costas were tantalizing, but almost offensive. "You fellows are playing penny-ante, my friends," Gaspar Ley told them. "Building a prison! Running a foundry and stone quarries. I'm sorry, gentlemen, but in private Don Rosendo Sarró calls you the stone cutters."

The Costas had a hard time swallowing that. But they knew that Gaspar Ley was right. Nevertheless, they had good reason to lie low. "How can you compare Don Rosendo Sarró's situation with ours? We're third-class citizens, like those ration cards. Every Saturday we have to report to the police."

"No, you don't have to," Gaspar Ley insisted. "You're still thinking the way you did before the war."

The Costa brothers' *amour propre* was pricked. For the time being, they were keeping their wives entirely away from business, although the ladies had become so "addicted" to it that they still signed all the papers. When the brothers went to Pálamos on Sunday and found their spouses playing bridge with other vacationing ladies—influenced by Esther—they put on the right sort of face.

"You might at least learn to play," the wives reproached them. "You could take part in the championship games."

"In the championship games? We have to be in Gerona again early tomorrow morning."

"Oh, sorry. We forgot."

Jorge and Chelo were another couple who left the city. They chose one of the farmhouses he owned, near Arbucias, surrounded by immense meadows, and began to renovate it to suit their taste. Carlos Godo was the architect recommended by Agustín Lago to draw the plans for them, and the young couple was enchanted with them. Of course, they installed a heating system in the house. And a grange near the tenants' dwelling. Finally, Jorge confessed that he would not mind staying in the farmhouse for a long period of the year and putting a grange on it. Ah, what turns the world could take! The former air force combatant, Jorge de Batlle, who once had dreamed of flying over Moscow, could have made his dream come true now by enlisting in the air squadron of the Blue Division. But he was spending his day surrounded by books on poultry farming. The "disaffected" people of Gerona could live in peace. Jorge was not going to persecute them or denounce them. He was more interested in incubators, feed mixtures, and the possibility of finding eggs with double yolks.

Chelo often said to him: "Do you know, you look better every day?"

She was right. Jorge was better. The air in Arbucias and the new life suited him very well, even though Arbucias was a village to which the Reds had sent any number of children during the war to protect them from air raids, later taking them to Russia, where their fate was a cause for concern to Cosme Vila.

Jorge adored Chelo. "You've been an angel to me. You're Martha and Mary combined."

"Careful, now! I'm just Chelo, that's all."

Only one cloud marred Chelo's horizon. She had received a letter from her sister, Antonia, dated in the convent where she was a novice. Antonia said: "Papa has written me from the penitentiary. It's evident that he's very depressed. We must pray for him." Chelo would gladly have taken a trip to Puerto de Santa María, but she dared not suggest it to Jorge. She did not know how he would respond to that particular suggestion.

One happy vacationer was Adela. The big beauty had talked her husband, Marcos, into renting a cottage in Playa de Aro for the entire month of August. Marcos had objected that he was taking his vacation in September. But Adela was thinking of Ignacio—they desired each other with unchanging ardor—and objected on the ground that the weather was sometimes bad in September. "I need sunbaths. You know that. The doctor said so."

Adela, stretched out on the golden sand of Playa de Aro! The moment the Civil Guards mentioned in Julio García's letter had turned their backs, she took off her beach robe and offered her firm skin to the sun—while she waited for Ignacio. Even in the afternoons she climbed to the roof and there, with no witness but the sky, stripped down completely and lay on a rubber pad, dreaming.

Tower of Babel was another happy vacationer. He went to Llafranch every weekend in a tiny Fiat that he had won in a contest put on by Potax Soup. The problem of the contest was easy: to give the exact altitude above sea level of the Sanctuary of Our Lady of Fatima. The prize was that very small car. So many people guessed right that Potax Soup resorted to a lottery, and the former employee of the Arús Bank won it. He was a lucky man indeed.

The Gerundians laughed at the sight of Tower of Babel in a *topolino.* But that in itself was a good advertisement for the Agencia Gerunda. Tower of Babel was so tall that in order to get into the vehicle at all he had to hunch himself up like Mosén Iguacén before the Bishop, and in order to drive he had to hold his legs grotesquely far apart. But he did it all with great gusto and whistled along those blessed roads on his way to Llafranch. Sometimes, but not often, he whistled old UGT songs.

The vacation dispersal... In the bullrings the so-called national sport was recapturing its old-time popularity. In the Café Nacional, Señor Grote declared that bullfighting always enjoyed popularity during dictatorships because they stirred up the so-called "heart of the race" with admirable zeal. "And you know how it is with Spain, my friends. If we really and truly gave the heart of the race a good stir, we'd find a bull in it."

The football season was over, however, except for an international game with "the sister nation" of Portugal. This recess had a strong influence on the conduct of Captain Sánchez Bravo, president of the Gerona Football Club. He made known to the other members of the board of directors that he did not want even to hear of players, umpires, or turf until the first of September. "I have to look after my own affairs, see?" he explained. "That would be the last straw!" Captain Sánchez Bravo's affairs were simple: poker, the horse races, and giving his father the *coup de grâce* with regard to the building of new quarters for the soldiers. He was able to tell the General that the bid was practically certain to be given to the Emer Company. As a consequence, the Captain expected five thousand pesetas to fall to him at any moment, in used bills. Meanwhile, he was pursuing all his aforesaid affairs—and Silvia, the manicurist. That is, he was competing with Padrosa, with the advantage all on his side. Silvia loved uniforms. And she longed to be a movie actress. She had read in *La Vanguardia* that the producers of Vizcaya Films were offering opportunities to young ladies from seventeen to twenty-five who would like to become stars. "After next Monday," *La Vanguardia* said, "you, too, may be a movie star. Apply to the Calle Aribau, 150, first floor, Barcelona, and your career will begin." Silvia was ready to make the trip, but Captain Sánchez Bravo said to her: "Better watch out. Most likely the manager of Vizcaya Films is a fat slob, much shorter than I, with the eyes of a satyr." Silvia exclaimed "Heavens!" and pressed her legs together. "Don't scare me, Captain."

The little boys for whom there was no room in the camps were whiling away the summer too. They spent their time swimming in the Ter, playing at killing Russians—not Englishmen any more—and throwing stones at passing trains. This last trick was a new one that only Dr. Andújar would have been able to interpret.

Paz Alvear was far from idle; indeed, one might have said that she worked too hard. The Gerona Jazz Band again. As soon as the owner of the Diana Perfumery gave her the necessary free time, she said to Cefe: "You won't see hide nor hair of me until October, Cefe." The Gerona Jazz Band took all her time. Sometimes they would stop at one place in the afternoon and at another in the evening. This gave the musicians a perfect chance to carry away food products in the luggage compartment of the taxi and in the bass drum, which was of such huge dimensions that Paz feared it would ultimately attract attention. Damián, the band leader, knew very well that a great part of the orchestra's success was owing to Paz. But she was becoming capricious and causing problems. Lately, for example, she had taken it into her head that she needed singing lessons. "Don't you understand?" Damián shouted again and again. "Your strength lies in the very fact that your voice is awful. You're not aspiring to sing in the Lyceum, are you?" Paz admitted finally that he was right, that he had always given her good advice.

August was a triumphal month for Ignacio's cousin. She moved into the apartment that the Agencia Gerunda had found for her. The rooms were pretty and cheerful, although for the time being there was no furniture. Nevertheless, what had to happen did happen: conflict with Pachín. He was given the expected discharge from the Army and left Gerona bound for Asturias to visit his family in the village of Cangas de Onís, a family of miners. He said goodbye to Paz, more in love with her than ever. He was crazy about her. And he promised to return soon and discuss the future with her as they had agreed. But at the end of three weeks, Paz had received only a couple of letters from her lover, in one of which he told her that his contract with the football club of Barcelona for the coming season could be considered a *fait accompli.*

"Just let him try any tricks on me," she said to Damián. "I'll kill him."

"Please don't talk like that, doll," the band leader reproached her. "Pachín will bring Spain many days of glory with his kicking. Respect him. Now that you have a new flat, you ought to start being a patriot."

"You're a fool," Paz growled, "a smart aleck. I'll sign up, too, with some orchestra in Barcelona."

"Don't even think of it," Damián replied, shaking his head. "You're sensational here. In Barcelona you'd be just one more vocalist, unless you should decide on some cabaret, and Pachín would take that like a kick in the pants."

Her Uncle Matías, whom she often visited in the Telegraph Office, was her best adviser. His smile when he saw her made up to her for many unpleasantnesses. "Come in, come in, little niece. You can help me paste up these telegrams." Paz would always put together a token message on the blue paper. Then she would sit down and smoke a cigarette with her uncle and the ever-worried Marcos.

"I'm ready to drop. We finished at four o'clock this morning."

"What's the matter with your voice? Have you lost it?"

"It's always like this in the morning. And I shouldn't smoke. Later, after I've eaten, it's all right."

"Would you like a cup of coffee?"

"Fine."

When Marcos heard that, he would get up and offer her the thermos bottle that he always brought with him, a much smaller one than those given the volunteers of the Division on its way to Russia.

Goal, the cat, was living in a dream world now in the flat; he was the girl's other comforter. But Goal missed the dirty corners of the flat that had belonged to El Cojo—and sometimes Paz did, too.

What about Marta? What was she doing that summer season?

The same as ever. She was at the Aiguafreda camp, named for the Blue Division. She took command of it two days after the departure of the volunteers and spent her hours there trying to forget Ignacio. That was why she made the little girls sing over and over again the patriotic song "Close Up the Lines" and a tune with a lyric that said:

Under the sun and face to the sea,
Lies our camp where we learn,
First we learn and then we *play.*

That did not mean, however, that her life was monotonous. Something was always happening and there was always something to celebrate. For example, on August 3 there was great merriment in the camp. The Day of Dawning had been declared, to mark the day when Christopher Columbus first set sail for America: America Day. Marta made a speech to the little girls in her care; she delivered it very well, telling the saga of the Catholic monarchs and the Castilian and Extremenian conquistadors. She added that, according to some historians, it was quite possible that Columbus was not an Italian but a Spaniard, and explained to her adolescent audience that the first cartographers in the world were Spaniards—Mallorcans and Catalans, to be exact—and that they could be thanked for the first map of the Mediterranean, that famous sea on the shore of which their camp had been built.

August 8 was another important date in Aiguafreda. Bruno Mussolini, the Duce's son, and the Indian poet Rabindranath Tagore, Gracia Andújar's favorite, died that day in very dissimilar circumstances. Bruno Mussolini was killed in an airplane crash on the outskirts of Pisa. His young and heroic life had leaned farther out of balance than the famous tower of that city; the Duce had gone to weep for him. As for Rabindranath Tagore, he died at the age of eighty in Calcutta, after a serious illness. His legendary beard was smoothed down forever, and all the young poets in the world wept for him.

Marta gave a quick sketch of the two men. She said of Bruno Mussolini that he had left school at seventeen to fight in Ethiopia and since then had served his country as an airman—and Spain, too, for he had fought with an Italian air squadron during the Spanish civil war. "He died like a hero while he was testing a new four-motor bombing plane." Concerning Rabindranath Tagore, she said that he was also a great patriot who all his life had defended the cause of his people in India against British colonialism. "Ten years ago he gave back to the King of England all the decorations that the King had conferred on him because he considered them symbols of dishonor in view of the fact that a cruel slaughter of the Indian people by the British police was going on at that time."

"Comrades, around the bonfire of our camp, let us say an Our Father for the soul of Bruno Mussolini, a symbol of heroic youth, and another Our Father for the soul of Rabindranath Tagore, a symbol of old age and wisdom. Each of them, in his way, has written his last line of poetry. May God receive them in His glory."

IGNACIO was leading a double life that summer: one in Gerona, with his parents, Manolo, his work, and Pilar; the other a weekend life visiting Adela in Playa de Aro and Ana María in San Felíu de Guixols.

During those summer months, Ignacio was able to see Ana María freely and often because Don Rosendo Sarró, very busy with wolfram and the like of that, was always traveling as acting head of his Barcelona office. He was able to squeeze in only an occasional visit to San Felíu de Guixols. This gave the young couple a clear field, for Ana María's mother had said to her daughter, finally: "You know what I think; I believe you're rushing things. But I consider you a grown girl. So do whatever you wish."

In Gerona, Ignacio's life was intense. The slow rhythm imposed by the heat did not affect him. He was so abounding in health that he had energy to spare. He had even dropped the habit of taking a siesta, and now he spent his time after lunch writing letters. Suddenly, he had acquired an itch for correspondence, in part because he had found it made him feel important to come home and hear his mother say: "Several letters came for you." He would rip open the envelopes with a bogus air of solemnity, knitting his brows a little. Later, he put the letters in his pocket without a word of explanation. Sometimes he went to the balcony off the dining room and threw the envelopes in the river in defiance of municipal ordinances.

Of course, he wrote to Ana María, and also to his old comrades in the Company of Ski Troopers, whose whereabouts suddenly interested him. Moncho was one of them. He had completed his medical training in June. Ignacio wrote to Moncho three times in two weeks, begging him to come to Gerona for a visit. Finally, Moncho agreed. Ignacio also wrote to Royo and Guillén, in the Valle de Tena, under the pretext of telling them about Cacerola. Actually, what impelled him to write was his discovery that the two ski troopers with whom he had shared so many guard watches and so much cold weather, and who had gone through the war talking about nothing but cows and women, were barely capable of executing a few lines on paper, and made more mistakes in spelling than Paz. He wrote to Madame Geneviève Bidot in Toulouse, inquiring about José Alvear, of whom he knew nothing. He answered Julio García. A long letter in which he gave the former policeman all the news of the Gerundian scene and asked him to send some magazines from the United States. He wrote to

Ezequiel. And to David and Olga, from whom he had received a Christmas card giving their address. Suddenly, Ignacio felt a need to be in contact with the teachers again. Summer had a lot to do with that; he remembered Olga coming out of the sea at midnight. What were they doing in Mexico, aside from publishing books that the Bishop of Gerona would have pronounced perverted? David and Olga answered him by return mail. Their words rang with affection and nostalgia. They repeated the words "dear Ignacio" a thousand times, it seemed. They were well, busy with their publishing business, planning cultural activities for the Catalan Club, and writing another Manual of Pedagogy out of their experience accumulated from defeat. They told him that "a Spaniard was not a Spaniard at all, not a complete man, unless he knew Mexico."

"That's funny," Ignacio said to himself. "Now it turns out that I'm only half a Spaniard."

He discovered that he was still very fond of the two teachers and that the vacuum left in his life by their departure could not be filled by anyone else.

In addition to his attack of the epistolary measles, Ignacio was working hard in Manolo's office. That very month of August saw the first clash between the two lawyers, Manolo and Mijares. The case concerned property boundaries. The Constructora Gerundense, Inc., had bought some land on which to build a paper factory, and the owners of an adjacent property had sued them. There was an ambiguous clause in the deed which gave the property owners grounds for claiming that their interests had been injured. Mijares would defend the Constructora Gerundense, Inc., Manolo the plaintiffs.

"It had to happen some day," Manolo said to Ignacio, "and now it's here. We're up against the Costa brothers. I'm going to make a prophecy. Before another year is out, there'll be a clash between us and your future father-in-law. It's in the cards. I don't know what's going to happen to cause it, but something will. And that'll be the first case you'll have to handle on your own, in court."

Ignacio put his hands to his head. "No, please! Not that!"

Manolo gave him an ironical glance. "What's the matter with you, Ignacio? You've got to make your voice heard in the courtroom some day, don't you?" Seeing that Ignacio still looked alarmed, he added: "When that day comes, we'll have to ask your cousin to lend you her microphone—unless you've recovered by then."

That was Manolo's great strength—his sense of humor. Manolo attributed it to his intensive reading of Chesterton and Bernard Shaw, but that was not correct. He had been born with it, and life amused him. He enjoyed living and finding the nuances in any situation. "If we couldn't give some color to that strange act of breathing, our days would be endless," he used to say.

Ignacio had seen ample proof of this during Esther's absence. Not only did Manolo cast off his initial gloom, but soon he began to take maximum advantage of his independence. At one of the dinners that the two men had together in the nearly deserted restaurant of La Barca, from the terrace of which they could hear the running water of the Ter and the nightly dialogues of the trees along the banks, Ignacio's boss admitted that he had done honor to the male of the species by being unfaithful to Esther for the first time since he had married her.

"Don't worry, though. It wasn't with the maid—that would have been humiliating for my wife. And for me. I picked up a lady who came my way. And so—well, I didn't pass up my chance. Perfidiously and at night I did it."

Ignacio was only partly surprised. He was used to hearing confessions of that kind. All the adulterous husbands he knew would have considered themselves less than a hundred percent Spanish even though they had never been in Mexico, unless they could tell a friend about their adventures. Ignacio, not yet a husband, was himself burning with the desire to tell someone about his relations with Adela. He needed that to bring out the full flavor of the affair.

"So, then," Ignacio said in response to Manolo's confession, "what you mean by giving color to breathing is that you don't want Esther to find you out of practice when she comes back."

"That's it exactly."

Manolo felt obliged to excuse himself, however. "I'm not proud of my conduct, you understand, but you know how it is in a sultry August."

He lighted a small pipe that he had just bought. But the air was so warm that he put it out at once and smoked a cigarette.

"You see—Esther is very jealous, you know. You've no idea! Oh, I see you're surprised. She wears slacks, plays tennis—she's a liberal. Nonsense! I'm a little bit scared of her about this jealous bit. I keep a tight control over myself. But now it turns out that she has reason to be like that, it turns out that I'm doing the very thing..."

Ignacio did not know what to say.

"All that control is hard for me, Ignacio. So as soon as I have the chance, I jump the fence, like everyone else."

Manolo's cigarette was a pinpoint in the darkness. Ignacio asked him: "Just out of curiosity—if Esther found out about this, would she forgive you?"

Manolo opened his eyes wide with a comical expression. "Not for a minute. She'd stay in Jérez with her mama and papa. And she'd wipe my picture out of my children's minds."

Ignacio persisted maliciously: "What if she should do the same thing to you?"

Manolo threw himself back in his chair. "I'd shoot myself."

Ignacio shook his head. "So much for all that stuff about Bernard Shaw and Chesterton, then. So much for Oxford," he said. "So now it comes out that you're about as English as my friend Cacerola."

Manolo shrugged his shoulders. "Just about."

Ignacio was thoughtful. After all, Manolo's unfaithfulness to Esther had made an impression on him. Realizing that, Manolo said: "All this goes to prove one thing, Ignacio, that marriage is a peculiar institution. In the best of cases, it's always hanging by a thread." He paused. "You know, living together, adjusting, is an extremely difficult thing."

Another surprise! Manolo's tone was reticent.

"But you've been lucky, haven't you? Your marriage is practically perfect."

Manolo still sat sprawled out in his chair. The waters of the Ter were still running to the sea in the shelter of the night.

"Don't you believe it! But, after all, I don't think I'm out of luck. Esther and I—we get along very well. But we get along best when other people are present."

Ignacio took a sip of his coffee, which he had let grow cold.

"Do you mean that you fight when you're alone together?"

"No. We never do that, or only on rare occasions, that is. We love each other. For God's sake, don't look at me like that! We love each other, kid, we love each other. Oh, it's very hard to explain it to a bachelor."

"I'm sorry, Manolo. But if you don't set an example for me…"

"An example," Manolo said coolly. "Well, you'll find out for yourself. You go into the bathroom when she's just taken a bath and find the mirror covered with steam. At first you take a deep breath of it. It's something intimate. It's exciting. Now it annoys me. I have to make an effort not to take a towel and wipe off the mirror so I can start to shave."

Ignacio scratched his left eyebrow. "You could shave some other time, couldn't you?"

"There you go! You aren't following me. Haven't you been listening? In the beginning, I enjoyed that steam."

"I see."

Manolo went on. "Another drama: you know we have vertebrae up our back, don't you? Well, the third, exactly the third vertebra pains Esther. I have to rub her back every single night with an ointment that she has to order from Gibraltar." Manolo paused again. "It stinks. That ointment stinks. Besides, there's nothing in the marriage contract that said Esther's third vertebra was going to start to ache."

Ignacio scratched his other eyebrow. "But you're joking!"

"Joking? Did you say joking?" Manolo called the waiter and ordered a cognac. "Okay! There's nothing worse than insensitivity. And you're being insensitive tonight, my dear Ignacio. Cognac, please."

The waiter turned and went for the bottle. Manolo smiled.

"Ah, marriage! I know all about it, Ignacio. Do you want to hear another phase of the problem? That's guessing what the other person is thinking and knowing in advance the gestures she'll make. Someone once said that was the source of happiness. He must have been talking about old age! And I've just turned thirty-six. Don't you think men are naturally polygamous?"

Manolo laughed. The waiter came with the bottle of cognac and two glasses, as if he knew that Ignacio also needed something stimulating. Manolo was silent until the waiter had gone, then went on.

"Esther—she's capricious. With her perfectly creased slacks. With her handsome sweaters. She's too elegant, Ignacio! And I've got to keep up with her; I've got to live up to her standard. Do you think I like that Tyrolean hat I wear in the winter? But I'm supposed to make an impression..." Manolo took a sip of the cognac. "Ah, my friend, my assistant, the same thing is going to happen to you with Ana María. And the truth is I like her a thousand times better than Marta, who may be in the Blue Division now for all I know. Yes, the same thing is going to happen to you, unless Don Rosendo Sarró falls into the hands of the price administration and they pack him off to Garrapinillos. Did you notice that Esther-Ana María duet the night of the procession? They looked like twins! Ana María will occupy the bathroom before you do, and you'll have to take a towel and wipe the mirror off before you can shave, too."

Ignacio managed to smile, with an effort.

"All right," he said. "But as far as I can see, I have one big advantage over you: I don't want to make an impression. I'll never be caught wearing a Tyrolean hat."

Away from Gerona, Adela and Ana María.

THE affair with Adela was like a flame. "I need you, Ignacio. Come here. Come closer. Put your arms around me."

Adela would send the children and the maid outdoors to play on the beach or to spend the afternoon at the Torre Valentina. Then she would wait for the bus to bring Ignacio. She could see it stop on the road from her window. The cottage that Marcos had rented at Playa de Aro stood on a knoll and had a door at the back which opened onto the woods. And Marcos had to be on duty at the Telegraph Office in Gerona on Saturdays and Sundays.

Theirs was an erotic coupling and nothing more. Nothing more on Ignacio's part. But Adela was falling in love with the young man. "This thing breeds affection, you know."

Adela was an expert on the subject of love. She knew the value of painting a mole here today, there tomorrow. And she knew how to take poses that she had practiced in front of the mirror—as Hitler reputedly practiced his speeches. Her posturings would have made Cefe nervous, even though he was a painter of nudes.

"Where on earth did you learn all this, beautiful?" Ignacio asked her. "It wouldn't be from the *Kama-Sutra*, would it?"

"The *Kama-Sutra*? What's that?"

"I mean I doubt that your husband is an expert exactly..."

"Marcos? That poor dope." She laughed. "Are you trying to get me to admit that I've known other men before you?"

Adela was trying to make Ignacio jealous.

"I'm trying to get you to do anything, Adela. Come on, I need you, too. Come closer..."

Before Ignacio could leave the house he had to admire the latest bathing suit that Adela had bought. And to climb up on the roof to where she offered herself to the sun. And then he had to eat a tremendous lunch.

"There's one thing that horrifies me—the thought that I might lose you some day."

"Why, my dear girl, you'll never lose me. Can't you see I'm crazy about you? Don't you realize I'm risking my neck?"

"Yes, but—what about after you're married?"

"Please, Adela! That's a long way off, and besides, we'll still see each other."

Fortunately, Adela could smile at the opportune moment. "Yes, you're right, Ignacio. We may as well live in the present. Oh, this blessed Playa de Aro." Adela gazed at the sea. "Would you like another piece of buttered toast?"

"Well—yes."

Their farewells were always frenetic.

"Now I'll be alone again! Another week of waiting for the bus."

In San Felíu de Guixols there was Ana María. A change of scene. There what mattered most was not the present but the future.

Every week Ignacio arrived in a simmering San Felíu. He always had to invent excuses because he never knew what time he would be there. Ana María wanted to go to the station to meet him, to see the little asthmatic train that amused her. But Ignacio said no. "Don't bother. Chances are I'll come by car with someone. I don't know what time I'll finish work. You know how it is."

That was all the same to her. Finally, they were together, and that deep, sincere idyl would begin and go on until Sunday night or Monday morning. The incident with Adela and her movable mole could not mar it.

San Felíu de Guixols was beautiful that summer. The scars of the war were disappearing. The breakwater had been cleaned and completely repaired, and the sea promenade had been conscientiously restored. A breeze always circulated around the breakwater, and from the rotunda of the lighthouse a great expanse of blue was visible. As the waves broke against the retaining wall of stone, they called forth mysterious, sonorous sounds that excited Ignacio's imagination.

"Did you know, Ana María, that there's a lighthouse keeper in the Insane Asylum who claims that fish can impregnate themselves?"

"What? How curious!"

Ignacio's imagination was a splendid antidote for Ana María's sometimes excessive logic. She was very sensitive, but it was not easy for her to invent new worlds. She would have been dismayed as much as anything by the sketches done by Félix, the Costa brothers' protégé. She felt certain that the intangible could not be seen. Ignacio, on the other hand, assured her that in spite of the theories of Dr. Chaos, the spirit was more real than the flesh, desire more real than the nose on her face, and that every thing had a poltergeist inside it.

"It's all subconscious—see, Ana María? We're moved by unknown impulses, like that water that comes from far away. By impulses not our own, that don't belong to us. Why should that be so? For example, you're frightened by wind. I've noticed that, but I like it. Why? Perhaps some of your ancestors were caught in a northwest gale or a hurricane. Now I loathe seafood, as you know. That comes from something occult, remote. You must read Freud. And then ask yourself what dreams really are. Gosh, if I told you what I dreamed last night! Oh, yes, everything means something, even that voracious hunger that sometimes seizes you when you see a piece of buttered toast."

A part of the beauty of San Felíu de Guixols was the sight of the fishermen sunning themselves on the benches that lined the sea promenade, watching the water curling beyond the port and the Punta de Garbí in an effort to forecast what the weather would be like. Ignacio said that fishermen rarely looked at the sky or, if they did, only for practical purposes, to orient themselves. The sea was what really interested them. "The people who look at the sky are the farmers, because the earth, the bare dark earth, is not at all expressive. The sea is much more so."

One object struck a displeasing note on the sea at San Felíu de Guixols: Don Rosendo Sarró's sloop. He had had it built during the winter to his specifications. There it lay like a flag, like a warning. White, with some lines of red trim. A little like the Red Cross. The name of it was *Victoria.*

"Why did he give it that name? He should have called it *Ana María.*"

"No, *Ana María* isn't a suitable name for a sloop. Although I don't like *Victoria* either. I don't know..."

"Well, I know," Ignacio said. "Your father named her for himself."

Ana María laughed.

More people were around that summer than the summer before. Friends of Ana María and their parents. Ignacio was introduced to them, but Ana María did not dare to say yet "my fiancé" or "the man I'm going to marry." She said: "May I introduce a friend, Ignacio Alvear."

Ana María's girlfriends liked the name. They thought it nice that he was a lawyer with black hair and eyes that looked inside things. What about his family? What sort of family did he come from? All this because Ana María had refused to go out with other boys on weekends.

"His father is an official in the Telegraph Office."

The speculations of the friends of the Sarró family stopped right there. But that made no difference to Ana María. "They're common. And my friends are still like little girls." Ana María was courageous because she was in love. So much in love that she had started to study typing and shorthand in order to be able to help Ignacio after they were married. Her mother had bought her a portable typewriter on which she practiced for a couple of hours every day. Three times a week she went to the shorthand class with a student of Esperanto in San Felíu, a man who took notes with incredible speed. He said: "If you keep on like this, you'll soon write faster than I do."

Ignacio was touched at that proof of good will.

"It's the least I can do. Because I can't study Roman law, can I? I'm too old for that."

No matter what she did, Ana María enjoyed herself. Dancing *sardanas*, of course. Following the steps with unusual grace. The old *sardana* fans would stand behind her to watch her feet and then look at one another as a sign of their approval. She also enjoyed going on bicycle rides with Ignacio. She had a gleaming bicycle, the latest model. Ignacio had to rent one, which was old and bent and had high handlebars, a ridiculous looking thing, but it served the purpose.

Sometimes they pedaled as far as Playa de Aro or even to Pálamos. The paved road, their youth, and the breeze inspired them to great efforts. "Ana María! Wait for me! Remember I'm riding a piece of junk." "Don't give me that! Show me how you fought the war."

Of course, he showed her. Suddenly, they would come to some solitary stretch of road where they could get off, sit down beside a ditch and kiss each other. That was all. Ignacio's respect for the girl was so great that Ana María could only be thankful for it. "I'm grateful to you, Ignacio." Ignacio could not tell her that the one she ought to thank was Adela.

The summer was splendid, almost cloudless. And after his conversation with Manolo, Ignacio kept on his guard, trying to divine what might cause friction with Ana María in the future.

He did not find much. A few differences between them. Once Ana María scolded him for his lack of interest in music and the theater and ballet. Ignacio asked himself whether those gaps in his education would come to be as important as steam on the bathroom mirror or a pain in the third vertebra. Well, was there ever a perfectly attuned married couple, even if they belonged to the same class? His parents, Matías and Carmen Elgazu, had never been able to agree on the way their children should be brought up. The problem was to know how to put up with things. Put up with? How could that phrase possibly apply while their bicycles lay there waiting for their young bodies, and the asphalt was gray but comfortable, and the breeze was bending the reeds at their back?

Ana María would be thinking her own thoughts at the same time. Especially in the mornings on the beach. The thing that worried her about Ignacio, aside from his chronic emotional instability—all of a sudden he would put on a mask and come out with something outrageous, just to mortify her—were his religious doubts. They went together to Mass on Sunday mornings, and he would simply be there, his thoughts far away. Sometimes he would even adopt an ironical attitude. And when the parish priest came out with some nonsensical statement, which happened often, he would nudge her and say: "That's sheer idiocy."

The worst of it was that Ignacio seemed to be well informed in his heterodoxy, for Ana María did not accept a number of outward and anachronistic religious customs either. And intolerance or an excess of self-assurance bothered her. But the Scriptures were sacred to her, as sacred as to Professor Civil. That was the precise point from which friction stemmed. Ignacio did not conceal from her that for some time now the Scriptures had seemed to him contradictory. He did not understand some of them, such as that about the "wise administrator." And it was very hard to know what were the exact words used by Christ, who had spoken in Aramaic—like Teresa Neumann, the girl marked with the stigmata when she was in a trance—and the Church could offer translations only. Frequently, translations of translations.

"Just what does spirit mean in Aramaic? Do you know? And men of good will? And the word 'father'? And the word 'heaven'? What did Jesus mean when he said: 'Except ye...become as little children, ye shall not enter into the kingdom of heaven'? That we must refuse to grow up?"

Ana María was suffering. "But why must you torture yourself like that? The Church has its learned men, hasn't it?"

"Yes, of course. But who can guarantee that those learned men are any more advanced than I am?"

"Ignacio, for heaven's sake! Don't talk like that!"

Ignacio tried to soothe her. "Ana María, baby, don't worry. I haven't lost my faith. I don't think I'll ever lose it. I love you and loving means believing in God. What happens is that I'm aspiring to be religious in a more conscious way. Yes, I know what you're going to say. You're going to say that I love a God created in my own image. That's not it at all. Quite the contrary. I feel that God is much greater than they want us to believe, than they've told us up to now. All right! Let's change the subject. Let's leave all this for now. Do you know what I need? I need to go to confession. I'll go to Father Forteza, make my confession, and hear Mass next Sunday on my knees, the whole Mass on my knees. Okay? All right, then, let's celebrate that. Let's go out on the breakwater and watch the sea."

A curious thing happened in San Felíu de Guixols on August 31. A dealer in flour was forced by Don Oscar Pinel, the administrator of price controls, to walk the streets all day with a sign reading: "I tried to sell ten thousand pounds of black-market flour to the Social Auxiliary. I'm a barefaced cheat."

People nearly split their sides laughing. But Ignacio and Ana María looked at the man with mixed feelings. Ignacio could not forget Manolo's words: "Before a year is out, we'll have to tangle with your future father-in-law." Ana María was thinking of her father, too, of the snatches of talk she heard when he was on the telephone.

The man with the placard looked to be about fifty. It seemed he was the owner of the Castillo de Aro, which operated several mills. He looked like a peasant, but probably he would gaze at the sky very little. He was so miserable that it was painful to see him. Ten thousand pounds of flour to the Social Auxiliary!

"Let's go. This is getting on my nerves."

"Mine, too."

They walked around window-shopping. Ana María liked to look at the perfumeries. In one of them they read a small sign that said:

Pimpinela advises you,
Brighten your lips with Marilú.
In place of lipstick, something new.

"Who's Pimpinela?" Ignacio asked as he stared at Ana María's unpainted lips.

She laughed. "A philosopher-manufacturer who knows more than you do about women."

Night came to San Felíu de Guixols. Ignacio and Ana María went into a café that reminded them of the Frontón Chiqui in Barcelona. They talked about the war. They both wished, in spite of everything, not only that Mateo would come back safely from his adventure, but also that, since he had no choice now, he would reach Moscow.

"Between the Germans and the Russians, we're on the side of the Germans, aren't we?"

Ana María put the little sugar envelope in her handbag to add to her collection. "Certainly, Monsieur Voltaire." Then she added: "And speaking of Moscow, when are we going to be married?"

Ignacio gave her a meaningful wink. "I'll tell you when: it'll be the day when I learn to like opera."

Ana María crossed herself. "Heavens! I might as well make up my mind to go into a convent!"

SIXTY

GRACIA Andújar and Ignacio were the first to receive letters from the volunteers in the Blue Division. Cacerola's name was signed to both.

Cacerola told Gracia Andújar, his pen pal, that he was well and so were his comrades in the Grafenhwor camp in Germany, near Nuremberg. General Muñoz Grandes had arrived at the camp to take command of the Division. For the time being, the men were spending their time on refresher courses, rifle practice, and playing cards with the decks that had been given them when they had passed through Vitoria. They did not know when they would leave for the Russian front. The German people had given them a marvelous reception. He, Cacerola, was in his glory, for he had always wanted to become acquainted with other lands. "Right now the only thing I'd like would be for you to send me a picture of yourself to keep in my tent where I could look at it as often as I wish." Gracia Andújar promptly went to a photographer, stopping along the way at the deluxe Dámaso beauty parlor, glad to gratify the first wish of her pen pal, whom Ignacio had described to her. "He has the purest heart of anyone I've ever known. The only danger to you is that he'll ask you to marry him before three months are up."

The letter to Ignacio also signed by Cacerola was dated July 18. It breathed homesickness and recalled the days with the ski troopers. "What a pity you're not here, Ignacio. I learned so much from you. I realize more and more each day how sad it is to be ignorant. Lots of the comrades start to talk to me about things I don't understand. Some of them already can jabber a few words of German. All I know is one word, *verboten*, which I figure means forbidden. I hope Mateo will wangle me an assignment as a cook, which is all I'm good for, although here you've got to cook with butter and everyone would rather have olive oil. I met a German girl named Hilda. Now don't you tell Gracia Andújar about her! I'll write to you again as soon as I can."

The next letter to reach Gerona was from Solita to her father, Don Oscar

Pinel, the price administrator. The letter was short; it exuded sadness. Solita said that she had made friends with another nurse named María Victoria, "who is José Luis Martínez's sweetheart, as it happens. She's a girl with a great deal of vitality; I've grown quite fond of her. She's a little nervous because she doesn't even know how to give a hypodermic, and everyone here has to be inoculated. But her gaiety is contagious, and that has done me a lot of good. I'm doing the best I can, but I find I'm a little unadjusted as yet. The change has been so sudden. And how are you? How is the General? Give him my kindest regards and write to me soon to let me know how you're getting along without me..."

Mosén Falcó, the religious adviser of the Falange, wrote also—to the Bishop—informing him that the religious life of the Grafenhwor camp was very intense, "with many communicants at the Sunday Mass."

Of course, Pilar carried off the honors; she received the most letters. Mateo wrote her four times within two weeks. The first epistle said:

> I hope you'll deign to read this letter in spite of your anger. I'm writing to you with all my love. And I hope, too, that in the course of time you'll understand that I had no choice. I did what I had to do. And I'm sure that later on, when it's all over and I'm with you again, and with our son, the son we're expecting, you'll be proud that your husband did his part in this new crusade against Communism.
>
> I've discovered that many of my comrades here are also married. And I've learned through talking with them that not all wives reacted as you did. There are some who were the first to want their husbands to enlist. One of those comrades with whom I've made friends, is named Olano; he has a five-month-old son! So there you are! Of course, he's much happier than I am.
>
> I can't deny that your behavior affected me as few things in my life have done. It will be hard for me to forget that you did not even want to say goodbye to me at the station. But I don't doubt that you'll think it all over and change your mind. Meanwhile, I have your picture in my writing case, and I never go to bed without looking at it for a long time and giving it a kiss.
>
> You told me that you could understand if I were a *soldier.* Don't you realize that being in the Falange is being a part of the Militia, that it's basically the same thing? What's the difference between wearing a khaki uniform and wearing a blue shirt? Either one changes questions of patriotism into questions of honor.

Goodbye, Pilar... I'm yours forever. I embrace you with all my love.

Mateo

The second letter was in a different tone. Mateo still alluded to Pilar's lack of understanding and repeated the same arguments, more or less. But he mentioned other things this time.

To my great surprise, I met Comrades Salazar and Núñez Maza here. As you remember, they were dismissed from their posts a little while ago and wanted to set an example. They were the first to ask for a place in the Division. Their attitude has been a great comfort to me. Núñez Maza, who can't live without a microphone in his hand, as you know, is going to speak one of these days on a special broadcast beamed to Spain. Perhaps you can find out the exact day and hour from the Gerona Broadcasting Station. And if you do find out, and turn on the radio, you'll have a good chance to catch a little of the enthusiasm that reigns here. It's possible that these broadcasts may become a regular thing, and in that case I may speak some day and tell you with my own voice how I feel toward you.

Of course, I'm still making new friends. There are all kinds of people in the camp, all united in a common aim. There's a boy who has a brother twelve years old in Russia; he was taken there in 1937 with one of the expeditions that the Reds got together in Asturias. His brother is the man in the greatest hurry to get to the front. Another individual, who likes to be called Difícil, told me that during the war he knew Miguel Rosselló in Madrid, while Miguel was working in espionage. If you see Miguel, tell him. This fellow is a bit odd; he always carries a ping-pong ball in his pocket, and he keeps playing with it.

Our morale is very high, thanks to the example set by the officers and the humane personality of General Muñoz Grandes. Besides, the Germans are knocking themselves out for us. We've had a trip to Nuremberg, one to Hof, and now they're going to take us to Bayreuth soon. That's the place where the great Wagnerian festivals are held.

This whole region is very beautiful, and the way it's organized is a marvel. Only to see it makes plain the admirable efficiency of the German Army. To give you an idea, I'll tell you that they've given us individual rainproof tents, but they've figured them out so that if four of them are joined, they make a campaign tent. They've also given an accordion to each company. The children in the Hitler Youth come to see us often—whenever I see them I'm reminded of our summer camps—and

> they shoot off rockets decorated with the Spanish flag. Bands play our national anthems everywhere. But to tell the truth, they do it so badly that we have to laugh...

And so on.

In his latest letter Mateo told Pilar that they were about to celebrate with great solemnity the ceremony of taking the oath of allegiance to the Führer for the duration of the war. And further that the Supreme Command had ordered them all to wear the German uniform, although with a patch on the right sleeve showing the Spanish flag. They were allowed to wear on their chests the medals won in the civil war.

> We're all very proud of being admitted to the bosom of the German Army, and proud to listen to speeches by the Spanish and German officers and to parade before them afterward.
>
> I haven't received a single letter from you yet. Don't you ever intend to write to me? Pilar, how can you possibly leave me without any news of you? All my other comrades have received letters from Spain. Your silence makes me very sad, and so does my father's.
>
> Perhaps it will be a little while before I can write to you again. We've heard rumors that we'll soon be leaving for the front. Goodbye, Pilar, they're sounding the mess call. My boys are standing in line. "*¡Arriba España!*"

Pilar opened all the letters with tears in her eyes. She read them avidly with Don Emilio Santos, then crushed them, into a ball and threw them away.

She was well. Dr. Morell had assured her that almost certainly the shock would have no effect on her pregnancy. But her attitude did not change at all. She had no regrets. She still believed that Mateo's departure was "the act of a cur," no matter what that Olano, who had left his five-month-old son, might say.

Of course, Pilar and Don Emilio were not the only people to turn on Radio Berlin and listen to the speeches of the members of the Blue Division. *Amanecer* announced the day and hour of the broadcast. Núñez Maza spoke first, giving a patriotic spiel that contained nothing new except that Stalin's eldest son, Jacob Dzhugashvili, had been taken prisoner in the Smolensk sector. Another time he talked about the men in the air force who had joined their camp. After that, an unidentified voice gave daily news of many of the comrades, beamed to their families. "Greetings from Divisionario Benito Tejada to his parents and brothers and sisters." "Comrade Crispín Gutiérrez wants his family to know that he's in splendid condition and high spirits." It all sounded somewhat like the records dedicated to someone which the manager of the Gerona Broadcasting Station had made popular.

In spite of everything, Pilar kept hoping to hear Mateo's voice some day. But it never came. On August 15, Radio Berlin said, however: "From Lieutenant Mateo Santos, a warm embrace to his wife, Pilar, and another to his father, Don Emilio Santos."

That night Pilar cried harder than ever. It seemed to her that the anonymous voice had come from the ends of the earth. But that oral greeting, which, fortunately, she had heard perfectly, did not persuade her to forgive Mateo. It did, however, prompt her to write a few lines at last, only a word or two to let him know "there was no news." *Amanecer* had published the instructions for mailing letters: they had to carry the first name and surnames, followed simply by "Spanish Division, Germany." Matías was given the letter to post.

Don Emilio wrote to his son, too, but on the sly, without a word to Pilar or anyone. Matías, Carmen Elgazu, and Ignacio did not want even to hear the name of Mateo. But each on his own account devoured the news that appeared in the newspapers concerning the Division.

By the end of August, however, Pilar relented enough to start to knit a sweater for Mateo, in preparation for the "Russian winter" that the newspapers were starting to describe. She alternated her work on the sweater with making garments for the baby, and the conjunction caused her much anguish.

Her visits to the Rambla flat were much more frequent now. If she had not been expecting a child, she would have thought at times that nothing had changed in her life, that she was still unmarried. And it was remarkable how much the frequent visits of little Manuel diverted her. With his always attentive manner, his willingness to help, Manuel Alvear reminded her somewhat of César. He had marked the name of Grafenhwor in his atlas. Pilar came to think of the child as a protective shadow over her, which would free her from something irremediable. Occasionally, Manuel brought her a clipping from *La Vanguardia* by a press correspondent in Germany. One report that impressed Manuel was that Radio Moscow had set aside an hour each day for a broadcast called "The Christian Hour," which provided its listeners with sermons, prayers, and hymns. They were beamed to the people in the villages who had kept their faith in God, with the hope that the program would help them decide to fight. The correspondent added: "A safe guess is that the stone tablet that stands in Red Square in the Soviet capital, proclaiming that 'Religion is the opium of the people' has been covered over."

Pilar made an about-face at that point and said to Manuel: "What do I care about all that? All I want is for Mateo to come back."

It was well for Pilar that she did not know the conditions against which the Blue Division was struggling at that time. The day finally came when the volunteers marched off to the front. Good Lord, what a trip! They traveled more or less comfortably by rail as far as Augustow-Suwalki on the Polish border. But from there on, they covered a distance of nearly a thousand kilometers on foot. This came as a great surprise to all the *divisionarios.* They all had thought that their division would be motorized and provided with something more modern for the journey. Not at all. For reasons they did not know, the regiment had only horse power. Some horses and a great many head of cattle were assigned to the Artillery and the Transport columns. Maintaining and caring for the animals became a great burden; the division needed many veterinarians for that, and they had only a few. So few that Alfonso Estrada finally thought: "I wish I'd studied veterinary medicine like my father instead of philosophy and literature."

Mateo, Rogelio, and all the others bore the march staunchly. They had not lost the skill acquired during the Spanish war. As the volunteers passed through the villages in Poland, they were hailed with enthusiasm on the part of the Catholic priests and the people in general. In Lithuania, on the other hand, they traveled through gloomy, poverty-stricken areas, where the people had turned somewhat hostile as a result of the reprisals wreaked on the communities of Jews by the German soldiers; many members of the communities had been tattooed on the back with a yellow sign.

The division reached Russia through the Vitebsk sector. Mateo and Cacerola, the section's cook, spat on the ground when they first set foot on Russian soil. Then, a few yards farther on, they knelt and kissed it. And they could hardly wait to see the first Russian faces in the villages. In Vitebsk they came to the end of their long march and moved northward, toward Shimsk by rail. Finally they reached the Volkhov to the east of Lake Ilmen, where they relieved German soldiers in the garrison, who asked them to sing "La Paloma." Captains Arias and Sandoval guessed that the reinforcement of that sector by the Spaniards was an indication that the great offensive for the conquest of Leningrad was in preparation.

The lively temperament of the Division astonished the Russian people, as did their devotion to their religion. The Spanish disposition, the accordions, and the innate gallantry of such young men as Núñez Maza and Cacerola opened a wide breach in the feminine youth of the nearby villages in spite of language difficulties and in defiance of the terrible penalties that the German military code threatened if they should contract a venereal disease.

Mateo saw for himself that the poverty in some of the villages was shocking. Nothing had made a dent in it—not the Revolution of 1917, the big talk of Cosme Vila, or the Five-Year Plans. Many of the Russian peasants had never made the acquaintance of a bed or sheets. They slept on straw. Everywhere there were tattered photographs of Stalin, Molotov, and Voroshilov. Many of the houses still displayed icons and "the samovar was softly whistling." The older people seemed resigned; they appeared to be so used to suffering that they paid little heed to it. The children stared at "the invaders" as if they were people from another planet. They marveled at everything: the canteens, the bicycles, and especially the phonographs. To them listening to a record was a miracle. They knew nothing that was not Russian; that was obvious a mile away. "Why are the Germans blond? And what makes you short and skinny and such great talkers?" they would ask through interpreters. Everything in the history textbooks apparently was distorted, and almost no mention was made of anything that had happened before 1917. The medical texts in the hospitals that had been abandoned upon the arrival of the German troops were very primitive.

Cacerola soon learned that he should knock at the door of the Russian hovels. He would pound with his knuckles and ask: "*Mozhno?*"

"*Da, da,*" someone would reply from inside the house.

"*Da, da*" meant that he could come in and sit next to the fire. Cacerola would enter and spend a while there in silence, thinking about Gracia Andújar or Hilda, the German girl—and the youngest Russian peasant girl in the house.

Aside from knocking on doors and asking "*Mozhno?*" the first thing the members of the division did, near Lake Ilmen, was to dig trenches, to which they gave the names of women. Certainly, one of the trenches would be named Pilar.

Russia—what a vast mystery! The speculations of Dr. Andújar seemed to be confirmed: the people were simple, the leaders complex. So complex that some of them invited the Spanish *divisionarios* through loudspeakers, and in astonishingly correct Spanish, to pass over into their ranks.

"That'll be the day, you pigs!" Salazar howled.

One circumstance was worrying Mateo: where was their air cover? He could not see any planes anywhere from their side.

"What if they bomb us?"

"Ah, well! That friend of yours, Mosén Falcó, will bless you…"

SIXTY-ONE

THE Civil Governor, Comrade Dávila, spent several weeks that he would not have wished even for Stalin's son, Jacob Dzhugashvili. He realized he could not stand living without Pablito and Cristina. When night came and he was alone at home, in the huge official mansion, he felt unable to breathe instead of feeling as free as Manolo. He spent long stretches of time in Pablito's room, sitting in his son's chair, feeling a smothering sensation of emptiness. Then he would go to Cristina's room and stay there with the little stuffed animals that the girl had lined up on a shelf along the wall. Her bedroom seemed cold to him in spite of summer. And when he decided to telephone to María del Mar in Santander, he always talked to her through the instrument that he had had installed on the night table while lying on their bed to feel more intimately in contact with her.

On the first of September, he decided that the separation had lasted long enough and started on his way to his home town to pick up his family. But first he had to go to Madrid to lay before several of the ministries important matters affecting the province, problems relating particularly to food supplies and the roads. The General lent him a chauffeur from the Army car pool, a boy from the province of Córdoba, a silent, respectful lad who had served with the Reds and had been mobilized since 1936.

"You've seen a lot of the barracks, haven't you?" the Governor asked him.

"Yes, a little," the boy replied.

In Madrid the Governor made good use of his time. He had hoped to ask for an audience with the Caudillo in order to solicit support for the petitions he was carrying in his briefcase, but the Caudillo had gone for a rest to Galicia, to the Pazo de Meirás, and was paying a visit to the North at the moment, distributing prizes to many families—one of them, a couple in Gijón who had twenty-five children, had been awarded twenty-five thousand pesetas—and to women who had given birth to triplets.

That did not matter, for the Governor was well served in the ministries, especially in the Labor department, the head of which, Juan Antonio Girón, the recently appointed Falangist, seemed disposed to give labor questions great primacy and to provide insurance for the "producers." The Governor also extracted a formal promise from the National Delegation of Syndicates that Comrade Arjona, the delegate in Gerona, would be shown the door and replaced by another, better informed, and more efficient comrade. "Before the end of two months," they promised the Governor, "you'll have such an active delegate there that you'll be sorry you ever complained." The Governor smiled and touched his dark glasses. The prospect held no terrors for him. He wanted to work.

After his official visits had been completed, he had a long conversation with his brother, the cavalry colonel who had been in Gerona for Christmas. The Colonel, in high good humor, greeted him with extreme cordiality.

"You must be sure to go to the Prado Museum," he said at the start. "Marshal Pétain has given us back Murillo's *Immaculate Conception* and the sculpture of the Dama de Elche. Both are on view there. They're marvelous. And of course," he added, "you can't go off to Santander without seeing the revue *Déjate querer.* Tomorrow's performance will be its hundredth. The girls on the stage aren't from Elche, but that doesn't matter, I'm sure."

Later the Colonel told him that on the day Germany declared war on Russia and Serrano Súñer made his speech, shouting: "Russia's got to be punished," some Falangists got so worked up that they went to the British embassy, threw stones at the windows, and broke some panes.

"Well, this goes to show what the English are like," he went on. "The Falangists were shouting, demanding, 'Gibraltar, Gibraltar!' A secretary from the embassy came out and said to them as cool as you please: 'It's not here.' And, boy, that broke up the demonstration."

The conversation was full of substance, too. The Governor learned a number of things from his brother. Not for nothing was Madrid the umbilicus of the nation. They reviewed the Basic Laws of the State, promulgated a few months earlier, and praised them unreservedly. "They were drawn with real shrewdness." They talked about the construction of the Valle de los Caídos, which was going to cost a mint. "It seems that all the fines levied by the Office of Price Control are being turned over to it." They talked about the Carlists' bitter campaign against the Falange and the power Serrano Súñer, Franco's brother-in-law, was exhibiting. "Have you heard the song that's making the rounds here? Well, this is the way it goes:

"Three things there are in Spain
Which go against the grain,
Grants by the State, the Falange's fate,
And the brother of Franco's wife."

The Colonel later confirmed the Governor's belief that one of the objectives dearest to the Caudillo's heart was to endow the country with a network of dams. "This will be done. Already work has started on several excavations. We hope no Von Filken is going to have a finger in that pie." "Von Filken?" the Governor inquired. "Yes, man. That German who was involved in synthetic gasoline."

Their evening together was so pleasant that it went on far into the night. And the next day, the Governor slept until lunchtime and dreamed that one of the dams would grace the province of Gerona. He started then for Santander, relinquishing both the Prado Museum and the revue *Déjate querer.*

In Santander he greeted María del Mar, Pablito, and Cristina with bear hugs. He found them changed and very happy.

"This separation has done you all a world of good."

"Don't say that—it's just that we've been on vacation."

The Governor shook his head. He could see that María del Mar had been in her element, much better off in Santander than in Gerona. With her family, the local customs, and the country. "Well, I can't deny that this spot has a hold on me."

It had a hold on the Governor, too, but he tried not to show it. With Pablito, he toured the area devastated in February and found the rebuilding going ahead at high speed. Contributions had flowed in from all over Spain and the Government had granted substantial aid. Later he went to the country to see his two brothers, who were taking care of the family inheritance, the Dávila patrimony. He found the elder of them, Mario Dávila, unwilling to talk politics. All his conversation revolved around cows, calves, pastures, and the cultivated fields. "Something's happened to Mario," the Governor mused. "He must be disappointed." He thought that this was not the time for starting discussions.

He stayed in Santander a day and a half before turning back to Gerona with his family. Pablito was very talkative throughout the trip. He had had a wonderful time during those three weeks, swimming and visiting a thousand times the section where he had spent his early childhood. And he went on outings all over the province with his cousins and his old schoolmates. But he was not sure that Santander had a hold on him. Catalonia had something that attracted him irresistibly. Something he could not define, but which Manolo had summed up as "the spirit of enterprise." "But what do I want to be enterprising about?" Pablito had objected. "All I want is to study and get to be another Cervantes or Aristotle." Manolo answered: "Well, I don't know. It must be the Catalan way that attracts you, now that you're beginning to understand it."

All the while Pablito chattered during the drive, the chauffeur lent by the General kept chewing blades of grass as he sat behind the wheel, not uttering more than one sentence on his own account the whole way, and that when he saw a bullfight poster tacked to a tree proclaiming the matadors Domingo Ortega, Pepe Bienvenida, and José Luiz Vázquez. "The only real bullfighter we've got in Spain right now is Manolete," the chauffeur declared. "Sure," Pablito replied, "since he's a *cordovés* like you."

Everyone in Gerona thought that María del Mar looked rejuvenated. "Why, you look ten years younger! You're lovely!" Flattered, she replied, "The air of my country..."

Pablito felt at loose ends, for he still had three weeks to spend before resuming his classes, during which Agustín Lago wanted to introduce some radical changes in the schoolroom. Pablito brought back with him so much accumulated energy that he started to pursue Gracia Andújar again; but she had grown up so quickly, had become so much a woman—old enough to be a "war godmother"—that he abandoned the field without needing advice or waiting to be called a brat again, and spent his time learning to know Gerona as well as he knew Santander. And since his friend Félix Reyes, "the avant-garde painter" was at the Tossa de Mar Camp, enjoying packages of sausages and other tidbits sent him by the Costa brothers, Pablito turned to Mosén Alberto, a man well-versed in his subject. Mosén Alberto gave him several brochures on the city and its environs—the ones that Ignacio had consulted while waiting for Ana María's Holy Week visit—and told him anecdotes about the famous sieges of the city during the War of Independence. Pablito reciprocated by visiting Mosén Alberto several times at the Diocesan Museum, still being embellished by the priest, and playing the harmonica for him, especially mountain melodies that acquired a special resonance beneath the arches of the old building. Manuel Alvear, the small, jealous guardian of those treasures which the priest had recovered, usually shunned the Governor's son, out of shyness, but whenever he heard the strains of the harmonica, he hid behind a wall as close to the music as possible and listened with delight.

Cristina went to the Blue Division camp at Aiguafreda to stay until its closing on October first, for the September days were not as stormy as Adela had prophesied to Marcos. The Mediterranean, much calmer and bluer than the Cantabrian Sea, charmed the little girl. "I'm not afraid to swim here," she said. "Lots of times I was scared in that other place, I don't know why." Marta paid a good deal of attention to Cristina and concluded that the child was less superficial and vain than she seemed at first glance. "She's not Pablito," Marta said, "but she has her own place in the world." Cristina was fascinated by fishes and butterflies. During a visit to the ruins of Ampurias, where she stood transfixed before the perfection of the figures in the Roman mosaics, she said: "Actually, when fish are swimming they look like they're flying, and when butterflies are flying, they look like they're swimming." Marta was so pleased by the conceit—perhaps because it was the sort of thing Ignacio might have said to her—that she repeated it to all the little girls in camp when they gathered to raise the flag.

As for the Governor, he found himself faced with problems far more serious than those filling the minds of his children. He had been away for ten days. Miguel Rosselló exclaimed: "Thank God you're back!" The Governor had left the province in the hands of Miguel Rosselló and Notary Noguer. The Notary tried to be as calm as the Mediterranean, and all he had to say for himself was: "If you'd stayed away one more day, this whole place would have gone to pot, if you'll excuse the expression."

What had happened? Nothing in particular. The mixture as before—the unscrupulous had been active. The Minister of the Treasury had just announced, with good reason, that in the second quarter of 1941 the Civil Guard had served papers on 9,289 persons in Spain charging them with smuggling and fraud.

Commissioner Diéguez brought the Governor up to date on the latest subtleties of unscrupulous Gerundians. Individuals who were collecting contributions for the Blue Division were stashing them away at home. Some doctors were prescribing enormous quantities of sugar and soap for "sick children," which was an abuse of a stipulation by the Supply Delegation giving sick children first call on such items. And two "ear, nose, and throat" specialists recently arrived in the city had found a way to empty their patients' pockets by taking out their tonsils. A person could hardly open his mouth to one of these specialists before he put on a look of alarm and exclaimed: "What a sight! Those tonsils will have to come out immediately. I'll expect you tomorrow at nine." And the next day, "Out with them!" And the day after, the bill.

As usual when he talked with Commissioner Diéguez, the Governor was crunching a eucalyptus tablet.

"My dear Commissioner," he said, "this is an ugly situation. Of course, I could take desperate measures concerning the donations for the Blue Division.

I could even speak to Dr. Chaos about those prescriptions of sugar and soap for children. But how can I prevent the ear, nose, and throat doctors from taking out tonsils? I spent my whole time talking about removing infections of all kinds. Not to mention that while my wife was in Santander a doctor friend of hers advised her to have hers out."

Soon the Governor had settled down again in his chair of office and made several decisions. The first was to hold a solemn funeral service for the repose of the soul of Bruno Mussolini, the Duce's son who had been killed in an accident near Pisa. Gracia Andújar said: "What about Tagore? Why don't we offer a Mass for Tagore's soul?" The second, to have copies of two patriotic letters from the Russian front, signed by Captains Arias and Sandoval, run off on a mimeograph machine, and distributed among the people. The third, to issue an official invitation to the chess champion Manuel de Agustín to play several games simultaneously at the club while blindfolded. "Simultaneous games without looking! Ten chess boards! Just think what the brain of man can do!" Next he ordered *Amanecer* to publish the two latest testimonials by Hitler to Spain: the dispatch of an autographed letter to a Seville man who had asked for it, and the gift of a portrait of himself to the Sabadell Town Hall, also in response to a request.

The most important step the Governor took after his return, however, was to arrange a private meeting with the General. He had several reasons for soliciting the interview: to bring the General up to date on the news that he had brought back from Madrid, to ask his opinion of the progress of the war, and, especially, to sound him out on a delicate matter having to do with his work as governor of Gerona, concerning which he did not dare to come to any decision on his own account.

General Sánchez Bravo received his distinguished visitor with great cordiality. "Please sit down. You know I enjoy so much exchanging views with you from time to time. Would you like a drink?"

"Why—yes. Cognac, if it's handy."

"Of course it is!"

The General pushed a button and Nebulosa appeared. "Bring a bottle of González Byass. If our supply has run out, then..."

Nebulosa blushed and left the room, returning at once with the bottle and two glasses.

The interview was a long one. The General disagreed with many of the slogans which the Governor was hammering into the citizens, although he esteemed the man himself. He knew him to be a man of integrity, and that was enough for him. Perhaps the Governor might be too theoretical, but that was true of all civilians. "You know," the General often said, "you can't force everyone to go through the Zaragoza Academy. But a taste of Army discipline would do every Spaniard good. Yes, I know there's such a thing as military service. But as a rule it doesn't last long and most of the boys take it as a joke. They can't wait to be discharged."

The conversation developed along the expected lines. They began by talking about Madrid and the impressions the Governor had picked up on his trip. The anecdote about the English diplomat and Gibraltar—"It's not here!"—was not at all funny to the General; on the other hand, he nearly split his sides laughing over the quatrain about Serrano Súñer attributed to the Carlists. And he was pleased that the Governor had been treated solicitously in the ministries.

"That means there's beginning to be some discipline. It used to be that the ministries were almost empty in the summer."

The Governor also told the General of the imminent change in the Syndical Delegation and repeated the praise bestowed on Juan Antonio Girón by the Minister of Labor. The General shrugged his shoulders. Obviously, nothing that had to do with the Syndicate, however vertical it might be, was of any interest to him. Speaking of the Minister of Labor, whom he knew only through his photograph in the newspapers, he asked: "Are you sure he's a competent man?"

"I'm sure, General."

"I'm glad to hear you say so."

The second subject they dealt with was the war. The General let himself go on that and more than satisfied the Governor's wish to learn his judgment of its progress.

Of course, General Sánchez Bravo was in complete agreement with the thesis set forth by the Caudillo in his speech on July 18—the speech that reached Cosme Vila and his comrades—to the effect that the Allies were beaten.

"They can't do a thing," the General stated so flatly that the Governor was impressed. "The German machine is irresistible. Stalin knows it, and that's why he's demanding that the English open a second front in Norway and France or in the Canary Islands. But what can old Churchill do? He can take it or leave it, that's all. He can ask the English housewives to turn over all their kitchen utensils for the construction of airplanes and even tear out the railings around the houses. He can step up the air raids. But none of that will stop the advance toward Leningrad in the north, toward Moscow in the center, and toward Odessa in the south. Both sides in a war make their boasts, don't they, my dear Governor? Hitler is getting ready for an assault on the Soviet capital—and when that happens I'll get drunk, I promise you, for once in my life. I'll do like my son, and do it again when he reaches Nikolayev in the south. By the way, have you seen the latest number of *Signal*?"

The Governor shook his head. "I have it in my office, but I haven't even glanced at it yet."

"Well, look at it as soon as you can. The Soviet generals in Nikolayev have sent even the insane into battle, crazy men. And boys of fifteen and sixteen. Do you realize what that means? It's as plain as daylight that they're in the same situation as the Reds were here at the time of the battle of the Ebro."

The Governor asked him: "How important do you think the meeting was between Roosevelt and Churchill on the Atlantic aboard that mysterious American battleship?"

The General was still very positive: "Not important at all in terms of the final outcome. They're trying to spread the area of the war even more widely, that's all. That's why England has occupied Abyssinia in Africa and Iran in the Near East, and that's why they oppose the Japanese request to establish bases in Indo-China. But I say again it's a mere matter of maneuvering to spread the war, and that it won't have any effect whatsoever."

The Governor persisted: "But what about 'General Winter'? Won't that make things hard? The Feminine Section has started to make overcoats for the volunteers in the Blue Division."

The military governor of Gerona made another dismissive gesture. "I doubt they'll ever need them. The conquest of Moscow is shaping up, and that'll be a knock-out blow. So final that Stalin will have to surrender and go off to Siberia with La Pasionaria and her ilk."

For some reason, the General liked to use the word "ilk" whenever he could and also the phrase "*tutti contenti.*"

At this point the Governor served himself a little more cognac before attacking the final subject, the one that directly affected his work as head of the province.

"Will you permit me, General, to use you as a consultant? Perhaps I should say, may I ask your advice?"

"By all means."

"Thank you." Contrary to custom, the Governor sprawled in his chair. "You know we have that Mr. Collins, the British consul, here in Gerona. We have to admit that, except for his little smiles, he has behaved correctly. Colonel Triguero—let me touch wood when I pronounce that name—assures me that up to now Mr. Collins has occupied himself exclusively with looking after the refugees from his own country or Canada. People who have been wounded, or without identification, or penniless. Let's say, then, that he's done only what his job entails. Very well, then. I'm under the impression, however, that the same thing can't be said about the German consul, Paul Gunther, or the German agents who are staying in the same hotel as Mr. Collins. In other words, I have to tell you that Commissioner Diéguez has concluded that for the most part they're agents of the Gestapo and that they're trying to pry out of the foreign refugees data that might be of interest to the German policy makers."

The General drew himself up like Dr. Gregorio Lascasas when he heard mention of Luther or the Encyclopedists. "Are you sure of what you're saying?"

The Governor was enjoying his second glass of González Byass.

"I'm afraid so. The fact is that I don't know whether we ought to provide them with the means—or do the opposite." He paused briefly. "That's what I wanted to consult you about."

The General pondered, far from ready to say "*tutti contenti*" at that point. Finally, he pronounced judgment.

"No facilities! Put your foot down. Don't permit such meddling. The Caudillo laid down the guidelines for us at Hendaye—Spain must preserve her independence. Good God!" The General got up and took several turns around the room. "It's one thing to send a division of volunteers to Russia, but it's something else again to permit one of the belligerent countries, even though a friend, to conduct espionage on our territory."

The Governor bit his lip. "Don't you think, General, that we might find a way to help those German agents—without letting it leak out?"

The General came to a halt in front of the speaker. "By no means! We'd be sticking our necks out too far. Mr. Collins is an Englishman, and if there's one thing an Englishman has it's a good nose." The General's attitude was stern. "It's absolutely necessary to avoid anything that would give that man cause to present a justified complaint against us to his government."

The Governor was thoughtful. He understood the General's reasoning. Spain had her obligations to England, not the least of which was a debt of several million pounds sterling.

"All right, General. I'll try to put an end to the matter. It won't be easy, but I'll try."

The General stared straight at him. "That's an order," he said.

The remainder of the conversation was on unimportant matters. Knowing that it would flatter the General, the Governor asked him when he was going to lay the cornerstone for the new, much-needed quarters.

Very soon," the General replied. "On the first of October. We've had the good luck to have been given some excellent vacant lots belonging to the widow of Don Pedro Oriol, beside the station in Olot. And the Emer Company, with whom we've signed the contract, has named a very reasonable price." The General added, "Of course, we have to recognize that there are good patriots in Catalonia, too."

At that moment, Captain Sánchez Bravo opened the door without knocking. Evidently he had eluded Nebulosa's vigilance. Seeing the Governor, he stopped in the doorway and said: "Oh, I'm sorry. I didn't know you were here."

The General's face changed; he looked at his son with open affection. He was very pleased with him these days.

"Come in, son. The Governor and I have said everything we had to say."

Captain Sánchez Bravo, who had just come from the Dámaso Barbershop, smiled and entered the office, closing the door after him.

"How were things in Santander, Governor?" he asked cordially.

The Governor adopted an attitude of reserve toward the Captain which did not go unnoticed by the General.

"Fine! It's started to make a come-back." He added immediately in an ironic tone: "The General has just been telling me that the construction business here is active, too, and reasonably priced."

Captain Sánchez Bravo did not blink an eye. He looked at the bottle of cognac. As there were only two glasses, he could not pour himself a drink.

"That's right," he said finally. "Yesterday I was looking at the work on the new prison in Salt. It's almost finished. It's turning out very well. Very comfortable."

The Governor, who had risen to his feet, seemed on the point of leaving. But, seeing that the Captain was holding in his hand a copy of *The World of Sport*, he asked him in a tone equally ironical: "How's the new football season going, Captain?"

"Oh, splendidly," the young man replied. "Barcelona has offered us three men on their second team in exchange for Pachín."

The General stared at his son with a comical expression. "And who's this Pachín?" he asked.

The Captain smiled. "How can you possibly not know that, Father? Pachín, our center forward! He was discharged only a month ago."

The General sputtered: "Football!"

The Governor, who had been moving toward the door, finally decided to say goodbye.

"General," he said, "give my kindest regards to your wife. We often think of her." The General nodded. "Good luck, Captain." Captain Sánchez Bravo, still smiling, nodded in turn.

As soon as the Governor left, the General turned to his son and asked: "What's wrong between you two? You're like a cat and a dog."

The Captain headed for the bottle of cognac. "Nothing, Papa. It's just that we like to kid each other."

SIXTY-TWO

AUTUMN came along at a snail's pace. Summer was refusing to die. Sunlight still gilded the façades of the buildings, but the nights were cool, and, according to the General, an expert in such matters, several stars would go into eclipse, not to reappear until spring.

The end of September was windy. The telegraph wires whistled. Goering, Dr. Chaos's dog, acted nervous; the leaves on the trees in the forest were curling as though begging for the miracle of rain which would cause mushrooms to spring up. Some of them would be poisonous. The ice-cream carts vanished. The drugstores were advertising all sorts of cold remedies, and the ever-apprehensive Marcos bought three boxes of pills from Dr. Andreu, with the excuse that they left a pleasant taste in his mouth. *Amanecer* again published advertisements for coal substitutes. The mannikins in the store windows donned coats and scarves. La Andaluza sighed: "The beginning of October is bad. But unless there's a flood, things will pick up again with the fairs."

Everyone came back to Gerona. Adela was the first. Alone in her apartment, she would suddenly stretch her arms as if casting off sloth; she was surfeited with happiness as she looked at a picture of Playa de Aro. Her instincts remembered.

Manolo went to Jérez de la Frontera as planned, spent just three days there, and returned with the children, Esther—and Esther's mother. This lady, familiarly known as Katy, had taken a notion to go to Gerona. "I can stay with you until Christmas. But if I bother you, you must throw me out." It seemed to Manolo that Christmas was an eternity away. He did not get along any too well with his elegant mother-in-law, a meddlesome woman and a pessimist by nature. Manolo said that what she liked best were funerals. But he smiled and said: "By all means!"

Ignacio met Esther's mother and said to Manolo. "My dear boss, I think your nocturnal escapades are over, until further notice."

"That's for sure!" Manolo exclaimed, stroking his little beard.

Dr. Chaos came back, too. He had not gone to any of the hotels on the Costa Brava that year. He had gone to the Balearies, bearing in the forefront of his mind Dr. Andújar's advice: "Try again with another woman, one not like Solita, younger, and more smoothly shaped." Dr. Chaos did the opposite: he backslid. He became involved in Palma de Mallorca with a sailor of twenty who was willing to tolerate him and his money. On his return to Gerona he showed the marks of his personal debauchery. Now he realized that a change had come over him: he could no longer yield with impunity to his abnormality. He was left in a no-man's land. Fortunately, back in Gerona, he found his clinic jammed with patients and his work kept him busy most of the time. Yet without Solita in the operating room—what could she be doing in Russia?—he felt helpless.

Dr. Andújar called him and said insistently: "You've got to try to cure yourself. Now you listen to me! Try it with another woman!"

All in vain. Within a few days, Dr. Chaos met a new young man in Gerona, a soldier from the same village as Nebulosa whom his comrades called "La Rosarito."

Warning Voice and Carlota came home two days after Dr. Chaos. They returned from Puigcerdá tanned by the mountain sun and had hardly settled down at home when Carlota raised with her husband the question of his sterility. Warning Voice had no recourse but to submit to a minute examination in Dr. Morell's office. The doctor's diagnosis was that the Mayor needed minor surgery.

"Are you sure, Doctor?"

"Completely."

"And who will perform it?"

"Dr. Chaos."

"No, by God, he won't." The Mayor flatly refused. "I'll go to Barcelona."

Carlota understood. "Very well, darling. Wherever you wish. But have it done soon."

Agustín Lago came back a few days later. After a short rest in Altea, where he had breathed pure air and read García Morente, both of which did him good, Agustín Lago decided to travel through the South, in Andalusia and Granada, Jaén, Seville, and along the coast from Almeria to Huelva. He felt depressed in Huelva at the sight of the conditions under which the miners of Riotinto had to work and at the news that there were cases of leprosy there. Lepers in Spain! But what impressed him most deeply was the desert-like country around Almería. He thought how it resembled a piece of Africa broken off from the other continent during some geological nightmare. Only God knew why.

On his way home he stopped in Barcelona, at Carlos Godo's suggestion. What an intelligent man! He declared that within the next few years architecture would undergo a complete transformation owing to the pressure of the population explosion—wars must end some day—and the need to use cheaper materials. He stated also that Agustín Lago was too much alone in Gerona and that to alleviate the condition and perform his apostolic and professional duty, he ought to try to attract some of his friends there into the Opus Dei. "We must broaden our field, Agustín. Our personal life is brief."

Agustín Lago returned to Gerona with the idea in mind of trying to draw some friend into the Opus. First he thought of Alfonso Estrada, the president of the Marian Congregations, but Alfonso had gone far away, to Russia. Whom else could he approach? He thought of several names: former Lieutenant Montero, Miguel Rosselló, Ignacio Alvear. Oh, how hard it was to break a trail! The Opus Dei demanded much and gave little. It was a direct contract, so to speak, between the soul, the person, and God.

Ignacio had caught Agustín's eye right at the beginning. But of them all, he seemed the least approachable. Well, that must not stand in his way. On the contrary, as a missionary, he must regard that fact as a challenge, a stimulus. And grace was there, waiting. If only he could win over the young man! He would be the ideal type to start the chain.

Agustín Lago finally made up his mind. "The Lord will show me the way to knock on the door when he considers that the time is ripe."

His decision was prompted at that moment by a personal problem: the maid in the pension, a great coquette, had discovered that Agustín trembled at the sight of her and consequently asked him each day: "Did I make the señorito's bed right?"

A scourge to the flesh! A lesson in humility. Agustín Lago immersed himself in meditations on the *Camino*, in which he read: "Saint Francis of Assisi rolled in the snow to preserve his chastity. Saint Benedict jumped into a blackberry patch and plunged into an icy pond. What have you done?" The thought was only a partial consolation, for there was neither snow or a frozen pond in Gerona, and he did not feel inclined to throw himself into a blackberry patch.

But what about the coming school year? And the teachers? Ah, there, too, the prospects were unpleasant! Madrid kept saying: "Patience, Inspector, patience. Don't you realize that Spain has been helpless for centuries?"

That helplessness was a fact. But could he brandish an argument like that before the people of the province who trusted him? The poor teachers! The summer had been ruinous to them. Overtime pay and a monthly paycheck had ended with the school year—and the same thing was true throughout Catalonia.

Overtime pay was based on the number of pupils in the preceding school term. The teachers were paid a base salary, with the result that most of them had to go around begging for translations or private lessons like the politically purged teachers who had had to solve their own problems—but only halfway. *Amanecer* was full of advertisements offering "Tutoring for a high school diploma. At home." "Review of assignments. At home." "Latin and French lessons." One advertisement said: "Use your summer vacation to improve your handwriting. To get ahead, good handwriting is essential."

When Agustín Lago read those notices, he felt anguished. And now, with the opening of the new term only a few days away, many incumbents simply decided to name a substitute and thus free themselves to look for other, better-paid jobs. Others had obtained a doctor's recommendation to resign for reasons of health. Still others were determined to arrange their class work so that they could read proof for publishers in their spare moments. What moral right did he have to forbid such malpractice? His responsibility was heavy.

The Costa brothers also put an end to their wives' summer vacations. They went to Pálamos to get them, and that same day, September 30, Carlos Civil, acting for Emer, officially turned over to the authorities the new prison built in the village of Salt, a building solid enough to warrant the praise of Captain Sánchez Bravo.

The inauguration of the prison went almost unnoticed, contrary to expectations. Only the families of the prisoners were aware of it. The opposite was true of the opening on the same day of the Ultonia Motion Picture Theater, which aroused the whole town's curiosity.

Yet the new prison did indeed exist. And on the second of October, the transfer of the thousand prisoners still in the Seminary began at night and continued until the building had been vacated and put at the disposal of the prelate of the diocese. The prisoners were transferred in trucks, and many of them felt a lump rise in their throats as they climbed into the assigned vehicle, fearing that the chauffeur would start them on their way to the cemetery. But that did not happen. When they realized that they were not being tricked and were heading for the village of Salt, they almost shouted with joy beneath the stars. To pass through the streets, even if only for a moment! To breathe the air of freedom with no walls around them! How beautiful the fronts of the houses looked, the street lights! How moved they were at the sight of the nightwatchman's silhouette, and how delighted to see the night owls who were still outdoors talking on the street corners.

What a pity that the transfer had not been made by daylight—they could have seen the shops, the cafés, and the bodies of women! Some of them had spent more than two years without ever leaving the prison. Their bones ached from the jolting of the truck. Those least moved were the men working off their sentences. They were familiar with the outside world, and they said to the others: "Don't be such fools! You wouldn't see anything by daylight but posters for the Falange."

Once the Bishop had blessed the new prison, he went to the Seminary to take possession of it. The stench shocked him; it came from the walls, from the toilets. How could it possibly smell so foul if air could come through the bars? The death cells stank of straw and blasphemy. What a job it would be to put it back into condition, to convert it into a building worthy of the new batches of seminarians who would have to study there and make themselves fit to be priests.

Autumn also brought back the sensational Paz Alvear, to stand once more behind the counter of the Diana Perfumery, now that the Gerona Jazz Band had completed its engagements. The orchestra's tour had been a smash hit, and furthermore, there were now two indispensable pieces of furniture in the new apartment rented by Paz. But the girl had to go through a few days of inner violence which took her back to the time in Burgos.

Pachín had gone. He had signed up with the Barcelona Football Club as expected. The boy came from Asturias to talk the matter over with Paz, but from the outset she realized that his mind was fully made up. The reasons he adduced were solid. Barcelona offered opportunity—he could even achieve the wearing of the international shirt. And within three or four years he could save up a large amount of money, which would enable them to marry comfortably. "Don't you know what all this means to me? I'm twenty-two years old. I think I must be dreaming!"

Three or four years! Paz was furious. "I'm going to Barcelona with you. I'll find an orchestra and a perfume shop there."

This put Pachín on the defensive. He hardly took the trouble to moderate his voice. "Be reasonable, woman. Your Uncle Matías and Ignacio are here. And I'll owe my time there to my club. Have a little patience! When the time comes, we'll do things as they ought to be done."

His meaning was plain to Paz. She bit her lips until they almost bled. Pachín essayed a smile and tried to put his arms around her, but she would have none of it. "So you're throwing me over, eh? As if I were a dumbbell from some village. I warn you it's not going to be that easy."

A stormy scene followed, ending in tears on the part of Paz. Pachín watched her cry, standing with his hands on his hips like a player waiting for the game to begin.

But the next day he left, and Paz was alone with her great chagrin. It helped her not at all to hear Dámaso say to her in the Diana Perfumery: "But, girl! You could twist a sap like that around your little finger." The girl's vanity kept whispering plans for revenge.

When Tower of Babel found out that Pachín had gone away "just like that," he said to Padrosa: "Now I'm going to put on a campaign."

Padrosa, chewing a paper clip as usual, answered: "I wish you better luck than I've had with Silvia. And after I promised her a battleship, too!"

Tower of Babel pointed to the Agencia Gerunda's letterhead and said: "Agencia Gerunda settles everything."

SIXTY-THREE

IF Jaime, the book dealer, had not already exchanged his kiosk for a small shop on the Calle de Albareda, to be paid for in installments, where romantic Catalans met in the rear, if he had been still delivering *Amanecer*, he would have underlined in red the following news items published during those weeks:

"The Pope, Pius XII, received twenty German soldiers in a special audience and offered them his ring to kiss."

"Northern lights appeared with solemnity in the heavens and were visible all over northern Europe. They aroused great excitement among astrologers."

"The miracle of the liquefaction of San Gennaro's blood occurred again in the Naples Cathedral on September 20, the date on which it happens each year."

"On the Russian front, two Spanish boys were among the prisoners taken by the Finnish troops. One, named Celestino Fernández, was a native of Ávila; the other, Rubén Vicario, was born in Santurce. Both boys had been taken to Russia in 1937."

"The Caudillo has signed a large number of pardons, and while continuing his journey through the north of Spain, he presided over the traditional regatta of sardine smacks in San Sebastián."

"The dam at Muedra in the province of Soria has been put into operation."

"The English people who have not been mobilized are still spending their weekends in the country, in the parks, or on the beaches."

"The Ofe Laboratory is offering nursing mothers who are the wives of the volunteers in the Blue Division a weekly tube of Madresol, which is beneficial to the child."

"Marcos Redondo, the talented *zarzuela* singer, made a tremendous hit in the Municipal Theater of Gerona."

All of these news items aroused appropriate commentaries in the Café Nacional, especially the ones referring to the audience granted by Pope Pius

XII, the miracle in the Naples Cathedral, and the performance of Marcos Redondo in the Municipal Theater.

Galindo, the bachelor, could not imagine why Pius XII had received a group of German soldiers. "The only way it would make any sense to me would be if he'd invited the same number of British soldiers for the same time." Señor Grote found it hard to believe that San Gennaro's blood would liquefy every year with such amazing punctuality. "Those Neapolitans!" he exclaimed. "They never miss, even in leap year!" Matías had gone to hear Marcos Redondo, and said that as long as there was a voice like his, the *zarzuela* would never die. "He made my hair stand on end. In Madrid, they'd have carried him out on their shoulders."

But one coming event, not of transcendental importance to the people of the town, had a much greater effect on Ignacio than all the foregoing items. This was a visit from Moncho, his unforgettable friend of the war days, the nephew of Don Carlos Ayesterán, who at that time had been Chief of Health in Barcelona. Like so many other exiles, Don Carlos had been most successful in South America, specifically in Chile. He had followed the advice given him in Paris by Julio García and had fitted out a very modern pharmaceutical laboratory.

Moncho announced his arrival by telegram, and Ignacio went to meet him at the station. The two young men embraced with as much warmth as Ignacio had shown toward Mateo soon after his return from the ski troopers.

"Moncho!"

"Ignacio!"

"My respects to the famous doctor!"

"And mine to the famous lawyer!"

"I almost thought you'd never come."

"When have I ever failed to keep a promise?"

Ignacio would not hear of letting Moncho put up at a hotel for his planned two or three days in Gerona. He wanted him to stay in the flat on the Rambla, which necessitated sending little Eloy to sleep at Pilar's house. This was a gay adventure to the boy, who was the Gerona Football Club's mascot and the best player on the youth team in the opinion of Rafa, the masseur.

Matías and Carmen had heard so much about Moncho that they received him like an ambassador. Carmen said formally. "I hope you'll tell me what you like to eat. And if you're cold in bed, I'll put on another blanket."

"Good Lord, you can treat Moncho like one of the family," Ignacio protested. "The same as me."

"Yes, please do," Moncho pleaded. "I'd feel more comfortable."

Moncho, a little taller than Ignacio and two years older, with golden blond hair, looked enviably healthy. He had not given up mountain climbing or skiing after the war. Much more firmly than Cacerola, he believed that the mountains were a source of health and the ideal remedy for dark moods. He had spent half the summer in the Pyrenees, in the province of Lérida, near the lake region, and was now waiting eagerly for the first snow to provide smooth slopes so that he could go to La Molina. When he learned that Ignacio had made only a couple of trips to Rocacorba and the hermitage of Los Angeles, Moncho smiled and struck the table with his fist.

"Ignacio that's worse than merely bad for you. Before long you'll be developing a paunch! And complaining that your kidneys bother you.

Moncho's words struck Ignacio like barbs. He had been thinking a great deal about him. He was left-handed and treasured an hourglass. He had collected photographs of the Himalayas, took quantities of sugar in his coffee, and had a part-time sweetheart whom he called Bisturí because during the war she had injected corrosives into the tires of the Reds' trucks being loaded for the Aragón front.

Their reunion was happy. They reminisced about the day they first met, at a cheap but clean pension on the Calle de Tallers in Barcelona. Four years had gone by since then.

"Do you remember the things you used to say to me, Moncho?"

"No, I don't suppose I do."

"You said: 'A whiff of ether and all men are equal.' And you said Luther couldn't have been such a bad sort as we'd been led to believe."

"Gosh, I said that?" Moncho thought a moment. "Well, believe it or not, I still think the same."

Moncho's arrival had much the same effect on Ignacio as the visits from his Madrilenian cousin had had in the past. With the difference that José was an earthquake—carrying prophylactics in his suitcase—while Moncho was a fertile field that would yield a harvest.

The next day Ignacio showed Gerona to Moncho with as much enthusiasm as he had to Ana María. "That old quarter is something you don't have in Lérida. But that's not your fault! You don't have a Montilivi either, or those houses hanging over the river. So, actually you've got nothing at all in Lérida. If the Bishop will forgive me, it's just a little Aragón now."

"You're a trickster," Moncho replied. "You're showing me only the good side of the coin. Why don't we walk around modern Gerona? I can't imagine anything worse."

Ignacio laughed. "That I can't deny."

They climbed up toward the hermitage of Calvario through the olive trees, the cliffs, and the memories of the Way of the Cross, which took the same route, with Carmen Elgazu chanting: "Forgive us, O Lord." It still looked like Palestine. They sat down at the top of the hill, from which they had a view of the valley. And there they began to catch up on each other's lives.

Ignacio told his friend in more detail what he had already sketched in his letters: his break with Marta and his engagement to Ana María. He described Manolo, his boss and friend. "I'm learning a lot from him. I think that within a couple of years I'll be able to open an office of my own. And get this: in December I'm going to do a solo in court, my first case. It happens to be a suit against the two outstanding black-marketeers in the city."

Moncho congratulated him. He realized that Ignacio had all the qualities needed to make a success of the law. "You have a good presence, a good voice, and a facility with words, plus integrity. A little mixed up in your mind. That's something you're going to have to fight."

Ignacio and Moncho were so alone up there near the small mountains called the Two O's that, had it not been for their clothes, they might have thought they were standing guard again on the Brazato and Bachimaña front.

"What about you, Moncho? What are you doing? Come on, tell me. Are you still at odds with your father because he denounced so many people?"

Moncho made a face. "Yes, we're still on the outs. I can never forget that."

Ignacio scratched an eyebrow. "I know," he said, "but after all, we were a couple of simpletons to think that wouldn't happen, weren't we?"

"Oh, of course."

"I remember you yourself saying when they asked you why you were fighting for the Nationalists that it was because the soldiers could ensure public order."

Moncho shook his head. "Yes, I said that. I didn't realize then that maintaining public order would cost such a price."

Ignacio stared at him. "You talk as though you had some regrets."

"Regrets? That's not quite the word, but after all…" Moncho's expression changed. He looked all around him. The whole scene was beautiful. "What do you say if we change the subject?"

"Not a bad idea," Ignacio agreed.

They talked about Moncho's profession. There he was able to talk fluently as he chewed a blade of grass. He was a bacteriologist. Near the end of his medical studies he had been undecided among surgery, anesthesia, which was his specialty—"Remember the Pasteur Hospital and all those drug addicts?"—and bacteriology. Finally, he discovered that his great enthusiasm was bacteriology.

"So what I have in mind is studying little bugs under the microscope. The truth is hidden there. You know there are people who look like athletes, but if you analyze their urine and blood, you might have to say they'll be dead in six months. Do you realize that? We bacteriologists are our brothers' secret police."

Ignacio was not at all surprised at the specialty chosen by his friend. Moncho was an inveterate observer. Ignacio in turn congratulated Moncho, for he knew that his friend had found the ideal niche for himself.

"Tell me something," Ignacio went on. "Bisturí: has she been a help to you?"

Moncho burst out laughing. "Gosh, Bisturí! She eats candy all the time and now she looks like a one-ton truck."

Ignacio laughed, too. "Then to whom are you reading Bécquer's poetry?"

Moncho made an expressive face and hesitated a moment before finally answering: "Maybe this will shock you, but I'm living with a German girl. She and I get along fine together."

Ignacio was astonished. Aside from the question of morality, he remembered that during the war Moncho had been allergic to anything German.

Moncho anticipated his objections. "You mustn't think she's a Nazi! Oh, no. Actually, she's quite the opposite. She had to escape from Germany. I met her at the hospital in Barcelona."

Ignacio wondered whether he had seen the girl's papers in Figueras while he was in the Frontier Service. And it occurred to him that she might be Jewish.

Moncho seemed able to read his thoughts. "Don't make too many guesses. It's all quite simple, really. She's a kid who hates war, like me."

Ignacio wanted to hear more about her, but that did not seem the opportune moment.

Well, well," he exclaimed. "That's about the last thing I'd have expected."

"When you meet her," Moncho said with a smile. "You'll understand perfectly why I recite Bécquer's poems to her."

They went on talking, heedless of the twilight chill that was beginning to penetrate to their bones.

Ignacio told his friend that he was reading Freud. Moncho gave a sign of approval.

"There you have a first-class analyst," he said. "Although he goes too far at times."

"Do you think so?"

"Of course I do."

Ignacio shook his head. "Well, almost everything he has to say strikes me as right. We're inscrutable creatures. When I think deeply about myself, I'm aware that other people haven't the vaguest idea what I'm like inside."

Moncho said ironically: "So much the better for you."

Finally, the cold grew so intense that it drove them down from the summit. They descended along the walls behind the Cathedral and looked for a moment at the windings of the Ter River, which they could see from the belvedere.

Moncho commented. "I'd have been glad to stay up there with a pup tent and a sleeping bag. Do you see?"

Ignacio was walking along the cobbled streets with his hands in his pockets, smoking.

"Moncho, may I ask you a question?"

"Naturally."

"If you had your choice, what would you ask the Three Magi to bring you?"

Ignacio supposed that Moncho would think a moment before answering, but he said with great promptness: "To keep all my faculties to the age of seventy, and then die suddenly."

Ignacio stood still for a moment. "Did I hear you correctly?"

"Why? Is there anything so unusual about that?"

Ignacio threw down his cigarette and stamped on it. "No, not really..."

They went back home. Supper in the Rambla flat was as cordial as on the preceding evening. At the end of it, Matías listened to the London BBC, then Carmen Elgazu, true to herself, suggested saying the Rosary.

Moncho passed his hand over his blond hair. "By all means!"

As usual, Matías paced the corridor the whole time, although now he could not walk as rapidly as before because of his rheumatism. At the routine responses to the litany, he swallowed the word "pray" and simply said "for us."

IGNACIO had made a plan for the following day. He wanted his friend to meet Professor Civil and Mosén Alberto, of whom he had often spoken, and Manolo and Esther, too, of course. He wanted him to meet Pilar and Don Emilo...

Moncho indicated with complete frankness that the only one he really was dreaming of meeting was Pilar. "Please don't make me climb so many stairs. Why don't we grab our knapsacks and go to Rocacorba? I'm actually not much of a visitor."

Ignacio was surprised. They were having breakfast, and the light was coming softly through the panes of the balcony windows facing the river. "Why? Have you gone anti-social?"

"Not in the least!" Moncho protested.

Ignacio's expression forced him to explain a little farther. He had come to Gerona to see him, Ignacio, and to become acquainted with the city. "That, and meeting your family are enough for me." He disliked doing things hurriedly, cramming his mind with fleeting pictures. "Don't you remember that? I like to savor things."

Ignacio agreed. But he was sorry not to be able to show off his friend, especially to Manolo and Esther. He insisted, but to no avail. "What would you like to do, then?"

"Nothing. Take another walk somewhere. Maybe through the Dehesa."

"All right. Later we'll have lunch at Pilar's house."

They started off toward the Dehesa. Moncho was carrying his camera, and he took advantage of the sunny morning to snap some pictures. First of the columns along the Rambla, next of the Oñar from the San Agustín bridge, next of the Telegraph building. Ignacio watched him indulgently, and it amused him to see Moncho snapping the shutter with his left hand. To him it was a noteworthy sight. Moncho said: "That isn't a mere nothing, I assure you."

They walked tirelessly, chatting. Moncho had developed in their years apart. He had come to certain conclusions. Ignacio's doubts seemed to him futile and wearisome. Everyone had to believe in something, he said. And an effective way to do that was to keep eliminating. "I need hardly mention the practice of saying 'a pleasure,' and 'I've had a lovely evening,' or of listening to such flattering words as 'heroism,' 'mysticism,' 'better future,' or 'a good, clean fight'—You've got to choose, Ignacio. But choose the simple things that are within our reach: work, friends, a brand of tobacco. They're enough."

"Then does one have to set ambition aside?" Ignacio objected.

"Ambition? I'm more ambitious than you are, ambitious to live within the reach of my strength."

The good thing about Moncho was that he practiced what he preached, as he was demonstrating at the moment by spending five minutes on the contemplation of a tree trunk. Moncho was a man who loved fixed things, although, as Ignacio knew, he also liked to watch the running of the clear water in a creek, "Think about this little item, for example. They don't put the 'Don't touch' and 'Danger of death' signs on trees, do they? They put them on electrical poles. You might also consider the fact that insects eat one another. They don't just argue. There's a difference, don't you agree?"

This was another of Moncho's elliptical allusions to the war. Ignacio understood that. The civil conflict had left a deep scar on Moncho. And now he was with a German girl who had fled from her own country. He admitted that it was all true. People were still what they had always been: half angel, half devil. Blonds like Moncho or brunettes like Ignacio. But the world, the collective and amorphous world, had gone mad. One had only to read the newspapers every morning. Air raids, tanks, enemy losses! Enemies of whom? It was a perpetual war among leucocytes. If society turned its back on nature, nothing would ever get straightened out. That was the worst of war, that it kept one from loving the minutiae of life and nature. People were being brainwashed to make them turn to war. Machines and the crowding into big cities were leading in the same direction. Wars meant promiscuity. They killed intimacy, and that was a serious matter.

Ignacio listened attentively to all that, and was impressed. But he could see one danger for Moncho: that his views might lead to inhibitions.

"Whatever happens, we must do our part to better things, mustn't we? Ordering our neighbor to risk his life, refusing to say 'a pleasure' are somewhat selfish in the end, aren't they? Working through elimination may lead to the serenity you enjoy, but it may lead also to personal vanity. But after all, I wouldn't like to turn my back on others, either."

"That's not what I said, Ignacio. I was talking precisely about paying attention to things. Feeling is more important than doing. Do you understand what I'm getting at?"

"I think so. The only thing is that such an attitude is basically pessimistic. As the saying goes, suffering purifies. Does that also sound too high flown to you?"

"No, it's one of the great truths. But what doesn't purify is hate."

"Do you believe, then, that all of us who fought in the war hate by definition?"

"Yes, without realizing it. And all those who are fighting now will also hate."

"Well, take another look," Ignacio said, "because in my opinion I'm better than I was before!"

At that moment Moncho was focusing his camera on a tall cypress tree. He could not decide whether to photograph its base or the tip that looked very like the bell tower of San Félix as it pointed at the sky.

"Don't talk nonsense. Before the war you were a pure creature. You were immunized. I tell you that as a doctor. And now, after meeting your parents, I understand why."

Those last words touched Ignacio. For a moment he felt himself really a saint. He loved that cypress, the collective world, amorphous and mad, his parents, Moncho—he loved everything.

"Thank you for the compliment, Moncho."

"You're welcome."

Finally, they stopped walking, sat down, and were silent for a long while. Memory brought back to them once more the hours they had spent together in the high mountains, beside a bonfire and beneath a starry sky. They could hear the distant murmur of the Ter, caressing the stones, wearing them down, thinning them in its bed.

Ignacio broke the pause. "I've been thinking over everything you said, and now I wonder if you'd want to have children."

As usual, Ignacio expected Moncho to take some time before answering him. Again he was wrong. Moncho said: "Definitely not."

Ignacio made a face. "So there you are. I was afraid of that. And it'll be a pity."

"Thank you for the compliment, Ignacio."

THE time had come to go to Pilar's house. Pilar, who was about to bear a child and whose opinions were quite alien to Moncho's. Dr. Morell estimated that the great event was only a couple of weeks away. Ignacio's sister had prepared a gala lunch in honor of his guest. Moncho tried to keep the conversation on frivolous subjects, but he found it difficult. *Amanecer* had just proved the truth of his earlier statements by publishing the news of the first *divisionario* killed at the front: Comrade Luis Alcocer Moreno, a lieutenant in the air force and son of the Mayor of Madrid. Pilar mentioned the subject and managed to keep from crying. Moncho refrained from citing his theories. He insisted, instead, on singing the excellencies of the baby about to be born. "I'm sure," he prophesied, "that he'll look like César."

Pilar was pleased. She thought as she watched Moncho and listened to him: "Marta would be happy with that man. If only I could arrange for them to meet." Don Emilio Santos was also taken with Moncho, for one reason because the guest showed a great interest in him and his illness, now conquered, and his term in prison. Don Emilio Santos told him what he had told everyone since learning it from Warning Voice: that the crosses he had scratched on the wall with his thumbnail had been turned into hammers and sickles by the prisoners who came after him. Moncho exclaimed: "Why, of course! That's the way it always is."

The luncheon lasted a long time. Moncho put such a quantity of sugar in his coffee that Pilar threw up her hands. Moncho said: "Don't worry! It's a sweet poison, isn't it?"

Pilar agreed, then said abruptly: "I wish you'd been here when Mateo went away."

Ignacio stared at his sister. "Why do you say that? He wouldn't have been able to do anything with him either."

Pilar was playing with her spoon. "No, of course not. I know that."

A few seconds later, something wholly unexpected happened. Pilar suddenly fainted and her head dropped. General alarm ensued, but fortunately Moncho was there. He opened the window and did what was needed. "Pilar, take a deep breath, like this. That's it."

When the girl came to, she asked: "What?" Then she stammered: "Oh, I'm sorry."

Don Emilio Santos advised her to lie down, but Moncho did not approve of that. "Why should she? It's all quite normal."

Pilar agreed. "Of course it is. I'm all right now."

But a few minutes later she burst into inconsolable tears.

Ignacio and Don Emilio sat motionless, not knowing what to do. But Moncho got up, went to the window, and closed it.

MONCHO and Ignacio left the instant the clock in Mateo's office, which Don Emilio Santos kept wound, marked the hour of six. They headed for the Café Savoy. Ignacio felt uneasy. When they came to the Plaza del Marques de Camps, he stopped abruptly. Evidently, an idea was simmering in his mind.

"Moncho," he said, "why don't you come to Gerona to live? Why don't you set up your laboratory here? I'm not entirely sure, but I think there's no real bacteriologist in the city."

Moncho kept walking. "We'd have a good time, wouldn't we?" he remarked, as though talking to himself.

"That I don't know," Ignacio answered, starting to walk quickly, not to be left behind. "But it would be wonderful for me."

Moncho started to look all around him. A pastry-shop window was displaying syrups and some little boxes shaped like standing cats which contained God knows what kind of candy. A passer-by stationary in front of the Diana Perfumery mirror was morosely squeezing a pimple on his nose. Couples were walking arm in arm. And dogs. And children.

"I'll have to think about it," Moncho said.

Ignacio almost leaped into the air. "So—you'd consider the possibility?"

Moncho answered: "Why not?" He seemed to be pondering the question. "It occurred to me as soon as I stepped down in the station. Besides, as you know, I don't want to live in Lérida."

"But—what about the German girl?" Ignacio hinted timidly.

Moncho raised his chin. "What about her? There's no guarantee that it'll last forever."

Ignacio was on the point of taking his friend by the sleeve and turning him around to embrace him. But they had come abreast of the Café Savoy, inside of which a solitary but elegant little old woman was drinking with relish the extraordinary concoction served there.

"Shall we go in?"

Ignacio stepped back to let Moncho precede him. Once they were inside, Ignacio stared around the place with the air of a connoisseur and greeted the waiters behind the bar.

"Where shall we sit?"

Saints alive! Ana María was right: Gerona was pocket-handkerchief size. There in the back at one of the tables usually taken by lovers sat Manolo and Esther. She had just risen, and Manolo was getting up as if they were about to leave.

Ignacio flew to meet them. "Just a minute," he cried. "Stay there."

Manolo and Esther looked pleased to see Ignacio. "What's up?" they said, believing he had come to look for them.

"I'd like to introduce you to Moncho."

"What? Is he here?"

Ignacio turned to his friend and signaled to him to come. "This is Moncho." A second later he added: "And this is Esther and Manolo."

Moncho did not seem displeased—quite the contrary. Manolo and Esther held out their hands to him, also visibly pleased.

"Gosh! Ignacio talks about you all the time."

"Let's all sit down," Esther suggested.

Suddenly, it was a gay meeting, in contrast with the time spent in Pilar's house. Unfortunately, the radio had been turned on, and an announcer with a powerful voice was giving the news. It was Sunday, the first day of the National Football Championship games. The Barcelona team, "reinforced by Pachín," had won 5-0. The Bishop was thinking of installing central heating in the Seminary, where the work of restoration had begun, and so on.

Ignacio, in a high mood, asked the waiter: "Would you please turn off the radio?"

The waiter, surprised at first, finally went to the counter and complied.

"What would you like to drink?"

The conversation moved along without difficulty. Manolo was twirling his green Tyrolean hat, while Esther, wearing one of her handsome sweaters, was coquettishly biting the little gold medallion that hung from her neck.

Inevitably, they talked cursorily about Gerona and the impression it had made on the stranger. "What can I say? There are only two institutions here: the Cathedral and Ignacio." Esther asked Moncho: "How do you manage to keep such a good color?" Ignacio anticipated his friend: "It's the mountains, Esther.

Surely you haven't forgotten?" "Oh, yes, that's right. Well, I'll have to take up mountain climbing."

Ignacio said with a flourish: "Moncho is a man who can spend five minutes contemplating the trunk of a tree."

Manolo looked astonished. "That seems to me a risky business."

They talked about jazz, Manolo's passion. Moncho did not like it. "But you do follow the rhythm by tapping you feet, don't you?" The young man admitted it. "Who could help it?" They talked about the Spanish Government and its recent creation of the INI—the Institute of National Industries—which planned to establish huge industrial plants all over the country. They discussed Barcelona, the University, bullfights. They saw Mr. Edward Collins sitting in one corner of the café, and Esther said: "He's the British consul." Moncho smiled. "That also seems like a risky business."

Ignacio realized that Moncho had made a good impression on the young couple, and he could not restrain a jealous reaction. He tried to take over the conversation, as had happened often before.

"Would you like to know the main fault of someone here?"

"Sure! Why not?"

"He's just naturally offensive. He says I've always been a pure being!"

Manolo stroked his short Balbo beard. "Whenever you want to, we can sue him, and that'll show him how wrong he is."

"He also says that the most important thing in life is to be able to choose three things: work, friends, and a brand of tobacco."

Esther made an expressive gesture. "That sounds good to me."

"But as it happens, he doesn't smoke."

Manolo raised his eyebrows. "You're right, then. He is a sly fellow."

Moncho laughed. He was enjoying himself. The radio had been turned on again. *Cante flamenco.* Mr. Edward Collins seemed to be listening with great concentration.

"You see?" Ignacio said. "There he is, poking and prying into our national secrets."

The Café Savoy was full; it was the smartest in the city.

"Too bad it's after dark now. I'd like to take a picture of this." As usual, Esther made a mock curtsy, happily.

THE day had ended, Moncho's last in Gerona. He was to take an early train the next morning.

In the course of supper in the Rambla flat, Carmen Elgazu and Matías did everything they could to make Ignacio's friend feel welcome. They wanted

Moncho to carry away a pleasant memory of their house.

"More soup? Just a little more?"

"No, thank you. I've had plenty."

During the dessert, Carmen Elgazu said to Moncho: "It's too bad you're leaving so soon. I can see how happy Ignacio is with you."

Ignacio said gaily: "Don't be alarmed. There's a chance that Moncho will come back—and stay."

His parents' eyes widened. "Really?"

"I don't know, I don't know. I'll have to think about it."

Matías nodded several times. "Yes, cheer up, man! There's a lot here to be analyzed."

MONCHO left the next morning. As he was ready to leave the house, the bacteriologist from Lérida found on the bed as he entered the room where he had slept a fine reproduction of Mount Everest dedicated to him with a line that said: "Don't touch. Danger of death." He gazed with undisguised affection at his closest comrade of the war.

"Ignacio, I meant in all seriousness what I said to your friends yesterday. You're an institution."

SIXTY-FOUR

SOON after Pilar noticed the first symptoms, she was taken to the Chaos Clinic, where four rooms were reserved for maternity cases. At the moment of the birth, Carmen Elgazu, Matías, Ignacio, and Don Emilio Santos were in the clinic.

Dr. Morell and a midwife named Mercedes, who had worked with Dr. Rosselló years earlier, attended Pilar. She took her labor with reasonable courage and everything proceeded normally. A miracle as simple as that of San Gennaro in Naples.

The men stayed in the corridor; Carmen Elgazu, however, wanted to be present at the delivery, and Dr. Morell let her. During the most important moments, Carmen was praying in snatches. She tried to help her daughter's breathing, and managed to do it. As soon as the small head appeared in the enormous aperture, she felt on the verge of fainting. The prophecies were fulfilled: the baby was a boy. A grandson, the first grandchild! A new life, a new being. A new soul for God.

Dr. Morell moved with great skill. His hands seemed actually to be receiving something that came from the beyond. When the newborn child cried, the Chaos Clinic was filled with joy; it was like the triumphal appearance of the aurora borealis over northern Europe a few days before. The baby weighed seven pounds, seven ounces. As soon as he was cleaned and swaddled, he was shown to the young mother, exhausted and only half conscious. She put her head close to the child's as if it were she who sought protection.

Everyone came in to see her then. She was heaped with congratulations on her courage and the beauty of the male child, whose eyes were blue.

Carmen Elgazu claimed that he was the picture of his father, but Matías and Don Emilio said not, that it was a miniature of Pilar. Ignacio could see no resemblance to either; the baby seemed to have been born by spontaneous generation.

From time to time Pilar moaned and stared around the room. Everyone thought: "She's looking for Mateo." Of course; he was the one absent. None of those around Pilar's bed ventured to speak his name, but they all thought of him and all with a feeling of resentment. Without Mateo, the baby was half orphaned.

Dr. Morell left them quickly, but Dr. Chaos came in his snow-white coat to take his place with a cordial and somewhat solemn air.

At the sight of Dr. Chaos, everyone remembered the day when Carmen Elgazu had undergone a major operation in the same clinic. This had resulted in sterility for her; now the birth that had just occurred was a kind of compensation, another sign of the pendicular movement that controlled human life.

Matías and Don Emilio were the most jubilant of them all. The knowledge that their own life would be carried on by that tiny body, helpless but not inert, filled them with a kind of bliss. They were somewhat overcome, but asserted that they had never seen Pilar look so beautiful; she was languidly holding out her hand to each of them in turn.

Carmen Elgazu felt a great sadness, however, a sadness she could not dismiss. She was crying. Perhaps she was a coward. Perhaps she was afraid of responsibility. Perhaps she was thinking that Pilar would belong still less to her from then on; or perhaps she was remembering her own pain when she had borne her three children, especially the first, Ignacio.

Ignacio was very much taken aback when Dr. Chaos said to him: "Now you see to it that you're married soon and that your wife brings us a baby like this girl's."

Great gaiety in the Chaos Clinic! The date was October 18. Mosén Alberto had been notified at once, and came bringing the liturgical calendar. After consulting it, he said: "The feast of Saint Luke," of the man who wrote the third book of the Gospel, a disciple of Paul and his companion on many journeys.

"Pilar, my daughter! Are you all right?"

"Yes, Mosén Alberto. Thank you."

Pilar wanted to kiss the priest's hand, but everyone was touched to see that it was he who took her hand and kissed it.

Her room, looking out at the garden in the back, was soon filled with flowers. The news spread around the city, and the Governor, Warning Voice, Manolo and Esther, Matías's friends from the Café Nacional, the Feminine Section, Asunción, and Miguel Rosselló and Chelo all sent flowers. Marta sent the best bouquet she could find in Gerona. It was bright and fragrant. Fresh roses, each of which had a secret significance.

Matías undertook to send a telegram addressed to Mateo Santos in Russia.

It said: "A son. All is well." He signed his own name, then hesitated between "love" and "greetings," but finally chose "love."

Next day the round of visits began. Paz appeared with a smiling, expressive face. She congratulated Pilar and looked at the child tenderly. She had brought a bottle of eau de cologne. Her comment was: "He looks a lot like you, Pilar. He's the very picture of you."

Manuel Alvear and Eloy also visited the clinic. Manuel came into the room on tiptoe, as if it were a church. He stood there a while before he looked at the baby. Like everyone else he thought as he stared at Pilar: "How lovely she looks." Finally, he looked at the baby; he was at a loss for something to say. He laughed quietly, as if he had won an undeserved prize. Eloy, all freckles and crew-cut hair—like Pachín's—stared at the infant and, seeing that he was sound asleep, looked so frightened that everyone was touched. Eloy was very innocent, too innocent to understand it all. Much more so than Manuel. He had no notion of the meaning of such words as "placenta" and "umbilical cord." He noticed the newborn fingernails, perfect, and very minute indeed. He wanted to go on studying them, but Manuel said: "I wish I could see his eyes." Pilar answered, "You'll have plenty of time for that, Manuel."

Carmen Elgazu saw to it that there were not too many visitors. She took care to avoid letting Marta see Pilar at the same time as Ignacio, who had sent a telegram to Ana María telling her of the birth. Marta kissed Pilar and burst into tears. Pilar stroked her hair. "Don't cry, Marta! Some day..." She did not finish the sentence, but merely added: "Come on, you'll wake up my baby."

"My" baby—Pilar had never used that word before. She herself was surprised to hear it from her own lips. She still had not taken in the idea that this little creature was hers. Until then she had looked at it somewhat as Ignacio had, as a neutral life that had arrived by mysterious paths. But suddenly, perhaps because of Marta, she became conscious that it was true. Then she, too, began to cry, and suddenly felt depressed. "My son," she said several times. She turned her head and looked at him with infinite tenderness, then reached her arm and pulled him close to her. And seeing how helpless he was, she closed her eyes and smiled, thinking that thus she was better protecting him against all the ills of the world.

AMANECER published a photograph of Pilar and her son, with a caption composed by Miguel Rosselló, a patriotic caption that Matías and Don Emilio Santos considered in bad taste.

Soon Pilar left the clinic and the child was baptized on October 25 at the parish church of La Mercadal. A crowd of people was there. Mosén Alberto officiated. The Governor and Carmen Elgazu acted as godparents.

Mosén Alberto pronounced the words of the ritual with feeling; Manuel Alvear served him as altar boy.

The infant was given the names of César, Emilio, and Matías. At the hour when people stopped at the Central Hotel for a pick-me-up, everyone was surprised to learn from Professor Civil that the name César came from the Latin and meant "he who is born with a head of hair"; that Matías came from the Hebrew and meant "divine gift"; and that Emilio came from the Greek and meant "amiable."

Pilar was touched when she heard that. She said jokingly: "Imagine calling that fuzz he has on his head hair."

Ignacio, who was beginning to love his nephew more than he ever would have expected, reproached Pilar. "It's not fuzz. Etymology can't be wrong. This child will turn out to be a Samson."

Matías was in constant fear that an agent for the Ofe Laboratory might suddenly enter the room and offer Pilar, as a nursing mother, a tube of Madresol, the product that "helps the child's growth." At the last moment, when the guests were on the point of leaving, Marcos arrived with a telegram addressed to Pilar which he had just received in the office. It was signed by Mateo and said simply: "Thank God!"

CÉSAR Santos Alvear was born on the day the German troops occupied Odessa. Forty-eight hours later, the Blue Division was to meet the enemy for the first time.

That sword had hung over the Alvear family every minute. *Amanecer* had started to publish a daily list of the *divisionarios* who had been killed on Russian soil. They were curt death notices, which would have evoked thundering comments from Moncho. "Ricardo Puentes Bejarana; Emilio Gómez Aguayo; Lieutenant Galiana Carmilla. All present and accounted for!" Pilar read the death notices and let the paper fall from her hands, exclaiming: "Why say 'present' when they're gone forever?"

The great danger was that any day *Amanecer* might come out with a black border and the name "Mateo Santos, present!" on the front page. If that should happen, how could her heart bear the blow? What would become of her, of Don Emilio Santos, of the flat on the Plaza de la Estación? What would become of the autumn, of the world, and of the newborn César Santos Alvear?

As if that worry were not enough, she did not know just where the Blue Division was fighting. The war correspondents never gave exact information; they merely said that it was "fighting victoriously, inflicting grave losses on the enemy." The name of Lake Ilmen was mentioned, of course. But were they still there? Where were they? Where was Mateo? The German dispatches occasionally mentioned the Blue Division, but merely to praise it. Only once did word come that it was fighting "in the southern sector." Well, that was a point of reference. According to Manuel's atlas, which the Alvear family kept consulting frantically, Lake Ilmen was situated "in the southern sector." Were they on the lake then? And why on a lake? The radio spoke of "a certain number of wounded Spaniards decorated with the Iron Cross by the Führer." Decorated? How fierce had the battles been? Was Mateo one of the wounded? She wished that she had sewed a protective patch over his heart.

What hung over her head was not a sword: it was martyrdom. The bureaucratic machine had started to operate with its bone-freezing coldness. All of a sudden, Pilar received an envelope from the Civil Government containing "Mateo's pay" for the month, plus some extras for "active service." The next day she received another envelope containing the notice that the city of Seville had sent sausages, bologna, and two thousand medals of the Virgin of the Magi to Russia. Shortly after that, she received an invitation to attend the funeral services in the Cathedral in memory of the first men in the division who had been killed. What could she do with her allotment? How could she spend that money? Would the time of the Three Kings ever come? Should she attend the memorial services in the Cathedral?

As it happened, everyone except those who had a member of the family fighting "in the southern sector" was hanging on the deeds of the *divisionarios*, full of euphoria. Memorial services and festivals were held for the Division, and people read aloud to their own cliques descriptions of "the sweeping German advance on all fronts," as well as news items reporting that several Russian generals had been dismissed for incompetence and that the Stalin government was preparing to abandon Moscow and move into the Urals.

The sword and the stake were two things very hard to grow accustomed to. And even harder when the newspapers began to mention "Christmas gifts" for the volunteers and what "all Spain ought to contribute."

The word "Christmas" rang through the Alvear household like a rifle shot. In Solita's father's ears, too, and the ears of Gracia Andújar, who went to Mass every day to pray for Cacerola. Father Forteza also heard it with a presentiment that he would never see Alfonso Estrada again. Christmas meant that the universally feared "General Winter" was about to descend inexorably upon the Division, contrary to General Sánchez Bravo's optimistic forecasts.

Pilar was upset; she was confused. Bologna, sausages, Christmas gifts? Was that all anyone could do? How could her own neighbor, a woman who lived on the same floor as Pilar and sold fruit in the mornings on the Plaza de Abastos, turn on her radio every afternoon to listen peacefully to a soap opera? What was the use of asking "all Spain" to contribute when the truth was that everyone was still involved in his own life?

Pilar realized that her anxiety was not transferable. She decided then to write to Mateo, and to enclose in her letter a picture of the infant César.

> I'm well, Mateo, and the baby is too, as you can see from his photograph. He weighed seven pounds, seven ounces when he was born. Mosén Alberto baptized him. His grandparents drool over him. My mother comes every day to help me, although, as I say, I feel perfectly well. How I wish I could be certain that the same could be said of you! How and where are you, Mateo? *Amanecer* publishes the list of fatalities every day. Oh, Mateo, may God take care of you!

Mosén Alberto was still calling on Pilar. He felt that his presence comforted her, as it did. He even went so far as to bring her some cookies because he had heard that Pilar liked them. The priest assured her again and again that nothing terrible would happen to Mateo. "You must understand, Pilar: bachelors are assigned the most dangerous missions." Mosén Alberto also had fallen in love with the baby, and he always asked Pilar to put him on the scales to find out how much he had gained. "A little over nine pounds! Good gracious! Ignacio was right! That child is going to be a Samson."

César Santos Alvear was the center of the household, its god, and its mystery.

"Pilar, the baby needs to be changed again. Bring me a diaper."

"I'm coming, Mama."

"Ah, my little darling, my king, my little boy!"

When Don Emilio Santos came home, he would stand in the doorway and shout: "Where's that great despot? Where have you put him?"

Matías went to Pilar's flat every day, too, after leaving the Telegraph Office. "May I come in? Or do I have to pay to enter?"

Ignacio carried in his wallet the first letter that Ana María had written him after César's birth. It ended with the words: "Our first boy will be named Ignacio."

SIXTY-FIVE

MATEO was alive—and perfectly well, like Pilar. He was one of the volunteers whose dearest wish was to meet the enemy. His second lieutenant's star shone on his chest. He had appointed Alfonso Estrada his aide. They got along very well together, and the cook in his section was Cacerola. On the other hand, he had lost touch with Captains Arias and Sandoval, Mosén Falcó, Solita, Rogelio, and even Salazar and Núñez Maza. The men in the Division had been scattered in the troop assignment that took place after it had relieved the Germans on the broad Lake Ilmen sector.

Mateo and his battalion took part in the capture of Tigoda and Nitlikino. The Russians had resisted so stubbornly that he saw the first of his comrades fall beside him; but the example shown by the officers and his own drive kept him from losing his coolness even for a moment. Cacerola and Alfonso Estrada had both been afraid for him. Mateo seemed to defy death, which was always stalking him in the Russian artillery fire. The Russian prisoners with whom the war correspondents for Spanish newspapers talked, however, were inexplicably submissive. Few sentries were needed to guard them. They maintained the roads and performed other work, but never took advantage of the chances for escape which came their way. At night they gathered in the *isbas* and reported on time to continue their work the next day. Mateo said: "The Russian language is an enigma, but even more so the Russian psychology; it's absurd."

The telegram sent from Gerona by Matías came on one of the rest days granted the section commanded by Mateo. When he read that a boy had been born to him, he gave a shout of joy loud enough to reach the stars. Alfonso Estrada heard him and went to his friend and commanding officer. On learning the news, he snapped to attention in front of Mateo and promoted him to first lieutenant then and there. Cacerola abandoned for a moment the letter he was writing to Gracia Andújar and swore by everything he loved best—by the flickering lantern light—that under the circumstances he would have to search one of the Russian shacks for a nursing bottle to give Mateo.

Mateo felt his paternity very deeply, and a mental and physical pang shot through him at the realization that he had not seen the little creature who would replace him some day in the service of Spain if he were to die in the present venture. But that knowledge also spurred him, like a Cossack spurring his mount, and infused him with the belief that because he had a son, he could never die.

Consequently, he volunteered for several dangerous surprise attacks, full of hazards: mud, the guerrillas hiding in the woods, and the mines and booby traps that the Russians had sowed all around them. He did not care. He accepted them all with such imperturbable calm that some of his men began to call him "The Suicide." The news of many losses suffered by the Division published in its newsletter, *The Campaign Leaflet*, did not dismay him. Someone had written in it that "it was an exact Division because it was not going to leave any remainder."

During one of their surprise attacks, Mateo and his men found several of their comrades pinned to the ground with stakes through their bodies. They were men who had infiltrated the lines the day before, and who had been described as "pinned to the ground" after being surprised by an enemy patrol. The sight was shocking, but Mateo and his men managed to pull the stakes from the corpses and to bury them with crosses of wood—not the Iron Crosses conferred by the Führer. Their voices were hoarse as they shouted: "Present!"

The volunteers' device against suffering was simply to say: "It doesn't matter." They all exerted their ingenuity to lessen it. Mateo did not feel the cold in his feet because he had exchanged his boots for those of a dead Russian. A Galician corporal put women's garments of silk between the wool and his skin, although that caused a great outcry. Cacerola had stolen a dynamo light from a German soldier. He had to use a small iron bar to start it and the bulb emitted a thin thread of illumination accompanied by a constant whistle that got on Alfonso Estrada's nerves. "Please, Cacerola, turn it off. I'd rather listen to the accordion or, even better, Pablito's harmonica."

Mateo lived with fear, but he concealed it; Alfonso Estrada did not. He suffered from a terrible fear, unlike any he had felt during the Spanish war when in the Tercio of Our Lady of Montserrat. He tried to conquer it by conjuring up the figure of Father Forteza, with his hair shirt and his faith. The young man who had told Pilar so many tall tales in the Supply Delegation was quaking inwardly now, but he managed to smile and pass out candy and honey on Sundays to the Russian girls living nearby.

Mateo's mind changed radically, however, after he received Pilar's letter one November night, thanks to the heroism of the men in charge of supplies, and saw the enclosed picture of her and his son, who had entered the world in the Chaos Clinic.

The picture seemed to come alive in his hands. César Santos Alvear became a creature of flesh and blood to Mateo. He asked Cacerola to lend him his lamp in order to see the baby more clearly by its thread of light. And when he saw him, sound asleep, he felt more awed than Eloy and shook more violently than Alfonso Estrada. From that moment, death held no more attractions for him. Mateo said to himself that he would die doubly if he died now that he had a son, for he would orphan a creature who had never heard of Marx, or Stalin, or the Kremlin, or the dismissed Russian generals.

Indeed, Mateo himself felt orphaned. It dawned on him then that they were existing in a vacuum, that they did not know anything, not even about the war. His world was the sector sown with mines, some of them made out of matchboxes, which was their theater of operations. How did it happen that St. Petersburg had not been taken yet? What was going on in Moscow and Odessa? He fancied that the fat in the Russian food was doing him harm. He was afraid that never again would his men call him "The Suicide." Mateo felt that it was all humiliating, but he said to himself again and again: "It doesn't matter. I'm doing my duty." During those same days an encouraging message came from General Millán Astray, the famous amputee, addressed to General Muñoz Grandes. And it was printed in *The Campaign Leaflet.* A rumor was circulating that the hero of the Alcázar in Toledo, General Moscardó himself, would soon pay them a visit. Had the General hesitated to sacrifice his son? Would he hesitate now to give up his own life? What was the source of courage? The Russian front was such a hard place to be! Besides, for unknown reasons, the Division was there without any air cover at all. The Blue Esquadrille, the Spanish air squadron whose first casualty had been Lieutenant Luis Alcocer, who had crashed during his training in Germany, had been sent to another sector.

Lieutenant Mateo Santos realized the wisdom of censoring many of the letters from Spain, of making sure that anything that might impair the morale of the fighting men was blacked out. A man might do anything at the front—except shed tears. It was bad enough to see some of the Russian girls crying because some insolent, ill-mannered fellow had asked them for something. Enough that the sky often wept. Enough that the accordion should weep in the hands of the "Charlatan," a legionnaire with a hundred tattoos on his body, one a portrait of a clown who, or so he said, had died laughing while the Legion was in Africa.

All in all, Mateo was almost sorry that Pilar's letter had reached him intact, without any blacked-out passages, and that the right to see his son had been respected, for his superior, Major Regoyos, had warned him that soon he would entrust him with "a very dangerous mission."

His son. "My son..." Mosén Alberto had baptized him already, not by fire, but by water and salt. The Governor had acted as godfather. The grandparents drooled when they looked at the baby. "Where are you, Mateo?" Pilar had asked him. "I'm here, my darling wife," Mateo whispered through the whistle of Cacerola's lantern. "I'm here, serving Spain in Tigoda and Nitlikino. Pulling up stakes that punctured the bodies of my beloved comrades. Calling the early morning shelling by the Russians 'drums rolling.' Calling some kind of gadget that fires thirty-six projectiles in succession through some sort of bore 'Stalin's hand organ.' Playing cards and throwing the bar in *la barra*, and pitching coins. Singing:

"A barge came down through Warsaw
With seventy Falangists shouting ¡Arriba, España!
To the rumble, rumble, rumble of the guns...

"Watching the Russian prisoners, who raise their heads when they hear us singing and listen with a smile of simple ecstasy."

Pilar's handwriting did not look the same as usual; it was not the handwriting in the intimate diary that she had begun to keep after he had given her that box of candy with an orchid on the lid. It looked shaky, like the flame in Cacerola's lantern, somewhat irregular, with the lines sloping downward, which meant sadness and depression, according to graphologists.

The final sentence of Pilar's letter, read a hundred times, said: "Oh, Mateo, may God take care of you."

This phrase pierced him like a dart. What would the "dangerous mission" mentioned by Major Regoyos entail? They had heard that a German company had been pinned down twenty kilometers farther south, in a marsh. So what? Hadn't many Germans, also with wives, been killed in the Spanish war? What if none of the women had been named Pilar?

"Alfonso, would you like to say the Rosary with me?"

"Count me in," Cacerola said.

The night was cold, bright, starry. Mateo, Estrada, and Cacerola crossed themselves as the Charlatan reprimanded the Galician corporal for the nth time because he put women's garments between the wool and his skin.

They started the Rosary, but Mateo could not "pace the length of the hallway" like his father-in-law, Matías Alvear, in the Rambla flat. Except for the sentinels, the section was quartered in an *isba*, and the place was so closely packed that they were almost unable to move. They warmed their hands at a plate in which a few drops of alcohol were burning with a violet flame that seemed to resemble the color of a newborn baby's skin.

When Mateo came to the litany, he said more than *pro nobis*; he stressed the *ora.* Yes, the Virgin, *turris eburnea, domus aurea, foederis arca*, would pray for and watch over him, Pilar, and the diminutive César. Mateo did not know whether Pilar would teach the child to love or hate his warlike father, that Falangist who had enlisted at the Plaza de San Agustín in Gerona one fine morning simply because he heard someone shout: "Russia must be punished!" and because he had believed it his duty.

Russia was guilty. Then what about those docile prisoners? What about those admirably modest girls, responsive to any kind look, to a taste of honey and some candy? What about those old people with their icons, who would suddenly cry: "Christus, Christus!"

No, Russia was not guilty. The blame should fall on the injustices of the Tsars, the hatred of the Bolsheviks, the powerful Jews of whom Professor Civil had talked with him and Ignacio, and the political partisans—and Cosme Vila, and those militiamen who had killed César, Pilar's brother, the seminarian whose memory always served Mateo as a stimulus and a consolation.

Russia, the Russian nation, the multiple Russian races, the Russian people who said *da, da* when they heard a knock on the door were guilty of nothing. They were broken by suffering and they were humble. They had lived like slaves for centuries beside their lakes, on their lands, and their sufferings and slavery had made possible the triumph of Lenin with his trim goatee—a man who loved chess and cats.

The Rosary ended. Silence fell within the *isba.* The Charlatan had gone to sleep, and Alfonso Estrada went out to urinate.

"Shall we have a game, Cacerola?"

"No, unless that's an order."

"Why? What's the matter?"

"I'd like to write a letter."

"To Gracia Andújar?"

"No, to Hilda, my German girl."

Mateo pulled out his blue handkerchief and his lighter. He lighted a cigarette, brand-name Juno. And said, "You've given me an idea. I'm going to write a letter, too."

"Send my regards."

"To whom?"

"To Pilar."

"Well, you're wrong. I'm going to write to my son."

"What? You're kidding."

"Go ahead and believe that. He's something special. He already knows how to read."

SIXTY-SIX

THE fairs and festivals took their normal course in Gerona that year; there was no flood. The Dodgem cars were a great success. The young people loved to attack one another in fun, as if they were taking sides in the war. The raffles were well patronized, especially those which said: "Everyone wins." The circus sent the small fry into ecstasies. Their gambits were eternal, although the clowns complained that they were not allowed to make puns on politics. Paz Alvear was missed at the Diana booth. "Soap for everyone! Diana soap for the most delicate skins." Perhaps the outstanding attraction was the fakir Campoy, the man who had had himself buried for several hours in the Dehesa years earlier, and had then come back to life. In this fair of 1941, Campoy walked barefoot, literally, on burning coals. A peasant in his Sunday suit who had come from the region of Breda looking for thrills decided that it was all a fake. To prove that to his companions, also in their Sunday best, he stopped down and touched the coals, and they burned his hand. Campoy, the magician, took off his top hat with an elegant gesture of his left hand and pointed the way to the dispensary with his right.

Then came the month of November. The mineral kingdom was done violence, the vegetable kingdom began to die, as if innumerable battalions of Stalin's "hand organs" were shooting them down.

Of course, that November was marked by events far from tedious. Someone somewhere in the city seemed disposed to threaten life itself. Perhaps it was Rufina, the half-witch of the rag peddlers. Perhaps some mythological giant hidden in Las Pedreras. Perhaps it might be existence itself, refusing to be tainted with vulgarity, with a lack of imagination.

However that might be, surprise followed upon surprise. Small ones like Pilar and Mateo's son. Normal ones like the removal of tonsils by the unscrupulous ear, nose, and throat specialists. Jumbo surprises, as big as the Cathedral—as Señor Grote, Torrus of the Grupo Escolar, Carreras the anesthetist, or Leopoldo, the Costa brothers' sharp secretary, might have put it.

One of the small surprises was that the weather did not turn cold. The mannikins in the shop windows were still wearing coats and scarves, but even the apprehensive Marcos did not fear to dose himself with his quota of Andreu tablets, stored up for his throat. The sun was still shining, a warm sun that rejuvenated the old men who walked along the railroad tracks. Of course, some people thought this must be a fake, too, because it was unheard of, and that Nature would take her revenge at the most unguarded moment, perhaps with a snowfall that would turn Gerona into a parody of the "southern sector" of Russia. But in the meantime, one was living, and that had not happened yet.

Another small surprise was the start of an idyl between Gracia Andújar and former Second Lieutenant Montero, the recently appointed director of the Municipal Library. No one thought it strange that another love affair should begin. Love was something unchanging, like the acts in the circus or the elegance of some birds. Love might hide for thousands of years, only to touch two persons at once when some predestined hour struck. The two persons might as well be the daughter of a Catholic psychiatrist who loved the Gregorian chant and a young man like Montero, thirsting for life after having had to shoot so many men sentenced to death by the military tribunal. Of course there were the usual comments, especially by the women. By María del Mar, Esther, the beauteous Adela. But no one was shocked by the news. The only adverse remark came from the girl's mother, the insignificant wife of Dr. Andújar, who said when she found her daughter inventing a thousand excuses for trips to the Municipal Library: "Don't you think you're too young, my dear?" An insipid, stupid remark. Warning Voice had said in one of his splendid "Windows on the World" only a few days before, as it happened, that among certain of the peoples in Oceania the girls were mothers at fourteen and fifteen years of age, and to set Montero's mind at rest, Gracia Andújar was old enough to begin to love him, and thereby to add another log to the fire of Marta's spinsterhood.

Another very small surprise: the proposed dismissal of the Provincial Syndical Delegate, the lazy Comrade Arjona, married with three children. He relinquished his position to active Comrade Jesús Revilla, also married and with three children. Comrade Arjona was thanked verbally and in writing for his services and left for Madrid, "where he had friends who would explain to him the reason for such a humiliation and lend him a hand." Comrade Jesús Revilla, who had taught business, was a most pedantic man with thirty-six years under his blue shirt. He had lost an eye during the war, but had won the friendship of several national advisers on his duty visit to the authorities by declaring that he was prepared to reorganize the syndical structure from top to bottom and to defend the rights of the "producers" against any oligarchical infringement.

As General Sánchez Bravo listened to him, he coughed several times in a manner that led Nebulosa, on guard in the passageway, to think: "That guy won't get a sniff of González Byass here." The Bishop, for his part, said to the newcomer as he gave him his blessing: "May God aid you in your work, my son." The Governor, however, was the most effusive of the three authorities. It seemed to him that Jesús Revilla, a Basque, had a flair for command and a store of good will. "I shall always be at your call whenever you need me." Then the Governor made clear that one of the main problems to confront the Basque would be Catalan irony. "You Basques are a bit rough-hewn, it's true. Here the people have a somewhat disconcerting mental agility. Their critical sense is extremely strong, especially with regard to those of us who occupy official positions. At first they considered us sharpshooters. They'd rather have had a good carpenter or a treasury delegate. Now try to be seen with your wife and children from time to time. A family makes an impression on them. A good father is greatly respected here. After all, I'll keep you informed. And never let it enter your mind to say that the Mediterranean looks like a lake! They'll never forgive you for that. And some Sundays you ought to wear civilian clothes—that will give you great prestige."

Another surprise, somewhat greater, was provided by General Sánchez Bravo on the day when at last he laid the cornerstone for the new quarters on the vacant lots donated by the Widow Oriol, near the Olot station. The General, normally terse in his speech, soared to the heights on this occasion, to the astonishment of his wife, Doña Cecilia, who asked him when he came home and was taking off his cap and white gloves: "Whatever happened to you? Did you eat a parrot for lunch?"

Actually, the fire from which the General was sending off sparks was built by a high military officer, his peer in the chain of command, who had telephoned him from his headquarters in Madrid to assure him that anything he could say about the skullduggery of Colonel Triguero was small beer compared with what was happening in the capital of Spain. "I said so in my letters. You didn't believe me, but that's how it is," his friend informed him. "Some serious things are going on. The English are consistently offering double what Germany is offering for our mercury, our pyrites, our hides, and so on. And some of your comrades and mine are taking a hand in the game. Can you hear me? Can you hear me? Yes? All right, then—come to Madrid some day and I'll tell you the latest, about the twenty thousand tons of powdered milk that the American Red Cross sent us." *Brrr...rrr...rrr...* "*Can* you hear me?" *Brrr...rrr...rrr...*

What a pity! The telephone was not functioning as it should, and the conversation had to be cut short. But the General thought he had heard his colleague in Madrid intercalate some important names among "those responsible for the serious things that are happening." Hence his long and impassioned speech at the cornerstone-laying for the new barracks. Carlos Civil, representing Emer, began to shake in his boots. The General ended by saying: "We must not permit the birds of prey, whatever their names may be, to profit from the blood shed by our soldiers. If necessary we shall unsheathe our swords again."

Everyone was somewhat awestruck. This was a large economy-size surprise.

Another in the course of that month of November was the doing of Carlota, Countess of Rubí. Carlota announced to her women friends that she was almost certain she was pregnant. Ah, the machinations of her husband, the Mayor of the city! Finally, he had paid attention to Dr. Morell and had gone to Barcelona for an operation, with the aforementioned result. Carolta noticed an unusual tremor inside her. "It could be a false alarm, but I don't think so. I have a presentiment that it will prove true." Her friends congratulated her with real sympathy. They knew what it meant to Carlota. A woman of the Catalan aristocracy must have children. The poor women living in the holes of Montjuich must not be the only ones to have them. "Oh, isn't it wonderful, María del Mar? It will be the best 'Window on the World' my husband ever wrote."

Another surprise had a more immediate effect on the people of Gerona. Gracia's father, Dr. Andújar, was the protagonist of that act. Finally, the man managed, and it was about time, to convince the people once and for all that he was no mere "crazy man's doctor," but could give effective help to many people who, although normal, nevertheless suffered vague and unlocalized disturbances that they themselves could not define, much less their families.

Dr. Andújar's prescription for success was to give some daily five-minute radio chats entitled, "Tablets for Thought." The Gerundians never had heard of such a thing, but the chats became as popular as the soap operas and the dedicated records. Incidentally, Dr. Andújar's prestige was already on the rise, owing to a pamphlet he had written under the title "Are You Sad Without Knowing Why?" The bookstores had just started to display its provocative question in their windows. Dr. Chaos added to the attention it attracted and merited by a highly eulogistic review in *Amanecer.* Added to that, Dr. Andújar had won warm liking everywhere by the model deportment of his eight children, none of whom ever whined and who might be expected to form their own orchestra of "chamber music." People said: "A man who can train his family like that has to have something in his head."

Indeed, there was a great deal going on in Dr. Andújar's head. His radio talks demonstrated that. He tried to adapt his words to the grasp of the common mind, to the people who were closing in upon themselves, refusing contact with others; those who suddenly felt elated and as suddenly lost their desire to live; those who noticed in themselves a growing aversion toward the people they loved; those who felt unable to breathe as soon as they found themselves in an enclosed place; those who felt dizzy when crossing an open space; women who shunned others when a little bird of theirs died and they buried it in a flood of tears, and so on.

"All these people," the doctor said, "are the victims of misunderstandings on the part of those around them, almost always. They are contemptuously pronounced 'hysterical' or 'neurasthenic.' They're told that what they are seeking is to be looked at, that they were born to make trouble, and that the best thing is to pay no attention to them or give them a taste of the stick. That's a serious mistake. The relatives should know that such people suffer a great deal, that their suffering is real, not imaginary or put on, and that the very fact they don't know what to say when they're asked: 'See here now, what's wrong? Why are you acting like this? Why do you spend half an hour staring at that big jug?' Doesn't mean they don't need help. It means the opposite. They need it more than if they had typhus or were suffering from anemia. Because their illness is not merely physical; their spirit partakes of it."

Language like that was new. Raimundo, the barber, said: "That's happened to me at the movies. I feel smothered and have to leave." The owner of the Crocodile said: "Conchi, the mother of Paz, was afraid of falling if she had to cross a bridge." Mijares, the counselor for the Agencia Gerunda and Constructora Gerundense, Inc., admitted that, contrary to appearances, he was exuberant only in the morning, whereas by the middle of the afternoon he usually had to go through a couple of hours when for two cents he would gladly let everything go to hell. Pablito drank in Dr. Andújar's words. "Things like that happen to Mama," he thought. "And me. And why did Cristina say she wanted to die the day when she found out she had become a woman?"

What Dr. Andújar provoked was more than surprise; it was curiosity, too. Particularly because at the end of the talk he announced that he would donate his time on Wednesday and Saturday afternoons to anyone who had some relative at home whose conduct seemed incomprehensible. Soon his waiting room was jammed on those days. The patient lines became so long that the doctor was confirmed in his belief that his chief weapon must be the soft word. He must talk about his science as Mosén Alberto talked about the customs of the fishermen on the coast, as if the public whom he was addressing were no more than twenty years old. And show a great compassion for the emotional universe of women.

As individual to individual, Don Anselmo Ichaso, the lifelong editor of *Navarrese Thought*, and Esther's mother, Katy, sprang their own surprises.

Don Anselmo Ichaso wrote to Warning Voice on princely embossed paper, passing on two juicy news items. One, that, implementing his statements in Pamplona during the Mayor's honeymoon trip, he had prepared for delivery to Franco a petition signed "by a number of Spanish personages," requesting him to restore the monarchy, "the only viable formula for saving the country, now at the crossroads, owing to the duration of the World War." The other item was that his son, Javier the amputee, had virtually abandoned his architectural studies and was devoting his time to writing novels. "I'm furious with him, but he doesn't care. He says he has a great deal to tell the world and that he wants to say it all with verbs and adjectives, not with buildings. Have you ever heard such nonsense, my dear friend? Ah, and he makes you responsible for his decision. He declares that while you and he were working together in San Sebastián, he discovered *the marvelous country of ideas.*"

As for Katy, she suddenly called her daughter, Esther, and told her that she had just received a letter from Jérez de la Frontera saying that her friend, the Duke of Medinaceli, had turned his Villarejo farm over to his workers in the province of Jaén, to be parceled out among the needy. "Do you know what that means, my dear? What with such fits of generosity, the syndicates, and your husband's mania for defending lost causes, we're going to have to sell our estate in Jérez."

Of course, one of the surprises inevitably was a death. This surprise was of great moment to adult Gerundians. Dr. Rosselló died of a "cardiac collapse" in the Penitentiary of Puerto de Santa María, according to the brief notice published in *Amanecer.*

The Governor received word officially and communicated it to Miguel Rosselló and his sister, Chelo. They were both stunned. Then it was Jorge de Batlle's turn to console his young wife by marshaling arguments not unlike those she had used with him. But who would console Miguel, Mateo's substitute in the provincial headquarters of the Falange? Miguel had learned to love and forgive his father during his absence. "What happened?" he asked the Governor. "When I visited him I could see that he looked tired, but he seemed healthy. And he never complained of his heart." The Governor hesitated a moment; finally, he made a gesture of helplessness. "Prison life is hard, my dear Miguel. You'll just have to resign yourself."

Miguel and Chelo would have liked to hold public funeral services in memory of their father, for they were sure that many people in Gerona had loved the doctor, but the Governor opposed the idea. "I'm sorry," he said, "but

I don't think it would be prudent." For the first time, Miguel Rosselló stared at his boss with angry eyes. As for Chelo, she went to see Marta and said: "It's a great pity that politics refuses to respect a man even after he's dead."

Pachín's name was not missing from the list of surprises. He triumphed all along the line with the football club of Barcelona. During the first week of the league championship games, he made seven brilliant goals, and that made him the most popular man in all Spain. So popular that he spent his whole day amusing himself, sleeping, reading comic books with a somewhat repellent relish, and forgetting Paz. Thus far he had never been to see her, on the excuse that "the trainer wouldn't give him permission." His letters were few, his excuse for that being that "writing isn't my strong suit." He telephoned her at the Diana Perfumery, calling her "my little pigeon" and promising her that they would be married when the right moment came—and then hung up. Paz threw a challenging look around the shop and at the world. She had promised herself that this man would not get away from her. But what could she do? For the moment she could only avenge herself by summoning the pluck to keep herself busy with the Red Relief and by asking Ignacio for the address of their cousin, José Alvear. Paz insisted that she "needed urgently to get in touch with him." Ignacio said to her: "We don't know where he is, Paz. I swear it. We wrote a letter to Toulouse some time ago, to his old address, but we haven't had an answer." The first person who really felt her wrath was Cefe, the portraitist. Paz said to the artist: "From here on out I don't take my clothes off in front of any man. You're all beasts."

The Bishop's name was also on the roll call of the surprise-makers. He was happy just then because his best friend, the Bishop of Salamanca, Dr. Pla y Deniel, had been appointed Archbishop of Toledo and Primate of Spain. In this good mood, he informed his parishioners of his plan to start another plea for beatification in the diocese on behalf of the martyred vicar, Mosén Francisco.

The Bishop had arrived at that decision not without effort. The fact that Mosén Francisco had gone with the Reds to the Aragón front as a volunteer had put him off so much that he had decided to think it over for a while. But as he kept receiving more and more data concerning Mosén Francisco, everything loudly proclaimed his sanctity. A militiaman imprisoned in Barcelona declared that he had been an eyewitness to the vicar's death in Gorki's Communist Cheka. He recounted the last moments of his martyrdom, which were truly moving. The Campistol sisters, who had hidden Mosén Francisco in their dressmaking establishment during the early months of the war, were summoned to the Palace, where they told Dr. Gregorio Lascasas, always sensitive to exemplary behavior on the part of young priests, so many details that he had to hold back his tears. Actually, the prime mover of the beatification petition was Mosén Alberto, who had affirmed again and again that there was no more reason for supposing that César was a saint than for supposing Mosén Francisco one. "They were twin souls, each according to his lights." That was the priest's theme song. Eventually he saw his wishes crowned, and was named vice-postulator. In this case it fell to Father Forteza to be "the devil's advocate." This reversal of their roles brought forth a dry comment: "Let's see if we can synchronize our shots."

The really great surprise, however, placed a proper colophon beneath all the others. The Gerundians were given it by the Government. On November 27, also declared Schoolteachers' Day, the Civil Governor, Comrade Juan Antonio Dávila, received official notice from the Ministry of the Interior that arrangements had been made to transfer him to the civil governorship of Santander.

The notice was terse; it ended by saying that on December 15, the Governor was to receive his successor in Gerona and would assume office in his new post on the twentieth of that month.

As the Governor read the communication, he felt that he could not pull air into his lungs; for a moment he was afraid that his habitual, expert breathing exercises were going to be of no use to him. What an unexpected blow of fate! He could not take it in or adjust to the idea. He was alone in his office, and he looked around with unusual detachment. He stared at the ceiling, the walls, the desk, the chairs, the carpets, the telephones—this time the yellow telephone brought no smile to his lips. It even occurred to him that there might be articles in the office that he had never seen. Since when had that lamp with the curved base stood behind the door?

His first impulse was to telephone Madrid and ask that the order be canceled. But he realized that it would be a futile—and ridiculous—gesture. Whom could he ask? The minister who had signed the document? The Caudillo, to whom he had sworn loyalty and obedience with his hand on the Bible?

After a moment, he told himself that the transfer could only be the fruit of some Machiavellian maneuvering. Immediately he thought of Colonel Triguero—even of his own wife, María del Mar. The last time he had talked to Colonel Triguero, the man had worn a more than usually enigmatic smile. That rascal had so many tricks up his sleeve! As for María del Mar, she had never become acclimated to Gerona, and only lately, when he had gone to Santander to pick her up, he had found her looking rejuvenated, with rosy cheeks, and in no hurry whatsoever to return.

Finally, the Governor felt annoyed with himself. Why should he think of

"Machiavellian maneuvers"? If he looked at it objectively, the transfer meant a promotion. Santander was a more important provincial capital than Gerona, and doubtless in appointing him the minister wanted to place in that province, recently lashed by fire and hurricane, a man like him, who knew it intimately and whose roots were in that earth.

But perhaps it was not even that. Shifts occurred frequently; they were a part of the old political game. He himself had moved mayors around like chessmen.

In the end, he reproached himself for thinking ill of María del Mar. She would be delighted at the transfer, of course. She would be so exuberantly happy that she would hardly be able to hide it. But she was loyal to him, and nothing in the world would have induced her to stoop to intrigue behind his back.

The Governor kept the news to himself for twenty-four hours without knowing precisely why he did so. But eventually he realized how absurdly he was behaving and decided to make the announcement.

Of course, he told his family first, next the authorities, and finally the public.

Ah, how true to type was the chorus of comment: "The vineyard of the Lord contains everything!" María del Mar covered her mouth with her hand while her eyes shouted a "Hurrah!" Pablito took a step backward and seemed to feel dizzy. "Oh..." he stammered. It was evident that his regret was enormous, greater than his father's. "Papa, why don't you call Madrid and try to arrange things?" Cristina stared at her family with round eyes, but it made no difference to her. For the moment things and persons were interchangeable to her. She had friends in Santander and a room there with little stuffed animals and pretty pajamas. And she would be "the Governor's daughter" there, too.

As for the authorities, they presented a united front of such gloom that the Governor felt flattered. The General, the Bishop, Warning Voice, the Chief of Police, all reacted alike. "How can that happen? We've never had anyone like you here." The General, more accustomed than the others to accepting facts, finally said to him: "Well, that's how it is. I'd like to go, and they keep me here; you'd like to stay, and they send you back to your own part of the country." What about the public? As soon as the news made the rounds of the city and the province, a puzzling situation arose. Many people lamented the Governor's leaving. On the whole, he had won the people's liking. Everyone, without exception, recognized that his work had always been guided by the wish to be fair. At times he had had to be hard. Of course. Rascals, scoundrels were flourishing like weeds and were as common. But at the height of the summary executions that had marked the repression, he had acted to rescue the accused when he could. And aside from that, people had to remember that when he had come to Gerona, in April 1939, the war had just ended. Gerona had been like an abandoned lot then. There had been no bridges, no electricity, no water or gas. Mountains of garbage and junk, and half-naked people marauding along the roads. Could anyone deny that, in so far as he had been able, he had corrected all those things through his work of a little over two years? The Gerundians, born workers, had helped him of course. But he had been their leader and protector who thought of everything from the pension assigned to widows to the metal ladders for firemen, now available to them because of his intervention.

The Governor, the first to be convinced that he had done his duty, dreamed for a moment that the people would be grateful and consistent and would give him a massive demonstration of gratitude. Yes, he was hoping that at any moment he would see a crowd gather before the Civil Government building and would go out on the balcony to speak to them.

But that did not happen. Indeed, there were some who believed that he had asked for the transfer. "Naturally, his farms are in Santander." Others shrugged their shoulders, saying: "What can we do about it?" before turning back immediately to their own concerns.

The Governor sensed briefly this fatalistic acceptance among the people who had been his constituents, and for a moment he showed the childish facet of his personality and muttered: "Ungrateful." María del Mar said to him: "You'll never learn, will you? You're very naïve. People also merely shrug their shoulders when they hear that a thousand Englishmen or a thousand Germans have perished in an air raid."

Her words, pregnant with good sense, restored him. What was the matter with him anyhow? Could he possibly have been "begging" for ovations, for deliria? If he wore dark glasses, it was to avoid the sight of flabbiness. If he wore the uniform of the Falange, it was to avoid the temptation to make a show of his office. If he chewed eucalyptus tablets, it was to clear his mouth of the pleasant taste of flattery.

"All right," he said. And did what he had to do, for nothing less could be expected of a Dávila. He ordered Warning Voice to be sparing of farewell eulogies in *Amanecer.* He found out that some official agencies—the Feminine Section and the aldermen—intended to put on a demonstration by escorting him in a caravan as far as the boundary of the province on the day of departure. He flatly opposed it. "Don't even think of it!" He meant to leave quietly with his wife and children, driven by a chauffeur whom the General would lend him. Commissioner Diéguez asked for an interview with him, to thank him for something or other. "Thank you for the white carnation I wear in my lapel." Dr. Chaos asked to see him. "Do come. But no mourning. We'll talk about the hospital's needs, if you think that as I go through Madrid I can do something for you." He called Professor Civil.

Ah, that was another story! He received the old man with pleasure and spoke with him in moving phrases. In spite of appearances, he had never forgotten the conversation they had had in the car on their way to acclaim Count Ciano in Barcelona. And Professor Civil's conduct, his peculiar mingling of intellectual vigor and meekness, had served the Governor as a constant example.

"Professor Civil, sometimes it happens that without realizing it we influence certain persons. That has been your role with respect to me. You and Father Forteza have been my two mirrors during the time I've been here. I can assure you of that. More than once when I was on the verge of doing something simple-minded, I've thought of those crosses you scratched on the walls of your prison with your thumbnail during the war, and I've made an about-face. So the least I can do now is to express my gratitude to you."

Professor Civil was touched by the Governor's words, for he was very fond of him.

"My dear friend, thank you. But I think you're exaggerating. I believe that your guardian angel has been not Father Forteza, much less I, for I'm old and old-fashioned, and I feel an excess of emotion at the sound of the Cathedral bells. I believe that the great controlling force in your life—and I beg you not to forget this—will be your son, Pablito, in the end. I want you to give him a hug for me. And now, goodbye. And please give my respects to your wife."

THE Governor was so impressed by his interview with Professor Civil that he felt inspired to plan a farewell party in the mansion. María del Mar took care this time to address the envelopes by hand. Everyone accepted. Comrade Dávila's home sparkled that night, and the guests, as Doña Cecilia noted immediately, were more or less the same people who had met at the gala ball in the Gentlemen's Club, at the end of the fairs and festivals of San Narciso.

An air of melancholy hovered over the gathering, to be sure, for everyone knew full well why María del Mar, with the help of Pablito, Cristina, and the maid, was offering them all drinks and sandwiches. But Comrade Dávila played the host with the utmost elegance. He did know how to rise above circumstances.

The party gave him an opportunity to chat briefly with all those who had shared his stay in Gerona in greater or lesser degree.

As usual, the first arrivals were Notary Noguer and his wife. The two men had a long private conversation that ended with the words: "You can leave with your mind at rest, Comrade Dávila. You've been efficient, no one can doubt that. And no one could have done more than you've done."

"Yes, perhaps you're right. But it always seems that one has fallen short. So much is needed."

"What your successor will be like is a great unknown."

"Ah, that I can't tell you. I wish him luck. I'll do all I can to bring him up to date and to summarize for him the conclusions I've come to during this time."

"Do you think, my dear friend, that you've finally come to understand us, the Catalans?"

"No, Notary Noguer, frankly I don't. You people are still an enigma."

Later, when he had a chance, he talked with Manolo and Esther, who came a little late.

At first the trio laughed a lot, reminiscing about the start of his official work, when his "door was always open to everyone," and recalling that some villagers had tried to bribe him with the gift of a hen or by leaving on his desk "a duro for a cup of coffee." They also laughed over the first official visit to Darnius, and the cries of "Sing it again, sing it again!" after he and Mateo and some other Falangists sang "Face to the Sun" from the balcony of the town hall, which the people of Darnius mistook for a folk song.

But soon they began to talk of more serious matters. Esther was the one who changed the subject. "May I ask you a question?" she said to the Governor.

"By all means! You're so beautiful tonight."

"Have you never considered the possibility of quitting politics?"

The Governor made a sign of negation. No, he had never thought of such a thing. He was more convinced every day that he was a political man. And that meant that, even though it had its drawbacks, as his present transfer demonstrated, and as he and María del Mar knew very well, politics had never ceased to be to him "a very noble and praiseworthy occupation," as the centuries-old saying put it.

"No, Esther, I'm not considering asking for a discharge as Manolo did. Our cases are different. Aside from the fact that Manolo's ideas have evolved while mine remain what they always were, he's a born lawyer and I'm not. I can't see myself making a mess for my brothers by getting myself involved in the problems of cattle raising either. I know nothing about it."

He stepped away from the wall to speak to Doña Cecilia, who was claiming his attention.

"Juan Antonio," she said. "You've been ignoring me. Tell me, have you a place to live in Santander, or are you going to live in the Governor's mansion there, too?"

"Honestly, my dear girl, I don't know. I haven't had time to worry about that."

"Now you listen to me, Juan Antonio," Doña Cecilia insisted. "You find María del Mar an apartment of her own. This sort of place doesn't suit her. Any more than the garrison suits me. But you're not a general, after all. You can give María del Mar that much pleasure."

His talk with Carlota was a somewhat uncommon colloquy, almost spontaneous in that setting. She was wearing a necklace that must have been two or three hundred years old. The question she asked him reminded him of Esther's query, for it pointed in the same direction. Carlota began with a flattering preamble, purporting to tell him that perhaps her husband would quit his office of mayor because the Governor was leaving. Then she asked him if he had ever thought of the possibility that Hitler might lose the war.

That was not the place for going deeply into such a question, with so many people there and Pablito and Cristina going from group to group with trays in their hands. Yet the Governor took the bait. Actually, Carlota never had been his cup of tea, he did not know why.

He replied that he had never thought of such a possibility and that she could rest easy on that score. In the first place, he was from Santander, not Barcelona, where it seemed the English had left a very strong imprint with their textiles, as they had on Jérez de la Frontera with their cognac. In the second place, he had a blind faith in thc absolute superiority of the totalitarian states over those which operated as democracies. Finally, and this was most important, he knew how to read. He could read both sides in the war. And both said as plain as daylight that in those very days the Russian campaign, which would be decisive by any lights, had entered its final phase. Hitler had stated flatly in his latest speech: "Russia is conquered. All that remains is merely a matter of procedure." Perhaps he had exaggerated a little in order to encourage and warm his soldiers, for the cold in Russia was apparently very intense. Nevertheless, that statement could hardly be far from the facts. St. Petersburg was about to fall—it was entirely surrounded; and Moscow would fall soon, too. And still the bulk of the German Army had not even gone into action. Therefore, in his opinion, the outcome was certain.

Carlota smiled, nodded her head briefly, and raising her glass she gave a toast: "Lots of luck to you!"

Next the Governor talked with Eusebio Ferrándiz, the Chief of Police, who came alone as usual. He talked with the Governor on the subject that he called his passion: the Costa brothers.

"You'll get a report on them, my dear Ferrándiz, identical with the one I'm going to send to the price administrator, who hasn't arrived yet, I see. I believe that after you've read that paper, you'll see that you have the famous industrialists in the palm of your hand—at last. Again thanks to Commissioner Diéguez."

Don Eusebio Ferrándiz disliked talking about such matters outside police headquarters, but in this case his curiosity won. The Governor satisfied it with a few words.

"Yes they've crossed the line this time. It seems they've been scheming with a Barcelona corporation, Sarró and Company, or some such name. Well, that outfit apparently persuaded the Costa brothers to offer a bribe to a poor brigadier who's in charge of the artillery batteries along the coast left over from the war. They were holding I don't know how many tons of copper in their warehouse. It came from Communications, and they've been disposing of it at a ridiculously low price. Of course, that's an important operation. And one that falls within the Military Code, I should imagine."

Don Eusebio Ferrándiz was dumbfounded. "Are you certain? Did you say Communications copper? Of course, you must be referring to cables..."

"Precisely."

"Then, who is that brigadier?"

"Ah!"

"Please be sure to send me that report."

"I'll have it on your desk tomorrow."

The Governor went back to his guests. He chatted for a while with Dr. Chaos, who said to him: "Are you convinced now, Governor, that a man isn't free, not even to choose his place of residence?" He said to Dr. Andújar and his wife: "Dr. Andújar, I shall miss your 'Tablets for Thought'!" He talked with Don Oscar Pinel, the price administrator, who finally arrived. "Tell me, have you had any news from Solita?" "Yes, just yesterday. And from what she tells me, I gather that she's in a hospital in Riga. Why Riga, I wonder?" He had a word with Agustín Lago. "Do I order a couple of stoves from Santander for your schools, friend Lago?" Lago smiled. He greeted Ignacio with: "I'm at your orders, illustrious lawyer." Marta was across the room, talking with former lieutenant Montero. "Marta, you're a brave girl. I congratulate you," the Governor said. He went next to the group composed of Jorge de Batlle, Chelo, and Miguel Rosselló. He felt extremely sorry for them. Among the secrets he would carry back to his own part of the world—to avoid hurting anyone—was one that affected the Rosselló brother and sister very directly. Their father, the doctor, had not died of a "cardiac collapse" in the penitentiary; he had committed suicide. Why should he give them such shocking news? "Chelo, marriage suits you marvelously." Jorge de Batlle said jokingly, "It's not marriage; it's the country, and the farm." "Good luck with the chickens, then." He talked with Jesús Revilla, the new Syndical Delegate, who exclaimed in an ironical tone: "Why, all this is a waste of money! It's not a first communion, you know." The Governor stared at the Basque as though it had nothing to do with him: "It's the last, Comrade."

He was spared a meeting with Captain Sánchez Bravo because that night the young man chanced to have guard duty in the garrison. In the end, everything turned out very well indeed. The General said for the nth time: "To think that you're going to leave us!" The Governor had taken care to invite his porter. But the man felt awkward standing beside his wife, who was very short and was wearing a red ribbon in her hair. The porter did not dare to mingle with the guests; he would have been happier to take Pablito's place with a tray.

At a very late hour, when all the guests were growing tired, the Governor asked for a moment's silence, which was granted him with general respect. He spoke a few words of gratitude to them all for their help, and begged them to wish him all success in his new undertaking, "for the good of Spain."

The Governor and María del Mar, who stood beside him with damp eyes, were given a long final ovation. Soon after that, the parlor of the Governor's mansion stood empty except for the family and the remains of pastries on the floor, some bottles in a corner, and glasses on all the furniture.

That was a difficult moment for Comrade Dávila and his family, who were numb with fatigue and nostalgia. They stared at one another, all captured by the inevitable sadness, which Pablito broke by saying: "Well, I'm tired. I'm going to bed. Good night." He kissed his parents and left the room.

Cristina also kissed them and went. But after only a few steps she turned around and said: "It was super, Mama!"

The Governor and María del Mar looked at each other and embraced. And to keep the scene from turning into a real soap opera, Comrade Dávila suggested taking a short walk before going to bed.

"Does that appeal to you? Let's stretch our legs a little. There won't be anyone around at this hour."

María del Mar was exhausted, but she complied. "Wait until I fix myself up a bit." She went to her bedroom and came back almost immediately. "My mascara was running.

A few minutes later the Governor and María del Mar were in the Calle de Ciudadanos. The Governor said jokingly: "Well, since the Bishop can't see us, what do you say if I take your arm?"

The street was deserted. They were impressed by the sound of their own footsteps in the Gerundian night. The night watchman recognized them and took off his cap. A light in a shop that sold orthopedic devices revealed a mannikin, a man's torso, which prompted María del Mar to make a surprising remark: "Why doesn't Agustín Lago get himself an articulated prosthetic arm?"

"Probably he's taken a vow," the Governor answered.

When they reached the Plaza Municipal, they stood looking at the balcony of the Town Hall, the great shield of the city, the clock. They heard the Cathedral bell strike, and it reminded the Governor of Professor Civil. The arcade along the square was dark, and the bootblacks' stands were shuttered with wooden planks. They came to the Puente de Piedra and leaned on the rail to look at the Oñar. To their left a strong stream of dirty water was pouring through an opening. "That's the waste from the Soler factory." The houses above the river seemed to stay upright only by a miracle.

The Calle José Antonio Primo de Rivera. The Diana Perfumery, with a lighted mirror. The Governor went up to it, took off his glasses, and stared at himself. And, as in his office earlier, he seemed to discover, this time in his face, something he had never seen before: several deep lines on each side of his nose. "Were they there," he asked himself, "before I received my transfer notice?"

"I'm cold," María del Mar said. "Let's go home."

"Yes, darling. It's been a hard day for you."

SIXTY-SEVEN

SUDDENLY, the lightning struck. For an instant the whole world closed its eyes, to open them again with a stunned expression. On December 7, the eve of the feast of the Immaculate Conception, Japanese aircraft made a surprise attack on the most important American and English naval and military bases in the Pacific and Eastern Asia. The most intense air attack was concentrated on Pearl Harbor, in Hawaii. A part of the United States fleet was sunk, and Japanese troops landed on the Malay Peninsula. Similar air raids struck Singapore, Hong Kong, and several points in the Philippine Islands. Meanwhile, an official statement was issued from Tokyo to the effect that Japan was at war with the United States and England. The declaration was signed by the Emperor himself.

On the twelfth, Germany and Italy made common cause with Japan by also declaring war on the United States, which in turn declared war on the two European powers.

What was happening on the earth? What was going on, O Lord? And what about the peace message that Pius XII was preparing for Christmas, already anticipated in every home?

Did such events modify the Governor's opinion? Would it be long before Mateo Santos found out in his *isba* that this bolt of lightning had fallen from the blue?

Gerona shrank inside itself. If the Andalusian women on Montjuich had ever gone to school or had had even a vague idea of the size of the oceans, they would have seen that the city stretching at their feet had indeed shrunk, like Eloy whenever he dreamed about Guernica.

General Sánchez Bravo stood in front of the map of the world, alone, without witnesses. And he meditated. Nebulosa, waiting in the corridor in case the General should call or give an order, heard nothing. The General stayed shut up in his office for more than an hour, staring at the map, sunk in absolute silence, almost motionless.

Warning Voice closed his dental office for a few days. Father Forteza went down to the convent chapel and knelt in front of the ciborium, thinking of his brother, the missionary in Nagasaki. Notary Noguer put in an appearance at the Deputation, but said to the janitor; "I'm not in to anyone." José Luis Martínez de Soria, on his way to the Military Tribunal, kept recalling some words that he himself had spoken in Valladolid during the war: "I believe that the present epidemic of political fanaticism will not last long. At the most, a century; the time it took the colonies to win their independence. Then I'm afraid that Satan will conquer the world through its very indifference."

Paz Alvear felt an indescribable joy, for some reason. The United States! The name sounded strong; it rang as forcefully and roundly as Damián's trumpet. The prisoners in the newly opened jail in Salt stared at one another, seized by a sudden vague hope.

But in the meantime an icy wind was blowing into the hearts of many of the "victors" of the civil war. They realized suddenly that the stakes had been raised, and that decades might pass before they were lowered again. They were helpless now to do anything. Everything depended on the actual power the nations that had signed the tripartite pact could call forth. If those nations lost their bet—for it had to be admitted that the name of the United States rang strong—perhaps on some unknown day El Responsable and Cosme Vila might come back to Gerona riding in British, or Belgian, or Russian tanks—and Julio García and his beloved spouse, Doña Amparo Campo, too, with her *pardon* and *okay.*

The vague hope of the prisoners in the Salt jail, of Manolo and Esther and Paz Alvear, of Jaime the Separatist bookseller, and Jorge de Batlle's tenant farmers, and Mr. Edward Collins, and the millions of men doing forced labor throughout the length and breadth of the nation—building roads, churches, and digging their own graves little by little—was simply and solely the United States. Bless Japan, which had the audacity to defy that giant. Hurray for General Tojo, who had attacked Pearl Harbor by surprise! Hurray for the Emperor, who had signed the declaration of war, whether he was a god or not!

The pendulum had swung so widely that Ignacio could not possibly climb up to a height of a thousand feet, as Moncho advised, in order to prove to himself, from that altitude, that man was an insignificant creature. No, man was right there with him, on ground level. Man was staining the whole world and all the seas with blood. Staining even the high mountains.

Ignacio felt an attack of vertigo and took refuge inside himself. He was afraid, as intensely afraid as Mateo had been when he had received the photograph of his son. He wanted to go to confession. And at the same time to telephone Adela. And to hang a veil over the Picasso reproductions hanging in his room, pictures that to Carmen Elgazu represented the breakup of the world.

Finally, he managed to pull himself together enough to send a telegram to Ana María, saying simply: "I need to see you. I'll be in Barcelona on the fifteenth. I love you. Ignacio."

Matías carefully refrained from making any comment whatsoever. All he did was to have two successive glasses of cognac in the Café Nacional. He went home then to the Rambla flat, and with his hat in his hand, suggested to Carmen Elgazu: "What would you think about our going to see Pilar? It seems to me that César looks a little peaked."

Carmen Elgazu joined Matías in the conspiracy of silence regarding the bolt of lightning. She answered in a serene voice: "Wait a minute till I finish this ironing."

Matías waited. He did not know what to do in the meantime, so, taking a slice of bread, he pierced it with a fork and went to the hot stove to make himself a piece of toast. He put a little olive oil and salt on it and ate it. "Hmm," he exclaimed, "this is really delicious."

Finally, they went out and walked, arm in arm, to the Plaza de la Estación. There they met reality face to face for they found Pilar inconsolable. César's supposed lassitude was of no importance. He had slept perfectly normally for hours, and now he was awake and content. But Pilar had the newspaper in her hand, and her eyes and heart were full of big words: Japan, the United States, Russia, Mateo.

"What will happen, Father? What does this mean?"

Matías made a gesture of sadness. "Nobody knows that, daughter." Then he added in a neutral tone: "May we see the baby?"

Don Emilio Santos, who came out of Mateo's office, from which the stuffed bird had been removed, answered: "By all means! Come on in. This way!"

They all went into the bedroom. César Santos Alvear, with his priceless little hands and a band around his middle, was lying in the cradle that Pilar had acquired for him and placed next to the bed. His blue eyes were open wide, although he could not focus them yet on any given point.

As if he guessed that he was the great star of the scene, he raised his legs and seemed to pedal an imaginary bicycle for a moment.

"César! Darling! Baby!"

Carmen Elgazu tickled him on the stomach, and he seemed to smile. He moved his lips as if ready to speak some big word of his own. But speech was beyond him and he drooled a little. Pilar took her handkerchief out of her sleeve—as the Bishop always did—and wiped his lips.

The innocence of Pilar's son suddenly touched everyone. What kind of world was he living in? Was it a world without war; a world of sensations; a world of pure love, the world before original sin?

They all had the same thought: "What will this child see as he grows up and comes of age? What inheritance will we, who have many years behind us, leave to him?" They felt responsible, although not for any definite act.

Pilar, who was looking at him in ecstasy, stammered: "I'm afraid—I'm afraid for him."

Carmen Elgazu supported her: "How I wish he would never have to grow up. I wish he'd stay like this, feeling loved and smiling."

Matías shook his head. That would be utopian, contrary to nature. César Santos Alvear would go on developing in time with events, and would grow up to be like Ignacio or Mateo.

"Let's leave him alone," he suggested. "It seems to me he knows we're trying to read his palm."

Everyone followed the suggestion and went toward the dining room. Everyone, except Carmen Elgazu. She stayed quietly in the bedroom, and as soon as she saw that she was alone with the baby, she leaned over him as far as she could to give him a kiss. But what she was really doing was tracing above the smooth forehead, slowly and with extreme tenderness, the sign of the cross.

GLOSSARY OF PERSONS

1. *Fictional Characters*

Adela. Wife of Marcos.
Agustín. An Anarchist.
Alvear, Arturo. Brother of Matías Alvear, killed during the civil war; husband of Conchi; father of Paz and Manuel.
Alvear, Carmen Elgazu de. Wife of Matías Alvear; mother of Pilar, César, and Ignacio.
Alvear, César. Son of Matías and Carmen Elgazu; killed during civil war; brother of Pilar and Ignacio.
Alvear, Conchi. Sister-in-law of Matías Alvear; widow of Arturo Alvear; mother of Paz and Manuel.
Alvear, Ignacio. Son of Matías and Carmen Elgazu; brother of Pilar and César.
Alvear, José. Son of Santiago Alvear; nephew of Matías.
Alvear, Manuel. Nephew of Matías Alvear, son of Conchi; brother of Paz.
Alvear, Paz. Niece of Matías Alvear; daughter of Conchi; sister of Manuel.
Alvear, Pilar. Daughter of Matías and Carmen Elgazu; sister of César and Ignacio; later wife of Mateo Santos.
Alvear, Santiago. Brother of Matías Alvear.
Andaluza, La. Brothel-keeper.
Andújar, Dr. Director of the Gerona Insane Asylum.
Andújar, Elisa. Wife of Dr. Andújar.
Andújar, Gracia. Daughter of Dr. Andújar.
Arjona. Delegate of Provincial Syndicate.
Asunción. Schoolteacher.
Ayestarán, Carlos. Uncle of Moncho.
Barroso, Lieutenant. Prosecutor at the War Trials Tribunal.
Batlle, Jorge de. Member of the Falange.
Bidot, Geneviève. Owner of a butcher shop in Toulouse.

Bisturí. Sweetheart of Moncho.
Cacerola. Comrade of Ignacio Alvear.
Cajal, Corporal. Comrade of Ignacio Alvear.
Camacho, Victor. Civil servant; member of Opus Dei.
Campistol sisters. Dressmakers.
Campo, Amparo. See García, Amparo Campo de.
Cándido. Son of Marcos and Adela.
Carreras. Anesthetist employed by Dr. Chaos.
Casal, Antonio. Socialist; exile in France.
Cervera, Julián. Civil Commissioner of Gerona.
Chaos, Dr. Maximiliano. Physician; health inspector.
Charlatan. Comrade of Mateo Santos.
Civil, Benito. Son of Professor Civil; Falangist.
Civil, Carlos. Son of Professor Civil; businessman.
Civil, Professor. Teacher of Ignacio Alvear and Mateo Santos.
Collins, Edward. British Consul in Gerona.
Costa brothers. Industrialists; leaders of the Republican Left.
Costa, Laura. Sister of the Costa brothers; wife of Warning Voice; killed in the civil war.
Dámaso. Perfumery owner.
David. Schoolteacher; Socialist; exile in France, then Mexico.
Dávila, Cristina. Daughter of Juan Antonio Dávila.
Dávila, Juan Antonio. Head of Civil Authority in Gerona; Governor.
Dávila, María del Mar. Wife of Juan Antonio Dávila.
Dávila, Mario. Brother of Juan Antonio Dávila.
Dávila, Pablito. Son of Juan Antonio Dávila.
Diéguez. Gerona Police Commissioner.
Difícil. Comrade of Mateo Santos.
Elgazu Letamendía, Victor. Father of Carmen Elgazu Alvear.
Eloy. Adopted son of Carmen Elgazu and Matías Alvear.
Estrada, Alfonso de. Student; soldier.
Estrada, Sebastián. Sailor; brother of Alfonso Estrada.
Ezequiel. Photographer in Barcelona.
Fontana, Clara. Daughter of Manuel Fontana.
Fontana, Esther. Wife of Manuel Fontana.
Fontana, Jacinto. Son of Manuel Fontana.
Fontana, Manuel (Manolo). Lieutenant; prosecutor on the War Crimes Tribunal.
Fontana Verges, José María. Father of Manuel Fontana.
Forteza, Father. Jesuit.
Galindo. Civil servant.

García, Amparo Campo de. Wife of Julio García; exile in France.
García, Julio. Childhood friend of Matías Alvear; policeman; later Chief of Police; exile in France.
Godo, Carlos. Architect; member of Opus Dei.
Gorki. Communist; former Mayor of Gerona; exile in France.
Grote, Carlos. Civil servant.
Guillén. Comrade of Ignacio Alvear.
Gunther, Paul. German Consul in Gerona.
Ichaso, Anselmo. Editor; Monarchist.
Ichaso, German. Son of Anselmo Ichaso; killed in the civil war.
Ichaso, Javier. Son of Anselmo Ichaso.
Jaime. Brother of Carmen Elgazu de Alvear.
Jaime. Fellow worker of Matías Alvear; poet.
Joséfa. Sister of Carmen Elgazu de Alvear.
Katy. Mother of Esther Fontana.
Lago, Agustín. Chief Inspector of primary schools in Gerona.
Lascasas, Gregorio. Bishop of Gerona.
Leopoldo. Head of the Spanish Frontier Service in Perpignan.
Ley, Charo. Wife of Gaspar Ley.
Ley, Gaspar. Manager of Arús Bank.
Lorenzo. Brother of Carmen Elgazu de Alvear.
Marcos. Worker at Telegraph Office.
María Victoria. Fiancée of José Luis Martíncz de Soria.
Martínez de Soria, José Luis. Son of Major Martínez de Soria; Falangist.
Martínez de Soria, Major. Commander of Gerona garrison; killed in the civil war.
Martínez de Soria, Marta. Daughter of Major Martínez de Soria; sweetheart of Ignacio Alvear.
Mati. Mother of Carmen Elgazu de Alvear.
Merche. Daughter of El Responsable.
Mirentxu. Sister of Carmen Elgazu de Alvear.
Moncho. Comrade of Ignacio Alvear.
Montenegro, Ramón. Son of the manager of the Bank of Spain.
Montse. Servant of Warning Voice.
Mosén Alberto. Priest; director of the Gerona Diocesan Museum.
Mosén Falcó. Priest; counselor of the Falange.
Mosén Francisco. Priest.
Mosén Iguacén. Priest; assistant to Bishop of Gerona.
Muñoz, Colonel. Mason; military man.
Nati. Typist for the Spanish Frontier Service.

Noguer. Notary; later Mayor of Gerona.
Núñez Maza. National Press and Propaganda Delegate in Gerona.
Olga. Schoolteacher; wife of David; exile in France, then Mexico.
Oriol, Pedro. Lumber dealer; owner of *El Tradicionalista.*
Oriol, Widow. Widow of Pedro Oriol.
Pachín. Football player; lover of Paz Alvear.
Pascual, Dámaso. Comrade of Ignacio Alvear.
Pinel, Oscar. Head of price control agency in Gerona.
Pinel, Solita. Daughter of Oscar Pinel.
Puigvert. Spanish exile in Moscow.
Quintana. Musician.
Raimundo. Barber.
Ramón. Waiter at the Café Nacional.
Relken, Dr. German-Jewish archeologist.
Responsable, El. Anarchist leader; exile in Venezuela.
Reyes, Alfonso. Former manager of the Arús Bank.
Rogelio. Waiter.
Romero, Colonel. Adjutant to General Sánchez Bravo.
Rosa. Wife of Ezequiel.
Rosselló, Antonia. Sister of Miguel Rosselló.
Rosselló, Chelo. Sister of Miguel Rosselló.
Rosselló, Dr. Physician; Mason.
Rosselló, Miguel. Secretary to Juan Antonia Dávila; son of Dr. Rosselló, Falangist.
Rubí, Countess of. Wife of Warning Voice.
Salazar. Fascist; comrade of Mateo Santos.
Salvatore. Italian legionnaire.
Sánchez Bravo, Captain. Son of General Sánchez Bravo.
Sánchez Bravo, Cecilia. Wife of General Sánchez Bravo.
Sánchez Bravo, General. Military Governor of Gerona.
Santi. Anarchist.
Santos, Emilio. Friend of Matías Alvear; father of Mateo Santos.
Santos, Mateo. Organizer of the Falange in Gerona; husband of Pilar Alvear.
Santos Alvear, César. Son of Mateo and Pilar Santos.
Sarró, Ana María. Sweetheart of Ignacio Alvear.
Sarró, Rosendo. Father of Ana María; businessman.
Senilloso, Carlos (*Warning Voice*). Dentist; husband of Laura Costa; journalist; later Mayor of Gerona.
Teresa. Maid of the Santos family.
Teresa, Sister. Sister of Carmen Elgazu de Alvear.

Tower of Babel. Fellow worker of Ignacio Alvear in the Arús Bank.
Vila, Cosme. Communist leader; fellow worker of Ignacio Alvear in the Arús Bank; fled to Russia.
Warning Voice. See Senilloso, Carlos.

2. *Historical Characters*

Alfonso XIII (1886–1941). King of Spain; dethroned in April 1931.
Alvarez del Vayo, Julio (1891–1975). Spanish Socialist leader and writer.
Attlee, Clement Richard, Earl (1883–1967). British statesman and Prime Minister.
Azaña, Manuel (1880–1940). President of the Spanish Republic (1936–1939).
Baden-Powell, Sir Robert Smyth, Baron (1857–1941). Founder of the Boy Scouts.
Balbo, Italo (1896–1940). Fascist leader.
Balmes Alonso, Amadeo (1877–1936). Military Governor in the Canary Islands.
Baroja, Pío (1872–1956). Spanish writer.
Becquer, Gustavo Adolfo (1836–1870). Spanish poet.
Beigbeder Atienza, Juan (1890–1957). Diplomat; Nationalist leader.
Belmonte, Juan (1893–1962). Spanish bullfighter.
Bergson, Henri (1859–1941). French philosopher.
Beria, Lavrenti Pavlovich (1899–1953). Soviet official; executed for treason.
Berti, Aleramo (1881–1964). Italian commander in Spain.
Blum, Léon (1872–1950). French Socialist journalist; Premier of France.
Calvo Sotelo, José (1883–1936). Spanish Monarchist leader.
Campesino, El (*Valentín González*) (1904–1983). Spanish Communist leader.
Carol II (1893–1953). King of Romania.
Ciano, Count Galeazzo (1903–1944). Italian fascist leader; Minister of Foreign Affairs.
Cid Campeador, El (*Rodrigo Díaz de Bivar*) (1043?-1099). Spanish national hero.
Cocteau, Jean (1889–1963). French writer, cinematographer, etc.
Companys, Luis (1883–1940). Catalan Nationalist leader; President of Catalonia.
De Gaulle, Charles-André-Joseph (1890–1970). French general and statesman; President of France.
Dmitroff (*Dimitrov*), *Georgi* (1882–1949). Bulgarian Communist; Comintern leader.
Durruti, Buenaventura (1896–1936). Spanish Anarchist leader.
Eroles, Dionisio (1900-1940). FAI leader.
Escrivá, Father Josemaría (1902–1975). Founder of Opus Dei.
Franco y Bahamonde, Francisco (1892–1975). Spanish soldier, statesman, dictator.
Gamelin, Maurice-Gustave (1872–1958). French general.
Gardel, Carlos (1890–1935). Argentine tango singer.

Goma, Cardinal Isidora (1869–1940). Archbishop of Toledo.

Goriev (*lan Antonovich Berzin*) (1881–1937). Russian Communist leader in Spain.

Gottwald, Klement (1896–1953). Czech Communist leader; Prime Minister and President of Czechoslovakia.

Graziani, Marchese Rodolfo (1882–1955). Italian soldier; Viceroy of Ethiopia.

Hernández, Tomás Jesús (1907–1971). Spanish Communist leader.

Hess, Rudolf (1894–1947). German Nazi leader.

Hoare, Sir Samuel, Viscount Templewood (1880–1959). British statesman.

Juan, Prince (1913–1993). Son of Alfonso XIII; candidate for Spanish throne.

Lalanda, Marcial (1903–1990). Spanish bullfighter.

Largo Caballero, Francisco (1869–1946). Spanish labor leader and statesman; Prime Minister.

Lister, Enrique (1907–1994). Spanish Communist military leader.

Llull, Ramón (1235–1315). Catalan philosopher and mystic.

Machado y Ruiz, Antonio (1875–1939). Spanish writer.

Maeztú y Whitney, Ramiro de (1875–1936). Spanish writer and publicist.

Mannerheim, Baron Carl von (1867–1951). Finnish soldier and statesman.

Manolete (*Manuel Rodríguez y Sánchez*) (1917–1947). Spanish bullfighter.

March, Juan (1880–1962). Spanish entrepreneur and businessman.

Marty, André (1886–1956). French (later Russian) Communist leader in Spain.

Millán Astray y Terreros, José (1879–1954). Nationalist general and propagandist.

Modesto Guillote, Juan (1906–1969). Spanish Communist military leader.

Mola Vidal, Emilio (1887–1937). Spanish general; killed in airplane accident.

Molotov (*Skryabin*), *Vyacheslav* (1890–1986). Soviet statesman.

Montseny, Federica (1905–1994). Spanish Anarchist leader.

Moscardo-Ituarte, José (1878–1956). Spanish general in defense of the Alcázar, Toledo.

Mosley, Sir Oswald (1896–1980). English fascist leader.

Muñoz Grandes (1896–1970). Spanish Nationalist general.

Mussolini, Bruno (1918–1941). Son of Benito Mussolini.

Negrín López, Juan (1889–1956). Spanish statesman; Prime Minister.

Paderewski, Ignace Jan (1860–1941). Polish pianist and patriot; Prime Minister of Poland.

Pasionaria, La (*Dolores Ibárruri*) (1895–1989). Spanish Communist leader.

Pétain, Henri-Philippe (1856–1951). French soldier; premier of Vichy regime.

Pius XII (*Eugenio Pacelli*) (1876–1958). Pope.

Prieto y Tuero, Indalecio (1883–1962). Spanish Socialist leader.

Primo de Rivera, José Antonio (1903–1936). Son of Miguel Primo de Rivera; founder of the Falange.

Primo de Rivera y Orbaneja, Miguel (1870–1930). Spanish general and dictator.

Queipo de Llano y Sierra, Gonzalo (1875–1951). Spanish soldier and propagandist.

Ribbentrop, Joachim von (1893–1946). German Nazi leader.

Romanones, Count (*Alvaro de Figueroa y Torres*) (1863–1950). Spanish statesman; premier.

Rommel, Erwin (1891–1944). German soldier.

Rosenberg, Alfred (1893–1946). German Nazi leader and theoretician.

Serrano Súñer, Ramón ("*Old Shirt*") (1901–2003). Generalissimo Franco's brother-in-law; head of the Junta Política.

Tagore, Sir Rabindranath (1861–1941). Hindu poet.

Tagüeña (1913–1971). Spanish Loyalist general.

Togliatti, Palmiro (1893–1964). Italian Communist leader.

Trotsky (*Braunstein*), *Leon* (1878–1940). Soviet writer and statesman.

Uribe Caldeauo, Vicente (1902–1961). Spanish Marxist theorist and leader.

Wavell, Archibald, 1st Earl (1883–1950). British soldier.

GLOSSARY OF ORGANIZATIONS AND TERMS

Carlists. Supporters of the claim to the Spanish throne of Don Carlos, brother of Ferdinand VII, and his descendants; reactionary Catholic movement opposed to liberalism, confined largely to the Basque Provinces, Catalonia, and Castile.

CEDA (*Confederación Española de Derechos Autónomos*). Coalition of right-wing parties under the leadership of Gil Robles attempting to organize Spain in the manner of the Austrian Corporate State.

CNT (*Confederación Nacional del Trabajo*). Founded in 1910 by Syndicalists to establish anarchism; opposed to the UGT (Unión General de Trabajadores).

Estat Catala. Catalan youth movement founded by Maciá; violently antagonistic to the Anarcho-Syndicalists.

FAI (*Federación Anarquista Ibérica*). Semisecret society founded in 1927; members of the FAI had to be members of the CNT; designed to prevent Communist infiltration into Anarchist groups.

Falange Española de las JONS. Fascist organization founded in 1932 by José Antonio Primo de Rivera.

JONS (*Juntas de Ofensiva Nacional-Sindicalista*). Several small fascist groups that merged in 1934 with the Falange Española.

POUM (*Partido Obrero de Unificación Marxista*). Rigidly Marxist group organized in 1936 from the Bloque Obrero y Campesino and the Federación Comunista Ibérica; especially hated and persecuted by the Communists.

Sardana. Catalan dance; its music.

SERE (*Servicio de Emigración para Republicanos Españoles*). Organization backed by Negrín for assisting Republican émigrés.

Socialist Party (*Partido Democrático Socialista Obrero*). Founded in 1879; in 1888, organized the UGT, trade union directed toward improving workers' conditions; grew most rapidly from 1910 to 1927.

UGT (*Unión General de Trabajadores*). *See* Socialist Party.

Zarzuela. Spanish light *opéra-comique.*

CLUNY MEDIA

Designed by Fiona Cecile Clarke, the Cluny Media *logo*
depicts a monk at work in the scriptorium,
with a cat sitting at his feet.

The monk represents our mission to emulate
the invaluable contributions of the monks
of Cluny in preserving the libraries of the West,
our strivings to know and love the truth.

The cat at the monk's feet is Pangur Bán, from the
eponymous Irish poem of the 9th century.
The anonymous poet compares his scholarly
pursuit of truth with the cat's happy hunting of mice.
The depiction of Pangur Bán is an homage to the work
of the monks of Irish monasteries and a sign
of the joy we at Cluny take in our trade.

"Messe ocus Pangur Bán,
cechtar nathar fria saindan:
bíth a menmasam fri seilgg,
mu memna céin im saincheirdd."

Made in the USA
Middletown, DE
24 September 2022